Absolutely True Retellings:

# The Saga of Shamus

Book the First

By

Jason DeGray

Illustrations by Marilyn Lyons

Outlaw Star Press

Also by Jason DeGray

*Those Left Behind*

*3VE*

*The Ruined Man*

*Prince Aidan and the Monster's Eye*

# Absolutely True Retellings

## The Saga of Shamus

Outlaw Star Press LLC
Albuquerque, NM USA

Cover Image: Rob Ewing
Cover Design: Chris Deichman

Interior Illustrations: Marilyn Lyons

Interior Etchings: Dead Medieval Dudes



ISBN: 978-1-969829-00-0

# A Note of Apology and Correction

Dear Reader,

Tis I, Infinity Jones, and I have been away for too long.

And in my absence, the tale I entrusted to the skald, Jay-Zun, was left incomplete. Do not think too harshly of your Realm's bard, dear reader. He did the best he could with what I gave him. Which, truth be told, was a considerable amount. And in this overwhelming state he chose to go to sleep and so lost sight of the place his heart truly lives: The Realm of Possibility.

But I was always at his side, waiting for the universe to shift so that I could parley with him once more. It was a reunion of tears and hope and the reigniting of dreams. And we begin this new journey into the Realm of Possibility by finishing a tale that deserves to be told. In these pages, you will find the Saga of Shamus as I always meant for it to be shared. And I offer this to you with a promise. I am here to stay. The Realm is alive and we welcome you to explore it and find yourself as Jay-Zun did. In a place he never left, but turned away from.

Yours,

*Infinity Jones*

There *is* (to be read with much emphasis, as a declaration) a place called The Realm of Possibility. I should know; I live there. My name is Infinity Jones and I'm somewhat of a something. Or something of a somewhat depending on whose side you are on. Now, because you are from where you are from, and I am from where I am from, I feel it necessary to clear up a few things before we plunge into unknown places. Perfectly good folk have been driven insane for less bold ventures.

First, understand that the residents of the Realm, or "Realmers" as we like to be called, don't speak or even write in exactly the same way you do. Not that there is anything *wrong* with your speaking or writing, we just find it a bit lackluster and mayhap a smidgen lifeless. Honestly, I've never known folk to be more irreverent toward the words they use to speak their realities into existence. Regardless, I have taken great pains in translating this for your reading pleasure as best as I could while still remaining truthful to the language of my beloved Realm.

Second, it is imperative that you understand universal shifts. A universal shift has occurred when something happens that makes you ask, "What the hell just happened?" Well, I'll tell you. You see, there are an endless number of paths to travel in your unconscious quest to find and realize your destiny. And all these paths run parallel to one another. A universal shift moves you from the present path you are walking to a parallel one. Most of the time you merely shift slightly in one direction or another without ever really leaving "where you are," but sometimes the universe shifts you into a different place and time altogether. As you can imagine, this can be a very traumatic experience or a very enlightening one (depending on how well-equipped your mind is to handle such journeys into foreign universes).

I know what you're wondering: "Is there anything I can do to stop the universe from shifting?"

The answer is an emphatic NO. However, there are some handy-dandy ways to determine when your universe has shifted. You see, certain objects are "non-universal." That means, when the universe shifts, these items get left behind on the old path. Hammers are an example of non-universal items. Every time a hammer "accidentally" falls the universe has shifted. Tankards, quills, eating utensils and other objects of that nature are also non-universal. Take a moment to examine your surroundings for non-universal objects, identify a few and watch them very closely. They may move at any moment.

Third, magic is something very real in the Realm. In fact, the thread of the Realm's existence is comprised of and sustained by a type of magic. Understand that Realmers consider any type of energy manipulation magic. Thus, there is Natural Magic possessed by the Realmers most in tune with Gaia; there is God Magic given to devout folk as blessings and protection; there is the magic of Fair's Folk and Oberon's Troupe used for deception and illusion called Tricksy (don't be fooled though, there are some very deadly illusions). Finally, there is Wyzrdry which is magic created by harnessing and channeling energies whether they want to be harnessed and channeled or not.

Lastly, I have a bit of advice to offer. Heed this advice well, dear traveler, for it has saved many a life (and pocketbook) in the Realm. That advice is: never trust a Gnome or make a deal with Fair's Folk. That being said, I welcome you to my home.

This, friends and foes, is the Realm of Possibility and all are welcome who are willing to let go and believe…just a little is all it takes. Can you see it? Here, let me paint it for you: Before me is a ship-laden harbor nestled atop a pristine ocean of blue that extends beyond the limits of ordinary sight. All manner of ships skirt across the surface of the bay in a whirlwind of activity, their crewmen acting as physical manifestations of that electric vibe. This is the great port of the City of Allure. And it was here amidst the emerald green hills that roll like rocks into the sea, with picturesque cottages and colorful colloquialisms, that I found myself sitting on the balcony of the beachside estate of the Countess De'Lis. I was sipping vino and entertaining a modest crowd when I was interrupted by the nauseating jolt that accompanies the more severe universal shifts.

Suddenly, I was no longer recovering in pampered luxury from the hardships of my dangerous exploits and adventures. Gone were the folk I was regaling with tales of my adventurous adventures. Gone was the beachside estate of the Countess De'Lis. Gone were the hypnotic sea and the salty winds that blow off it. Gone was my beloved Realm of Possibility.

Instead, I found myself sitting outside a plain, brown building with a bustling street to my right. Horse-less carriages zoomed hither and thither and busy folk scuttled by without ever raising their heads to take in the world around them. I was seated at a small table with badly inlaid mosaic upon which sat a white mug full of steaming black liquid. The table was already occupied by a gentleman who looked like he was about to keel over from fright. He bore a slight resemblance to myself, but lacked most of the charismatic qualities that have made me a living legend. I sensed within him great potential coupled with a great lack of confidence.

"You're Infinity Jones!" the man exclaimed, face white as unblemished paper.

"Indeed I am," I replied with a flourish of my hand.

"You, uh, you aren't supposed to be real."

"I'm not? Well, this does cause some problems, then, doesn't it?"

"Just a few. But I've suspected I was going insane for a while now. I can finally admit I cracked. It's actually a relief. I can move into a tiny padded cell, all stark white and soft. Not have to worry about the normal world anymore. Yeah, this will be better. Definitely."

"Insane? Why? Because little old *me* popped into your universe?"

"Well, yeah."

He was trying (unsuccessfully) to convince himself of his own insanity. In my experience, this is a sure sign of not being insane. "I've heard it said that insanity is merely a state of mind brought on by extreme circumstances."

"Then I'm *definitely* insane," the man said. His orbs never left mine. "Are you..." he leaned in close, "are you really from the Realm?"

"Indeed."

"Then what are you doing here?"

"Where exactly is *here*," I wondered, "Where have I landed this time?"

"Earth. This is Earth."

"Of course it's earth! I can feel that much under my feet. But what is your realm *called*?"

"Um, Earth?"

"Let's move on," I said. I have no patience for circular conversation. "What's your name?"

"Jay-zun," or something to that effect was his answer.

"What a marvelously odd name. Tell me, Jay-zun, what are you going to do now that you are insane?"

"Probably get put on prescription drugs and then shut in a little room until I'm loopy enough to admit none of this ever happened. That's what they do with insane folk here. Dope 'em up and lock 'em up."

"Huh. Sounds like quite an adventure." I absently sipped out of the mug. The substance was warm and bitter, similar to what we call *Express Go!*™ in the Realm. "What do you call this?"

"Coffee."

"Is that so? I know a fellow named Coffee. He's a bit high strung, but all in all he's a stand-up guy."

"Yeah," said Jay-zun still staring at me, "I know Coffee."

"Verily?" This fellow was becoming more intriguing by the moment. "How did you and Sir Coffee meet, pray tell?"

"I wrote about him in *The Incarnations of Princess Plum*."

"Is that so?" It was then I noticed a pad of lined paper with sloppy handwriting littering the pages lying on the table. "What are you writing about now?"

"You."

"Fascinating. May I?" I took the tablet and began flipping through it. "Not bad. You're quite the tale-spinner. You know, I've been accused of being a raconteur myself. I'll tell you what, why don't you run in and get me some of your 'coffee' while I read over what you've written. Just to check it for facts and all."

"Yeah, sure. Why not? Might as well let the figment of my imagination give me writing advice. What's the worst that could happen?" The young author disappeared inside the shop and I scanned through his writings. Most of them were indeed moments taken from my life. Bits and pieces, mind you, a memory here, a fantasy there, but all unmistakably my own.

He returned shortly with a fresh, steaming mug of coffee.

I sipped it in delight, "Delicious stuff."

"Yeah," said the writer, "but addicting."

"All vices are. That's what makes them so fun." This lad was obviously green. He needed a few life lessons lest he meet his fate in the jaws of some despicable demon or another. I decided right then and there to set him aright. I've a weak spot for such charity. "Let me tell you, you've written some interesting personal accounts of mine. How is it you came to know them?"

Jay-zun shrugged. "I just kinda saw them. In my mind."

"Ah. Imagination truly is our greatest gift. Well then you won't mind if I offer you some creative criticisms in order to help you get it right? I won't be misrepresented, no matter which realm I'm in."

"Of course. Misrepresentation often leads to slander."

"Right you are. Now, understand that these incidents occurred during some of my travels. Travels which I later recorded in an *absolutely* <u>true</u> retelling. Not just any tale, mind you. This tale is larger than life. It has to be, for the hero himself was larger than life. Would you like to hear it?"

"Sure."

"Great!" I gathered my thoughts while sipping coffee. It really was delicious. "I'll give you the shortly-long version to save us a few ticks of the tock. Right, then. Good sir," taking a breath, I gathered all my bardic energies into my Voice, "allow me to present to you: The Saga of Shamus.

Part One

The Rise and
Fall of Shamus

Shamus McFamus was a giant among giants. He was so giant that he dwarfed all the other giants in the Realm of Possibility. Shamus had monstrous hands teeming with thick forests of coarse hair. His arms were as massive as the trunks of ancient Redwood Trees, and they bulged with muscles as big as hills. His enormous head was accentuated by the chiseled lines on his forehead that flowed like rivers when he sweat. His nose, a colossal onion shape, resembled the domes atop the churches and palaces made by the Frosty Folk of the Frozen Lands.

Because of Shamus's immense features, the other giants feared and hated him. But all giants have massive egos to maintain, and their egos couldn't admit to fearing anyone. So, the giants kept their fears hidden and only whispered about them when they were alone in their secret giant places. What the insecure colossi didn't know was that no place is truly secret. And while no other giants were around, other things were. Invisible things that listened with sibilant ears to the giants tell their secrets[1] and repeated these confessions with breezy tongues to anyone or anything that would listen.

Shamus heard the rumors, but he didn't mind that the other giants disliked him. They were smaller and weaker and it seemed like every time he tried to help or play with them, they ended up getting hurt. Not because Shamus wanted to hurt them, but because he didn't know his own strength. So, Shamus kept to himself and plotted a grand future in which he would be adored and loved by all. This future would indeed come about, but not in the way the lonely giant imagined.

Shamus's biggest problem was his taste for the finer things in life. He liked expensive clothes, gourmet food, and first-class travel. He liked to have huge luxury carriages with lots of horses to pull them.

---

[1] The Secrets of the Winds: The sibilant North Wind heard the somber confessions of jealous giants and shared the secret with his brother the South Wind and his sisters, the East and West Winds. Then, the four winds spread the secrets of the giants all over the Realm of Possibility. Because that's what the winds do. They carry the stories and dreams and secrets of the universes upon their breezy backs and sing these stories to any and all that care to hear them. That's how I found out about it. I just closed my orbs and listened to the winds sing.

Most of all, Shamus liked to be treated like nobility, even though he wasn't. Shamus yearned for these material possessions with all of his insurmountable being because he thought that they would make him happy and content. His giant's logic figured that if material possessions brought happiness, then more possessions meant more happiness.

Being a giant among giants didn't help Shamus in his pursuit of the rich and famous life style. Shamus was so huge that he needed bigger quantities of the finer things more frequently than the other giants. The finer things in life cost a lot of dingle and dingle doesn't grow on trees (around there anyway). It was gossiped around Giantdom that Shamus alone used forty percent of the entire Realm of Possibility's resources! This created problems in Giantdom and Shamus was eventually "voted off" by the rest of the giant community. So, the giant among giants left his home in search of prosperity and a bit of elbow room.

He packed everything he owned and left Giantdom to farm land he inherited from his father. The truth of the matter is Shamus inherited the land after a ruthless court battle that ended in broken hearts and broken bank accounts. The court battle actually seemed to be going in his father's favor when a surprising turn of events changed the course of history.

In the end, Shamus's father, Amos McFamus, abruptly proclaimed in court, "Your honor, just give the brat what he wants. I'd much rather be on a beach somewhere enjoying what's left of my life and my estate." Then he walked out of the courtroom with his head held high and never looked back. Fathers do that a lot, I think. They fight with their sons because all fathers want to see their sons succeed. But sons are stubborn folk who seem to enjoy making mistakes and driving their parents crazy. That's why parents eventually stop fighting. They get tired of being crazy.

The land was some of the best the Realm of Possibility had to offer: a beautiful expanse of territory just outside Giantdom with rolling hills, rivers, waterfalls and everything else that a realmly paradise needs. Shamus surveyed his new domain and noticed the Forest of Hidden Things, an enchanted ecosystem populated with all manner of exotic plants, animals and trees, spanned most of his land. Shamus reasoned that the absolute best land for farming must be *under* the forest because there were already a lot of plants growing there. The way he saw it, there were an awful lot of trees crowding up prime farming real-estate and he needed lumber to build houses, barns, and fences. Little did the giant know, his task wouldn't be easy.

Among the populace of the Forest of Hidden Things lived the shadowy Tree Folk. Distrustful by nature, they lurked about in the safety of the forest's eldritch gloom. Nothing Shamus did managed to lure the reticent forest dwellers from their sanctuary. They denied all his diplomatic rhetoric with silent responses and spat on the giant's name[2] when McFamus offered to let them stay and farm the land after he cleared it of trees. The frustrated giant even tried yelling threats at them, but the Tree Folk remained unmoved. In a last ditch effort, he decided to try luring the Tree Folk out of the forest by giving them some dingle and a few sacks of old potatoes he picked up at the farmer's market. I mean, who doesn't like potatoes?

Surprisingly, this worked…kind of. Shamus managed to trick one tribe of Tree Folk into leaving the safety of the trees.[3] He placed the dingle and potatoes just outside the forest and hid by disguising himself as a large hill. Soon, the curious Manhattans crept out of the forest of primitive notions and into the open plain of progression. Once they did this, Shamus snatched them up in his titanic hands and dropped the confused Tree Folk into a glass jar. He corked the top and went about his business with the jar dangling from his belt.

Without the frivolous luxuries of air, food, and water the jarred Manhattans dropped dead like cultists around a punch bowl. The survivors desperately cried out to Shamus for mercy, but his head was so far above his waist that their pleas fell on deaf ears. Instead, the giant set his mind to clearing the Manhattan's portion of the forest.

The South wind happened to be passing through that day. He watched the intrepid giant obliterate thousands of trees with one apocalyptic swipe of his more-giant-than-giant axe. A great outpouring of agony sallied forth from Gaia[4] as the mammoth lumberjack littered the forest floor with felled trees and bleeding stumps.

This sudden destruction caused woodland creatures to stir in their dens, burrows, and nests. In an attempt to stave off Shamus's assault,

---

[2] After speaking the name of a disliked individual, a person spits on the ground in disgust at having uttered such filth. To spit on someone's name is like spitting on them personally. In the Realm this is sign of disrespect and disgust. Wars have been started because of it.

[3] The Manhattan tribe was a bit bolder than other Tree Folk when it came to dealing with strangers. Their land skirted the very edge of the forest and the Manhattans had actually come into contact with a smattering of travelers and traders over the years.

[4] Gaia is the name of the spirit that inhabits earth in the Realm of Possibility. She is the daughter of the Lady of Pleasure and the Jolly Man.

thousands of animals amassed to form a wall of furry beasties. Wily foxes, timid deer, albino squirrels, courageous foozlebunnies, pythonic owls, sibilant serpents, and even the great and massive Ted Bears (that slept in the forest's hidden caves), gathered as one to protect their home and Mother Gaia.

They desperately attacked the indestructible mountain that was Shamus McFamus as he went Paul Bunyon on the outskirts of the forest. The wind witnessed the surge of animals slam into the part-time lumberjack and either fall harmlessly to the wayside or be crushed under the giant's feet. Shamus never missed a step. The animals gave everything they had to stop the giant's progress, to no avail. The brave critters added their corpses to the scores of fallen trees, and the mighty woodland wept at the loss of her many children. For the first time in history, fear crept inside The Heart of the Woods[5] and it beat a little quicker. All appeared lost.

The self-appointed farmer king wasn't all bad though. The benevolent landlord gathered lumber from his deforestation project and built a small village for the dislocated Manhattans in the foothills of Giant Mountain. He named it the "Tree Folk Reservation Village" and generously supplied the Folk Rez with seeds and hoes so they could farm the rocky terrain. If one ignored the fact that the Folk Rez was on the least farmable part of Shamus's property and one didn't look too closely at the shoddily constructed cabins, Shamus appeared to be a swell usurper.

He uncorked the bottle and dumped the natives onto their new home, never realizing that a great majority of them had already expired. The survivors were so elated to be somewhere besides a glass jar they didn't complain much about the removal from their ancestral home and subsequent relocation to a glorified shanty town. The Manhattans didn't even gripe when they discovered the land was actually rocky, barren, and nearly devoid of resources. Shamus took their silence as gratitude and continued his arborous conquest with a clean conscience.

As you can imagine, the remaining Tree Folk weren't the least bit amused with Shamus's lumberjacking venture. Using every ounce of resistance their primitive spirits could muster, they gathered their best warriors to attack Shamus with furious arrows and prickly spears. But

---

[5]The exact center of the Forest of Hidden Things. This is the oldest part of the Forest, the first grove that gave birth to a natural wonder. The Heart is a very magical place to many folk of the Realm and is connected to Gaia's essence. Legend says if the Heart dies, so does Gaia.

Shamus moved unperturbed as he destroyed their homes. Their arrows bounced harmlessly off of the giant's thick skin and their wooden spears were broken by his rock-hard muscle. Even the cries of primal rage and determination were drowned out by the giant's thunderous laugh. Like most giants, Shamus was a massive, unstoppable machine with a keen sense for battle and conquest. Tree by tree, tribe by tribe, the Tree Folk were driven out of the forest and forced to wander as gypsies or farm under Shamus's rule. Most chose to become gypsies.

Shamus fully intended clear out the forest and turn it into farm land, but Gaia had other plans. Deep in her belly anger boiled over into rage. Shamus had to be taught a lesson. Gaia bellowed a great cry for aid, which the South wind took up and spread throughout the Realm. But Shamus was a force to be reckoned with. All the Realm's inhabitants were paralyzed with fear at the thought of defying the giant. All except one: Jo-Joe, King of Mount Simian, was the lone hero confident enough to stand up to the destructive colossus and halt his progress. The Monkey King gathered his army and fearlessly awaited Shamus in the Heart of the Woods.

When the murderous lumberjack finally cleared his way to the Heart of the Woods, he found himself on the shore of a literal sea of monkeys. Monkeys stationed in trees, perched on rocks, swimming in rivers, monkeys everywhere. There must've been millions of them covering every remaining square inch of the forest. The sight of innumerable monkeys glaring with bestial rage at Shamus made him guffaw outright.

Shamus laughed until he trembled, "Do you honestly seek to challenge me, *monkey king*? I am the way of progress. Do you defy advancement?"

Without hesitation, the loquacious King Jo Joe marched over to Shamus's pinky toe and shoved it. "I find your advancement highly offensive and so does Mother Gaia. You have plundered your way too far into her precious bosom and now she suffers. The steely grip of death seeks her Heart. Your rapine progress has gone far enough! Filthy reaver! Cease your plundering! Turn around and be gone! Make haste back to your ill-begotten farmland before I am forced to move against you!"

Shamus did his best not to burst out laughing again. He raised himself up to his full height and said, "This is my land. I can do anything I want with it. I defeated Nature's onslaught and that of the forest's native dwellers. I am indestructible. So, stand aside, Monkey King, before you get hurt."

"That's fine," said Jo Joe, "For some odd reason, folk only respect action. Diplomacy is usually taken as a sign of weakness. I prefer action to diplomacy, as a general rule. It's much more fun." The Monkey King raised his long arms above his head, "Monkey Sea! Monkey Do!" he screamed and drums began beating…beating…beating to a slow and steady rhythm.

In response, the monkey army started to sway with the rhythm of the drums. From a griffon's gaze, the sea of monkey warriors churned with sluggish and erratic waves. Jo Joe began a dance, shaking his out-stretched arms in the air and shuffling his feet. The drums responded in rhythm with the king's movements. Jo Joe moved faster and faster and his haphazard movements morphed into a calculated choreography. The primal flow gathered him up in rapture. As the king gyrated, the drums increased their rhythm to a frenzied pace. Jo Joe's subjects mimicked their liege and the sea became violently agitated. Shamus swatted at the churning tide with no effect. Every time he opened a hole it was immediately filled with more primates. Scattered screams began to erupt and quickly gathered in force and duration until a cacophonous roar deafened the stupefied giant. The roar matured into a horrendous crescendo and the waves began to uniformly swell into one giant tsunami. When the screaming peaked the furry tsunami broke! Suddenly, primates of all shapes and sizes washed over Shamus in sheer and unconquerable numbers. There was no resisting. Even a giant among giants has his limits.

The primates clung to Shamus like primordial glue and continued to rock to the beat of the drums. The giant uncontrollably swayed with the crowd of monkeys and was unable to keep his balance. With a shout of fear and disbelief, Shamus toppled backward to the clearing's floor.

The drums abruptly quit, plunging the forest into a tense silence.

Shamus's bellow shattered the uneasy quiet. "Alright! Alright! I'll leave! Just GET OFF OF ME!"

The drums began beating again, softly this time, and the sea of monkeys whispered, "Giant, giant go back now," while retreating into the forest as if fleeing the embrace of a sandy beach. Soon, Shamus was alone in the clearing staring up at the blue sky thoroughly dazed and confused. He hadn't expected that outcome at all. But he had learned a small lesson. He learned very swiftly that the bigger you are the easier it is for monkeys to topple you. With effort, he got back on his feet, picked up his axe and went home to begin farming.

Shamus quickly discovered he needed help. He had ample land to farm, but he couldn't farm it by himself. To alleviate this problem McFamus enticed thousands of folk to farm for him by organizing "The Great Dirt Derby," which promised free land to any who entered. In order to be fair about it, Shamus divided his land into sections called plots and put a marker flag in the middle of each plot. Folk that wanted a free plot were given a marker flag with their name on it. When the race began, folk scattered throughout the land in search of plots to claim. They "staked a claim" by replacing Shamus's marker with their own. Once a person staked a claim, the land was theirs.

The problem with competitions such as the Great Dirt Derby is that they tend to bring out avarice in some folk. The night before the race began, these nasty cheats, dubbed "earliers," tried to sneak onto the land and stake their claim before anyone else could. But fear not, for it was announced that any apprehended earliers would be fed to the Ravenous Vampires of Velhampshire. This seemed to be a good deterrent as only three earliers were caught and devoured (much to the vampires' dismay).

Once the Derby was over and the plots claimed, the farmer-king put his folk to work. They farmed from sun up to sun down, day in and day out. Shamus and his subjects worked the land ruthlessly. Year after year, they planted, tended, and harvested. This may have been good for making dingle, but it wasn't good for the land. Farming constantly without ever giving the land a break sucks out the nutrients and eventually nothing grows. That, amigos, is exactly what happened to Shamus McFamus's Land of Farmly Paradise.

Sadly, when the land couldn't give anymore neither could the folk. King McFamus tried to be a good leader and keep his folk's spirits up by giving encouraging speeches and work incentives like extra food and clothes. The farmer-king even tried to make up with the Folk Rez by giving them more food and acquainting them with whiskey to take the edge off a hard day's work. As grateful as they were, the problem wasn't with the folk. They still worked very hard, but the land was tired and worn. Seeing no other recourse, the colossus begrudgingly accepted his failure.

He waited for the cover of night, gathered all he had that could be sold and secretly fled, leaving his folk to fend for themselves. I know it sounds despicable, but we must not hate Shamus McFamus for this, good reader. It is only natural for a being to want to live. Life is a struggle for survival at every turn. Some folk believe that ultimately only the strongest beings will survive, while the weaker ones will fade into extinction. This is called *natural selection*. Since Shamus was one of the strongest beings in the entire Realm, he was very much in favor of natural selection. I guess you could say it came naturally to him.

The once-fertile land is what suffered the most. The stories say it was so wasted no plants could grow to absorb the sun's fierce energy. Gaia's flesh had been rendered defenseless to his heated fury. Every morning the flaming orb leapt into the sky with red anger. He shone as hot and bright as he could, relishing his withering effect on Gaia's tender flesh. "Look at me!" he screamed. "I am brilliant! I am powerful! I cannot be denied!"

The winds found the nuclear sphere's boasting rather hilarious and made it a point to taunt the sun by blowing cool breezes that acted as a salve for the wounded land. Not surprisingly, the sun *hates* to be taunted, especially by the four winds. In response, the sun grew angrier and burned increasingly hotter until the rest of the plants shriveled and most of the wildlife dispersed to more temperate climes. Devoid of vegetation to shield it, Gaia's flesh became a dry and arid desert. Rolling hills of green morphed into sifting dunes of sand, lakes shrunk into tiny oases and the rivers dried up except for the Great River of Destiny that flowed through the center of Shamus's farming colony. Eventually, all that was left of Shamus McFamus's Land of Farmly Paradise were ruined cities, dead fields, and lots of ghosts. The desert was christened, "The Desert of Lost Causes," to serve as a reminder of what happens when folk abuse the land that gives them life.

Most of Shamus's workers fled, joined the gypsies, or died during the sun's brutal scorching. Folk unlucky enough to survive the relentless barrage and remain in the desert developed hopeless spirits and defeated attitudes with impressive speed. They felt the gods had singled them out personally, which, knowing certain gods, was not entirely out of the question. This bitter chip on their collective shoulder made them suspicious of outsiders and convinced them that civility was a luxury they could no longer afford.

They built a city on the banks of the River of Destiny that reflected their hollow and angry spirits and named it, with a flair for the obvious, the City of Lost Causes. Its first citizens anointed a queen to rule them — the first Queen of Swords — and she proved to be exactly the kind of leader a city like that deserves. Her dynasty of cruelty has continued uninterrupted ever since.[6] The motto inscribed above the city gates reads: "Survival first, civility later." They mean it.

---

[6] I would like to take a moment to note that the Queen's daughter, the Princess of Swords, is a rather nice young lady, though she is given to bouts of drama

The city boasts a thriving black market, a booming slave trade, and what its Chamber of Commerce optimistically calls the "involuntary organ donation" sector, which is growing faster than any other industry in the Desert of Lost Causes and considerably faster than anyone who visits it.

Naturally such a city attracts organizations that prefer to conduct their business in the dark. The City of Lost Causes is home to the Assassin's Union, the Associated Union of United Cutpurses and Cat Burglars, the Mercenary Placement Agency, the Society of Non-Goodly Aligned Wizards Sorcerers Jugglers and Clowns, the Mad Scientists and Evil Doctors Club, and the ever-popular Guild of General Miscreants. I have had dealings with most of them. I don't recommend it.

and histrionics. Though I suppose that comes with having such a vicious, narcissistic woman for a mother. I have recorded an Absolutely True Retelling about this dysfunctional family entitled *Frederico's Flamenco and Other Tangoes to Live By*.

Shamus spent his remaining dingle investing in the West Feather Trading Company, a small shipping company located in the lively port of City of Allure. The company was involved in a growing triangle of trade between the Continents of North Vespucciland and Oldhome and the West Feather Islands. The West Feather Trading Company was actually a conglomerate of smaller shipping companies that decided to pool their resources for more effective business. It was the first company in the Realm's history (but not the last) to issue stocks. Each investor bought a certain amount and their dividend yield depended on the amount of their initial investment. Shamus was sitting at a cool forty percent yield and quickly found that being a merchant was much more profitable than being a farmer. He was making twice the dingle and only doing half the work. All he really did was sign forms and check shipments before they left port. The managers and ships' captains took care of the rest.

The West Feather Trading Company rapidly gained momentum as the leading commercial power in the Realm. The company grew exponentially and at its peak employed 55,000 folk, had 1,000 merchant ships, 250 warships, a personal army of about 10,000 mercenaries, and outposts scattered all over the trade route. These trading outposts were really a pseudo-military presence that often interfered with the governments and societies of the native tribes and even constructed internment camps disguised as plantations. Or maybe it was the other way around. Either way, innocent folk greatly suffered for the profit of a few men thousands of leagues away.

Shamus was overjoyed to discover that for the first time in recallable history, he had ample time and dingle to do with as he pleased. The first thing he did with his spare dingle was buy all the fancy clothes he could never afford and the luxury carriage that used three gulps of hay juice just to get down the block. He splurged on gourmet meals, cheesy artwork, overpriced furniture, and superfluous accessories. Oh, and let's not forget the beachfront mansion in the City of Allure. This palatial home boasted fifteen bedrooms, five baths (with running water), a dining room, a ball room, a full-service kitchen, a library, stables, and private beach access. Desiring to show-off his wealth and abundance to others, the merchant saw Gatsby's distant green light and began throwing lavish parties that are still legendary to this day.

The parties attracted noble and famous folks from miles around. Luxury carriages would line the road for blocks. Nobles like King Jo Joe of Mount Simian attended Shamus's galas (after the giant merchant issued him a formal apology) and famous folk such as the Minstrel Lord Bard[7] performed the most heart-breaking concerts one's ears have ever been privy to. Shamus's manse was always abuzz with revelers partaking in his generosity and wealth. But the good life wouldn't last forever. As the saying goes, "You can't throw a stone in the sky and expect it to fly."

The West Feather Trading Company soon became too big for its britches. The investors and merchants running the company amassed a great deal of material wealth in a relatively short span of time. This wealth went right to the "conquest centers" of their brains, turning honest, hardworking businessmen turned into greedy, shifty power-mongers. Since demand for goods rose sharply, supply needed to be maintained. To ensure this, the West Feather Trading Company took matters into its own hands and began to engage in less-than-honorable practices such as assassination, extortion, slavery, and genocide.

To nobody's surprise, open rebellion flared up on many of the islands and coastal cities ravaged by the terrible presence of the West Feather Trading Company. No folk can handle the boot of oppression on their necks forever. Eventually, freedom is the only option and that at any cost. Think of it like wanting personal space, but your parents keep bursting into your room to demand things when all you want to do is read a good book. For a while you grumble, then you yell for your space, and finally you slam the door in their face and lock the door. It's like that, but with much more bloodshed.

In order to protect its assets and land, the company used its private army and warships to quell these violent outbursts. Those in Charge decided the warships would best serve by battering the coastlines and ports of any folk aggressively resistant to the company's expansion—a policy which quickly extended beyond the savage

---

[7] The embodiment of creative sound. He is everything that is chaotic and passionate about music. He is the reason that music moves folk and changes lives. He serves She of the Benevolent Chaos.

islanders and began affecting city-states on the main continents. Thus, the West Feather Trading company became highly unpopular with the nobles of the Realm and action was finally taken to stop the expansion of this destructive commercial beast.

A gathering of rouge captains and nobles joined together to form the greatest sea-faring dynasty in history: The Pirate Kings. The first Pirate King was Lord Protector Principle of Singing Duck Island. Originally a company man placed on the island as governor, Lord Protector Principle turned on the company after it sold all his island's native tribes into slavery. Disillusioned, he gathered like-minded heroes around him and together they struck at the commercial behemoth that was the West Feather Trading Company.

The Pirate Kings began their rebellion by attacking the company's interests in the West Feather Islands. With the help of indigenous tribes, the Pirate Kings captured or destroyed many of the company's weaker outposts and retook possession of the islands for their native folk. Using the conquered outposts as bases, the Pirate Kings assaulted the shipping interests of the company.

The Pirate Kings started with small raids on unprotected merchant fleets and lone warships, striking suddenly and disappearing quickly. No ship flying the West Feather Trading Company colors was safe from the ravages of those vigilantes. Attacks on West Feather Trading Company ships became more violent and bold, and before long no company ship could sail the open water freely. The company's trade got hit square in the dingle pouch, and the Pirate Kings started a parallel economy by redistributing West Feather's reappropriated goods throughout the Realm.

Without frequent contact and support from the mainland, the company's remaining outposts fell to native rebellions and Pirate King attacks. The company organized a last-ditch effort in the form of a massive assault on the Pirate Kings. Throwing everything it had into the war, this bold and desperate ploy severely sapped West Feather's resources and dingle. This war lasted for seven years after which time the company lost the epic sea battle and slid into bankruptcy. The Pirate Kings assumed the sea trade in the Realm, and to this day, it is a thriving business founded on honorable principles.


As one of the trading company's most staunch financiers, the war against the Pirate King's quickly dwindled Shamus's bank account. And like all folk who live outside their means, he sank into the sticky mire of debt.[8] Shamus not only lost his business, but also his mansion, fancy clothes, luxury carriages, gourmet food, and everything else. And remember all of those famous and noble folk that came to his parties? Yeah, well, no one wants to party with a broke indigent. Shamus McFamus was now a very broke and very broken giant with loan sharks constantly nipping at his heels.

Loan sharks are experts at turning fake dingle into real dingle by any means necessary and are very menacing when it comes to getting their due. Bones get broken, houses catch fire, it's a whole ordeal. Shamus found this out one morning when the loan sharks showed up at his front door with a squad of hired goons. The tradesman McFamus was forced to flee the city, not out of cowardice (well, maybe a bit) but out of fear for life and limb.

The bankrupt tradesman wandered the Realm as a homeless vagabond scorned by all. Not even the gypsies, the vagabond's vagabonds, would have anything to do with Shamus. I suspect they were still a bit wounded over the whole Forest of Hidden Things debacle. This rejection was the final catalyst that sent the giant spiraling into the period of his life known as "The Great Depression."

During his Great Depression, Shamus traveled the Realm from village to village. A hungry and pathetic sight, he took any odd jobs he came across. If a village had no work, the giant plopped down, sitting for days on the outskirts of the town consuming any and all surrounding resources. With frequent pitiful sighs, he ate away his pain and negative emotions, while his huge body cast an enormous shadow that plunged the entire town into an artificial dusk. To make matters worse, every time he sighed, his hot breath scorched the soil and kicked up clouds of dust and debris that blotted out the sun even further! These extended periods of giant induced nights became to be known as "Shadow Spells."

No amount of pleading could get Shamus to move. No amount of food, treasure, or beautiful women could motivate him to move either, although, he always accepted these gifts with a half-hearted word of thanks. Except for the women. A giant among giants has no need for teeny women. They're like chatty dolls and the last thing Shamus needed in his Great Depression was the responsibility of

---

[8] Debt is when folk give you fake dingle to spend then demand you pay it back with real dingle (which is also largely fake). Then when you don't, or can't, pay it back, they come legally steal all your stuff. Debt is bad, dear reader, don't do it.

taking care of a slew of teeny women. He wasn't even responsible enough to take care of himself.

Eventually, the giant would consume all of the town's available stock piles and natural resources from the surrounding area. Then, he would heave himself to his feet and move on to the next unsuspecting hamlet. You'd think Shamus would've realized the pain he was causing others, but he didn't realize anything except his depression. Those were dark days for many folks on many levels. And just when the Realm thought it'd be plagued by Shamus's Shadow Spells forever the tables turned and something wonderful happened.

It came about that a traveling salesman/ motivational speaker/ doctor of the mind and body/ licensed creditor extraordinaire/ entrepreneur/ and purveyor of all things fantastical and rare (at discount prices!), named Man Man, happened across Shamus during the giant's Shadow Spell outside Curry, now a ghost town.

"What's the matter with you?" asked Man Man as he slowed his cart to a halt at the giant's feet.

"I don't wanna talk about it," mumbled Shamus without looking at the peddler.

"Good. Neither do I really, but my mother always told me it was polite to care."

"Your mother was a smart woman."

"She was something," said Man Man, his voice carrying a longing for bygone days, "Anyway, I can tell from your slumped posture and oppressive sadness that you are a very big giant who is down on his luck. By the looks of it, you could very well be right smack dab in the middle of a Great Depression. Am I right?"

Shamus nodded. "How did you know?"

Man Man bowed. "I, Man Man, am a seer of much and a doer of little. I sell, I tell, I smell, once I even fell."

"Do you have any food or dingle? That'd be swell," said Shamus, awestruck and enchanted by this traveling salesman.

Man Man bowed. "Of course, milord, but that will cost you."

Shamus leaned down very close to Man Man so he could see him face to face. "I don't have any dingle. If I did, I wouldn't be in the middle of a Great Depression and asking *you* for it."

"Well then, today is your lucky day. Fortune smiles and lights the way. For I have exactly what you need."

The homeless McFamus raised his orbrows ever so slightly, orbs glimmering with the tiniest spark of interest behind their melancholy gloom, "Yeah? What might that be?"

"I happen to have a correspondence degree in motivational speaking."

"What is motivational speaking?"

"Motivational speaking is the greatest thing since voluntary indoctrination," said Man Man. "See, what a motivational speaker does is he makes depressed folk happy again. He makes them feel good about themselves and their lives. Motivational speakers also help folk make lots of dingle by selling them books of dingle making secrets. For instance…" Man Man rummaged around in the "Books" section of his cart until he came across a huge tome which he presented to Shamus with a triumphant smile.

"Awwwww. A book," whined Shamus, "I hate to read."

"Now, now. Give it a chance. That's not just any book, sir. No. That is a copy of *Mark's Book of Consumptionism*. A rare treasure indeed."

"Who's Mark?" asked Shamus, still not sold on the whole book idea.

"Oh, he was just a guy that knew a lot," the motivational speaker paused dramatically like in your realm on reality television when they are about to kick someone off the show, "about making dingle quickly and easily."

The sound of that made Shamus's ears perk up. "Well, how does he make dingle?"

"You'll have to read it and find out," said Man Man like a school teacher to a student.

Shamus opened the book. On page one was "Lesson One." It read: When low on dingle, never hesitate to ask for a loan from a licensed creditor extraordinaire. This is called establishing credit. Credit is good. Any good practitioner of orthodox consumptionism has credit. Shamus closed the book. "I need credit," he announced.

"Excellent! I happen to have credit right here," Man Man replied. He reached into his cloak and pulled out a scroll and a large dangle of dingle. "Now, in order to receive credit, you have to sign my contract. It sets up a repayment plan with reasonable vig.**"

Shamus was confused. "What's vig?"

"Vig is a small monthly charge you pay me on any dingle you haven't paid back. I'll start you out low…how's forty percent sound?"

"I don't know that seems a bit steep. First tell me how much is in the bag."

"Enough for you to get back on top if you follow Mark's lessons to the tittle. Minus the cost of the book and the motivational speaker seminar, of course."

Shamus was torn. He didn't quite trust Man Man. Something wasn't right about the mysterious peddler, something that he couldn't quite put his finger on itched at the back of his mind. But the giant was desperate to change his life, so he ignored it, "Alright, I'll do it." Shamus signed the contract.

As he handed Man Man's contract back to him, he felt a weird sensation in his gut. Like his Sacred Fish[9] had just gone belly up. Shamus ignored the peculiar feeling and snatched the dangle of dingle from Man Man's hand. Consumptionism makes one ignore all sorts of pertinent feelings.

"And that's that," Man Man said while rubbing his hands together like a greedy child in a candy store. "Now, the next step is to help you stay out of this depression. I have just the thing, being a Doctor of the Body and Mind." He went over to the medicine section of his cart and sorted through vials until he found what he was looking for. He handed the vial to Shamus.

"What is it?" asked the giant, scrutinizing the contents of the bottle.

"It's a Potion of Happiness. With one drink, your troubles go away and you become happy again…for approximately 24 hours."

"Then what?" questioned Shamus.

"Then, you simply take another one," replied Man Man.

"Sounds easy," said Shamus.

"Oh, it is. Here, I'll tell you what I'll do. I'll start you off with a month's supply for half the cost and throw in an open prescription. It'll be good with any druggist[10] in the Realm who handles my product, except the naturalists. Nasty lot there, I'd avoid them if I were you. Safest thing to do."

Now that Shamus had dingle, he was ready to spend it, so he bought Man Man's potion of happiness and drank a bottle of it.

---

[9] The king of the Fair Folk, Oberon, gives the best description of what a sacred fish is. He says: It is thy inner self of inner most inner self's in one's own innards. It is what keeps a person most vibrant, energetic and faithful. Without it a person becomes dull, boorish and given to attend social functions like a meeting of city councilmen. Verily I tell you, that without a Sacred Fish a person is reduced to an everyday, normal bureaucratic or corporate mode of profession. The person is unaware of their drudgery and misery because they are so sedated all the time. In short, folk without their sacred fish will be reduced to a state of complacent cowness. From: *The Incarnations of Princess Plum.*

[10] Druggists are like pharmacists. Except, here in the Realm, druggists sell potions. In your realm, druggists sell mostly pills. Druggists only make dingle when they sell their drugs. So, they sell their goods to anyone who will buy them, especially doctors, because everyone who is three-plus-one knows that doctors and druggists help each other make dingle. Doctors prescribe drugs and send folk to druggists to buy them. In return, druggists hook doctors up with all kinds of perks. Around here, that's called a "racket."

Instantly, Shamus felt happier. He began to laugh, which was something he hadn't done in a very long time.

Man Man smiled a secret and evil smile. "Good luck, milord. I will return every month to collect the payment you owe me for your credit." Without another word, Man Man got on his cart and left.

Reading Mark's books never made anyone smart. But folk like Shamus don't read books because they're smart. They read books so other folk's ideas get into their heads and become their own. This is called learning. Shamus learned a great deal about making dingle from Man Man's book. He learned how to buy low and sell high. He learned how to seize the means of production. And, once seized, he learned about supply and demand, mass production, and low overhead costs. He learned how to make folk buy stuff they don't need and how to make folk continue wanting the things they buy, even if those things are bad for them. But most importantly, he learned how to manipulate the folk he was exploiting by spreading lies about how everything would be better if it were free. And those that had more should be obligated to share with those who had less. So, folk constantly fought among themselves over who was entitled to what, and never paid attention to Shamus who was manipulating them all to get what he wanted, which was lots of dingle and the power to use it.

He quickly spent the money Man Man gave him on some land, a huge palace, and startup capital for his corporation. Shamus named his corporation *Shamuscorp*, and following Mark's Lesson number 13, he put his stock up for public trade. Now, anyone with enough dingle could buy and sell stock in Shamus's corporation. Then the giant built his palace/ office on his highest hill and named it Headquarters Hill.

Shamus's palace was truly a sight to behold. It was hundreds of feet high, so Shamus could have plenty of head room, and was made of the whitest marble. He had seven towers with seven spires and from each spire flew seven flags, each emblazoned with one of the seven sacred animals. The wall surrounding the palace was one hundred feet high and fifty feet thick. After he built his headquarters, he hired a staff and a bunch of vice presidents to help him run his business efficiently. Then, he built a factory so he could start producing goods for his corporation to sell.

Shamus began producing and selling and buying and selling and producing and selling and producing and selling and buying again. He bought shoes, shirts, tunics, lutes, guitars and carriages. He sold horses, medicine, food and entertainment. And just like Man Man predicted, Shamus quickly rose back to the top. Soon, others began to see Shamus's prosperity and moved to his land in hopes of sharing in "Shamus's Dream." Shamus named his land the Undividable Land of Shamus and built his folk a city to live in. The city was named "Shamusville" and its citizens were dubbed "Shamusans."

Man Man rolled into Shamus's palace monthly to collect his payment. On Man Man's sixteenth visit, Shamus expressed some concerns that had come to light.

"It's just, I don't know. I'm not as happy as I used to be anymore…like the happiness potion quit working," said Shamus.

Man Man nodded sagely. "Tolerance."

"What's that?" asked CEO McFamus.

"It means your body is getting used to the amount of the potion you are taking. You need to start taking more in order to be as happy as you were."

"More?"

"Did I stutter?" snapped Man Man, "double your usual dose."

Shamus was uneasy about this.

"What seems to be the problem?" asked Man Man.

"It's just that I can barely afford the dose I'm taking now. What with the gourmet meals, the trips to the theater, and the shopping excursions in the marketplace. I'm broke."

Man Man patted the giant's massive pinky toe in understanding and sympathy. "I understand and sympathize with you. The answer is simple: work harder and faster. Make even more dingle."

"But then I won't have time for anything else, like golf or going to the theater," protested Shamus.

"Then I suppose you'll have to ask yourself what is more important: Your happiness or your free time."

"But I want both," whined Shamus.

"Tuff. 'You can't have your muffin and eat a doughnut too', my Uncle Bill Z. Bub used to say. So quit whining. Look, I'll loan you some more dingle so you can get your first month's double dose now. You'll just need to sign another contract…"

Shamus signed yet another of Man Man's contracts. As soon as he made the last quill stroke, the giant swore that he felt *smaller* and not so giant and strong anymore. However, Man Man looked a bit larger and more vibrant than he did when he arrived.

The next time Man Man came to visit, Shamus was bedridden from exhaustion.

The peddler looked annoyed to find Shamus lying in bed instead of out working for dingle. "What's the matter with you now, giant?"

"I've been working so hard and so fast for so long that I burnt myself out. I'm sick now and I don't have any energy. I can't even move to get out of bed."

"And my fee?" asked Man Man knowingly.

Shamus lowered his gaze in shame.

"I see you don't have it this month. Tsk. Tsk. What am I going to do with you, my massive mound of muttering matter?"

"Give me one more month?" Shamus queried weakly but not without a certain tone of hopefulness in his voice.

Man Man tapped his temple to rattle around any loose thoughts and snatched the first one to fall out of his brain pan. "O.K. here's what I'll do. I'll give you that extra month to pay me. Plus," Man Man reached into his cloak and produced a vial of Black Sludge, "this."

"What is it?" asked Shamus.

"It's Black Sludge. Helps to keep you going. Gives you energy. Zip! Zoom! Zing! I'll give you the first month's dose in advance. You can pay me next month."

Shamus groaned. "But I already owe you so much. I don't think I'll ever be able to repay you."

"Well, you need not worry about that now," said Man Man handing the vial of Black Sludge to Shamus. "Here, the first shot is on me."

Shamus drank the sludge with a grimace and before he knew it, he couldn't sit still. He was awake and full of energy. "Woo! That'll put hair on your chest." Shamus paced excitedly across his room making vice presidents scatter to avoid being crushed by his massive feet. He halted abruptly, "Hey, I've got an idea," the CEO said excitedly, "We'll mass produce it. Start selling this stuff to *everybody*. I can see it now: Keep yourself moving with *Express Go!*™!"

"*Express Go!*™?" wondered Man Man, "It's called Black Sludge, not *Express Go!*™."

"No it's not. Mark's Lesson Number 175 says, 'Folk don't want stuff that has a gross name or looks disgusting. So, you need to make it look cool and give it a super neat name so folk will buy it and use it.' Black Sludge is a disgusting name. But, *Express Go!*™ That's a name that has potential. You could get behind something called *Express Go!*™. I've got to get started!"

With his trademark smile of vile, Man Man left Shamus to his work once again.

Shamus assembled his best folk to help him produce and sell *Express Go!*™.

First, he got Russell Bugtussell from Research and Development (or R&D) to take the Black Sludge into his special lab and run experiments on it. Bugtussell wanted to know exactly what the Black Sludge was made of. He wanted to know everything about it, from why it was black to why drinking it gave a person so much energy. Using his complicated scientific machinery with all its tubes and hoses and Bunsen burners, he ran every scientific experiment he could think of and even some he couldn't. Finally, he discovered the very thing that gave folk energy and made them shaky and talk a lot! He called it zing. Russell took zing and began putting it in other things like food and candy and soda pop. Then, the R & D staff added all manner of additives, preservatives and other chemicals to Black Sludge so it would taste better and have a longer shelf life.

Next, CEO McFamus got Bobby From Marketing to change the name of Black Sludge to *Express Go!*™. Bobby had bottle labels designed and ready for production and decided on three different flavors of *Express Go!*™ to sell: regular *Express Go!*™, Diet *Express Go!*™ (for those folk who enjoyed the delusion of thinking a sugary, syrupy concoction loaded full of zing could be healthy), and Lemon-Lime *Express Go!*™.

Then, Shamus enlisted the help of the Totally Awesome Duo of Paco Production and Danny Distribution. Paco's job was to make as much *Express Go!*™ as he could as fast as he could. Oh yeah, Paco also had to make *Express Go!*™ as cheaply as he could to keep the overall price of *Express Go!*™ down and make it more affordable for the masses of consumers in the Undividable Land of Shamus. In order to keep costs low, Paco built a factory in the destitute Desert of Lost Causes instead of building a factory in the Undividable Land of Shamus. Paco did this because folk in the Desert of Lost Causes were so poor they would work for any amount of dingle no matter how despicably low the wage was. Also, the Queen of Swords, who ruled over the Desert, wasn't interested in safe work places or proper sanitation. She was interested in bringing industry to her land in order to help build her economy. This saved Paco a lot of dingle in the long run because the Safety and Sanitation Inspectors in the ULS could be downright bastards when they inspected places. Not having to worry about the inspectors made Paco's job that much easier and cheaper.

As soon as Paco Production began producing *Express Go!*™ it was up to Danny Distribution to make sure that *Express Go!*™ was available on every street corner and in every marketplace in the Realm. He did this by hiring a lot of wagon drivers. The wagon drivers loaded barrel after barrel of *Express Go!*™ onto their wagons and traveled the land in all directions selling *Express Go!*™, giving out free samples and delivering orders to every merchant, woman, or child they came across.

Finally, it was time to launch the marketing campaign. Shamus got Bobby From Marketing to design commercials and advertisements for *Express Go!*™. The vice president designed t-shirts, cups, and even action figures. Bobby paid playwrights to write plays promoting *Express Go!*™ and bards to sing songs about it. He designed huge banners to hang at jousts and tournaments and had noble and famous folk tell others about *Express Go!*™. Normal folk have an odd tendency to copy the things that noble and famous folk do, hoping to be like them.

But Bobby's crowning achievement was opening *Express Go!*™ *Stops*, cafes that served *Express Go!*™ drinks and zing pastries. Then the VP founded a restaurant that sold nothing but quickfood, which was food injected with zing and other unhealthy chemicals. He called the restaurant, *Famous McShamus*, in honor of his boss and king. Marketers made sure folk saw commercials and pictures for *Express Go!*™ everywhere they looked. Bobby and his team did all of these things because that's what marketers do. Marketers know that the more something is on a person's mind, the more that person wants it. So, if all you ever see, hear and think about is *Express Go!*™, then you want to buy it and drink it all the time. Marketing was very important to Shamus. It made him a lot of dingle. Soon, Shamusans wouldn't be able to breathe without inhaling zing.

A year after Bobby's marketing campaign started, Shamus had his entire population hooked on *Express Go!*™ and other zing-injected products. Citizens of the ULS took so much *Express Go!*™ they never stopped working to eat, sleep, play, or do anything else fun or non-work related. As a result, blood pressure, heart disease, and stroke rates rose to epic levels, but nobody noticed because they were working so much. Before too long, the local newspaper, *The Giant Gazette*, began to report on the skyrocketing divorce, abuse, and crime rates that "mysteriously" appeared at the same time *Express Go!*™ and other zing-based products hit the scene. Shamusans thought that *Express Go!*™ was doing so much good there was no possible way any bad could come from it. The paper contributed the rise to an influx of deviants into the area. What the paper failed to report was that the majority of the deviants were long-time citizens who had fallen into the dark pit of *Express Go!*™ addiction and the rest were insurance salesmen.

Man Man entered Shamustown, population 140,376, and immediately noticed the effects of his Black Sludge. He smiled his evil smile as he passed dirty folk shivering on streets and in alleys. These hopeless addicts gave a bad name to all the honest and down-on-their-luck homeless folk doing their best to reclaim their place in society.

Then there were the quickfood addicts. They were perhaps the saddest Shamusans in all the land. You see, quickfood gave folk a rush while they ate it, but afterwards they felt tired and lazy. The only way to feel the rush again was to eat more quickfood. So, quickfood addicts would eat quickfood *all the time*. This made quickfood highly popular and highly addicting. All the chemicals and additives in the unhealthy cuisine were bad for folk's bodies, but they ate it anyway. Because of their blatant denial of the food's harmful effects, quickfood addicts became very sick. The "foodies"[11] as they were

---

[11] Zing addiction doesn't announce itself. That's what makes it so effective. The sacred fish doesn't go out like a candle. It dims so gradually that most folk don't notice until the fishome is nearly dry. By then the zing moves beyond pleasure into need. The difference between a man who enjoys Express Go!™ and a man who needs it is the difference between a swimming fish and a fish that's

stereotyped, became permanently lethargic and eventually died from either obesity or toxic chemical shock to the internal organs. But Shamusans ignored this as well, claiming the foodies were responsible for their own bad health.

"No one *forced* them to eat all that quickfood," Shamusans would mumble as they sipped their drinks at the *Express Go!*™ *Stop*. But those folks were duped as well. In their snide ignorance they became addicted to *Express Go!*™. And soon, that addiction would rip their Sacred Fish from them in a horrible manner.

Man Man saw all of this as he made his way to the gate of Shamus's giant palace on top of Headquarters Hill. The gate had an elaborate archway with an image carved into it of Shamus holding a smiling infant. Below the picture was the inscription: "Giantly gentle stands our Lord." Man Man always laughed out loud whenever he read that. And that day was no exception. The peddler was in the middle of his loud laughing when he was approached by a homeless man begging for dingle outside the gate. Something was familiar about the bum trying to mooch change off Man Man. But the swindler didn't care, he just pushed his way past the man and said, "Get a job, you stupid bum."

Man Man found Shamus juiced up on *Express Go!*™, jabbering and pacing excitedly in the courtyard of his palace. His humongous feet had worn huge grooves into the ground that came to be known later as "The Canals of Worry."

Man Man cleared his throat and the giant, who was feeling even smaller and weaker than he did at Man Man's last visit, came to an abrupt halt. Conversely, Man Man seemed that much bigger. So much bigger in fact, that he was almost to Shamus's shoulder.

The CEO's face contorted with anger as he peered down at Man Man, "Where have you been?" demanded Shamus angrily.

"I've been about my business," replied Man Man haughtily. "What is troubling you, milord?"

"What's troubling me? What's troubling me? I'll tell you what's troubling me! It's all falling apart! Everything! My folk are sick and depressed and a lot of them are homeless and starving. There is crime! Can you believe it? Crime like murder and robbery and it is all because of *Express Go!*™!" shouted Shamus, his voice cracking as if he were going to burst into tears.

---

forgotten how to swim. The tragedy being that from the outside they look almost identical. Until they don't.

"Now, now. Let's not be too hasty to blame things that might not be at fault. I gave you my Black Sludge—"

"*Express Go!*™," corrected Shamus immediately.

"Yes, of course. I gave you my *Express Go!*™ in order to help you and your folk work harder and make more dingle. Are they?"

"Yes! That's all they do. They work and guzzle *Express Go!*™ or eat a Zing Brownie or whatever. Until they get addicted and run out of dingle."

Man Man nodded in approval, "I noticed. Quite the brilliant marketing campaign."

"Yeah, Bobby was a good fellow," Shamus said with a regretful sigh that blew a hot wind of rancid sadness over Man Man.

"Was?" queried Man Man, his right orbrow raised in interest.

"Yeah. He was the first *Express Go!*™ addict. Called it 'method marketing.' His work performance became awful and the Marketing Department collapsed because of it. Thankfully, it had already done its job. Now, all he does is sit outside the gate, begging for dingle so he can get another shot of *Express Go!*™ or a Cheezy Zingerburger from the Famous McShamus."

"Tragic!" Man Man exclaimed in fake surprise and concern.

"I don't know what to do. I'm ruler and CEO of a sad and sick corporate state. I'm tempted to quit selling *Express Go!*™ so folk can start being themselves again."

Man Man was not amused. "I'm not amused, Shamus. If we quit selling *Express Go!*™ then Shamusans will quit working so diligently. I've been keeping tabs on folks' credit and, let me tell you, they can't afford to quit working hard. It'll make them go bankrupt," Shamus looked confused, so Man Man helped him out. "The First United Bank of Man Man would take all their property and sell it to pay off their debts."

Horror flooded Shamus's face as repressed memories of his own bankruptcy began to plague him, "Like loan sharks? That'd ruin my entire land!"

"Precisely. But don't worry," assured Man Man, "I can solve your problems. First, we must mass produce and sell Happy Juice to help Shamusans forget about their sadness. Next, we'll mass produce my brand new Potion of Sleep to alleviate all the sleep issues folk seem to be having."

"We'll call it Sleepy Sauce," interjected Shamus offhandedly.

"Right. The Sleepy Sauce will help them sleep at night. Poof! Problem solved. Just like magic, only better. So what do you say? Do we market the Happy Juice and Sleepy Sauce?"

Shamus lowered his head. He really did hate what he was about to say. "O.K. Do it." When he looked up, he was at even orbs with the sinister peddler.

"Right on. You know," began Man Man in a practiced off-handed manner, "I am an official licensed doctor of the body and mind. I could stick around for a while and help out with the relief effort."

"You'd do that?"

"Of course. Anything for my gentle giant…and the right amount of dingle. But, first things first. Get Bobby From Marketing in here. We'll need him if we're going to sell our new potions."

"Didn't you hear a word I said? Bobby is an *Express Go!*™ addict now."

Man Man tapped his temple to rattle around any loose thoughts and snatched the first one to fall off the idea shelf. "Well then, he'll be the first patient in Dr. Man Man's Center for Recovering *Express Go!*™ Addicts. I'll even give him premium rates for being the first patient in the program. First class all the way for Bobby."

"He's broke, remember," said the not-so-giant-anymore colossus.

Man Man laughed, "Silly giant, Lesson Two in *Mark's Book of Consumptionism* says: 'There is no such thing as broke when you have credit.' What I'll do is tell the bank to give Bobby a 'New Beginnings' loan so he can get back on his feet. Of course, since he is a credit risk, the loan will have to be at a higher vig."

"That doesn't make sense," protested Shamus.

"It most certainly does. It will be a good motivator to keep him working hard. He'll want to pay back the loan fast so he doesn't have to pay that outrageous, but wholly justified, vig. Now let's get started!"

Bobby was in Dr. Man Man's clinic for exactly twenty-eight days. When Bobby was released it appeared he was no longer addicted to *Express Go!*™. Instead, he walked around guzzling Happy Juice and acting disgustingly chipper all the time. Well, except for when the Happy Juice wore off. Then Bobby was sluggish and moody. To alleviate this problem, Man Man gave Bobby twice the normal dose of Happy Juice so the VP could maintain his cheeriness levels and work on the new marketing campaign. It appeared that Dr. Man Man had cured Bobby after all. At least that's what the paper, *The Giant Gazette*, said on the front page. But the East Wind knew a secret. She said Dr. Man Man didn't cure Bobby's addiction; he just traded it out for Happy Juice. That's method marketing at its finest.

Now, brave adventurer, we must skip ahead a few years. Why? Because *Mark's Book of Consumptionism* tells us in lesson 63, All good institutions take time to institute. Yup. Just like that. So here we are three years later and this is the state of the Undividable Land of Shamus:

Thanks to all the positive publicity from the paper and Bobby's marketing campaign, Dr. Man Man's Center for Recovering *Express Go!*™ Addicts had a six-month waiting list. Dr. Man Man not only set up a booming practice in psychology and health/nutrition, he also established several medical schools. Even Man Man's expectations for *Express Go!*™ were exceeded and he needed help in dealing with the influx of patients. The new doctors' main job was to give Happy Juice and Sleepy Sauce to every patient that came into their offices regardless of the actual diagnosis.

It wasn't long before eighty-percent of the ULS's citizens were using Happy Juice and Sleepy Sauce to help them cope with the side effects of *Express Go!*™.[12]

What about Shamus, you ask? Unfortunately, Shamus wasn't doing so well. He looked a lot smaller and skinnier, not to mention much weaker. I'd guess he had shrunk to a measly ten feet high. He was no longer a giant among giants. This didn't help with his mood. Depressed, he mostly stayed in his room bawling because things had gotten out of hand…again. He began to think that everything he touched was doomed to failure and he would never succeed at anything, despite his best efforts.

Shamus got up early after he'd gone to bed very late, leaping out of bed with a fierce determination to set things right and fix the problems he allowed Man Man to cause. Then, he did ten pushups and ten sit-ups and ordered a breakfast of eggs, bacon, gravy, and zing juice.

---

[12] Side effects are other things potions do to your body besides what they are supposed to. All potions have side effects. For some reason, folk can't make potions without side effects. So, instead folk make new potions to fix the side effects of the older potions. And these new potions have their own side effects, so in turn even newer potions have to be made to alleviate the new side effects. You can see the downward spiral already. Can't you?

While he ate, he read the daily paper. And every day the paper was full of stories about natural disasters and destruction and folk who were doing nasty things to other folk for stupid reasons. He would read these stories and think, *there is too much bad going on. Way too much bad for just one (former) giant to change on his own. It's hopeless. We're all doomed.* Then he'd cry. And once he started crying, he wouldn't stop until he cried himself to sleep at night to dream fitful dreams. I know what you're thinking, because I'm thinking it too. That really doesn't sound like a very fun way to live life. Something had to happen and it had to happen soon.

One day, while Shamus sat in his room pondering all the bad things in life and reveling in his sense of hopelessness, he got an odd craving for Azen food. He promptly grabbed the take-out menu from Lum Chow's Magnificently Sedative Grub Palace and picked up the carrier pigeon.

Between thirty and forty-five minutes later, there was a rap rap rapping on his chamber door. He opened it to find Lum Chow with MSG in hand. Shamus gave him the exact dingle and shut the door.

"This exact change! You forgot tip!" yelled an irate Lum Chow through the door. Getting no response, Lum Chow muttered a few choice words under his breath and left the giant McFamus to his melancholy. Little did Shamus know, that act of insensitivity would cause the wheel of Karma to turn against him. Lum Chow, humiliated at his treatment, coerced an army of folk to deliver food for him so he didn't have to do it himself. He paid them disgustingly low wages and assured them they would make up the difference in tips, knowing full well most folk were cheap like Shamus and would under-tip if they tipped at all. And so, the delivery prole class was formed. He was also the first business man in the Realm to institute a delivery fee. And for that, he's a jackass.

Shamus ate the food in depressed silence. After his meal, he broke open the fortune cookie. Little did Shamus know that the fortune he was about to read would be the harbinger of change he so desperately needed. It read:

> *Don't cry to me cuz you lost your spirit.*
> *You stupid Jerk, I don't wanna hear it.*
> *You have power! Write your own fortune,*
> *All epic journeys begin with step one.*

Ah, fortune cookies. Verily are they society's overlooked oracles standing erect in forgotten Delphi. True beacons for wayward travelers lost in the fog obscuring the Path of Destiny.

The fog on the Path of Destiny lifted one fateful morning when Shamus was awakened by a demanding knock on his bedroom door.

"Go away, I'm not seeing anyone today," bellowed Shamus from beneath his sheets and rolled over into a more comfortable position.

"Milord, tis Man Man. I would speak with you."

Shamus sighed and a wispy breeze stirred up a tiny dust devil on the marble floor. "I don't really want to talk to you, Man Man."

Man Man ignored this comment and entered the room, ducking his head to clear the massive doorway. Man Man had certainly grown during his stay in the ULS. The peddler was more expansive than Shamus had ever been. (Un)Fortunately, because of this change, a new story has to be told. Call it a universal plot shift, if you will. Most times the universe shifts without asking for our permission (it can be a jerk like that). When that happens, *new* stories are told about *new* lives. It isn't a bad thing necessarily; it's just a different thing. That being said, this new story begins thusly:

Man Man was a giant among giants. He didn't come by it honestly, though. He stole his giant-ness from Shamus McFamus, who as we know, *used* to be a giant among giants. But, sadly, the once-great CEO had been reduced to a shell of his former self, sucked dry by Man Man. The evil wizard's contracts enslaved Shamus's body and the potions seized McFamus's mind and spirit. Shamus was now a very tiny ten-foot giant—or a very large ten-foot man—but Shamus didn't see it positively like that. Ten feet is an embarrassing size for a giant, so embarrassing that he developed Little Giant's Syndrome.[13]

On the other hand, Man Man had grown so large that he was no longer able to do many things for himself. It can be annoying being an over-sized giant in a little man's world. To fix this, Man Man surrounded himself with many regular sized folk to take care of all his mundane and regular-sized tasks. For instance, while Man Man slept at night, scores of ant-like custodians swarmed his being and cleaned

---

[13] This is common in most small giants. LGS makes those who suffer from it very touchy about their size and they will get very upset and might even cry when confronted. It also espouses confidence issues. In rare cases it has been known to breed machismo, but these instances are few and far between.

him from head to toe. Whenever he wanted to eat, tiny chefs frantically scrambled around to cook the insurmountable amount of food it took to satisfy Man Man's appetite. In order to clothe the new giant, teams of seamstresses and tailors were commissioned and sixty percent of all available textiles in the Realm were redirected to garb the ginormous peddler. During the height of Shamus's Shadow Spells, he never consumed resources like Man Man now did.

Vice Presidents covered Man Man at every possible location to make sure the evil wizard kept running effectively. Each toe had a junior veep with the big toes being the departmental leaders. That was followed by the VP's of Feet Management (Right and Left respectively). Then there were the Vice Presidents of the Lower Legs and Vice Presidents of the Upper Legs who were all overseen by the Senior Knee VP. Man Man couldn't walk unless the overall Legs and Walking Department VP's administrated their departments properly. I know this seems like a lot of veeps, but Man Man was so monumental that he had to establish this type of system for his entire body. This diverse, but necessary, group of folk came to be known as Man Man's Peanut Gallery. The Peanut Gallery constantly surrounded Man Man with a bustle of activity: ceaseless chattering, sending and receiving carrier pigeons, bickering, and a few very secretive Inner Gallery romances.

The Peanut Gallery was a glamorous assortment of individuals led by management teams who achieved their accomplishments in life through sheer charisma. That is to say, they are good at appearing competent and rerouting the blame for their mistakes to the clerical proles that do the actual work. Some call that "delegation of responsibility." I call that, "blatant professional laziness using social status as justification." Peanuts in the gallery didn't really do a lot other than talk on the phone, have power lunches, play a round of nine in the afternoons and meet their fellow Gallerians after hours for drinks in the pub. The Gallery's personal assistant proles handled all of Man Man's day to day affairs. Safe to say, without the support of his Peanut Gallery (and their proles), Man Man would collapse. On this particular morning, Man Man and his Peanut Gallery hovered at Shamus's bedside causing noise pollution even a severely depressed giant could not ignore.

"Have you seen today's *Giant Gazette*?" Man Man's booming voice kind of hurt Shamus's ears.

Shamus pulled the blankets over his head, "Don't read it anymore. It's depressing."

"Tsk. Tsk. You really should keep up with the news. Remember Mark's lesson 13: 'Current events are dingle making opportunities.

Especially events that are currently causing suffering. Vast amounts of dingle can be made from suffering.' Which leads me to ask again if you've read today's paper?" Man Man snapped his fingers and a peal of thunder resounded off the chamber walls. A peanut stepped from the bustling activity of the Gallery and tossed a newspaper in Shamus's lap.

Shamus ignored it. "I'm tired of suffering, I'm tired of making dingle, I'm tired of credit, I'm tired…just tired."

"Well then, today is your lucky day. If you would only glance at the front page, you would see that you have just *re*-tired."

Shamus picked up the paper and glanced at the front page. What he read made his orbs stick and grow ever so slowly wider as the realization hit him.

"That's right. I've bought you out. I purchased fifty-one percent of *Shamuscorp's* stock. That means *I* own your company now. And my first act as the new CEO of *Shamuscorp* was to fire you and your entire staff. You know the saying, 'Toss out the trash if you want greener grass.' So, all your Veeps, along with your president and board of directors, have been ground into a delicious feed and served to my Giant Albino Chickens."

"What's a Giant Albino Chicken?"

"You'd love them. I had Bugtussel grow them in the lab. Amazing beasts with a violent appetite for chaos and pain. Going to be great for my next quickfood craze, the Nuggie."

"Even Bobby?"

"Alas, even Bobby. It broke my heart too, believe me. I tried to recruit him, but he insisted on his loyalty to your regime. That's business I suppose. I pondered killing you as well, but thought better of it at the last moment. Can't sully my public image, or gods forbid, turn you into a martyr."

"You're too kind."

"Thank you," replied the usurper. "Now for the unpleasant news. I had a severance check written out for you, but apparently you had some debt on the books. It is with the greatest regret I must inform you that the First United Bank of Man Man got to your final paycheck before you did. Further, my gentle lord, I am afraid your debt was sufficient enough to render the remainder of your check unworthy of your noble consideration. So, I took the liberty of donating it to Daddy Man Man's Home for Impoverished Children. The good news is all of your debts have been paid. You are now completely free to become an indigent…again." Man Man couldn't help but snicker.

"You-you can't do this!" Shamus roared. He leapt out of bed and made a desperate lunge for Man Man's big toe. Out of the Gallery stepped two peanuts in dark suits and sunglasses. They intercepted the former giant and wrestled him to the floor with bone-cracking precision. Shamus howled in anger and pain as he was handcuffed, dragged down stairs, and tossed into the Canals of Worry to rot.

"So?" I asked Jay-zun, "What'd you think?"

"I think that's a pretty depressing story. I mean, Shamus didn't ever seem to learn. He just messed things up and ran away to somewhere else so he could mess them up again. Man Man probably did him a favor."

"Well, yes, Man Man sure thought so. But then again, Man Man is an evil bastard. And evil bastards love to justify their wickedness by casting them in a favorable light. Why, that's exactly how I ended up with this millstone around my neck." I pulled a plain chain with a smooth, blue Orb attached to it and showed it to the author.

"What is it?"

"It's a pain in the ass."

"I heard that," said the Orb aloud. Jay-Zun's face turned white as the Countess D'Lis's sheets.

"You have a talking marble?"

"Unfortunately," I grumbled and stuck it back inside my tunic before it could begin a tirade of insults. "So, you say the story is too depressing. What would make it less so for you?"

"It'd be better with dragons. Aren't there dragons in the Realm? You know, overgrown, fire-breathing, virgin-eating, treasure hording lizards? I haven't seen any when I write. Do you have them in the Realm?"

"No," I said in immediate defense at the mention of those distasteful creatures. But I do my best not to fib (even a bit for it impedes personal progression), so I came clean. Live in truth is a proverb I hold fast to, and so should you. "Well, kind of, but not exactly. There *are* dragons, but Realmers don't exactly dig the Dragon essence so most of us kinda try and forget they are around."

"What does that mean?" asked the author.

"It means that dragons aren't dragons here like dragons are dragons there. In the Realm dragons are the species most in tune with the creative energies, so they make exceptionally brilliant artists, if you get into Dragon Art, that is. They have voices to rival that of the Minstrel Lord Bard if you can get past the nonsensical lyrics they spit. They don't breathe fire, but they do sneeze smoke out of their noses. And they absolutely *hate* eating folk. We're much too gamey for their taste.

They prefer succulent buffets of seasoned goat meats and veggies with sugar cubes in warm milk for dessert. Oh, and very few of them actually have treasure hordes. They're broke. Most dragons live very long lives as starving artists and bards."

"What do they look like?"

"What kind of question is that? They look like dragons. Between six and eight feet tall, bipedal, scale-covered, uber-intelligent reptiles with razor sharp teeth and forked tongues that can work wonders on bare flesh."

"You mean you actually have carnal relations with these creatures?" Jay-zun asked in disgust.

"Not carnal relations in the way you're thinking. Pull your head out of the gutter and pay attention. Now certain types of dragons called Drakes, have tails and wings, and others, like the Draco, don't. Just depends. For now, why don't you fetch me some more coffee so I can continue my tale."

Jay-zun went into the café and retrieved more of the delicious black liquid. I drank it greedily, "Are you *positive* this isn't *Express Go!*™?"

"Yeah, it's coffee. I told you."

"Well then, I suppose it won't give me the Gaunt."

"I wouldn't be so sure about that."

"Indeed? Best enjoy it while I can, then. Now, as I was saying, Man Man had stolen everything from Shamus. His fortune, his home, his folk, and his land…"

Part Two
The Redemption
of Shamus

This is where I come in. The wind told such a fantastic story that I had to see it for myself. Gathering my things, I set out to find the giant, Shamus McFamus. I traveled over hills and into valleys; I walked lonely streets and dark, dark alleys. I crossed brutal deserts without any rain; and I even traversed the grassiest plains, until I found myself in the Undividable Land of Shamus.

The city was just like the South wind said it was: a beautiful place filled with majestic towers and lush gardens. Folk loitered in quaint little cafés that served *Express Go!*™ and Zinger muffins. Minstrels and entertainers littered the streets, and folk tossed dingle into their pots without stopping to watch the performance. Vendors and artisans peddled wares that upon closer examination revealed them to be rushed, almost carelessly made. Regardless, they charged premium prices for them. Some were more expensive than those of the master craftsmen in the City of Allure! Everywhere I went, the streets were crowded with jittery folk racing to and fro like chaotic ants, all very shaky with glassy, hollow orbs. Haunting. To me, it seemed like the Shamusans walked around living their lives without being aware of it.

When I stopped someone and asked for directions, the person noticed me long enough to snap an unfriendly greeting and continue along his way. After a few unsuccessful attempts to locate the whereabouts of McFamus, I decided to wander around the city seeing what there was to see.

After drinking in the sights, I meandered to the town square—a vast plain of white granite that drew one's attention to the gazebo and fountain in the center. Every visible inch of the place was covered with advertisements for the plethora of zing products and Man Man's cures for the problems he had caused. Shamusans zipped and zapped across the white stone oblivious of one another and the calculated majesty of the city around them. I alone stood still within that swirling mass of unaware folk.

"They can't notice you," said a voice from a nearby alley.

Suspicious, I drew my blade because I never trust talking alleys. You shouldn't either. Talking alleys always have ulterior motives. I peered into the blackness trying to decipher the gloom, and the shadows slowly parted revealing a very tall man (or a very small giant).

"They can't bother to stop. If they do, they'll lose dingle and go bankrupt."

"What's wrong with them?" I asked.

"*Express Go!*™ gave them the Gaunt," said the tall man, his voice carrying a tone of lament.

"What's the Gaunt?"

"It's the end result of *Express Go!*™. See, eventually folk get "zung." That means zing fried their Sacred Fish and served it up with a side of chips. Never really the same after that. They get all jittery and nervous and paranoid, scuttling around with glassy orbs, and they lose their ability to dance the Dance of Tongues."

"No!" My outburst was involuntary, properly reflecting my shock and awe.

"Aye. Then the depression sets in. Man Man's doctors write prescriptions and my folk start taking potions hoping to fix all of their problems. It's not long before all those potions start to pollute the pure waters of their fishome[14] and then all of a sudden, SNAP! They get the Gaunt. After that they scurry around in a half-life daze doing the same things over and over, day in and day out. They become increasingly irritable and violent as the disease progresses…something to do with the effects of zing on the brain Russell told me once. But I think it's the glassy stare that unsettles me most."

"You must be jesting!" I exclaimed.

"I wish I were. But the good thing is that it *does* make them good workers."

"Yeah, but what about all the other non-work type things?"

The small giant shook his head sadly.

"Is anybody trying to help these folk? Attempting to free them of their evil bonds?"

The large man scoffed. "Man Man is too powerful. He can't be stopped." Shamus tossed me a newspaper and I glanced at the front page:

---

[14] A fishome is where your sacred fish lives. It's like a divine ocean filled with the life giving waters of truth. If it dries up, your sacred fish can't swim or breathe anymore and it goes into a deep sleep. But the more you fill your fishome, the bigger it gets and your sacred fish swims happy and free. How big or little your fishome is all depends on you. That's why it's a good idea to be a free thinker and to keep your imagination alive and well.

The Giant Gazette: Second Day Waxing, Summer's Bloom

*Man Man's Power at All-Time High! There's no stopping him now!*

**Yesterday**—Delegates from Man Man's Peanut Gallery reported a record-breaking increase in Man Man's power. "We've never been so formidable," states Pamela Gnoot, Public Relations Representative for Man Man and *Shamuscorp*. "As a matter of fact," she continues, "We're having to remodel the Palace in order to accommodate Lord Man Man's ever-expanding boundaries." Construction is set to begin on the Palace in coordination with the next Spring Thaw. "Man Man has been talking of needing a bit more room to stretch, so we'll see where that leads us." No word yet if Man Man's new strength has caused political unease with any of the neighboring city-states. "We only expect good things from here," says Ms. Gnoot in response to questions of the future, "Personally, I'm excited to see where progress will take us."

"Wow," I said flatly, "that's pretty gloomy."

"Yeah, and besides, even if we could get close to him, we'd have the Black Suits to deal with and let me tell you, they *aren't* fun like birthday party clowns."

"Unless they are *evil* birthday party clowns," I added.

"What brings you to town?"

"Looking for Shamus McFamus. You know where I can find him?"

"Aye, you found him, er, me," confessed the wee giant, lowering his gaze in shame as he claimed his identity.

"Fantabulous!" I exclaimed. "I've been looking for you."

"You have? What for?"

"To see if the East Wind sang true. I'm Infinity Jones," I said extending my hand. The giant warily accepted my handshake.

"Shamus McFamus. CEO," he began, but caught himself and his orbs became cloudy with a forecast of rain, "*Former* CEO of Shamuscorp."

"So I'm told," said I, "Had to see it, though."

The giant orbbed me with open skepticism and distrust. "Are you a motivational speaker?"

"Nope."

"A doctor of the Mind and Body?"

"Nay."

"A certified physic?"

"You mean psychic," I corrected.

"That's what I said," retorted McFamus.

"Nah. I don't do that anymore. Depressing business. Folk aren't interested in the real truth. They only want to know when they are going to find their next true love or lots of dingle."

"What about a registered dingle lender?"

"Can't claim that one either."

"A purveyor of fantastical and wondrous items at discount prices?"

"I'm offended you would accuse me of such unwholesome business."

"Well, what are you then?"

I shrugged. "I'm Infinity Jones."

"What do you do, Infinity Jones?"

I thought about this for a moment. "I do lots of things. But sometimes, when I get tired, I do nothing."

"Do you have a *trade*?" the giant asked, the huff in his tone ratifying his frustration.

"My good giant," I began as I am wont to do when I get full of the Chattering Winds, "This is the Realm of Possibility. I can have any and all of the trades I can conjure. Mostly, though, I get the trades that no one else wants."

"Like?"

"Well, I sold cheap furnishings to folk who couldn't afford it."

"Scandalous!" gasped Shamus.

"Tell me about it. Told some fortunes for a while, then went into aluminum siding. Tended a pub or two, you know, that sort of boring stuff."

"I see," said Shamus. His orbs flashed with a glint of haughtiness as he compared his so-called list of accomplishments with mine. "Doesn't sound too lavish."

"Yeah. It sucked, so I started wandering around seeing things. I guess you could call that my trade."

"Seeing things is what you do for a living?"

"Yeah. I mean, someone has to see things, otherwise there's no point to things at all. Now, Mr. McFamus, I've traveled a long way seeking out your story and I'm rather famished. I could use a bite to eat. Is that Azen food?" I asked and began walking toward Lum Chow's MSG Palace.

We reached the restaurant, a combination of ancient Azen and modern tackiness in design. The roof was shingled and painted a gaudy red trimmed in gold. On either side of the front door crouched two plaster lions lathered in the same flashy gold as the trim. We entered with ravenous looks in our orbs and terrible thunder in our guts.

"Welcome Lum Chow MSG Palace, I Lum Chow!" exclaimed a tiny, bald Azen with a bit too much enthusiasm. He had an almost feral manner about him. Old and wizened, leathery skin distorted his figure. A long, peppered mustache drooped down past his chin and he wore a bright red shirt displaying a yellow smiling face and the phrase "Lum Chow's MSG Palace." The old man's orbs constantly darted around as he talked and he rarely made orb contact. I sensed something sinister in this man's aura, but my grumbling stomach overrode my sense of danger (as it tends to do).

"Table for two, please," I said and held up two fingers.

Lum Chow nodded and grabbed a pair of menus. He wove through an empty restaurant and sat us at a small table next to the kitchen doors.

"Why are you sitting us here?" I asked.

"This special table for special big tippers," Lum Chow winked at Shamus and the former giant blushed a radiant shade of red, but he took the seat offered him without a word of protest. We scanned the menu, but like any true connoisseurs of Azen food, we settled on the buffet. Then, good folk, we ate. And ate. And ate. Until our orbs bulged with Admiral Yo's Chicken, Shrimp Fried Rice, Spicy Minty Bovine, Rolls of Egg, Sweet and Sour Swine, Hot and Sour Soup, Fried Cheese Tontons, Orange Chicken and Vegetable Noodles. Chopsticks blurred as we shoveled food into our mouths with reckless abandon. For a brief instant, I had a Zen moment and felt at one with everything that is "the buffet." When I finished, I sat back with a gluttonous sigh and loosened up my belt to allow for extra room.

"Garcon," I called out to Lum Chow, "bring on the fortune cookies."

Lum Chow obeyed promptly and presented us with a pair of fortune cookies on a little white platter with black dogs etched around the edge. With a small bow he retreated to a nearby corner cackling to himself in suspicious satisfaction. I shrugged it off and cracked open my fortune cookie.

"What's it say?" asked Shamus who was beginning to sound a wee bit groggy.

"Says: 'You need to improve your exercise routine. Try Sumo,'" I read with a big yawn. "What a crappy fortune! That's offensive. Lum Chow!"

"How can I help you?" he called from the kitchen. We could hear clanging and banging, easily written off as stacking pots and pans.

"This is crap!" I yelled and waved my fortune in the air.

He responded by cackling and saying, "So sorry."

"Stupid jerk," I mumbled and turned to Shamus. "What's yours say?"

Shamus cracked open his fortune cookie and read, "Fame haunts the man who visits Hell. Caged away till his spirit do quell. Now a trapped delivery prole, never to soar as a carefree soul. Whatchoo think it means?" he asked, his orblids drooping heavily.

"I think yours…is much…cooler…than…" I trailed off and Lum Chow's cackle escorted me into oblivion.

When I awoke, I noticed I was the occupant of a large cage suspended high off the ground by a burly looking chain. The bottom of the cage was covered with wooden planks. Lum Chow was obviously shooting for a "rustic" motif. At the opposite end of the cage sat a huge, steaming pile of rice and a vat labeled "Lard Sauce." I looked to my right and noticed that Shamus was also the proud new tenant of a suspended metal cage.

"Lard sauce? What is Lard Sauce?" I wondered aloud.

"Lard Sauce for making you fat fat," sounded a reply from below.

"Lum Chow? Is that you?"

"Yes. Now eat! Get fat and become Sumo warrior. I train you. Lum Chow have fights. Make big dingle off Sumo."

"So you've nabbed us in order to make us fight for you?"

"That master plan," admitted Lum Chow. "Make me lots of dingle."

"Listen," I said, "I've seen a lot of plays like this. This kind of thing never works out. You should really reconsider your karmic investment."

"What you getting at already?" yelled Lum Chow.

"I'm saying that either way, the evil slave owner dies. Your own noxious greed inevitably kills you. That's how these stories always end. So, you might want to let us go now and save yourself the bad karma later."

There was a brief moment of silence as Lum Chow considered this. "Shut up and eat!" shrieked the evil little man and slammed the door. The boom roused Shamus from his slumber.

"What's going on?" he wondered, staring around. I dutifully filled him in as to our situation. Shamus thought for half a second and then said, "I'll have to eat on it. Rice and Lard Sauce you say?"

Before I could warn him, I heard the unsettling sound of a wee giant gorging himself on sticky rice and that filthy lard-based concoction. The distasteful symphony of gluttony ended moments later with a climatic belch and a sigh that took a soulful decrescendo into sinful satisfaction.

"Well, I'm feeling a nap coming on," said Shamus and immediately following that statement the sound of snoring cascaded into my ears.

Before we continue you should probably read my secret.[15] "Six hundred and four thousand, eight hundred," spoke an incorporeal voice. It followed that up with, "He's an idiot. We're leaving. Now."

"And what? Leave him here to suffer the fate of Sumo fighting for the remainder of his days? That's not very cool."

"You know what else isn't very cool?" asked the voice.

"What's that?"

"Being stuck in this cage to suffer the giant's fate with him. We are definitely leaving." That being said, the Orb around my neck began to glow a soft blue and hum ever so slightly, like the sound of fairies tuning their flutes. Then, the universe shifted with a sickening jolt and I found myself standing on the floor staring up at the cages.

"That's better," said the Orb, oozing self-satisfaction. Didn't I tell you he had a tendency to be smug?

"I *hate* when you do that." I took three deep breaths to settle my stomach. Universal shifting upsets the innards. "Now, how are we going to get Shamus down?"

"We aren't. We're out of here. Making like trees and bananas. Leaving and splitting. I'll keep watch on things and let you know if you need to rush in like an idiot and save the day."

I protested, but it's very hard to resist the Orb. It's very insistent and somewhat more willful than I am. When it wants to do something, we usually have to do it. I suppose that's why it is the Orb of Power and I am merely Infinity Jones. I glanced one last time at the

---

[15] A small blue globe no bigger than a barble hangs on a chain about my neck. Tis nothing grandiose or particularly gaze catching, but merely possessing it has made me the object of many a madman's obsession. And I did it to myself. See, I once thought it would be neat if, as a skald, I had a magical artifact that allowed me to see things I wasn't around for. What better way to test the accuracy of your verses? That artifact was the Orb of Power. And though it delivered spectacularly on that (becoming the sole reason I alone can claim absolutely true retellings), my decision to seek it and the quest to find it, remain two of my biggest regrets to this day. And in that order. Trust me, magical artifacts are more curse than boon. Some things are best left to the power of Imagination.

The Orb is intelligent, that is to say, it has a personality and will of its own, not to mention it can do some incredible things. It can speak and often does so for the sole purpose of being smug. It's been silent up till now because it lost a bet and since I won, it couldn't speak for a week. It's been counting the seconds, let me tell you.

dangling cages and left, but I want you to know that it was against my better judgment. I haven't always been so chaotic. In times before magical items, I was a selfless and courageous hombre.

I was none too excited to realize that Lum Chow had imprisoned us far below ground in some ancient and forgotten catacombs that smelled of grandfathers. The walls were chiseled to a uniform smoothness and decorated with an expansive mural depicting an epic, though forgotten, history. How Lum Chow came to know of these passages I never knew.

"Well," I said out loud as I came to a fork in the passage.

*Well what*, responded the Orb, this time as a voice in my head.

"Which way? Left or right?"

*Follow the mural*, spoke the Orb. As I walked, the wall mural traveled back in time. I saw portrayals of the fall and rise of the first civilizations. I saw the heroes and battles that make the ancient past so great. I saw how the gods rose to power and were born. I saw the Chaos Unfolding as history in reverse until it ended suddenly in an entire wall of black.

"What does this mean?" I mused.

*It's the beginning.*

"Of what?"

*Of everything.*

My curiosity piqued, "You mean it all begins with black?"

*Yup*, said the Orb bluntly. Then, *Did you hear that?*

"Hear what?" I asked straining my ears to hear.

*Somebody had a thought*, said the enchanted marble.

"I don't hear thoughts."

*Well I do. And I'm telling you, I heard one. It came from behind the Black.*

"Impossible, that's solid rock." I rapped my fist against it a few times to prove my point. The wall was hollow. "Oh. Wow. You're right."

*I always am. One day you'll learn that. Hopefully before you meet an untimely end eaten by some beast or fallen into a dungeoneer's obvious trap. Never mind. The secret switch is on your right. Push in and pull up. Now open it.*

I did just that and discovered...

RICE RIBS
Lard Sauce

Shamus awakened feeling even more groggy and bloated. He sat up with a groan and looked around. "Yup, still in the cage," he said. No one answered but his echo. "Hello? Anyone there? Mr. Jones? Anyone?"

"No one but your echo," said the giant's echo.

Shamus sighed and retreated to a corner to soak in self-pity. He had just dozed off when the chamber door creaked open. From far below the giant heard the clanking and rattling of chains. As he strained to hear more, his cage shuddered and lowered ever so slowly.

"What's going on?" he asked as the lock to his cage was removed. "Jones? Izzat you?"

"Why it be Jones?" came the reply, "my name Lum Chow."

"Oh," stated Shamus. "What's going on, Mr. Chow?"

"Begin second part of training. You exercise so you not get slow fat. Slow fat no good for fighting," answered Lum Chow. "You deliver food to hungry lazy folk. Keep in shape. You wear this."

Shamus was hit in the face with a large piece of cloth. He strained his orbs to make out the phrase: "Lum Chow's MSG Palace" and below that was a picture of a smiling face. "What is this?"

"It delivery uniform shirt. You put on. You wear."

Shamus pulled the shirt over his head and Lum Chow shoved his torch into the cage to inspect the former giant's new skins. "Look good. Now, you officially delivery prole."[16] Shamus heard the clanking and rattling of the other cage as it was lowered. Lum Chow thrust his torch into the cage and I was nowhere in sight. The evil man howled with such intense fury that Shamus shivered and goose pimples ran up and down his spine.

"Where he go?" roared Lum Chow at Shamus, "Where other man go? You tell now!"

---

[16] A delivery prole is only one type of prole. Proles are what some civilizations called "slaves," your civilization calls them "the working class." Proles get the kind of jobs that no one wants, but that folk in desperate need of dingle always take. They clean restrooms, serve your food, deliver your mammonly possessions, clean up the messes you leave behind, and pretty much do all the other jobs that folk are too lazy or snobbish to do for themselves.

"I-I don't know. He must've gotten out while I was sleeping somehow."

Lum Chow muttered to himself in unintelligible vexation. He retrieved a small flute on a chain from his tunic. No audible sound came out when he blew, but within moments he was surrounded by panting henchmen dressed in a motley and distasteful black. Lum Chow began chattering to them in Azen and gesturing wildly. In moments, five henchmen filed out of the room, leaving Shamus alone with Lum Chow and two of his cronies.

"This Lam Jerk," said Lum Chow motioning to the biggest henchmen, "he top Black Dog Ninja. He train you how to be real good delivery prole. Don't worry. It first day as delivery prole. I tell him take it easy on you. Not burn you out too fast. Now get started!"

Lum Chow slammed the door and a wicked smile broke out across Lam Jerk's face like a nasty rash. He sized up Shamus with unhealthy delight sparkling in his orbs. The prole let out a tiny whimper as his cage door opened and his training began.


I uncovered an elaborately hidden room that was not so elaborately decorated. The walls were smooth, but bare of any tapestries or hangings. To the right of the door hung a sconce with a sputtering torch in it. In the exact center of the room was a big iron ring and attached to the ring were big iron chains and attached to the chains was what appeared to be a child. She was small, no more than five feet tall and didn't look to be more than sixteen. She had a long black topknot that kinked oddly at the bottom and was garbed in dark, loose-fitting garments. I could make out a huge red dragon on the torso of her tunic.

"Are you alright, child?" I asked.

The girl groaned and stirred a bit. She tried to speak but was interrupted by the sound of approaching footsteps. I hit the switch on the outside of the chamber and shut myself into the room.

"Who is it?" asked a weak voice.

"Tis your liberator!" I proclaimed boldly.

A short laugh was my instant reply. "Liberator? How are you going to liberate me when the only door switch is the one on the *outside?*"

"I…well…just let me think…"

A frustrated outburst erupted from the center of the room and it was answered by the shuffling of feet outside the door. A few seconds of silence was broken by a faint scratching on the rock face.

"Stupid Black Dogs," spat the girl, "Can't even find their own secret switches. You better not let them find you in here. I'm a very important prisoner. I'm a princess," she said with an obvious tone of self-importance.

"Care to help?" I asked the Orb. It answered me with stubborn silence. I'm not kidding, I really do hate that stupid thing sometimes.

Thinking quickly, I reached into my mag and grabbed a clear barble.[17] I mumbled,

> *Ho, Ho, Ho.*
> *Hee, Hee, Hee.*
> *I can see you*
> *but you can't see me.*

The barble shattered in my hands and I felt the tingling of the Energies as they raced up from Gaia and into my veins. I disappeared with an audible pop just as the door slid slowly open.

Shamus hated being a delivery prole more than he hated anything in the world. He hated it even more than he hated being an indigent. True, when Shamus had been indigent, he didn't have any of the finer things in life that he craved so vividly; but he didn't have any of them being a delivery prole either. Besides, even when he had all the finer things he wanted, the more he accumulated, the more he needed. Collecting material objects was like feeding a hoom worm and all hoom worms did was burrow into hills and eat entire groves of trees without ever being satisfied. That's why they got the nickname "Bottomless Gulches." During the peak of his affluence, Shamus had stuffed a palace full of junk and never got happier for it. He still had to guzzle Man Man's Happy Juice just to get out of bed in the mornings. Could

---

[17] A mag of barbles is one of the most fantastic things to have. Barbles are globes made from glass, wood, metal or whatever else can be rolled into a sphere and infused with different types of Magic. Each barble is a unique and colorful work of art that has its own special power. Most barbles are used in barble competitions among Fair's Folk and Oberon's Troop. But certain folk paid attention and learned a secret. I learned that when the right phrases are spoken one can release the magic in a barble. When it's been used like that a barble shatters, which is why most of the elfin folk don't use them as such. When you put lots of barbles together, their Magic gets pretty excited and unstable which can lead to unsavory explosions of energy. In order to keep all the barbles in one place and settled down like mature globes should be, they are kept in a mag, which is a bag made of spectral silk and enchanted with magical protections.

it be that things didn't bring happiness? Could it be they were a source of enslavement and unquenchable desire?

As he thought this, a wellspring of hope bubbled up from the dry bed of the ex-giant's fishome and Shamus's Sacred Fish woke from its catatonic slumber to swim in the refreshing waters (even if it was only the size of a small mud puddle).

The reawakening of the delivery prole's Sacred Fish also rekindled the spirit of life in Shamus's orbs and very unprole-like thoughts began to cross the enslaved giant's mind. Thoughts like, "This sucks," and "These folk aren't better than me!" resounded in Shamus's head over and over. And as everyone who is three plus one knows, the most dangerous thing for a prole to do is to think for himself. It makes Those in Charge very uneasy.

The lowering of his cage roused Shamus from his insubordinate thoughts.

Lum Chow and Lam Jerk waited for him. "Good you awake. How you feel after first day?" asked Lum Chow.

"I hate myself," muttered Shamus.

"Good," said Lum Chow and tossed Shamus a bucket of rice and Lard Sauce, "Now eat. We start sumo!"

Sumo training was a tortuous experience for the miniature giant. He wasn't used to exercise. For the past few decades, he had survived mostly by sitting on plush couches and stuffing his face with fried zingo chips while indulging in a bit of live theater. Shamus didn't ever really *exercise* in the pure sense of the word. Oh sure, every once in a while, he got an odd hankering to do something physical, but that hankering would pass a few tocks after he'd start exercising. I'd say Shamus averaged about ten minutes of exercise a week and about half of that time came from the effort it took to walk from his couch to the john. Couple his poor physique with Lum Chow's sadistic streak and working out was a living hell for Shamus.

He began the routine with light cardio. Shamus was made to run in place until Lum Chow told him he could stop. If the sumo-in-training were to slow or stop from exhaustion, Lam Jerk was there, whip in hand, to keep Shamus motivated. After an hour or so of cardio warm-up McFamus was allowed a few ticks so that his stomach could return the rice and Lard Sauce in a most retched manner and then it was time for weight training.

Lam Jerk strapped a few extra pounds onto Shamus's arms and legs for good measure and led the ex-giant over to the squat machine. It didn't take long for Shamus's muscles to begin howling in unbearable pain.

"AHHHHHHH!" bellowed McFamus and then collapsed.

"UP!" commanded Lam Jerk, "Now!"

"Please no…please don't make me."

Lam Jerk answered with a smart crack to the Sumo's bare back. Shamus yelped and sprang into action.

"See?" said Lum Chow with a sadistic laugh, "I whip you into shape real good."

Once Lum Chow was positive that Shamus's legs were thoroughly ripped he moved him over to the bench press. As he worked every muscle in his soft body, tears streamed down the poor giant's face, sobs intermingling with outbursts of painful exertion.

Sounds pretty awful, doesn't it? Believe me; Shamus thought that he must be stuck in some outer layer of Damnation—an outer layer that gives you a taste of how dreadful eternity can be, but without the inconvenient eternal qualities. A place in time akin to a holiday resort in Hell.

But do not be disheartened, brave adventurer, for some good did come of this. Shamus's Sacred Fish started to swim again and the former giant's ego had its prideful butt kicked by humility. Thank He Who Is Not A Pronoun[18] for difficult life lessons that goad us into action.

"He had enough," announced Lum Chow abruptly. He motioned to two Black Dogs standing in the door snickering at Shamus's anguished yells. "Take him back to cage and feed him. Lam Jerk come with me. We go find where rest of pack is. Should be back with Jones by now.

---

[18] He Who Is Not A Pronoun is the most ordered of the Lords of Order and Chaos. He embodies "Goodness and Right thru Structure and Might." He is very hierarchical and bureaucratic. Thus, he has established various committees to oversee his religion.

I could make out five shadows in the torch light. They stepped in and scanned the room, first with their noses and then with their orbs. Lum Chow's Black Dog Ninjas scoured the tiny cell from top to bottom, but I was nowhere to be found.

"I smell him, but I no see him," spoke the jailor Ninja. He glared at the small prisoner, "Where he at?"

"Huh?" she asked innocently. "What was that? I'm so weak from hunger that I can hardly hear you."

"You hear just fine," said the spokes-ninja, "Where man at?"

"Oh! Of course! You mean that weird dude who came in here looking for the way out! He'll be back. I sent him after the keys."

"Ha! Stupid Red Dragon Ninja! I have keys right here!" The jailor dangled his keys in front of the prisoner.

"Ah, Plum! You guys outsmarted us. Guess you dogs better go look for him."

"No. We wait," said the jailor and sat down in front of the girl, facing the door. The remainder of the pack mimicked their leader and sat in a circle around the prisoner.

I picked a few choice vocabulary words to mutter under my breath. True, I had done a disappearing act, but I was still only one man against a group of semi-intelligent brutes. Seeing no other choice, I snuck out the open door very quiet like to think of a plan.

Whilst thinking, I heard the rattle of the prisoner's chains inside. I poked my head in to see what was what. Nothing had changed. It was still five Black Dog Ninjas circled around a helpless girl chained to the floor. Then the chains rattled again, followed by a brief pause, then more rattling. The jailor turned his head to snarl at the prisoner and a manacle met the Ninja's jaw with a dull thud. The poor schmuck didn't even have time to finish his snarl before he slumped over in an unconscious heap. The other Black Dogs jumped to their feet with weapons drawn.

The escaped prisoner wasted no time. Taking a length of chain, she whirled it around a few times to give it momentum and flung it at the Ninja nearest the door. Another Black Dog Ninja crumpled to the floor. Then, the girl sprang into the air (much higher than any normal person could) and brought her right foot around to the brute directly behind her. SMACK!! was the sound of sweet unconsciousness when her foot met the Black Dog's head. Three back springs later she was outside the room with a sword in one hand and a torch in the other! She smashed the door switch with a yell of triumph and smiled coyly as the remaining Black Dog Ninjas stumbled over their fallen comrades to get out before the door closed. It sealed shut and the Black was seamless once again. The girl's orbs flashed and she violently smashed the switch with the hilt of her sword until it was completely destroyed.

"Ha!" she exclaimed, "how's that for Amontillado's Cask, you filthy beasts?"

"What will they do now?" I asked and the girl spun around in a flash.

"Who is it? Who's there?" she demanded through clenched teeth. Every muscle and nerve were tensed and ready for action.

"No need for pokey sticks, lady. It's only me, your liberator."

She scoffed. "Yeah, a lot of good you did. Saying some stupid poem and then just disappearing like that."

"I had to retreat to think of a plan."

"Well you think too long. And come out where I can see you. It's getting real old talking to air."

"I am most definitely, Highly Visible," I stated and the Tricksy dissipated. The girl glared at me with open suspicion and sniffed the air. "You stink like Fair's Folk and you've caught their Tricksy."[19]

I shrugged, "I summer there sometimes and I listen to the lessons they teach. Now, about those men…"

"Hopefully they'll starve and have to start eating each other," said the girl without a trace of jest in her voice.

"Um, right. So, I'm Infinity Jones," I said hoping to change the subject.

"My name is Lola Fa Lona and I am a Red Dragon Ninja," she said as she raised herself up to her entire height of 4 feet 10 ¼ inches. The quarter inch is necessary. Believe me, she won't be sized without it figured in. I still have a scar from the last time I forgot it.

"It's nice to meet you, Ms. Fa Lona," I said with a bow, "So, how'd you get out of those chains and all?"

---

[19] Fair's Folk are the folk of Queen Fair. They are the mischievous creatures who are cousins to the entourage of Lord Oberon. A fun loving and chaotic bunch of beings, they delight in meddling in the lives of the mundane. Tricksy is their form of magic and it mostly involves building illusions that appear real. So, I don't really turn invisible, I just appear to be that way to everyone else.

She sighed and flung her sword around carelessly, "I know many ways. I'm impressive like that. Stupid Black Dog shouldn't have put the keys in my reach. We better go before the rest of them come looking. I know a way out."

"How do you know of a way out?"

"Oh, I saw it in a dream," she stated without fanfare or self-consciousness and plunged ahead into the depths of the ancient caverns beneath Shamustown.

"Do you dream of escape routes often?" I asked.

She stopped dead and whirled around to face me. Despite her small size and stature Lola Fa Lona was a very imposing figure. "No, I don't 'dream of escape routes often,'" she sneered. "It just so happens that in this particular dream I wasn't dreaming. What I was really doing was walking Over There and while I was exploring, I happened upon the way out."

"That's lucky. Did you happen upon anything else?"

"There's some nasties down here, but I saw where they lived too. We should be good…except for the giant spiders. They like to wander, so they could find us and end up eating you. I would escape of course."

"Of course." I began to notice something wasn't right with this young Red Dragon Ninja. She seemed easily distracted and unable to focus on anything for more than a few moments at a time. She claimed to dream of escape paths in forgotten caverns that she discovered while walking Over There. And she spoke of danger and the possibility of death as though they were nonexistent in her universe. Not to mention, Lola had an obvious mean streak that could turn violent without much provocation and knowing this I still followed her. What was I supposed to do?

We twisted and we turned and we zigged and we zagged and we stopped for breaks and to turn around and go back the way we came until after a countless time in near complete blackness we came to a rock face that boasted a tiny pinprick of light way off in the vertical distance. Thankfully, we didn't encounter any of the Red Dragon Ninja's nasties.

"Now what?" I asked.

"Now, we climb," Lola answered and tossed the torch to the ground. She nimbly climbed up the rock face. I was somewhat humbled by her impressive skill and agility.

I followed suit, but not with any semblance of nimbleness and I lacked any measure of skill. To be honest, I could barely climb the wall at all. I couldn't find a proper hold and I kept pulling small rocks down on top of me as my hand searched vainly for a grip.

"Go toward the light," Fa Lona hissed down to me, "I'll meet you on the other side," she scampered up the wall and out of sight. I sighed and resumed my relentless climb toward the light and freedom.

I scaled about ten feet in half an hour and had to take a break on a small outcropping of rock in order to quell my mutinous muscles.

"Tired already?" mocked the Orb, "My, my. Aren't we the manly man? Machismo indeed! Ha!"

I couldn't answer for my panting and wheezing so I mentally glared at it.

"You know that *little girl* is probably out already," continued the Orb.

"I'm…not…hearing…you," I managed to wheeze between huge gasps of air that filled my lungs with fire.

"Let me tell you how this inevitably goes," began the Orb, "because I know how your kind is, and I know the thoughts that play out in your dim little brain-cases. The biggest obstacle you face, although you don't believe it at the time, is that you can actually see your goal, though it's far away. It's this tiny pin prick of light off in the distance that jazzes you with motivation. Folk always start with high energy and excitement when they strive to scale the impediments to their dreams. But this high energy doesn't last long. After climbing for a while, you get winded and think that minutes seem like eternities in complete blackness. And blindly climbing towards distant lights always makes the eternities seem longer.

"So, you climb and you climb and you climb for what feels like an endless amount of time and your goal never appears to get any closer. Before long your muscles start to burn and your bones get tired, and still, your light is nowhere near being reached. Tired and a little discouraged, you quit 'for a while' and give yourself a 'moment to catch your breath.'

"Little do you know; your ultimate defeat lies just ahead. While you are resting thoughts begin to creep in. Thoughts like, 'I'm never going to get there,' 'This is impossible,' and 'I can't do it anymore,' pop into your dull noggin and without fail, you give in to them and quit. You don't even want to climb anymore. Even after you've rested and are ready to go, you'll stay where you are. Why? Because it's much easier to fantasize about reaching your goals than it is to endure the actual suffering and self-sacrifice required to reach them. Sadly, but like so many folk before you, your dreams fade into fantasies and then you forget why you started to climb in the first place. Welcome to life in the dark."

"I…really…hate…you…some…times," I said because the Orb was right. With one last inhalation of determination I resumed my climb.

"Shifting you out would be counterproductive," continued the Orb as I scaled the rock wall. "You wouldn't learn a damn thing. I've no use for a codependent fool, but I will contribute to your cause," the Orb glowed a faint blue that illuminated my immediate surroundings. Not extremely helpful, mind you, but it was better than nothing.

After unfathomable torment I managed to I scramble into sunlight and fresh air. I collapsed at the edge of the hole and lay there staring at the stars in my vision. Lola Fa Lona wandered over to me chewing on a piece of apple. "Huh. I thought you fell."

"I wish I had… It would've…been less painful," I panted.

"Oh what, you don't have any Tricksy to zoom you out of holes and stuff?" asked Lola sarcastically.

"No…apparently that…would be…counter…productive." I sat up to get a sense of where I was. We were in a small grove of apple trees on the outskirts of Shamustown. Directly to the East was the haunted Forest of Hidden Things and to the West were the hill lands of the Undividable Land of Shamus. Here, for a while at least, we would be safe. No one would've expected us to escape the city by now. If any search parties were being mobilized, they would likely scour the city's sewers and back alleys first. I had to give it to the little Ninja; she really came through brilliantly.

Vibrant, plush grass blanketed the grove. On the edge of the forest, the crumbled remnants of a stone cottage whispered of times forgotten, and the remains of a stone wall ran to the North and South. The hole we climbed out of was actually a ruined well. Next to the well was a large rock and tied around that rock, oddly enough, was a rope.

Storm clouds of anger rolled in and I turned to the Red Dragon Ninja. "You had rope this entire time?"

"Yeah, I mean, I got up here and there it was coiled around the rock like that."

"You could have thrown it down to me!"

"Yup. I could have, but I was busy picking apples. Besides, you didn't want that rope. It's old and just waiting to crumble. I actually saved your life by *not* dropping it down to you."

I was absolutely livid. "You could've helped in some other way, then! Instead of going right for the stupid apples and leaving me down there to die!"

"Hey, I was *starving*! I've been choking down rice and Lard Sauce for the past few months! When I crawled up from that well, I saw apples and I had to eat. Don't look at me like that. I was gonna help you after I finished picking apples…if you hadn't fallen that is. Besides, I barely know you. How was I supposed to know you're a weak pansy that couldn't climb a simple wall?"

"I can't believe-How could you just—" my anger was a torrential flood looking for an innocent village to destroy.

Lola rolled her orbs. "Get over it," she said, plopping a brush inhabited by a tangled mess of black hair into my lap, "Brush my hair."

"Why?"

"Because! It helps me go to sleep and I can't brush my topknot by myself. In my clan, this would be considered a great honor."

"Oh, I'm sure it would," I said, "Where did you get a brush?"

"The Ninja Code prohibits princesses from being imprisoned without a brush. It's like a law of all Ninja or something. Now get to it."

For some reason I felt compelled to do as she asked. I brushed her hair until I heard the princess begin snoring softly. I carefully put the brush down and propped myself up against the rock.

A chuckle echoed inside my head.

*I suppose you think this is funny*, I thought at the Orb.

*Oh yes,* replied the Orb, *Not just funny, but down right hysterical.*

I tried to retort but only mumbled gnomesense as my exhausted body gave in to sleep.

Two weeks had passed since our escape from Lum Chow's dungeon and the caverns below. My muscles were doing little to help in the way of recovery and even after a fortnight I still felt the sharp pain of injury when I tried to do anything too strenuous. Since I was literally too sore to walk, we stayed in the grove. Lola Fa Lona tended camp when she felt like it and left me to sleep in the cold when she didn't.

On our twelfth midday in the grove, I was resting against the rock, sunning myself in the afternoon's warmth when I felt something land in my lap. I opened my orbs to a bright red apple waiting for me.

"So, I'll tell you what happened to me. If you really want to know," Lola Fa Lona offered.

"That's great," I mumbled and closed my orbs again. "I really want to hear it…later."

"Man Man stole my Harmony. Without it I'm kinda broken."

I sighed. "What do you mean," I asked without opening my orbs.

"My folk believe that Harmony is necessary in order to fuse mind and body. A true Ninja is a singular being with mind and body acting in flawless unison. Harmony is also vital for your spiritual growth. It allows you to manage your light and dark sides. Keeps one from overtaking the other. Without Harmony you get what my folk call Advanced Depletion of Harmony Disease and the true Way of the Ninja can never be realized."

"I get it," I said, "So Man Man stole your Harmony and now you are thrown out of whack and your destiny impeded. I'm gonna get back to my nap now."

But she wasn't having it. "Exactly. Plus, I am a Red Dragon Ninja," Lola Fa Lona sat down beside me. "We are a noble tribe of Ninja who live in the forests surrounding High Azen. But we are not the only clan struggling for survival in that area. There is our arch nemesis the Blue Dragon Ninja clan, the powerful White Tiger clan, the cunning Green Serpent clan, the ferocious Bronze Fighting Cocks clan, the—"

"You mean 'roosters?'"

"Did I *say* roosters?"

"No."

"Then I must've meant cocks. Can I continue or do you need to interrupt me some more?"

"By all means, continue."

"The ferocious Bronze Fighting *Cocks*, the chaotic Maroon Monkey clan, the stoic Brown Ox clan, the sneaky Gray Rat clan and the lowly Black Dog Ninjas."

"I get it," I said, "Ninjas here, ninjas there. Ninjas, ninjas everywhere. Go on."

Lola glared at me for a moment before she continued. "I'm extra special because I am a *Pure* Red Dragon Ninja," she studied me looking for a reaction of awe or reverence. Receiving neither, she continued, "That means I'm not only a stupendous Ninja with unsurpassed skill, I'm also noble about it. During our sixteenth year, all Pure Red Dragon Ninjas are given a troop of twelve warriors to command. As I am only now approaching my sixteenth year, I was the youngest Pure Blood ever to receive a troop. Guess why I got it early?"

"Because you are a stupendous ninja with unsurpassed skill," I said flatly.

"Maybe you aren't so dumb. That's exactly the reason. Not only that, I was given the best troop the Red Dragons had to offer. My father, who happens to be the Samurai Chief of our clan, handpicked the best fighters to accompany me. You can't imagine the honor."

"I don't suppose I could."

"Well, shortly after I was assigned my troop, we were called to investigate a building that seemingly sprang into existence overnight. I was convinced it was the tower of an evil wizard who had fled persecution and thought our territory perfect for an isolated lair in which to commit despicable acts of sorcery. I was later proven correct, but that's no surprise because I've never been wrong."

"That doesn't surprise me," I yawned.

"When my troop arrived at the tower, I couldn't believe my orbs! Before me towered a ginormous structure of solid gray stone. An immeasurable plain of black stickiness extended to the very doors of that palace of doom. A monstrous sign illuminated the surrounding area with a pale, sickly glow. There was no way my Ninjas and I could breach it, even utilizing the sneaky ways of the Peeking Duck. We would have to assault the menacing building head on. My first impulse was to attack it with the ferocious Way of the Tiger."

"What'd the sign say?"

"Said, Super Mark's Mart."

"With a Famous McShamus inside?" I queried further.

"Yeah, how'd you know?"

"They've been springing up 'out of nowhere' more and more places as of late. Like tumors of social cancer."

"Well, this isn't about the tumors in 'more and more places.' It's about the tumor just outside of High Azen," said Fa Lona rerouting the conversation with a subtle narcissism that could only come from a noble upbringing, "So my troop and I began to traverse the black plain. By midday, we were about half way across. As the sun's daily glory peaked, heat magically radiated from the black plain and the ground became sticky goo that stuck my troop where we stood! We were immobilized for the remainder of the day and the heat emanating from the plain caused two of my best to dehydrate and swoon before the sun shadowed.

"As night fell, the black plain quickly cooled and the bright sign became an unmistakable beacon in the velvety darkness. I sent the two ninjas who swooned back to the village and the remainder of my troop marched onward without sandals. The sticky goo had claimed them for itself. Curious travelers and the duller tribes began to creep around the boundaries created by the artificial light. We shooed them off to the best of our abilities, but many folk disappeared into the tower. Once they did, horrible screams would emit from the place. But that didn't stop others from entering. I suspect it was mostly Black Dog clan, that's about how smart they are. I tried to warn them, but they didn't listen. To Black Dog clan, apparently entering glowing portals with screaming coming from them is smart. Stupid Black Dogs. After the second one I stopped trying. You can't save folk from themselves and a Red Dragon Ninja doesn't waste effort.

"We reached the transparent doors of the wizard's tower as quickly as we could. To our great surprise, the doors opened for us, as if driven by some unseen spirit! We crossed into that den of evil with our weapons drawn and our senses primed for battle." As she told her tale, she acted the part out, which added a layer of charming whimsy.

"My troop was immediately set upon by two screaming banshees who attacked our flanks.

"'Welcome, lost souls, to Super Mark's Mart! Offer your Sacred Fish and join us!' the things screeched as they flew toward us, blinded by rage or stupidity…or more likely stupid rage. Every time one of the hell-fiends dipped in for an attack my ninjas darted and dodged the banshees' deadly claws. The demonic manifestations shrieked as they succumbed to our superior skill. I managed to pierce one in the throat and the banshee expired with a hiss. Her companion redoubled her efforts and unleashed a maddening screech. The weaker of my troop fell to their knees and covered their ears, but we who were strong withstood the scream, though our eardrums ruptured and seeped blood.

"The second banshee was slain by my First Ninja, Kim So Kim. She slit the creature's throat from behind while I distracted it with my dizzying acrobatics. But such a victory does not come without cost, as I found two of my soldiers lying in warm pools of their own blood. My band now totaled nine. But we are plucky Ninja who do not cower in the face of fear. We ventured even further into the Super Mark's Mart only to discover ourselves trapped in an unending maze of torture and horror."

"Unending maze of torture and horror, can I use that?"

Fa Lona ignored me. "We explored the building and stumbled upon a portion of Super Mark's Mart named Sandal Lane. I motioned for two Ninja to scout the area for possible threat of ambush or traps. They returned and told me that they had disabled two traps, one at either end of the lane. We crept into Sandal Lane, never lowering our guard. You should've seen it. Sandals and boots and shoes of all manners and varieties were *just sitting on the shelves*, unattended and everything. So, we helped ourselves to new sandals. I decided it was justified since the black plain claimed ours. With new footwear, we delved further into the eerie lair.

"Our next encounter proved to be even more deadly than the first. Succulent smells wafting throughout Super Mark's Mart spiked our hunger. We followed our noses to the Famous McShamus within the market's walls. But once we laid sight upon the deadly bounty that was spread before us, most of my troop turned their noses to it. The food was disgustingly presented with grey meat and potatoes soaked in some sort of super heated chemical. Any Ninja worth their weight in dingle knows when food has been poisoned.

"Alas, four of my party members couldn't contain their hunger. Ravenous, they stormed the Famous McShamus and uncontrollably stuffed themselves with disgusting food and drank grease out of large vats with straws. I tried to break them of the enchantment, but they wouldn't heed my calls. My heart broke and I cried out to them. 'Brethren! Return to the Path! Remember the Way!'

"But they only snorted at me as hogs would do. I tried to physically remove them from the confines of that culinary dungeon, but the enchanted ninjas lashed out at me with furious orbs and razor sharp ninja claws.[20] My fellows and I watched helplessly as our cursed comrades began to bloat and contort while they ceaselessly gorged themselves. They were becoming misshapen monstrosities, part person, part hog and wholly evil. I couldn't bear to look upon it. I shed one tear of sorrow before I sent them to properly feast with the Jolly Man."

"You mean you—"

"Yes. Better me than others. Better quick and merciful than slow and dishonorable. My folk believe that abstinence in this life grants us indulgence in the next, or vice versa. It's part of keeping the Harmony. I did what I thought was best and moved forward. What more can you expect in life?"

"Good point."

"The remainder of my troop and I met our demise when we came upon the Aisles of the Box. We were naturally attracted to it from a distance because of the flashing lights and unintelligible chattering that we beheld from afar.

"We rushed over thinking to catch the evil wizard in the midst of some vile spell and thus take him off guard, but it was not to be. Instead, we found ourselves instantly enthralled by flickering and chattering boxes that lined the shelves. We could only stand and stare dumbly at the odd contraptions as they continuously flashed pictures and jabbered at us.

"'Fascinating, aren't they?' asked a voice from behind me. I came out of my enthrallment and spun around to find myself face to face with the evil wizard! He wore blue pants and a white tunic that hung on him as a father's clothes hang on a child. He also wore a large blue vest that bore a name plaque that said 'Man Man.'

"'What are they?' I asked.

"'Chatter boxes,' replied Man Man. 'They provide entertainment,' he said with a smile which I didn't trust in the least. Smiles like that always mean there's a knife hidden somewhere and it's looking for your gut. So, I drew my sword and called my men to arms. Alas, they didn't answer me because they were enthralled by the Chatter Boxes. Orbs glazed over, stupid stares on their faces, dripping drool, they looked as if they were dead but alive. I still shudder to think of it.

---

[20] All real ninjas have ninja claws. They are fingerless gloves with small blades woven into the knuckles. The ninja clenches her fist and the claws extend. Very classy and surprising in a bar fight.

"'I SAID TO ARMS!' I roared with every ounce of energy I could muster. Only my first ninja Kim So Kim broke the enchantment and came to my side.

"'This is no place for you, wizard. Leave now and do not return,' I demanded.

"Man Man laughed, 'This is exactly the place for me, little Ninja. Your folk have just what I need.'

"I commanded Kim to engage and she drew her pokey stick, attacking Man Man with unrelenting wrath. Her sword was a silver smear on the canvas of reality. But no matter where she struck, she couldn't connect with the diabolical wizard's flesh. Her blade was literally deflected by thin air.

"Man Man smiled that infuriating smile and simply pointed at Kim and said, 'Poof!' Kim instantly disappeared in a puff of smoke and I haven't seen her or the remainder of my company since."

I could tell this bit was hard for the little Ninja, that recalling it brought her much pain and torment. I tried to place a reassuring hand on her tiny shoulder but she shrugged it off, her orbs hardening with a resolve only the Ninja possess.

"With a yell, I lunged at Man Man, thrusting my blade at his chest. He didn't flinch. He patiently clapped his hands together and caught my blade inches before it connected with its intended mark. The sorcerer began to shake it back and forth and said something like 'wobble wobble noodle bobble' and my sword went limp."

"Limp?" I asked.

"Yeah, like wet Lo Mein. Then he conked me over the head and I woke up tied to a chair seated in front of hundreds of Chatter Boxes. And that's where I sat for I don't know how long. One morning during meditation, I noticed I couldn't focus or concentrate on anything for more than two ticks at a time. My mind became increasingly distracted and thoughts bounced around inside my head in a chaotic jumble. With dawning horror, I realized that my Harmony was slipping from my grasp.

"Shortly after that fateful day, Man Man showed up with a black vial. It was the first I'd seen of him since our battle. He entered the room all smiles and cheeriness, but I wasn't having it. 'How are you today, little princess?'

"'I'd be better if you'd untie me and give me a blade.'

"The wizard laughed, 'I don't doubt that for a moment. But don't worry, you'll be out of here soon enough. I've discovered just the place for you. But before that, I need to get something from you.' He pulled a straw out of his pocket and jammed it in my ear. I screamed while Man Man sucked through the straw until I felt something give inside my head. I felt a sharp pop and then Man Man spit something into the black vial and put a cork on top. After that, he sold me to Lum Chow, because being a captive of lowly tribes like the Black Dog Ninjas is a huge disgrace among my folk."

"Wow, that's quite a tale. This Man Man really needs to be stopped."

"I know. There's no telling what he's done to my folk since I've been gone and above all, he stole my Harmony, disgraced me, and vanished my warriors. For that he must die," seethed Lola Fa Lona. "We better go find him."

"Whoa," I said, "A fortnight ago, I scaled an immeasurable rock wall to escape the clutches of said Lum Chow. That's exhausting and traumatizing. I need to rest. I suggest we stay here and sleep until our next plan of action comes to us in a dream."

"That's nuts from squirrel butts," said Lola.

"Like demanding the return of stolen essences from entities who are obviously stronger and better equipped isn't?"

"Fine!" snapped Lola. She couldn't dispute that bit of logic. She stuck her sword in the ground and lay down next to it.

The princess fell asleep in seconds and I followed shortly thereafter.

"What do you want from me?" Shamus roared into the stale blackness. There was no answer. He rattled his cage until it swayed, outpouring his anguish in a great bellow and collapsing onto the floor of his cage, sobbed quietly to himself. He didn't understand why he was being forced to be a delivery prole and amateur Sumo. But we don't always get the answers we like to the questions we ask. Ah well, Sacred Fish will swim and ignorance really is bliss.

The delivery prole longed for the Gaunt. He actually began to crave an automatic and dead lifestyle. But that just angered his Sacred Fish and the waters of his fishome began to thrash in defiance. He didn't deserve to suffer like this. Why was he being singled out? What did the gods have against him? It seemed like every time Shamus made a come up, someone or something was there to knock him back down. He couldn't get a break.

In case you haven't noticed, Shamus was prone to crippling bouts of self pity. What he couldn't see is the Sacred Fish requires friction to wake up. A fishome filled with comfort and ease produces nothing but a sleeping Fish. Tis the friction that makes the Fish fight. Shamus took the suffering personally. Then again, most folk do. They make it about injustice and bad luck and gods with grudges. And what happens when you pour energy into a "woe is me" story? The grievance grows. Why, the Fish sleeps harder. The fishome dries a little more. Tis tempting to fall into the notion that the Divine tailors its friction specifically. And tis more tempting still to fall into the trap that we are unique in our suffering. We are not. Everyone suffers, dear reader. What separates the baaah's from the bleats is what we do with that suffering. We either use its fire to evaporate our fishomes or embolden our Fish. Sacred Fish want to swim, they want to fight. So choose to swim against the currents of friction, always moving toward growth, no matter how uncomfortable, because when it comes to Sacred Fish, tis always sink or swim.

Shamus lay on his cage floor, as limp as Lola Fa Lona's blade, sobbing to the heavens. "Please, please help me. Get me out. I hate Lard Sauce; I hate being a prole, and I hate sumo training. Help me. I promise I'll change; I promise I'll be a better person. I'll do anything you want," he repeated this to himself over and over and made it his mantra that carried him into Dreamy Land.

The giant's prayer traveled through the forgotten tunnels until it quietly escaped into the open air. There, it was picked up by the North wind and carried to the dwelling places of Fair's Folk. The North wind blew a chilly entrance into Fair's royal court and presented the prayer to the Queen for her enjoyment. The North wind sought to trade Shamus's prayer for the sweet scent of summer, a delectable smell that he craved over all others (because his harsh and frigid destiny did not lend itself to the aromatic scents of vibrant life). The sweet scent of summer was a rare commodity bottled by Fair's Folk and could only be gifted by Queen Fair herself.

Fair delighted in the bittersweet harshness of Shamus's plight, but she also felt pity for the caged sumo warrior in training. "Pan, send this along," she ordered. "Find a way to secure this pathetic giant's freedom and watch his progress. And fetch the wind his scent."

The mischievous elf bowed and left to do his Queen's bidding. In order for prayers to be answered they have to grab the attention of some deity or another. And everyone who is three plus one knows that deities don't pay attention to just anybody. Pan rode atop the chilly back of the North wind scouring the Realm until he found the perfect vessel for Shamus's supplication: the Ever-Divine Minstrel Lord Bard. Pan floated into the chambers of the Minstrel Lord Bard and whispered the prayer to him in a dream.

The Minstrel Lord Bard immediately awoke with a burst of inspiration. Grabbing the lute resting next to his bed, he settled in and closed his orbs. Shamus's Prayer sang in his mind's ear and he, in turn, offered it up in praise for his Lady:

*Shamus sighs a hollow wind*
*Winter's gloom*
*Inside cold ancient tombs.*

*His Sacred Fish revived*
*New Spring beginnings*
*Locked within iron chains.*

*Suspended he cried*
*Lonely bird's songs*
*Fall like withering summer blooms.*

*Where is my release?*

*North Wind moans tearfully*
*Desperate pleas chill my dreams.*

*A slave to a curse*
*A victim of karma*
*A lover of the Fates.*

The Benevolent Chaos, She Who Becomes, clapped with delight and blessed the Minstrel Lord Bard with a golden kiss. She decided right then and there to grant Shamus's prayer. "Where is it you came upon this hymn, sweet?" she asked the Bard.

"'Twas given to me as I slept by Pan of Fair's Children."

The Blessed Lady reached down with her delicate hand and plucked Pan from his place in Fair's court. "Pan," she commanded, "This is your charge: Answer the giant's prayer. Set him free."

Pan bowed humbly, "An honor, my Lady." But Pan can never do anything simply. When Fair's Folk are involved expect complications and mischief. It's just their way.

Pan flew through the Realm until he found exactly who he was looking for. He leaned in real close and whispered a teeny tiny white little lie into slumbering ears that would set into motion a most chaotic chain of events (which is exactly what Pan had hoped for).

Lola Fa Lona's orbs popped open. She sprang to her feet and crept over to where I was sleeping.

"Hsssst!" she hissed in my ear and slapped my face.

I thrashed my arms wildly and bolted up right, "Who-What?"

"We need to go," she said.

"Huh?" I mumbled while trying to clear the Sleep Mist from my head, "Go? Go where?"

"Well, you know your idea that we should stay here for a few days and sleep until we dreamed up what to do next?"

"Yeah," I said, "But I'm still sore from the climb and the dreams aren't quite here yet. I'm gonna need a few more days."

"Yeah, um, no. Cuz *I* dreamed up what to do next."

"Oh yeah? What's that?"

"We go back inside."

"What?! Why?"

"Because," said Fa Lona, "Man Man gave my Harmony to Lum Chow."

"That doesn't make sense," I protested. "I don't think Man Man would go through all the trouble of stealing your Harmony just to give it to Lum Chow. Something isn't right."

"Yeah, something isn't right. We're being played. Played by that filthy Black Dog Ninja and his evil wizard chum! It was right there the entire time!"

"I don't think so. Sounds very familiar though…mischievous even. I think—"

"I hate when you think. When you think, nothing gets done. Now let's go." Without further argument Lola Fa Lona grabbed the rope and tossed it into the well. She expertly scampered back into the vile pit of blackness I struggled so hard to clear. The rope held up famously.

I moaned in protest and followed the princess.

The darkness hit us like an impenetrable force. "I can't see," I muttered. "Wake up Orb! Give me some light." The orb remained silent, choosing to ignore my impetuous demand on its smug persona.

"Shhhh," chastised the little ninja, "Remember nasties roam these corridors. So shut your mouth."

I glared in her general direction and reached into my belt pouch, retrieving three poofy balls of cotton. I closed my orbs and cupped the poofs in my hands.

*"Little light, little light,*
*Help dispel this gloomy night."*

I felt a buzz of energy race through me and a tiny flash of light escaped through my fingers. The poofs began to glow with an ethereal light. They slowly rose into the air and circled my head in wide arcs that lit a twenty-five-foot circle around me.

"That's better," I said in triumph.

Lola Fa Lona shrieked in an odd combination of terror and anger—"terranger." "You fool! You've led them right to us!"

"Led who right to us?"

"Them!" she replied and pointed to the edge of the circle of light.

I noticed three sets of ruby red orbs peering at me. "What are they?" I whispered to Lola.

"Giant spiders with poison dripping from their fangs," she whispered back.

I rolled my orbs. "You're kidding. Giant spiders? C'mon! Must we plummet right into a played-out cliché? I mean, this can't be how it *really* ends."

"Hey now," said a decidedly feminine voice from the darkness. Something rustled against the stone floor and three spiders as big as ponies scuttled into the light. "What do you mean by that?" The female spider stepped forward and challenged us with a threatening glare.

"By what?" I asked innocently.

"That you've just plummeted into a 'played out cliché.'"

I chuckled nervously. "Oh that. Nothing, really. I was just saying…" I trailed off, unwilling to keep putting verbal nails in my coffin.

"Uh-huh. You were just saying," prompted the female spider, who was more than happy to supply the hammer with which to nail my coffin shut.

I sighed. If I were going to be eaten by giant spiders, I might as well express my frustration at such a pitiful and embarrassing demise. "It just seems to me like there are an," I had to choose my words carefully, "…overwhelming number of giant spiders in the fantasy mythos. It's almost obscene." I'm trying to compose an original tale."

"Who says this is an original tale?"

"It will be later, hopefully, if I live long enough to write it down. So, I'm asking…no, I'm begging you, don't do this to me. Verily, must you be giant spiders of all things?"

"What would you rather us be?" asked the spider, her voice dripped annoyance like her fangs dripped poison.

"I don't know. I'm not your career coach. But honestly, this is the Realm of Possibility. You can be whatever you want and you mean to tell me that all you want to be is a *giant spider*?"

The spider shuffled her multiple legs. "Well, not exactly. When I was a wee arachnid lass, my Pa caught an Emperor Butterfly in our web one day. Have you ever seen an Emperor Butterfly?"

"Once or twice," I admitted. "They are a rare sight. Very large and regal. Been known to move folk to tears for merely gazing upon them."

"Exactly." The spider trailed off caught up in a moment of sweet recollection then abruptly continued, "I watched it fly from a distance. It seemed to dance on the breeze and play with the fickle winds. It was one of the most beautiful and amazing things I've ever seen. I watched it until it stumbled blindly into our web.

"Pa whooped with joy when he saw what we'd snagged. Butterfly is good eating; it's a delicacy. I remember watching Pa as he spun it up and prepared to suck the life-juice out of it."

It should come as no surprise that magic in the Realm is only limited by one's imagination. That being the case, I have a very active imagination. So, I've got all kinds of unique and whimsical barbles at my disposal. While the spider was lost in her memory, I drew my only Changeling barble from my mag and rolled it toward her mumbling, "There's truth in appearance and appearance in truth. Let nothing you believe rob you of youth."

The spider continued uninterrupted, "I kept thinking, how beautiful it is! Look at those magnificent wings. All those colors and patterns. And look how graceful and noble it is—even unto death. I squeezed my orbs tightly shut and wished I could be like that butterfly. Beautiful and graceful and free to play with the carefree winds." As the spider talked, she began to remember. As she remembered she began to visualize herself. And as she visualized herself, she believed herself to be.

"Don't forget free to be snagged by your Pa's net," interjected Fa Lona.

"Yes, well, I'd avoid spider webs. Seeing as how I know about them and all."

As the barble slowed to a stop at the spider's feet, it shattered and saturated the area with a brilliant emerald light. Before my very orbs, the light condensed and concentrated on the female spider. She hissed in fright, but remained immobile. The other two spiders scurried into the shadows to watch their sister's fate unfold.

The arachnid's bulbous torso elongated and turned a fantastic green. Next, numerous tiny legs sprouted from her chubby cylindrical body. She was no longer a giant spider, but a massive caterpillar. The caterpillar attached herself to the wall of the old well while a cocoon of golden light surrounded her and solidified with an audible POP!

"Whoa!" said Fa Lona in disbelief, "How'd you do that?"

"I know many ways. I'm impressive like that," I said.

"Sorcerer! I'll have your Sacred Fish for that!" One of the spiders in the shadows sprang toward me. I jumped to my left and the eight-legged monstrosity flew over me.

Lola drew her blade and leapt vertically into the air; her topknot actually grazed the cavern ceiling which must've been a good fifteen feet in height. She had timed her jump so that on her descent the spider would be directly beneath her. The Red Dragon Ninja guided the blade expertly between the fiend's orbs and drove it down to the hilt as she landed on the creature's back, forcing it to the ground. With an evil hiss, the red glow dimmed and the arachnid's life expired. The remaining giant spider fled into the darkness with promises of revenge and death falling off its fangs.

Lola wiped her blade on the defeated foe's body (as is the custom of her folk) then turned to me. "You ready?" she asked and without waiting for an answer, plunged into the darkness.

I dusted myself off and followed her with light poofs leisurely orbiting my head.

Shamus was jolted awake by the rough swinging of his cage being lowered. A singeing stench permeating the air assaulted his nostrils…was it smoke? Panic triggered adrenaline and Shamus was wide awake. The door to his chamber stood open and he could see the playful shadows of flames dancing on the walls. He made out two shadowy figures flitting about in the smoky gloom. One was noticeably taller than the other. Shamus instantly assumed it was Lum Chow and his head dog Lam Jerk.

*This is crazy*, thought Shamus, *What's going on?*

His cage settled onto the ground with a thud and the smaller figure began to manipulate the lock with slender metal tools. After a moment of desperate rattling punctuated with an audible click the lock fell away and the cage door swung open. The taller figure stepped out of the smoke and into the giant's vision.

Shamus the prole hollered with glee. "Why! Infinity Jones! My prayers are answered! I thought for sure you left me to rot in here!"

"Not me," I proclaimed defiantly, "But the Orb speaks for itself."

"I do, and I will. I need your head, Jones. And you need my help."

I scoffed. "Please. Now you choose to grace us with your asinine prattle? My head belongs on my shoulders—"

"And your head-pole is my chain's drape. It's not an ideal situation, but it serves us both. Get used to it."

"Can we do this later?" Lola asked impatiently. "This place is burning down around our ears and the nasty Dogs are still about," she turned on her heel and stalked out of the room.

"She's right," I agreed, "We don't have much time."

"So what happened?" asked Shamus as we made our way back to the old well and freedom.

"Well, Lola was convinced that Lum Chow was in possession of her Harmony. She claims to have come about this knowledge in a dream. So, after we went through all the trouble of escaping, we came back. We burst in on Lum Chow while he was sleeping. He had a huge four poster bed in his room that covered most of the chamber's available space. Night tables stood on either side of his bed and he had a chest at the foot. Lots of wood within those cold, stone walls.

"The little Red Dragon Ninja didn't waste any time in losing her cool. She sprang onto his bed and demanded the return of her Harmony while holding her ninja claws at Lum Chow's throat.

"'Where is it, you disgusting lout?! Give me my Harmony! Give it or I swear I'll slice your head-pole from ear to ear.' Her fury was more than a little unsettling.

"Lum Chow cackled, disturbingly cool for someone who was a hair's breadth away from having his head-pole slit by an unstable girl with a superiority complex. It was then that I caught him deftly fooling with a button at his bedside. Before I could voice a warning, three whooshes of air...WHOOSH! WHOOSH! WHOOSH! Then silence. Lodged in the wall opposite the bed were three barbed darts. Lola was nowhere to be found.

"Lum Chow bolted upright and blew some little flute he has on a chain around his neck. Within a few ticks I heard guards assembling in the hallway and moving in our direction. Then, with a fantastic scream, Lola Fa Lona leaped up from the opposite side of Lum Chow's bed, flipped in mid air and landed next to me holding a lit candle that she procured somewhere. Her orbs flashed with some kind of weird ferocity and she did her own maniacal cackling.

"'You wouldn't!' screeched Lum Chow. 'I Samurai Chieftain of Black Dog. My personal sanctuary protected by Code of Ninja!'

"'There is no Code here, filthy dog,' she said and tossed the candle on Lum Chow's bed. The whole thing immediately went up in flames. Cheap furniture. I recognized the brand."

"Where'd she get the candle?"

"I thought it best not to ask. Anywho, Lum Chow howled in comical terranger and flew out of the bed faster than a foozlebunny in a cheese scurry. He continued to scream as he ran from the room. We fled shortly after. But not before Lola stopped to loot the wooden trunk at the foot of Lum Chow's bed. By an amazing stroke of luck, her stolen gear was stored inside."

"That's convenient."

"Tell me about it. After that, she set a few more fires to 'ensure a finished product,' as she called it, then we came upon your chamber."

"Is she crazy?" the giant's question was thick with worry.

"Not exactly. She's just out of Harmony. Oh, and she has absolutely no attention span."

"What happened to it? Did Lum Chow have it?"

"No, he didn't. But from what I understand, Man Man captured her and forced her to sit in one spot for months on end in front of this evil box that continuously flashed pictures and spouted repetitive nonsense."

"Wow. And that steals your Harmony?"

"Apparently. First goes the attention span. It takes some kind of focus to maintain your Harmony, you know. It's like taking care of your fishome. Without focusing on it and paying some attention to it, you forget to clean your fishome and feed your Sacred Fish. That's when folk get broken and sick because their fishome either gets polluted or dries up. Same thing with her Harmony. If she doesn't put some focus into its maintenance, it makes it vulnerable and easy to abduct."

"So then..." Shamus began and then stopped, as if the words he wanted to speak got caught in his throat, "How would one go about cleaning their fishome?"

"You just do it," I said for lack of a better answer.

"So, I could just say, 'I'm cleaning my fishome' and then it's clean?"

"Well, yeah, kinda. That's one way of doing it. But say 'I'm regenerating my fishome,' it's more inclusive."

"I'm regenerating my fishome," Shamus proclaimed with absolute certainty in his heart and mind.

Deep inside Shamus's inner self of inner most inner selfs in his own innards the puddle that was his fishome grew into a playa lake.

The former giant's Sacred Fish, which happened to be named Senior Commander Gilli Gali, became so excited that he did flips of happiness that sent ripples of pleasure throughout McFamus's body.

Shamus smiled to himself and the fog of depression lifted from his mood. "Wow, I feel better," he admitted.

"Yeah. Makes all the difference when you *mean* what you say."

Shamus didn't reply. He walked in silence until we reached the dilapidated well that was to be the means of our escape.

"What in the name of the Flawless He is that thing," asked Shamus pointing to the cocoon in wonderment.

I relayed the tale to him and he shook his head.

"Emperor Butterflies are worth a fortune. We could get a king's ransom for the enormous wings alone. Do you know how many shirts can be made with just one wing? Scores!" said the ex-CEO in a calculating tone.

"We don't have time to wait for stupid bug eggs to hatch. Lum Chow and his goombas are hot for blood. I think I may have upset their balance a bit," announced Lola and scurried up the rope as fast and deftly as she had before.

"Yeah, she's right. I hate to leave it here for Lum Chow to find, but I've suffered his torture long enough," said Shamus and climbed steadily after her. His Sumo training had hardened his muscles and improved his endurance in record time.

With a final glance toward the cocoon, I lowered my head in shame and began to climb after them. I had scarcely begun my ascent before I felt the screams of my muscles echo the screams of Lum Chow and his cohorts as they followed our scent. I tried to climb faster, but couldn't. My body, still sore from the first escape, went on strike and I fell to the rocky floor next to the cocoon. I laid there in a daze and couldn't help but consider the cocooned spider's plight. I imagined her one true wish becoming reality only to find her demise at the hands of the greedy Lum Chow. I pictured that beautiful and rare existence snuffed out and transformed into a blouse for some noblewoman or another; or perhaps ground into a fine powdered aphrodisiac for noblemen who have two right feet when dancing the Dance of Tongues.

"I can't let that happen," I said through gritted teeth.

"Oh yes you can," the Orb blurted.

"Oh what? Now you have something to say?"

"Don't get all heroic on me. You were going to let her die anyway. You have one disappearing act left. I suggest you use it on yourself and let the cards fall where they may."

"No," I said.

"Yes," responded the Orb, "you don't want to test me, Jones."

I could hear the voices of the Black Dog Ninjas getting closer. I only had a few seconds left. With all the will I could muster I reached into my mag and pulled out my last Vanishing barble.

*"Ho, Ho, Ho.*
*Hee, Hee, Hee.*
*I don't see you,*
*But you see me."*

I dropped the barble over the cocoon. It quickly grew into a large, clear bubble that encompassed the entire surface. The image shimmered for a moment and then disappeared.

"You're a fool," said the Orb and then its blue glow went cold.

Lum Chow and his goons found me lying underneath the dangling rope. "Oh, ho, ho," hooted Lum Chow. His mouth gave birth to a grin that displayed his decayed teeth like a trophy case. "Look what we have here! Mr. Jones all alone. No friend to help him."

"What makes you think I need friends to defeat you?"

"Oh, Lum Chow know you very Tricksy," he said wagging a finger at me. "You smell like stinky Children of Fair. You escape my cage. You and Red Dragon Ninja seal Black Dog Brothers in dungeon. They starve and eat each other before we get door open." His orbs briefly misted over and then they were once again hardened by evil. "You come back and set place on fire, but that don't matter. I win in end." He motioned for his henchmen to overtake me.

The pack of Ninjas growled and mumbled in anticipation. I struggled to my feet and drew my sword so I could meet Mother Death somewhat respectably. The pack drew closer and fanned out around me. Just as Lam Jerk was about to engage me a large, dark shape fell from the ceiling and landed on the advancing pack of Black Dog Ninjas. I was struck heavily in the chest and thrown backwards out of the fray. Screams, yelps, hisses and flailing hairy limbs of all sorts comprised the midst of that rumble. Then it suddenly quit.

Silence, thin and taunt like lute strings, snapped and the very spider who had promised death to me earlier emerged from the pile of bloody and broken bodies. It glared at Lum Chow with ravenous red orbs. At the sight of the oversized arachnid, Lum Chow let go a high-pitched scream that could have shattered fine china and fled back the way he came.

"Now what?" I asked, but I didn't really want to know the answer. My first thought was that he had dispatched the Black Dogs in order to kill me himself. I swallowed hard and raised my sword with a shaking arm. It appeared death by giant spider was to be my fate after all. "Infinity Jones, killed by clichés," would be inscribed on my tombstone…if I even had one. Chances were, there would be nothing left of me to bury.

"Now, I give you a ride up top," it replied, struggling to get the begrudging words out.

This was an unexpected, yet pleasant turn of events. "But I don't understand. You promised curses and death upon me."

"Yeah," it sighed, "And I was really looking forward to it, too. I waited and waited and waited for the perfect moment. I was going to pounce on you after you fell when I saw what you did for my sister. I saw you struggle with the curse around your neck in order to make a selfless sacrifice. You did what was right and for that, I will repay you…and besides," the spider glanced over at the heap of bodies, "I've enough food for a while. Shall we be on our way?"

We surfaced from the ruined well into the crisp morning air. I was welcomed by the sights of a glorious sunrise and of Shamus sitting at the edge of the well sobbing. Lola's keen ears heard the scuttling of spider's legs as we climbed and she met our arrival with sword drawn.

"Mr. Jones!" Shamus stammered in disbelief, "I thought for sure you were dead, or worse, a delivery prole."

"Not so my good giant!" I exclaimed as I jumped off the spider's back. "I was aided by our friend here," I motioned toward the spider.

"I wouldn't go that far," answered the spider. "I have repaid your kindness with one of my own. We are square," he said while making a square shape in the air with his front two legs, "but we are not friends. I still owe your party for my brother." He glared at Fa Lona and backed into the hole, disappearing into the darkness of his forgotten caverns awaiting both rebirth and revenge.

After our escape from Lum Chow's dungeon, Shamus, Lola Fa Lona, and I fled the ULS. We didn't run in fear for our lives, but in fear of what our lives would become if we were caught. We assumed it was only a matter of time before Lum Chow ran screaming to Man Man about what happened. This knowledge would no doubt anger the new CEO and he'd send search parties to find us. Know this dear reader: There are fates worse than death and Man Man knew them all. We ran blindly eastward into the ancient Forest of Hidden Things and further from the evil peddler's influence.

Unbeknownst to us at the time, Man Man did send folk after us in a manner of speaking. He did what Those In Charge always do, because they don't want to sully their karma with unpleasantness and bloodshed: they had others act at their behest. But make no mistake, everything that happened did so because Man Man willed it. First, the new CEO charged us with a multitude of bogus and vile crimes. Then, his Peanut Gallery put out a bounty on each of our heads. They printed wanted posters with our likenesses and dispersed them to all the seedy back alley joints in the Realm. Others they posted in inns, general stores, and anywhere else folk frequented. It was only a matter of time before every scuzz-bucket bounty hunter in the Realm was slithering after us. Speaking of slithering, Man Man himself put Slither Faust on our tails.

The Drake, Slither, stood about nine feet tall (which is large for a dragon) and was covered in shimmering black scales. Faust was of the winged and tailed race of dragons with hands and feet that ended in razor sharp claws. He carried a devilish looking blade that was as long as Fa Lona was tall and wore an elaborate breast plate made from the shells of the peaceful and majestic Flying Turtles of West Feather. As a bounty hunter, Faust built a Realm-renowned reputation for merciless efficiency. He possessed many tricks and techniques that few of his peers could—or would dare—emulate. He was easily the most feared and sought after bounty hunter in the Realm. And for good reason. Objectionable folk often require unwholesome services. In fact, one could consider unwholesome services somewhat of an industry. Slither, being the best, could snatch anyone he set his mind to without much effort. He never failed. And for this reason, the petty bounties offered for menial criminals dulled Slither's interest in his profession. He had moved to the slums of Shamustown hoping for a change of scene and a decent corporate bounty—a fat, juicy bounty that paid well and offered him some kind of a challenge.

Slither lounged in the common's room of a seedy joint named, "The Drunken Sow," pondering ways to exterminate whole caravans of gypsies (his natural enemies) when a cloaked female and her two bodyguards approached him.

The woman's features and physique were obscured by her cloak. Only the smooth and practiced grace of her movements signaled her femininity. Her two bodyguards were dressed in very clean, black suits and wore sunglasses, even inside the dark and smoky bar. The entourage approached Slither's table with an unmistakable air of authority. The bounty hunter's orbs shrank to thin reptilian slits and his hand found the hilt of his blade.

"Slither Faust?" asked the female.

"Who wantsss to know," asked Slither.

"I am Media Tron, public voice for Lord on High, Man Man. I bring a proposition for you." Tron tossed a handful of rolled parchments in front of the bounty hunter.

Slither scanned the posters and tossed them back at Tron. "Why me? Doesssn't Man Man have hisss own gooniesss for thisss kind of thing?" He was obviously a lower-class dragon; he hadn't had the proper speech training needed to remove their natural lisp.

"He does, but none that are as good as you. Word is you're the best."

Slither smiled. "That I am, lovely. That I am." He paused, "Tell Man Man that I'll ssstart onccce I've cleared up the gypsssy problem in Ssshelldown."[21]

"Gypsy problem? What gypsy problem? Our allies in the area haven't mentioned it."

"Jussst a rouge band I got word of. Came up from the desssert, I hear. They're sssuposssed to be led by Fallen Tree." Slither's orbs flashed with hate.

---

[21] Dragons and gypsies are natural enemies. A very long time ago when Realmers were still tribal, dragons ruled folk and used them as slaves. Eventually, the Realmers rebelled and overthrew their dragon masters. As Realmers evolved, so did their attitude toward dragons. What began as a seething hatred eventually softened into a strong, but civil, dislike. However, Tree Folk (later to become gypsies) retained their traditional way of life and their racial hatred never quite dulled into the pheasant posturing and scorn of civilized men.

"Lord Man Man won't be happy about delays. He expects this search to be started immediately. There are others searching as well. You don't have a lot of time if you hope to collect these bounties."

"Let othersss sssearch. I'll be the one that collectsss the bounty," boasted Slither.

"That remains to be seen," goaded Tron.

"Fine. Tell your lord that I've ssstarted immediately, if that will make him happy." The dragon's forked tongue played across his lips as he stuck the posters into his belt and stood up. "Pleasssure doing busssinesss with you." Slither shoved by the Black Suits and left the inn.


We made camp in the obscuring density of the woodland. Desperation seized us in its icy clutches, denying us any peace whatsoever. The forest cast frightening shadows that our paranoid imaginations turned monstrous and, to us, every sound we heard was an approaching search party. We tried to sleep in shifts, but nobody really slept. The next morning, we masked the campsite with irritable dispositions and continued our flight. Sometime during the night, a soupy fog descended into our moods like a second misery. I couldn't help but think that, though I had lost track of the days, it must assuredly be a Moonsday.

Around midmorning we heard the unmistakable rumble of horses approaching from behind. Thinking it to be some sort of pursuit, we took cover in the mist laden forest. In order to properly hide the dwarfed giant, Shamus and I ran until the road was nearly swallowed by the hungry fog. Lola stayed in the underbrush near the road to see who was on our tails. We held our breath as the sound drew closer and then passed us by.

A few moments later, the Red Dragon Ninja materialized. "Just some stupid nobles in their big carriages. Got a couple 'a guards, but nothing I couldn't handle with both arms tied behind my back and blindfolded."

"Just the same, let's stay off the road for a while," said Shamus in a trembling voice.

We walked parallel to the road in silence for the rest of the morning. About midday, the fog dissipated and sunlight slipped through the leafy fingers of the trees. We stopped for a meager meal of apples and some rabbit that Lola caught earlier then continued on our way.

Shortly after we resumed our trek, the road abruptly disappeared around a bend and an orchestrated symphony of noise pollution signaled heavy construction nearby.

"What do we do?" asked Shamus nervously. "That could be Man Man! What if he's setting up some kind of roadblock for us? Or got ahead of us during the night? Oh man! We're as good as busted!"

"Will you shut up!" snapped Fa Lona. "Big baby. I swear. Guys like you always die first. Weeds out the spineless nancies before the real fighting starts."

"Don't say that," Shamus whined.

"Then don't act like that. It's whatever. I'll go check it out while you stay here and wet yourself." Lola stealthily made her way toward the bend to see what awaited us. Shamus and I waited for an excruciating amount of time before the Ninja princess returned, leading with a broad smile on her face, "You guys *gotta* see this."

Just around the bend, sweaty construction workers were erecting tollbooths on either side of the road. Oddly, for every one man working, two looked like they were on break. Chatting workers used shovels and other construction type implements as handy leaning poles. Behind the workers stood two groups of well-dressed men wearing powdered wigs and white stockings. The "powdered wig posses" held firm positions on either side of the road, one on the left, the other on the right.

Members of the groups scurried about, scribbling on papers and ceaselessly arguing with one another. Every so often small sub-groups separated, it appeared for no other reason than to yell at the powdered wigs on the opposite side of the road. When this happened, all construction ceased while spokesmen for the respective groups verbally slapped each other. Then the arguing suddenly simmered down without reaching a resolution and the spokesmen once more assimilated with their peers. Construction resumed as soon as the workers finished their union mandated breaks.

"They've been doing this since I found them," whispered Fa Lona. "And remember those nobles that passed us earlier? Yeah, those powdered wig guys must've harassed them for a good half hour before the carriage driver forked over some dingle and was allowed to pass."

"Wish I could've seen that," I mumbled, cursing the Orb's control over my sense of courage.

*I heard that,* the magical globe whispered in my head, *it's a fine line between courage and stupidity. Leave the stupidity to the brash little one. Save the courage for when you really need it.*

As our band pondered how to get around the construction without being seen and extorted from, a small party of gypsies approached from the opposite direction. Once they were spotted, all construction halted and the powdered wig spokesmen stepped to the edge of the road, careful not to step into it.

"Welcome gentlemen and ladies," said a frail older man standing at the forefront of the group on the right, "Let me be the first to welcome you to the Harry T. Burrhoffmanshauer Expressway. Proudly brought to you by the Traditionalist Party."

"Don't listen to that twig!" yelled an equally old and frail man standing at the forefront of the party on the left. "He doesn't care about you. He just wants to pilfer your dingle the first chance he gets. The Traditionalists are bloodsuckers!"

"We are not! We are the folk's champions! Advocates for independence and individualism!"

"Ha! I can't believe the drivel that comes out of your mouth Lyle! Advocates for independence indeed! The only thing you advocate is the continuous filling of your dangle! And it's the Francis C. Smithshipston Memorial Expressway." He returned his attention to the gypsies. "Anyway, on behalf of the *Libertine Party* of the Greater Forest Area, I, Kyle, welcome you to the brand-new Francis C. Smithshipston Memorial Expressway. It is our latest public works project," said Kyle proudly. "We're using the dingle we raise to help starving gypsies in the Desert of Lost Causes."

"We are doing no such thing!" Lyle cut in. "Some of the proceeds will be used for highway improvement. The rest we are giving to the Merchant's Union in order to stimulate the Realm's economy."

"How many times do I have to tell you, brother? You won't stimulate the Realm's economy by giving *more* dingle to folk who already have an abundance of it! Do you see the absolute *ignorance* we Libertines must suffer when in the company of the Traditionalists?" Kyle asked the gypsies.

"There you go! Starting again! Do you have to disagree with everything I say?"

"I wouldn't!" spat Kyle, "But everything that comes out of your mouth is pure balderdash!"

"That's it! We're coming over! Traditionalists to arms!" proclaimed Lyle. The Traditionalist mob milled around for a while and whispered to each other, but they stayed to the right, never stepping over the apparent boundary the road represented. After forming committees and sub-committees that deliberated plans of action, a middle-aged man separated from the main Traditionalist mob and conferred with Lyle.

The caravan tried to use the distraction to move past the groups, but they were cut off by Libertine Party Guard. "It is five dingle per booth per person," said Kyle.

"But we *are* gypsies!" exclaimed the leader, a tall bronze young man with black hair cascading about his shoulders. "Surely you wouldn't make us pay when you are raising dingle for our aid. Perhaps you kind gentlemen could make a small donation to the very gypsies you are raising dingle to help and let us continue on our way in peace."

"You dirty gypsies aren't getting a *single dingle* from the Harry T. Burrhoffmanshauer Expressway project. And even if you were, we couldn't give you any coinage right now anyway!" shouted Lyle.

"Why not?"

"What's your name?" asked Kyle in a smooth voice.

"Fallen Tree," said the young lad proudly.

"Well, Fallen Tree, It's just not how the system works," explained Kyle. "See, the dingle has to be put into a general fund and redistributed that way. To take advantage of this program, your caravan would have to register with the Gypsy Aid Committee and apply for assistance through all the proper channels. Then, if you met all of our predetermined requirements, we would issue you an amount of dingle based on your level of need. Despite my brother's protests, we *will* use this money to aid the impoverished. But we have to be very careful and make sure only folk who deserve aid get it."

"Listen to you! Running your cake hole off like that! Do you have to undermine everything I say?" interrupted Lyle.

"I wouldn't if something other than poppycock came spewing forth from your mouth!" Kyle turned his attention back to his nemesis across the road.

"I never! I'll have your powdered wig for that!" Lyle screeched.

Still, neither party attempted to cross the road into the other's space. They simply stood on their respective sides muttering and glaring at each other.

Fallen Tree shook his head in disgust and reared his horse around. "Turn it around," he commanded his caravan. "We'll find other passage."

"Um sir," interjected Kyle.

The gypsy leader spun back around. "What now?"

"There's still the matter of the consultation fee and tax for consumption of party time. I've had our accounting committee draw up your bill." The Libertine handed the gypsy leader a rolled parchment.

The leader unrolled it, scanned over it and handed it back to Kyle. "It means nothing. I cannot read that. Please let us go our way in peace."

"I'd be happy to oblige, after you've paid your due. What it says here is that the total comes to three thousand, five hundred and two dingle."

"How much do we get?" asked Lyle. "The Traditionalists were involved as well."

"If you'd like, we can work out a payment plan for—"

"Ride!" yelled Fallen Tree and galloped off with his caravan following closely after him. Gypsies have fast carriages. They modify them with shocks which allow for speedy flights and smoother rides.

"We've been attacked by thieves! To arms!" howled Lyle.

"We've been attacked by thieves! To arms!" yelled Kyle in agreement.

"After them!" commanded Lyle and Kyle in unison.

Both parties drew their blades and swarmed the road attempting to pursue the caravan, but so many folk moving in individual unison caused forward progress to be a challenge. The throng of powdered wigs moved like a river of molasses flowing slowly after the swiftly disappearing caravan.

The construction proles must have taken this as a sign of a lunch break or something because they promptly ceased all work and sat down. Some began eating, others dozed, and still others huddled in corners having a smoke.

"Hey. They finally agreed on something," noted Shamus.

"We should probably dip out before the powdered wigs get tired of looking for them and come back," said Fa Lona. We skirted around the lounging construction workers and resumed our trek.


After traveling one more day in the forest we came upon the small hamlet of Middle Road. It's what Realmers like to call a "one street beat" because the majority of the village is built around the main road. The good thing about one street beats is that you are able to see most of the town with one glance. The town consisted of a few small huts, an inn, a general store and the headquarters of both the Libertine and Traditionalist parties…each on their respective side of the road, of course. A commotion greeted us outside the parties' headquarters on the eastern edge of town. The Libertines and the Traditionalists had finally caught the gypsies that fled from their debt. As the caravan's wagons were impounded, guards marched the gypsies into the

Traditionalist headquarters to be jailed. Only She Who Becomes knows how the powdered wigs managed that seemingly Herculean feat. Those fools weren't even competent enough to manage themselves.

A traveling tent revival lurked on the western outskirts of the village. Being a devoutly spiritual man myself, the droning rhetoric emanating from the tent drew me in, so I ducked inside to see what was what. Please note, dear reader, that I was attracted out of curiosity, not the impulse of a wayward sheep looking for a home. I have a home, but who doesn't like to visit other folk's homes from time to time to see how they live and (most likely) silently judge them?

Inside, uniformly placed wooden benches cut grooves into the dirt floor. Obviously, their placement sought to direct all attention to the small stage occupied by the preacher. To this day, I'm not exactly sure as to the proper name of the cleric delivering the sermon. For lack of a better title, I dubbed him "Hollow Monk," for reasons that will be revealed soon.

Hollow Monk wore the simple brown robes of a monk. The robe's hood covered his face so completely that no light could penetrate the shadows obscuring his features. In an ironic contrast, gold adorned his entire person, accessorizing him with exceptional bling. He wore rings, chains, bracelets, necklaces and even a solid gold belt buckle to hold his hemp belt around his waist. He gripped a solid oak walking staff adorned with icons of his religion and precious jewels.

Hollow Monk had managed to captivate a small assortment of construction proles and elderly folk with his charismatic dullness. We entered during the middle of his sermon.

"And so, the true colors of Science are brought to light by its near obsessive desire to obtain Religion's role as a faith container for the folk. Science, in seeking to *replace* Religion, must first disprove Religion while simultaneously supplying rational and modern folk with a universe to believe in and make sense of.

"Science must offer a better rationale to explain the mysteries of the universe. In order to do so, Science must also willingly accept the burden of effectively proving that the Divine, which is the heart and soul of Religion, does not exist.

"It first attempted this by giving us the fable of the Grand Boom so that we may rationalize creation without having to explain the existence of a Divine Artist molding the chaotic Nothing into an ordered Something. Science tells us that just like that! And with a BOOM," the monk threw his arms into the air with a theatric flare, "the Universe was born. That makes for wonderful yarn spinning, but I have questions for the oversized brains of Science: How did the

Boom come about in the random and chaotic Nothing? What—or Who—lit the fuse to the explosive singularity that spoke us into Reality with a solitary Word? And in response, Science stares dumbly through their looking glasses to find an answer. An answer other than the one their Sacred Fish whisper with every flick of their fins: 'The Flawless He…'" Hollow Monk trailed off in a very dramatic whisper and passed around a golden, jeweled-encrusted collection plate he produced from the folds of his robe. I heard the tingling of dingle as it was dropped into the golden platter and left as quietly as possible to avoid the whole collection process.

"What was he talking about?" asked Lola as we stepped into the dusk.

"Just muttering religious mumbo jumbo and nonsense," said Shamus stiffly.

"Don't be so sure. He's rambling truths," I corrected, "they are just truths that very few folk understand and even fewer folk actually believe in."

"Why?" asked Fa Lona.

"Because believing that a tree is a squirrel is a very hard thing to do."

"That's dumb. How can a tree be a squirrel?" challenged Shamus.

"How can it not be?" I countered and walked toward the village in hopes of a hot meal and a warm bed.

I had taken only a few steps when Hollow Monk materialized out the darkness in front of us.

"How did you—?" Shamus started, but Hollow Monk held up his hand for silence.

"I noticed that none of you gave during collection," he chided in a hollow but oddly enchanting voice. "Is it that you hate the works of the Lord?"

"Not exactly," I said, "We're just kinda short right now and I'd hate to offend the Lord with a paltry offering."

"The Church appreciates any amount you can spare," said Hollow Monk extending his hand.

"You seem to be doing just fine from the looks of all that bling you have slung around your head-pole," spat Fa Lona. "You don't need our dingle."

Hollow Monk went rigid, "Young lady, this is not measly bling you gaze upon. These are holy relics bestowed upon me by the

Excitement[22] in order that I may better battle the legions of He That Is In Grammatical Error."

"Whatever. I don't care. You aren't getting a single dingle from any of us," stated Fa Lona definitively. She shoved past Hollow Monk, heading towards the village with Shamus close behind.

I gazed at Hollow Monk's energy looking for his intentions, but all I could discern was a transparent and empty shell where his aura should be. Empty. Vapid. No Sacred Fish or fishome to speak of. He truly was a hollow monk. I shook my head and turned to follow my companions.

It was during our after-dinner refreshments in the common's room of the Hornless Unicorn that our party once again crossed paths with the Hollow Monk. He appeared in the doorway clutching a copy of the Book of Absurdity[23] to his chest. The smoky candlelight of the room glinted on his menagerie of golden jewelry and accessories. He walked directly over to the bar and ordered a drink while scanning the crowd for potential converts. His hood turned in the direction of our table and a firm resolve straightened his posture. He marched stiffly over to crash our party. "It seems that the will of He has crossed our paths yet again."

"We still aren't giving you any dingle," said Lola.

"I came not in search of tithe, but to issue you and your cohorts a challenge," replied the monk, "You look the adventuring type. And everyone who is three plus one knows, the Realm thrives on adventure. What I offer is no mere fetch-and-return. But a noble quest, epic in scale, to be undertaken with the purest of intentions."

Lola rolled her orbs, "Boring! I'm going to my room. Infinity, you need to brush my hair. Don't be long, Mr. Jones," she scolded, "Royalty waits for no one." She downed the remainder of her sweetmilk and stomped upstairs.

Hollow Monk claimed her empty seat. He cleared his throat to begin his pitch. When he spoke, his voice was a melancholy rasp emanating from the shadows that hid his face, "I'm questing to reclaim something I foolishly gave away."

---

[22] The Excitement is a pure force. A loving force. A force that wants to fulfill the lives of those who follow it. It has no roots in sin. The Excitement is a celebration of life and spirituality. Tis an energy that consumes you and fills you with passion and desire. Tis a beautiful thing. Once it becomes you, doors open that you would've never known before.—*Coffee, The Incarnations of Princess Plum.* Yeah, Hollow Monk was lying. The Excitement doesn't like bling.—IJ.

[23] The holy text of He Who Is Not A Pronoun.

"Which was?" I asked.

"My faith."

"How would you give away your faith?" asked Shamus trying to wrap his brainpan around such a concept.

"I suppose I should enlighten you as to my situation," Hollow Monk sighed and it sounded like dry leaves scraping on a sidewalk, "I was not always thus," he began while presenting his bling dramatically, "At one time I was a devout cleric of He Who Is Not A Pronoun." The fallen monk fell silent for a moment and then he continued, "Even though I was supposed to rebuke the quest for material gain, the niceties in life always appealed to me."

Shamus nodded in approval and signaled the barmaid for another round.

"And so it was that happenstance sent a wandering peddler my way named Man Man."

The giant inhaled sharply at the mention of the ne'er-do-well's name.

"Ah. I take it you have heard of him."

"You could say that," he replied.

"Then you are well aware of his Cart of Wondrous Items at Discount Prices."

"Oh yes," concurred Shamus, "Chock full of grandiosity."

"Exactly. Well, there I was, browsing his cart when I saw this." The monk held up an oversized symbol of He Who Is Not A Pronoun suspended by a thick chain of gold. It sparkled in gaudy pretension as the flickering candlelight made love to its surface. "I was fascinated…and maybe even a bit enchanted," he admitted while running his hands across it like a lover would his beloved.

"Man Man came over to see what had caught my attention. 'Ah,' he said and nodded, 'One of my finest pieces. You certainly have a discerning orb for tasteful jewelry. Should I wrap it up for you?' he asked with a peculiar smile.

"'I'm sorry, but I can't afford it. I am but a humble servant of the Holy He,' I told him.

"'I'm sure we can work out a deal,' he cooed, 'I'll let you have it in exchange for something you'll never miss. I just need you to sign this contract,' he produced a scroll and a quill. I read over the contract carefully:

> *I (the undersigned) do hereby allow for Man Man to gain possession of my Faith in exchange for this Fantastic Bling*
> *Signed.*

"'Why my faith?' I asked amused, 'Why not my Sacred Fish?'

"Man Man scoffed, 'Nasty little buggers, those. Disgustingly chatty and chipper. High maintenance too. Faith doesn't try to foil your best laid plans from its fishbowl while you sleep. Faith is much cleaner and neater. More abstraction, less substance.'

"I shrugged it off. You see, I truly believed there was no way a filthy rat such as Man Man could affect, much less abduct, my faith. Verily, I was a holy child of He. I was positive that this creepy man before me was loony. I mean, how can you actually extract someone's faith? By shoving your hand into their chest and pulling it out? Do you put it in a bottle with a neat little label? Do you see how ludicrous this sounds?"

"Um….," I didn't know how to answer that one and neither did the giant. Seeing no immediate response, the monk continued.

"I signed the contract with all the confidence in the Realm that I was getting something for nothing. Man Man snatched up the contract and tucked it inside his coat pocket. He asked me to kneel and he put the bling around my neck very ceremoniously. As if it was some grand occasion or another—a coronation or a knighting. The chain was heavy, but it was so beautiful and shiny and…gold. I stood up feeling energized by the bling's sense of false confidence. Man Man held up a mirror and my reflection seized me. It was the most beautiful, most elegant, most regal I had ever looked. Why, I even had a tiny, shameful thought that I was more majestic than Pompus I, himself! I thanked Man Man and turned to leave, but the peddler halted me.

"'Ah, ah, ah,' he chided, 'Now it is my turn to collect.' And right there before my very orbs, Man Man literally *plunged his hand into my chest.* I stood frozen in place. All I could do was watch him in dumb amazement. I felt no pain as he rooted around. Finally, he shouted with glee and pulled out his closed fist. He opened it gently and I saw a glowing white ball for a brief moment before the evil mage put it in a bottle neatly labeled, 'Faith' and corked it. 'That's that,' he said in satisfaction.

"Something happened to me then. I actually *felt* the shadows creeping over my face. I cried out and to my surprise my voice had changed! No longer did it contain the silvery smoothness of His grace. It was now hollow and without life. All around me was darkness. I saw everything through a veil of empty blackness. I desperately grabbed at my hood, trying to pull it off my head and expose my face to the light. Man Man's orbs widened with fear and he grabbed my wrists.

"'That is not who you are anymore. You must never lower your hood in the presence of *any* folk.'

"'Why not?' I asked with a tremor in my voice.

"'Ever heard the saying: if looks could kill?'

"'Yeah.'

"'Well yours can now, and they will. Literally frighten folk to death.'

"'How?'

"'Well, you've no faith. And regular folk do not have the spiritual strength needed to look into such emptiness without going insane. You've a void *inside* that is to be replaced with things from the *outside*.' He pulled a book off his cart and handed it to me, 'This should help with your new beginnings.' Then he got on his cart and left." Hollow Monk fell silent.

"Was the book called *Mark's Book of Consumptionism*?" asked Shamus.

"No. It was called *The Principles of Pious Rationality*. It was a guide book on how to be religious without actually having any faith. Turn religion into a business is what it said to do. And it worked like a charm. I was making dingle hand over fist. With teary orbs, folk literally begged on their knees to join the Church of Pious Rationality. They confessed themselves at my feet and groveled for forgiveness. I became their father, their Voice of Reason that guided them through the pagan darkness of superstition and into the glorious enlightenment of Religious Rationalism.

"It all comes about by controlling emotional responses. If you control folk's emotions, you can control the folk themselves. First, you must work the congregation into an emotional frenzy. Then, when the congregation is good and emotional you 'pass the collection plate to the right-hand side' and ask for converts. It's all about forgetting the spiritual emptiness and manifesting material replacements. You see, materialism is much more tangible than faith and it makes it easier for folk to believe in. Show them immediate results and they sign up immediately.

"Never could do that with the Church of the Flawless He. We were always crammed into some sparse monastery or another chanting and doing monotonous chores in hopes of having a divine experience. Not very fun at all."

"So why ask for your faith back?" asked Shamus who couldn't understand giving up dingle to find salvation.

"It's hard to explain, but I feel...empty now," said the monk sadly. "I did like *The Principles of Pious Rationality* instruct and substituted more dingle for my faith, but it hasn't worked. I've even tried buying fine clothes, houses and carriages. Still nothing. There's a hungry black hole inside and the dingle doesn't fill it like Man Man claimed it would.

"In desperation, I quit the path of Pious Rationality and returned to preaching the testaments of He Who Is Not A Pronoun, but He hasn't answered my call. Man Man lied to me. I *do* miss my faith. I can't live without it. I *need* my faith back. Will you help me?"

"Sure," I said lightly. "We were just on our way to remove his blight from the land anyway."

Shamus laughed, "Have you *seen* Man Man lately?"

"Well…no," I admitted.

"He's huge. No, he's huger than huge. He's damn near *universal*. And he's surrounded by countless Peanuts night and day. We'll never get close to him without the Dark Glasses stepping in. And let me tell you, they aren't fun like Ferris Wheels."

"We could always ask the Oracle for help," I suggested.

"What Oracle?" asked Shamus.

"The one in the Desert of Lost Causes. Legends say he's in the fallen city of Remembrance. It'd be good for you anyway, Shamus. All true heroes have to visit the Oracle at least once during their journey."

"Legends are legends are fables," said Hollow Monk.

"Sounds like you're still stuck in your rational frame of mind. You have any better ideas?" I challenged.

He never got the chance to answer. The inn's front door flew open and a group of powdered wigs paraded in and seated themselves at the tables surrounding the fireplace. A small patrol of heavily armed guardsmen filed in after them and sat surrounding the wig-heads. They called for the barmaid in boisterous voices and began discussing something in mumbled tones.

"Nasty chaps there," said Shamus quietly.

Hollow Monk turned to see whom he was talking about. "The Traditionalists aren't so bad. It's the Libertines you have to watch out for."

"They're building a tollbooth just up the road, you know," said Shamus. "And we saw them harassing gypsies."

"I know these things," spoke the Monk. "'Tis why I was holding a revival and collecting dingle. That I may pay their toll and cross unmolested. Business is business and dingle is dingle. I'll not fault them for ingenious profiting."

The group of powdered wigs fell silent and stared intently at our table.

Whenever shady characters are staring at you, it's best to get ahead of the situation. "How might we help you gentlemen?" I asked them.

"Yes, I am Charles Fonzworthingtonshire, member of the Traditionalist party and champion of the simple way of life. And might you be the infamous Infinity Jones?"

"Infamous? When did that happen?"

"I'm guessing it happened about the same time these started circulating." Charles held up the wanted posters for Shamus and I. "I assume little miss Lola Fa Lona is also in your company? Perhaps the one with the dark hood?"

"Nay sir," said the monk, "I've no connection to these folk. I am a humble traveling cleric seeking to spread the truth of the Nonsensical Paragraphs."

"Perhaps you should lower your hood then. As a sign of good faith," said Charles slyly.

"Nay sir. I cannot," informed Hollow Monk, "To do so would surely be the death of all."

"Are you threatening us?" yelled Charles. "Guards!"

The Traditionalist party guards leapt to their feet.

"Arrest these folk," demanded Charles, "They are wanted in connection with heinous crimes in the ULS and they have threatened our lives!"

The guards orbbed our table, clearly unsure as to the appropriate plan of action. Shamus was a good head and shoulders taller than the tallest guard, who was obviously the group's enforcer. And how can you enforce someone that towers over you and is double your girth? Well, he tried. The enforcer let out an incredible howl and charged our table while we were still seated.

Shamus reacted first. He leapt to his feet and sent the table sprawling. The monk sprinted to and through the closest doorway. I drew my blade and yelled for Fa Lona.

The enforcer barreled into Shamus and both went tumbling to the floor. A tangled mess of flailing arms and legs jockeyed for position until Shamus managed to get the upper hand. The shrunken giant's wildly waving fist accidentally slammed into the guard's temple, knocking him out cold.

Lola Fa Lona appeared in the hallway behind me. "I thought you were going to brush my hair," she snapped and then saw the advancing guard. She fled back into her room and I followed.

Shamus was close on my heels, but in his haste, he failed to duck under the doorway and instead met the wall with a resounding smack. Lola and I heard Shamus fall from inside her room.

"We have Shamus!" called Charles from outside. "Come out! There is no escape for the rest of you." The sound of something very large being dragged across a wooden floor met our ears. "Throw him in with the gypsies. We'll collect the rest and meet you back at HQ," said Charles. "This is your last chance!" he called to us. "Come out or we are coming in!" Without waiting for a response, the Guard began to assault the door.

"Out the window," hissed Lola. She opened the window and leapt lightly into the arms of a guardsmen stationed out back for just such an escape attempt.

"Crap," I said and dropped my sword in surrender.

Lola and I were manacled and led to the Traditionalist Party's headquarters where we were stripped of all our possessions…except for mine. You see, the Orb of Power cannot be removed by *anybody*, even me. The desk sergeant found this out as he clasped his hand around it and yanked the chain. The man yelped and jerked his hand back. Smoke and the scent of scorched flesh filled the air. Instead, the guards manacled my hands and feet together with a short length of chain so I couldn't reach for the Orb or manipulate my hands. I was slapped around a bit (to nurse wounded egos) and tossed into a small cell with about twenty-five gypsies, a sassy Ninja, and a snack-sized giant. Needless to say, quarters were close and I'm no fan of close quarters.

Shamus came around thanks to the aid of Fallen Tree's great grandmother. This ancient woman kept the old ways of healing and Nature Magic, and I learned quite a lot from her during our stay. She taught me the incantation to close wounds and gave me a tea she claimed would show me to my totem. I'll tell you about that in the next book.

The next morning, guards escorted the gypsies to the Main Hall to await their trial. They were back before midday with guilty verdicts hanging over each of their heads. Their sentences varied from labor camps for the women and children to death by hanging for the men.

"This is not right," said Fallen Tree smoldering, "We harmed them not."

"Well, they think you did. And right now, what they think is what matters," I said.

"Who are you, outsider, to speak to me thus?" the gypsy leader bristled.

"Sit down you hard headed fool," said Fallen Tree's great grandmother poking a bony finger into her great-grandson's chest, "This gent not say what ain't but truth. Ain't nary a storm raging inside you ta break these walls down," the old woman chided, continuing to poke the large brooding man in the chest. She turned to me, "Go on. Speak you peace, maybe this boy knowing something when you through. Got his pappy's blood innem, he do. Runs hot!" The old healer chortled to herself as she sat down against the wall and closed her orbs in meditation.

"You heard her. Go on then. Speak your peace, stranger," demanded Fallen Tree as he plopped heavily to the floor.

"First of all, I am Infinity Jones. And you are?"

"Fallen Tree."

"Pleasure to meet you, Fallen Tree. Now we are no longer strangers. See, friend, my companions and I witnessed your encounter the other day."

The gypsy's countenance darkened, "Then I need not inform you of the rank injustice inflicted upon my folk for our inability to pay."

"True."

"And yet you comment as if you side with them."

"You misunderstand, my good man. I don't side with them at all. I only see where they are coming from. Their reasoning behind it, if you will."

"Then explain to me your insight, if you will. What twisted logic would lead them to such a conclusion?"

"They are as misguided and imperfect as the rest of us. They chose their paths and now they walk them. For better or worse. It's all part of the Divine's great tale. In their minds they believe they are doing right, because that is their part to play."

"Paganistic hogwash," somebody whispered outside the barred windows.

Fa Lona hoisted herself up to peer outside. "It's that stupid monk," she announced. "What do you want?"

"I've come to set you free. We've a quest to undertake."

"No, no I don't think we do. I'm pretty sure my *subjects* wouldn't undertake quests or make new plans without first consulting me and seeking my approval." The princess shot visual spikes toward me and Shamus before she readdressed the monk. "Get out of here you stupid jerk. We don't need your help." She lowered herself back to the floor and glared at Shamus and I with burning vexation. "I really don't like that guy."

"Our impetuous princess may have the details wrong, but her context is correct," I said out the window, "You flew your true colors when the trouble brewed back at the inn."

"I'm no coward! I merely slipped away so I could give aid later."

"Be that as it may, we'll not abandon these innocent folk in their time of need."

"Suit yourself," hissed the monk and then disappeared.

"Infinity Jones, huh? I knew he one of the good ones," the wizened gypsy cackled and made her way over to the barred window. She spent the rest of the night yelling animal calls outside. When the sun began to redden the horizon, she started getting answers.

At dawn, guards escorted the gypsy men to their fates. We followed with the women and children to witness the public example of what happens when Those in Charge don't get their dingle. Lola bounced ahead of me, while Shamus brought up the rear. Directly in front of Fa Lona was Fallen Tree's great grandmother. A good crowd of townsfolk and construction proles gathered around, mumbling in anticipation. Apparently, the various labor unions treated execution days as holidays. Everybody loves a good hanging, more so a head lopping. But that's far messier.

In the trees that encompassed the sylvan village, birds had gathered in disturbing numbers. Additionally, small woodland creatures like raccoons, squirrels, chipmunks, a few of Jo Joe's monkeys, and even some very rare tree-otters joined the ranks of fowl already in the trees. I caught the gaze of Fallen Tree's great grandmother. She winked and gave me a toothless smile.

Guards led the men to the second floor of the Traditionalist Party HQ. A scaffold ran the length of the building's front. A very large man wearing an executioner's hood stood near the scaffold release at the east end of the building.

Guards shoved each gypsy out a window and onto a small wooden plank, where their head-poles were gifted with nooses. Some of the men wept and begged for mercy. Others, like Fallen Tree, stood proud and refused to flinch as they gazed into the hypnotic gaze of Mother Death.

Kyle and Lyle stepped forward to address the crowd.

"Good folk," Lyle said, "I welcome you all today in the name and good graces of the Traditionalist party."

"Oh lord," said Kyle rolling his orbs, "Good graces indeed. Gentle folk, it is with great regret that we must gather here today. We stand before you in shame for we have failed these poor gypsies. In our endless struggle to help those less fortunate, some inevitably slip through the cracks."

Lyle continued, "In these instances we must be willing to demonstrate the serious level of commitment that the Traditionalists *and* the Libertines," Lyle shot a self-righteous glance at his brother, "possess in our collective pursuit for a better and more wholesome society that all may enjoy."

"In order to achieve a comfortable society, we require the help of *all* Realmers. All must abide by the same laws and receive the same punishment. This is the nature of equality," Kyle said.

"We do not wish to be part of your wholesome society!" yelled Fallen Tree rebelliously.

"Well tough!" shouted Lyle. "You're part of it whether you like it or not. If everyone got to pick and choose it'd be chaos. And we can't have chaos. That's anti-social."

"Chaos negates peace. My misguided brother isn't always wrong!" shouted Kyle, "All must participate or all are lost." Interestingly, the brothers weren't wrong about this. A folk must be unified, not divided. Societies and civilizations cannot survive when fractured. Within the Realm are many different folk, each with their own lands and cultures, as it should be. But there is a difference between ensuring social cohesion within one's own society and trying to force others to conform to push political agendas. That's how revolutions happen. Speaking of...

"In keeping with that spirit of participation, we are taking this moment to officially announce the Traditionalist and Libertine alliance with Man Man and the Undividable Land of Shamus! Our alliance is secured with the *Traditionalist* apprehension of the ULS's three Most Wanted Vile and Wicked Criminals!" Lyle pointed to us and all gazes fell on Shamus who towered above the crowd, attracting much interest. "The dingle collected from the bounty will be split among several economically stimulating programs that the Traditionalists have drafted in order to speed along the process of—"

"Speed along the process of fattening your wallets you stupid oaf! The dingle we get for the reward is going to fund social awareness programs among the lower classes," interjected Kyle.

"You stupid jackass!" Lyle screeched.

"You oafish Oompalump!"

Tension between the two groups escalated; wigs on both sides quivered with restrained anger.

"Hang 'em already!" someone yelled from the crowd and the rest bleated in agreement.

The tension faded as suddenly as it had arisen. "Yes, well, er, of course. That is why we're here, isn't it? Well then, let the hanging begin!" announced Lyle.

Everyone looked toward the executioner so they wouldn't miss that juicy moment when he pulled the rope and single handedly snuffed out multiple lives.

At that moment, Fallen Tree's great grandmother raised her left fist to her mouth. "Shaman dart," she said and blew into her closed fist.

The executioner raised his hand, but instead of grasping the rope and beginning the carnage, the agent of death clutched his throat and fell over dead.

For a moment, no one dared move or speak. Everyone simply stared around in the dumb, half-frightened silence of uncertainty. But the carnage began anyway.

"Somebody pull the blasted rope!" screeched Lyle and the Traditionalist guards advanced toward the scaffold release.

Hollow Monk appeared around the corner carrying a thick oak staff. "Halt!" he commanded and his Voice froze the men in their tracks. They gazed around in a stupor for a moment and then glanced back at the bickering brothers.

"What are you waiting for!" yelled Kyle. "He's just one man!"

The guards took a few more leery steps and Hollow Monk raised his right hand, palm out. It was covered with a fine glove of black silk and each finger was adorned with at least one ring. "I said YOU SHALL NOT ADVANCE." This time, the cleric's voice was a physical force that knocked the armor-laden guards to the ground. Despite his lack of faith, Hollow Monk could still use the Voice.[24]

The gypsy women used Hollow Monk's interference to strike. They began to sing a fast-paced, brutal tune that told of the fiery spirits held by an uncompromising folk. Their manacles unclasped and fell to the ground, and the hot-blooded gypsy women circled their young, countenances aflame with defiance toward the advancing guardsmen. Their hips began to sway in seductive agitation like a battle dance tempting the overconfident guards closer. Once the soldiers stepped into range, the women whirled in unison using outstretched legs as fleshy clubs.

The leather skullcaps of the guards did little to protect their heads from the forceful strikes of the spinning gypsies. The first onslaught of guards collapsed to the ground without ever raising their weapons. The remainder drew their blades and rushed the group. The children jumped onto the backs of their mothers, clinging tightly to them as

---

[24] The Voice is a physical ripple in the OM of creation. It is the true weapon afforded to all clerical folk of the Realm. The more authority and confidence a holy man puts in his Voice, the stronger and more effective it becomes. Truly devout and spiritual folk can command just about anything with a strong enough Voice. Legends say they've even moved mountains into the sea.

the women sought to merge with the crowd. But the frightened mob scattered quickly, attempting to disengage from the action while remaining entertained spectators.

The old medicine woman laughed hysterically and threw her hands in the air. On cue, the birds in the trees took flight as one giant, black cloud. Without warning, the fowl dropped stones, nuts, hardened pieces of dung—anything that inflicted pain—into the crowd.

On the Headquarters rooftop, raccoons overwhelmed the guards and chewed through the nooses around the male gypsies' necks. Their manacles also unclasped and fell harmlessly at their feet. The freed gypsies sprang back into the windows and attacked the guards with bare hands. It appeared that Pandora had come to play uninvited. But honestly, when is that carefree daughter of Chaos invited anywhere?

The Traditionalists and Libertines quickly lost control and their leaders could not have that. In keeping with the tradition that all despots losing control turn to, they resorted to violence.

"Kill them before they escape!" Kyle yelled.

"Kill them all!" agreed Lyle. The fluid scraping of metal on sheath added to the cacophony of screaming birds. Powdered wigs and guards alike prepared to slay anyone remotely resembling a gypsy. Even the Libertines had lost their previous humanistic bleeding-heart approach and were primed for slaughter. Remember this, dear reader: violence is always on the table for politicos. Never be fooled into thinking otherwise.

A call for archers was sent by carrier pigeon when the commotion started. Unfortunately, the nervous powdered wig that sent the request forgot to include the Permission Override Form A-00. So, a squad of archers was geared up and ready to go, but had to wait while their superiors sought the proper clearance in the convoluted maze of bureaucracy. I don't know if you've ever been trapped in a bureaucratic maze, but personally, I'd rather be lost in a Minotaur's labyrinth. It's far more exciting and you don't have to wait long for the bull-headed brute to sniff you out and get down to the business of battle. Anyway, the archers arrived just in time to fire arrows into the cloud of birds from atop the HQ. Truly, an impotent and fruitless use of resources, as most bureaucracies are.

On the ground, large bucks and Ted Bears burst from the foliage and assaulted the guards bent on wreaking havoc among the innocents present. Woodland critters darted in and about the crowd, seeking the women and children and leading them to safety. I felt a tugging at my chains, and, to my amazement, a small tree-otter had his paw inside the locking mechanism of the cuffs. I heard a click and the manacles slid from my hands.

*Now you can be of some use to me. We might be able to save your pathetic life yet*, the Orb sneered inside my head. *Listen. Clasp me in your left hand and hold out your right hand like you saw the monk do.* I did as the Orb commanded and immediately felt myself seized by the energies. *Now yell, "Blue-haired killer!!"*

"Blue-haired killer!" I yelled. Tiny blue orbs of flame burst from my palm and landed neatly atop any powdered wigs in the crowd. The wigs caught fire in rapid succession causing Traditionalists and Libertines alike to frantically roll around in the dirt trying to put them out.

"Our wigs!" they screeched as they stuck their heads into mud puddles or threw their expensive pieces on the ground and stomped them into the soil.

Being freed, we forced our way through the crowd, trying to break loose so we could bolt for safety. It was a slow and frustrating process—one step forward two steps back kind of progress.

And if that jumbled mess of Chaos wasn't bad enough, a large shadow appeared overhead and instantly scattered the cloud of bombardier birds.

Slither, as it turned out, had been busy. A few days prior he'd come across the Traditionalists and Libertines dumbly milling through the forest after the gypsies gave them the slip at the tollbooth. The dragon sniffed out the caravan in record time (something the powdered wigs hadn't managed) and delivered them to the politicians for processing. Then, not knowing we'd already been caught, he'd settled in to wait and see if we'd turn up. The battle was, from his perspective, a delightful bonus.

"Dragon!" one of the archers called and the small squadron, being uninformed of Slither's role in the gypsies' initial capture, fired on the winged horror hovering above the scene.

The dragon hollered in anger and, landing atop the Traditionalist HQ, wasted no time in cutting the archers to pieces and heaving their bodies into the crowd below with a booming laugh.

Hollow Monk materialized out of the bedlam, finding us stuck between a Traditionalist and a Libertine (which I understand the saying for in your Realm is "stuck between a rock and a hard place."). "Come with me, quickly. We must escape without catching the dragon's attention." The crowd parted for that mysterious cleric like the Primary Colored Sea parted for Joses, and we followed him around the side of the building to the impound stables.

"Shamus and Jones, watch our backs. You pick that lock," Hollow Monk commanded Lola and pointed to the corral of gypsy horses, "set them free."

"You are no one to give me orders, monk," spat the princess.

"For crying out loud!" I yelled. "We don't have time for this! I'll do it."

"Good. I'll return briefly," said the monk and disappeared into the stables.

The lock didn't look too complicated, but unfortunately, my picks had been confiscated with the rest of my gear.

"Don't tell me you need picks for this," sneered Lola from over my shoulder.

"I thought you weren't helping."

"I'm not. I'm only saying that if you grab it like this," she moved around me and clasped the lock in both hands: one on the metal loop and one on the lock. "Then move it like this," she jerked the lock to the right, "then here," to the left, "and finish it off with a little twist," she twisted the loop while simultaneously pulling the lock and it fell apart in her hands, "you can open it without your picks. Duh. Everyone who is three plus one knows that."

Without another word, she darted over to stand with Shamus and I opened the gate. The agitated horses rushed out of the corral and around the building, all too willing to add to the confusion and mayhem.

After he tossed the last archer over the edge of the building, Slither noticed Shamus and Lola keeping tabs on the battle's progress. Slither smiled at his wonderful luck and glided down in front of the pair. "Ssshamusss McFamusss, I presssume?" he hissed. "I am Ssslither Faussst. I am here to collect you and your party for crimesss committed againssst the mossst noble tyrant, Man Man. Leaving already?"

"Yup. And you can't come," snapped Fa Lona and took a shot at Slither's inner thigh, aiming for any major joints or easily breakable bones.

Faust dropped his sword and brushed the ninja's kick aside with the flat of his blade. With his free hand he delivered a harsh blow to the princess's head that sent her careening into the side of the building. She collapsed in an unconscious heap.

"It appearsss I've caught you jussst in time."

Shamus backed up a couple of steps and held his arms in front of him protectively. "Look, Mr. Faust, I don't want any trouble. But you gotta understand I'm not going back there to Man Man. I—I can't." Fear built a dam inside him that kept any courage from flowing into Shamus's heart. Ever since his reawakening, Commander Gali worked to alleviate this, but breaking through dams of fear is tedious work and ultimately a labor of love. Thank the Divine that we have Sacred Fish to care for us thusly.

"Yesss you can," said Slither seductively, almost sweetly. "You jussst come over here and we are on our merry way. We'll be home in three daysss time. Man Man longsss for your return." Slither's forked tongue danced across his scaly lips.

"I—I—don't—I mean I can't," Shamus backed further away from the dragon.

The bounty hunter merely smiled a toothy smile and followed Shamus nonchalantly like a mass murderer in a horror drama. McFamus ran behind the Traditionalist building just as a few gypsy men, led by Fallen Tree, burst through the back door brandishing bloodied swords.

Slither rounded the corner and stopped dead in his tracks. "Fallen Tree!" he hissed, "I thought I'd collected you already."

"You speak truth, dragon. But, some of us escaped," he informed Faust, "no chains exist that can hold a gypsy."

"Then now you ssshall essscape the binding chainsss of life!" roared the dragon and sprang on the group of gypsies.

Shamus was forgotten for the moment. You see, some things mean more to folk (and dragons) than dingle. These things are emotions and beliefs that live deep inside folk's hearts. They are the unconscious but intuitive understandings of one's place on the Great Neutrality's Scale of Duality that governs all realms beneath the One. Fortunately for us, dragons and gypsies are diametrically opposed to one another. Neither can stand the sight of the other and when the two species do come into contact the inevitable result is battle.

Shamus capitalized on the distraction and rushed to where I was tending the injured Ninja. A dark bruise already covered the right side of her face.

"I'm sorry, Miss Fa Lona," the giant whispered and gathered the girl into his arms. "We gotta go, Mr. Jones."

"This way," Hollow Monk called. He stood at the stable doors, waving us over to him. "I've procured us a wagon and some supplies." With a flourish of his gloved hand, he drew our attention to a very nice tarp-covered wagon made of reinforced wood laden with supplies and pulled by two horses. Both were strong and fine beasts that might've been war horses in another life.

"Politicians always have the nicest rides," noted Shamus.

"Marvel about it later," I said.

"Indeed," agreed Hollow Monk. "We must leave now lest the dragon finish with his diversion and return his attentions to our number. Come, we escape into the forest! We will return to the road when we can!" The monk climbed into the driver's seat and I rode crossbow beside him. The princess was gingerly laid in the back and Shamus ran beside us. We fled south and east, deeper into the forest. The sounds of the gypsies battling and the frantic confusion of the powdered wigs fell off into memory.

"Yeah, but does he have to come with us?" whined Fa Lona when she regained consciousness and discovered the monk among our party. "This doesn't help my headache, Infinity Jones."

"What do you want?" I asked as I applied a healing salve to her bruise. "The guy had his Faith stolen for crying out loud! He needs our help! Plus, he helped us escape."

The ninja pulled away from me and spat on the ground. "He'll have our purses and slit our throats while we sleep. Mark my words." She stormed off to sulk as a good princess should.

"Well then you get first watch!" I yelled after her. "If you're so worried about it!"

"She's a bit melodramatic, don't you think?" asked the monk, seeming to materialize beside me. He did that often and it was often creepy.

"She is a bit high strung," I conceded, "but that comes with no-bility, I suppose."

"Ah, of course," murmured the monk, "she is Pure Ninja. I should've seen it before."

"How do you know that?"

"They tend to be smaller and finer than their brutish cousins who are essentially a new sub-race springing from centuries of interracial mingling between the Ninja clans and the more barbaric minded Frosty Folk who roam the hills and forests around High Azen in search of plunder."

"Wow," I said mildly impressed at Hollow Monk's display of triv-ial knowledge.

"The Pious Rationalists believe that true awakening comes from a deep and intimate understanding of the mundane workings found in the Realm," his voice took on a teacher-ish tone, "Knowledge, not faith, is the key. And with the right knowledge, you can properly ex-ploit the time-honored traditions and rituals that folk hold sacred and dear, effectively cutting faith out of religion altogether. Of course, this leaves a hole and that hole is filled up with *profit*, this is true. However, knowledge must also be sought in order to reconstruct beliefs and morals without having them based on faith or the supposed utterances of an invisible deity."

"Pious Rationality seems to have quite a grip on your persona for one who gave it up."

"It's hard to get away from," Hollow Monk admitted, "I would liken it to an addiction."

"So, you traded Man Man your Eternal Afterlife Pass to Paradise Land and Waterpark[25] for a shallow life of luxury and pursuit of ill-used knowledge?"

"When you put it like that it sounds so bad."

"Yeah."

He marinated in his own absurdity for a moment and then said, "I recovered your possessions from your captors. They are in the wagon. Perhaps this will be sufficient to prove my good intentions."

"Really?" I could hardly contain my excitement, "My mag, my belt, my pack, my blade?"

"Everything," said the monk simply.

"Far out," I said and rushed over to dig through the wagon like a kid at a toy shop. Lola soon followed, gathering all of her items before storming off again without looking at any of us.

The next morning, we made our way north and east so we could meet the road further ahead and maybe avoid any nastiness or pursuit. We reached the road leading into Velhampshire at sundown. High above the mountain peaks, sky giants battled in their great cloud chariots in the sky. You could hear the cracking and rumbling of the chariot's wheels and see the flashes of gods' steel in the sky as the combatants struggled.

"Storm heading towards us," said Lola. "We better stop here for the night."

"I'd rather not," said Shamus uneasily. "This is Velhampshire. Do you have any idea what they keep in the mansion on top of that hill?" Shamus pointed and on cue, a flash of lightning lit up the area of the wee giant's discontent. An ancient manse of brick and stone loomed atop a rocky plateau outside of town. Surrounded by a moat, it was only accessible by ferry.

Another flash of lightning revealed the mansion's looming architecture. Three separate wings jutted haphazardly about; their design obviously inspired by some raving lunatic's nightmare. The angles were all wrong, in a way that was offensive to the glance. It literally

---

[25] The heavenly abode of He Who Is Not A Pronoun.

*hurt* to look at the place for too long. Carved from cold, black stone, nightmarish creatures of lore and myth perched atop the parapets of that cursed building. Devilish looking gargoyles, terrifying were-wolves, and vicious Maidens of Lilith patiently sat on the ramparts, as if daring the sun to go down so they could flee the confinements of their stony prisons and lay waste to the innocent countryside. In the center, over the front door, stood a statue of an exquisite woman carved out of white stone.

"What is that place?" Lola, orbs wide, breathed that question, like she was afraid to speak it aloud lest that hideous manse somehow hear her and turn its attention her way.

"It's the Sanitarium for the Ravenous Vampires of Velhampshire. And believe you me, it is best if we avoid contact with this place and its residents as thoroughly as possible." Shamus then related his experiences with the Great Dirt Derby and the fate of the earliers that were caught. He also explained the function of the Sanitarium and its attempts at vampyric reformation.

"That's irrational," said the monk as Shamus finished his tale. "First of all, vampires don't exist. And even if they did, popular vampire lore says that those who become vampires do so willingly. They see it as a *gift*. You have to ask for vampirism. That they would denounce their gift and seek reform is wholly impossible."

"Exactly," reinforced Shamus, "Smells fishy to me too. We should keep going."

"You jerks have fun," said Fa Lona impatiently, "but princesses don't sleep in the rain when there is a perfectly good inn within walking distance." With a flip of her hair, she sprang off the cart, walking toward Velhampshire.

"You can't just go into town looking like yourself," I called to her.

She stopped and turned around; tiny fists balled at her sides. "Just why can't I, Infinity Jones?"

"We're wanted. Posters and everything, remember? What if Slither is in town waiting for us?"

"So what?" she demanded. "Because I'm *not* <u>not</u> **NOT** sleeping outside in the wet and cold!"

"Then I'll disguise us." I dug through my pack until I found my jar of magical, black stage makeup that comes in handy when fleeing the wooing of certain persistent (to put it delicately) noblewomen. The makeup really is extraordinary. Fair's Folk use it all the time. You merely put a smattering under each orb and speak the cantrip,

*"When you see me,*
*how cool it'd be;*

*if you could see
me differently!"*

Then you just picture what you want to look like and viola! That causes the Tricksy in the makeup to activate and disguise the individual. The problem with disguising Shamus was that he was ten feet tall. It's damn near impossible to disguise a ten-foot giant as anything or anyone else other than a ten-foot giant without disguising him as some creature or another that would terrify the life out of most of the general populace. So, I disguised him as the "Realm's Tallest Man" and myself as his promoter looking for a well-paying circus. Lola masqueraded as a gypsy acrobat and Hollow Monk was still Hollow Monk. I couldn't see his face to put the makeup on and he wouldn't let me reach inside his hood. Being mostly camouflaged, we descended on the town in hopes of a few mugs of ale and a warm bed safe from nocturnal predators.

The town itself was quaint enough: Simple one-story houses surrounded by wooden fences with pickets sharpened to fine points. Black iron rods barred all the windows. Symbols of He Who Is Not A Pronoun decorated the majority of the doors and windows, accentuated by garlic braids swaying in the wind like silent, smelly windchimes.

The inn, creatively christened the Bloody Turnip, was located in the center of town right across from the temple of He Who Is Not A Pronoun. Aside from the towering temple, the inn was the tallest building in the village, reaching a bold three stories into the crisp, forest air.

The crowded common room's impressive size easily rivaled many noble ballrooms throughout the land. I should know. I've seen most of them. However, it wasn't nearly as clean and pretentious. Wooden tables littered the room with no discernable order. When there were no more tables to sit at, folk took to standing in small groups. A young barmaid wove in and out of the crowd expertly dodging groping hands while serving her orders. The western wall housed a roaring fireplace burning whole tree trunks. At the north end a bar/front desk lined most of the wall with stairs on either side. And tucked in the corner by the front door was a small and poorly constructed stage with a shivering bard performing for folk who weren't paying the least bit of attention to him.

We entered to find scores of folk singing, yelling, and acting like children at a birthday party. Nobody even stopped to take notice of our arrival. Shamus and the monk went to find us a table. Lola and I went to secure rooms. Fa Lona walked deliberately through the thickest part of the crowd as she made her way to the bar/front desk. Once she reached it, the impatient Red Dragon Ninja began slamming her tiny fist against the counter to gain attention.

The innkeeper appeared from the kitchen wiping dry a glass. Though she was young, she had obviously been through numerous tough times. Fierce determination had chiseled itself into her features. Her right orb reflected a fiery spirit, while a black patch covered where her left orb should've been; this accentuated by a jagged scar that began at her temple, ran down her cheek and ended abruptly on her chin. A disheveled crop of blonde hair was held in place by a bandana made of varying browns and greens.

"Whaddya want?" she asked gruffly.

"Four private rooms for the night," demanded Fa Lona and dropped a dangle of dingle on the counter.

The innkeeper snatched the bag and weighed the contents with a few slaps against her open palm. "These bloody Adventure Trails tourists bout got me booked up, but I'll see what I got," she said and disappeared into the back.

"Where did you get that dingle?" I whispered to Fa Lona while the innkeeper was away.

"Dunno. One of these drunks must've dropped it. And you know I can't just announce to a crowded room full of proles that I found a dingle dangle. There'd be a lot of folk missing their purses all of a sudden, if you get my drift." Out of the corner of my orb I saw a brief glint of metal that quickly disappeared into the ninja's loose-fitting garments.

I was about to call the little rogue on it when the innkeeper reappeared carrying a handful of wooden room keys.

"Check out after breaking fast. Name's One-Orb Goldie if ya needs anything, but I'd rather ya didn't bother me if it's all the same. Oh, and don't be wandering around outside twixt High Dark an' Pre-Dawn."

"Why?" asked Fa Lona with her characteristic and obnoxious curiosity.

"Just not a particularly good idea, is all," snapped the innkeep, "especially for travelling strangers who don't know their way round these parts."

"That's no answer," said Lola. "That's just you trying to scare me so you can make fun of me later with all your stupid backwater friends," the little Ninja's orbs narrowed into tiny slits of seething rage and her hand crept slowly towards her blade.

I placed my hand on the princess's shoulder. She whirled around, orbs flashing with anger as her harmonic imbalance shifted toward yang. "Back away. Before I add your hand to my collection."

I jerked my hand away and hid it from her sight. "I was only going to say that you might want to let it go."

"Why would I want to do that?" hissed Fa Lona.

"What if I told you that I needed an introduction to this part of my retelling so I kind of...added a bit of flare? She's really guilty of nothing more than partaking in her own destiny."

"Now wait just a tick," Goldie interjected, "Are ya saying that my *destiny*, my entire reason fer being, was to provide *ya* with a bit of flare for some story?"

I lowered my gaze sheepishly. This, I have noticed, usually settles the smoldering feminine volcano that is a woman's wrath. "I mean, I'm on an adventure; and all my adventures become absolutely true retellings. If you wouldn't have said what you did, then the tale wouldn't flow right." I chanced a glance to see how Mt. Fem-Fury was faring. She was set to erupt at a moment's whim. I felt it wise to back away slowly.

"I'll have ya know," began the innkeeper calmly, but it wasn't a good calm. It was the tense calm that comes seconds before the world goes all topsy-turvy. And the look in her good orb was just as unsettling. It was the look your mom gives when she uses your full name. "I am a *real* person with *real* memories and *real* feelings and *real* thoughts!" Mt. Femfury had begun to erupt. "I was *born* sir, do ya follow? I have a birthday, which happens to be the second day of Waning during Wolf's Moon!" Her angry reinforcement was a lava flow that swallowed whole the fragile huts of doomed villagers. Hers was the burning anger of individualism, of each person's secret desire to be something *more* than just another letter or comma or space between the words that God uses to write the history of the universe.

"I had a husband and two strong boys who just up and vanished three years ago, collecting firewood inna woods. I miss them so," she began to cry, tears like falling pumice and debris that blotted out her sun and resurrected the cold, dark reign of grief. She quickly turned away to hide her moment of weakness and recollect herself.

I felt awful. "Of course, you are somebody special. With free will and your own memories and everything. I didn't mean it like that. Clearly you are a very complex individual with depthless emotion and being. Besides, realizing your destiny early like this isn't a bad thing."

"Why not? Ain't I going to die now?"

"Lords no! When folk fulfill their destinies, they are free."

"Free?" her tears began drying up.

"Of course," I said. "Free. You've done your duty. Helped the universe and my retelling progress as they should. Your life is your own, do with it what you will."

"Hum," Goldie said thoughtfully. She shot one last glare in my direction and returned to the back.

"We can't hang out if you're going to act like a jackass in public," Lola informed me as we fought our way through the crowd to the only available table, which happened to be right next to the stage.

Shamus and Hollow Monk were conversing with the bard who had given up trying to capture an audience for the evening.

"Any news of the ULS?" asked Shamus.

"I've just hailed from there," said the bard. "The Gaunt is worse than ever. It was haunting to watch them. And their new CEO, Man Man, is a living monument at this point. I heard," the lad leaned in closer, "I heard that Man Man actually gave folk the Gaunt on purpose. He's building an army as we speak. Oh, sure he *says* it's for the security of the ULS and all, but I pose a question: If he is only concerned with his own, then why is he trying so desperately to spread his influence and build alliances *outside* the ULS? New Super Mark's Marts are erected daily. Famous McShamus has become the number one quickfood eatery in the *entire* Realm."

"No!" I exclaimed a bit too loudly.

"Aye," responded the bard somberly, "Not only that, but the United Bank of Man Man has opened branches in Sense City, The City of Lost Causes and a new branch is going up in Middle Road, last I seen. I'm telling you, that monster has bigger plans. Say, you wouldn't mind helping me out with an ale, would you?" the bard asked after he'd finished his story. "I didn't do as well tonight as I'd hoped."

"Of course," I said, "and thank you for your information. Now, lady and gentlemen, if you don't mind, I do think I'll retire for the evening. The last few days have been exhausting." I left a couple of dingle for the bard and went to my room.

The storm broke shortly thereafter. Thunder crashed against invisible walls of air and lightning flashed across the night sky like nature's fireworks display. Then the rain hit. Torrential sheets of furious droplets slammed into the building and rapped on the windows with a horrific cadence. I tumbled into sleep and dreamt of nightmarish creatures sniffing about for my blood.

Later that night, a faint scratching on my window roused me. As I was on the third and topmost floor of the inn, this struck me as something worth investigating. I pulled back the curtains, and, much to my surprise, a beautiful, yet strangely white woman floated on a cloud of mist outside the window. She smiled at me, flashing teeth like porcelain pillars of desire proclaiming my divinity. I couldn't help but stare at her. She was perfect in shape and form and moved with a practiced, sensual grace. She beckoned me with both her glance and her figure. My first thought was that she was probably terrified from the unsettling experience of being whisked away by a cloud of mist to float where the wind takes you. I've been there, and it isn't as fun as it sounds. I fumbled around for the window latch and ushered the lady inside.

*Jones*, screamed the Orb inside my head, *snap out of it fool! She's a mmfmmfhmff…*

The white lady clasped the Orb in her hand and whispered something to it. The blue glow went cold and the Orb fell silent. She looked into my orbs and smiled. "Follow me," she purred in a sexy whisper.

I was powerless to deny her. I grabbed her hand, stepped onto her magical carpet of fog and flew into the stormy night.


An almost imperceptible scratching accompanied a click outside my door. The door creaked softly as it opened. The only other sound was the soft pitter patter of feet on wood.

"Hsst! Jones," whispered Fa Lona, "Wake up! I want you to brush my hair." Lola waited, but there was no answer. "Jones!" she shouted. She scanned the empty room with trained orbs. I was gone! Vanished! Fa Lona walked to the open window to see if I had plummeted to the ground in some fit of sleepwalking or other such gnomesense. I hadn't. Lola glanced up just as a flash of lightning outlined the Velhampshire Sanitarium.

NEW
HAMPShire

"Jones. Wake up," came a whisper from the Void.

My orbs popped open. I was immediately aware of being bound to a table in a room lit by flickering torchlight. The walls were built of huge granite blocks sporting chains and manacles at various intervals. My first thought was that I'd somehow ended up in a seedy nightclub with the lady in white, had a bit too much katzpuh, followed by a memory lapse, and was about to be prepped for involuntary organ donation.

My second thought was that I had been enchanted by the lady in white, spirited away to her haunted abode, had a memory lapse, and was currently awaiting some sacrifice or death. I weighed my options while I waited for my fate to present itself. Involuntary organ dona-tion would be violating and assuredly painful, but I would most likely survive. However, sacrificial death still ended in death, no matter what adjective you put in front of it. Needless to say, I was desperately hoping for the reality of the first thought.

The reality of the second thought manifested itself later with the arrival of a very round and very bald man in a doctor's coat. He was built almost exactly like a snow man and the stark whiteness of his attire only enhanced his likeness. Round, rimless spectacles gro-tesquely magnified the beady little orbs behind them.

"Welcome, sir!" he yelped and topped it off with a jovial smile. "I trust your trip was comfortable and to your liking? Jewel can be a bit rough sometimes when she gets a dark humor in her."

"It was most pleasant," I said.

"Jolly good then. I am Dr. Wikket, warden of the Sanitarium for the Ravenous Vampires of Velhampshire."

"Fascinating. Pleasure to meet you. I am—"

"You are Infinity Jones, possessor of the Orb of Power," the doc-tor finished for me. "I know all about you," he said and waved my "wanted" picture in front of me. The reward wasn't half bad—five thousand dingle. I've had bounties put on my head for less.

"Wonderful. Always good to meet a fan." I always try to be hum-ble when taking compliments. "Now, good doctor, perhaps you might help me remedy a small dilemma. You see, I seem to be strapped to this table and was wondering if you might be able to, oh

I don't know, untie me perhaps? I'll autograph your poster for the trouble."

"I can see how you would wish for that," returned the doctor. "But I'm afraid you'll be staying right where you are for the moment."

"I was afraid of that too," I sighed.

"I do think it was horribly cute of you to ask, though," laughed the warden. "Gives me a chuckle to spread along to the staff later. First, though, I must alleviate you of something that is far beyond your simple understanding. I was hoping we would get the pleasure of crossing paths," he cooed to the Orb as he ran pudgy fingers over the blue smoothness of its unresponsive surface. "So beautiful. So much power, I cannot believe you have fallen so effortlessly into my grasp." I could feel the Orb's silent anger racing through me. "You really have no idea the favor you've done me Infinity Jones," he peered at me with avarice openly displayed on his face. "But that is no longer any of your concern. Soon, we shall separate you from your chaotic curse. Soon the Orb will *serve* instead of *being* served.

"Very good Tricksy, by the way. Very clever disguise. Bit of Fair's Stage Makup, I take it? Too bad my agents aren't prone to such trifling illusions. They saw right through it." Wickett tied a strip of rope around my upper arm to expose a vein. Then, he retrieved a syringe from an attending orderly and flicked the needle a few times. "I admit, I almost cried with joy when my spies told me who had entered *my* town. Literally fell into my lap! Of course there is the matter of the bounty for your capture, and thankfully, Man Man didn't rightly say if he preferred your corpse or your life. This will undoubtedly bring about the tragic and utterly un-heroic end of Infinity Jones," giggled Dr. Wikket. "Ah well, not every adventure can have a happy ending," he jammed the needle into my arm.

I screamed as my whole body was consumed by the evil doctor's concoction of liquid fire. The burning reached my brain and a bright red light flashed inside my head. The sensation left just as quickly as it had come and in its wake was a feeling of throbbing numbness. I was completely unable to move. An orderly materialized out of the shadows and undid my restraints.

Dr. Wikket spoke during this process. I think he was a sucker for a captive audience. His tongue was as loose as his morals. "Isn't it exquisite? Un Pequeno Fuego Muerto. Little Fire of Death, I call it. It's my own invention," said the doctor swelling with pride. "The beauty of this potion is that the intense burning isn't only physical, but spiritual as well. It can completely burn out any connections you may have to enchanted items or even enchanting folk. In this case, it severed your connection to the Orb of Power, see?" Dr. Wikket grabbed the Orb in his pudgy hand and jerked violently, snapping the chain that suspended the magical barble around my neck.

The orderly heaved me off the table and into a wheelchair. "Now," Wickett said as he slid the Orb into his coat pocket, "I'll give you a tour of the facilities and introduce you to some of our guests. They absolutely *love* to meet the meal before they eat, just to prove that it's not dead flesh," the doctor finished with a whisper in my ear.

What happened in the woods while I was otherwise occupied being slavered over by crazed vampires and even crazier doctors was later related to me by the Orb, who witnessed everything and took considerable pleasure in describing the parts where Shamus nearly soiled himself. I have reconstructed events as faithfully as the Orb's editorial bias allows.

"Where could've he gone?" wondered Shamus, sitting on the cot in his room. Lola Fa Lona paced and Hollow Monk gazed out the window.

"I don't know. But I'm blaming the monk," Lola's orbs narrowed and she glared at Hollow Monk.

Hollow Monk ignored the comment. "That place reeks of pagan evil; if anyone could have spirited him away so it would be the unwholesome devils that lurk there. At first light we should—"

"No!" roared Shamus in a fit of uncharacteristic bravery, "It may be too late by then. We have to leave now."

"The innkeeper said there were nasties in the woods at night," said Fa Lona.

"There are no such things as 'nasties,'" snapped the monk, "They are a product of the overactive imaginations of country yokels who fear their own shadows."

"Is that so?" The Red Dragon Ninja bristled. "Your stupidity will be your undoing, monk. And don't expect *me* to step in when the overactive imaginations of country yokels come to claim your pathetic life!"

"Stop it!" yelled Shamus. "You guys are driving me crazy!"

"Me too!" yelled a muffled voice through the wall, "Shut up and go to sleep!" The outburst was accentuated by a brief fit of pounding.

"Listen, we've got to go now. The Sanitarium feeds at night, and if Infinity has been captured, then we don't have long. We'll ask the innkeeper for help. If she knows so much about the forest and the things that crawl there then she can show us the quickest and safest way to the Sanitarium," said Shamus. He felt good taking charge of the situation, as if he was accomplishing something worthwhile. Was that a crack that appeared in the cowardly giant's Fear Dam?

Incessant knocking on her door jerked One-Orb Goldie from her slumber. She opened it to find three of the four strangers who had checked in earlier. "Where's the other one?" she growled. "Mr. Fancy Pants Destiny Decider?"

"That's what we need to talk to you about," began Shamus. "He's kinda disappeared from his room. We think that the 'unwholesome devils' up at the sanitarium may have—"

Goldie slammed the door with a curse and fell back into her bed, trying to ignore the presence of the strangers still outside her room. "Go away!" she yelled from underneath her pillow.

"Not until you help us!" Shamus screamed from behind the door.

"Look," Goldie said, "if that's really what happened, ya'll better go back to bed. Yer friend is as good as caviar on toast."

"No he's not!" bellowed Shamus, his yell a windstorm that threatened to burst the solid oak door at the seams. "Now get out of bed and help us!"

All was quiet for a moment and then the innkeeper's door slowly creaked open. Goldie's good orb glared at the small group, "Fine. Come in. I got an ort to pick with those jerks about my husband and boys anyway."

Small and sparsely decorated, Goldie's room wasn't what you'd expect from an innkeeper's quarters. A small bed was tucked into the north western corner, and in the southern corner sat a single wooden chair and table with a smoky lantern acting as the centerpiece.

"How're ya'll armed?" asked Goldie as she reached for a huge wooden trunk under the bed.

"I can handle my own," said Fa Lona haughtily displaying her assortment of weapons.

"I, also, can fare for myself with the help of the Lord," said Hollow Monk, ignoring Lola's sharp laugh.

Goldie opened the trunk and began to arm herself with an impressive array of weapons. Many were unknown even to Lola, who prided herself on knowledge of weapons and warfare.

"What are those?" she asked as Goldie lifted two funny looking hand-held contraptions from the trunk and added them to holsters on her belt.

"Pellet Shooters. Most of my gear is military issue," she grunted and snapped a belt peppered with metal pellets across her chest. "What about ya, tall boy?" Goldie asked Shamus. "Where's yer gear?"

"I, uh, well you see, I had an axe," Shamus lowered his gaze. "But I'm not...," he trailed off into embarrassed silence.

"Yer not what?" asked Goldie.

"I'm not big enough to use it anymore, ok?" he sobbed. "I've *shrunk*."

"Huh," Goldie said, "We can't have ya roaming around out there naked of weaponry." She reached under her mattress and pulled out an exquisitely crafted double headed battle axe. Its surface etched with ornate silver and gold runes glimmering fiercely in the light.

"It were my hubby's and before that it were his pa's and before that it were *his* pa's axe. He was going to pass it to our oldest on his Coming of Age." Goldie's orb misted over briefly, but anger quickly burned it away. "Now ya can have it." She shoved the axe into Shamus's hands.

Shamus didn't know how to accept such a gift, so he did it quietly with a mumbled thanks.

The rescue party left the inn just after High Dark and made their way toward the trail that would lead them through the woods and to the sanitarium.

"What manner of military did you serve under," inquired Fa Lona as she watched Goldie turn a crank attached to the side of a pellet shooter.

"None from around these parts," she said. The pellet shooter clicked and Goldie put it back in its holster. She retrieved a much longer pellet shooter slung across her back and began loading pellets into it.

"What are *those* called?" continued Fa Lona.

"We always called them Attitude Auditors inna Corps."

"How do they work?"

"Here," said Goldie. She pulled a pellet shooter from the holster and handed it to Fa Lona, "The pellet goes in that groove. The crank pulls the spring back and loads it. Then the hammer holds the pellet in place. If ya wanna fire, pull the hammer back to loose the pellet, then pull the trigger to release the spring. Oh, and make sure yer pointing at what ya wanna hit."

"Right," said the ninja as she pulled the hammer back and squeezed the trigger. TWANG! The spring released and the projectile made an audible zipping sound as it shot through the air, connecting with the axe blade strapped to Shamus's back. He spun around and watched the pellet ricochet back toward Goldie and Lola. The women ducked and the lead ball zipped overhead, finally lodging itself in the front door of the Bloody Turnip.

"By the Jolly Man's jowls! I said watch yer aim; ya blasted loon! You coulda killed them!" yelled Goldie.

Lola shrugged, "He's fine. I could've *really* hit him if I wanted to. I've got skill like that," said the princess with a flick of her long, black hair. She tossed the pellet shooter back to Goldie and trotted ahead of the group to scout the scene.

"Where did you come across such a manner of weapon?" asked Shamus as he fell back to walk with Goldie.

"My husband invented them when we was inna Corps. Got the idea in a dream. He used to have lotsa crazy dreams," said Goldie, her gaze drifting into memory, "He used to say that there was this *other* place, not the Realm, but kinda like the Realm. He said it had lots of the same things we have, just in different ways, ya ken?"

Shamus nodded like he knew, but he really didn't.

"He'd dream about some pretty crazy stuff," Goldie snapped out of her daze. "Anyway, he invented these babies and brought our Corps to a whole new level."

"What was your company's name?"

"We called ourselves the Fightin' Marines," said Goldie proudly.

"What are Marines?" wondered Shamus.

"My husband said that inna land across his dreams they was some of the toughest sons a battle ever to grace a soldier's uniform."

"Ah. Was he touched with insanity?" Shamus's question was padded with sympathy.

Goldie glowered at him with her good orb. "Not all are touched with insanity, ya ken. Some are touched with truth and lots of folk mistake that for insanity. Alright, hold up!" she called out as they reached the fringes of the woods. "Once we step inna forest, we're in *their* territory. This is *their* house; we're just coming to play innit," she said pointing toward the Sanitarium. "We're already being watched and followed. Be on yer guard."

Goldie drew her two pellet shooters from their holsters and stepped into the woods.

"And this is the staff cafeteria. We call it the 'staff caff' around here. It's kind of our little employee joke," chuckled Dr. Wikket.

Still unable to move, an orderly wheeled me through a plethora of white coated individuals stuffing their faces with what looked to be the edible version of the color gray.

"We keep them healthy on a steady diet of protein enhanced gruel," the twisted man of science said and instructed the orderly to wheel me back into the hallway.

The middle wing was the admittance wing—the only part of the sanitarium shown to the families of prospective patients. It had a luxurious receiving area designed to look like the lobby of a grand hotel. Thick, burgundy carpet sprawled across the floor, ending abruptly, as if kneeling in inanimate reverence, at the room's center where a circle of marble tiles marched stoically to a stone fountain carved in the semblance of a young, winged child holding a bow nocked with an arrow while standing on one foot. The water feature happily spit a constant stream during business hours. Ornate woodwork covered the walls, painted in the gaudy colors and design of Baroque gauche. Offices lined the long hallway and at the very end of the wing was the staff caff.

"I see you're drinking in the opulence. Mayhap it even seems a bit out of place? Not so. A majority of our patients are the wayward offspring of nobles and high society merchants. Mostly spoiled brats desperate for power and influence that they are mentally unequipped to handle. Thus, when they do receive vampirism, their brains snap, if you will, and their fishomes are rendered uninhabitable. Their own Sacred Fish are their first victims, more often than not. Their loving parents bring them here in hopes that we can restore their minds and regenerate their fishomes. We like for our patrons to think that their children are maintaining a life of luxury. This is all for show, of course. You see, vampirism is viewed as a gift amongst its recipients. So, to reject the gift isn't a feasible act amidst the vampire population."

"So I'm told," I tried to mutter but all that came out of my numb lips was a lot of slobber and an, "Ahhhahh."

"I couldn't have said it better myself. Let's move along to the east wing," Dr. Wikket's face broke out in a wicked smile, teeth gleaming much like his bloodsucking charges. "I have such sights to show you there."

The east wing was where the "restoration and regeneration" took place. This part of the hospital was much less luxurious; its opulence stripped away in favor of utility. Fluffy illusion was replaced with hard reality. Walls made from hewn granite blocks covered with bright white paint clashed with the smooth, cold-looking material that tiled the floors. While rooms did line the hallway, they weren't offices. Instead, rooms secured by harsh metal doors with tiny windows at orb height dotted the hall, each door labeled Examination Room followed by a number, chiseled into the metal with precise uniform lettering. The utility was rather ruthless and the whole vibe of that stone corridor gave me a chill. Each examination room housed all sorts of horrid looking machines and diabolical implements arranged around a metal table with manacles dangling over the edges. I didn't want to even offer a guess as to their use.

"This is where the magic happens," Dr Wikket informed me. "We bring the patients here for their spicy tomato juice transfusions. I see you've an interest in the table restraints," said the Doctor noticing my intense gaze at the implements. "I assure you; they are completely humane and necessary. Vampires are known for their unnatural strength and often resist the infusion of the spicy tomato juice concoction. Let me tell you, they howl and scream Bloody Mary, no pun intended—no, no actually the pun *is* intended, but anyway, the treatments really are helping integrate them back into society. My concoction has shown tremendous results in curing the infection of vampirism."

"Why am I being fed to them then?" I managed to slur, sensation creeping back into my limp frame.

The doctor laughed, "You can't expect a vamp to go cold turkey when getting off the Life Sauce. They'd go absolutely mad and tear the place down around themselves. Thus, they are allowed to feed only on that blood provided to them by the sanitarium. We aren't all bad, Mr. Jones. We hire a priest to perform the bleeding ceremony and give the donor's last rites. Then, the donor's body is carefully portioned and fed to the patients. It's actually a lovely ceremony. Strangely, it's hard to find living donors willing to undergo such selfless sacrifice. To circumvent this, we grease the pockets of a few local governments who, in turn, ship us prisoners from time to time. We supplement this with the occasional invading vampire hunters or commando teams. But when I got word of you entering town, well, you can imagine my excitement. You've no idea how long I've sought that Orb. Possessing it is my true desire; you just happen to be an inconvenient complication that makes for a convenient snack. And as a bonus, it saves me a few dingle this month in the process. Speaking of that, let's go meet the flock."

The west wing housed the patient's quarters. In reality, the quarters were nothing more than cells furnished with dirty straw mats. The doors and hall-facing walls were all made of rough, black iron. The entire wing was devoid of windows, sunlight never pierced the thick darkness of this damned place. It was lit by torches interspersed along the entirety, coughing oily smoke that gathered along the corridor's ceiling. As soon as we entered, a bloodthirsty cacophony erupted. Dr. Wikket's orderly wheeled me into the Patient's Commons to mingle before the patients sucked the blood from my body and the flesh from my bones. The room was made of the same whitewashed granite as the rest of the place, as if Dr. Wikket had attempted some semblance of decency and decorum in his patient's care, however thin the veneer. Growling, snarling, or sobbing vampires of all shapes and sizes filled the room.

The vamps themselves were a sorry lot. The forced denial of blood had obviously cost them dearly in body and mind. All were muzzled and their hands wrapped in fuzzy mittens. Upon my entry, a howl of delight went up in unison from the denizens of that unholy place. The evil doctor wheeled me into the center of the room and stepped back. The vamps swarmed me like a pack of starved chickens, sniffing, prodding, and running their hands over me with varying degrees of molestation. I closed my orbs and withstood that onslaught of violation as best I could.

After the meet and greet with the patients, I was returned to the basement and strapped back onto the table by the orderly.

"I'll be back shortly," Dr. Wikket said. "Dinner won't be long now." He bowed and left the room with the orderly in tow.

After they left, I noticed a vent directly above the table. I heard the faint whistling of the wind and my heart leapt with hope. I listened closer to identify which wind it was. The playful giggling of summer afternoons tickled my ear.

*It's the South Wind*, I thought. "Hear me, oh South Wind. Tell me of my companions," I sighed at the vent.

The wind burst from the vent and spun around me like a small vortex. "Infinity Jones…Infinity Jones is alive" the South Wind murmured and shot up the vent with a whoosh. Moments later, I felt the brush of invisible lips across my face as the wind returned. "Listen," it whispered into my ears.

Goldie guided the small group to a well-worn trail that wove its way deep into the woods.

"What manner of place is this? Looks like you're leading us even further into the darkness…should we question your intentions?" Hollow Monk turned his shadowed cowl toward Goldie. If he'd had visible orbs, the innkeeper would've felt them probing her for lies.

"Question my intentions, question my honor. I'm leading ya to the Sanitarium like ya asked."

"Yes, well we seem to be traveling parallel to it instead of toward it," pointed out the rational holy man.

"I figured ya guys would want to skirt around the nasties instead of plunging into the thick of them."

"Oh yes. We definitely want to avoid as much nastiness as possible," assured Shamus.

"Well, the main road to the place is crawling with a single-minded evil. Those hell-spawn sitting up top the sanitarium are its security. What do ya think they're for? Decoration? Ha! At High Dark they come to life and protect the sanitarium from unwanted invaders."

"Who would want to invade *that* place?" asked the wee giant.

"Tons a folk. Vampire hunters, for instance. Despite the agreement, there's a few rebels who'd like to eradicate the vampire population not reform it. And whatever secret things those docs do up there has a lot of powerful folk jealous. Spies and small commando teams get sent up there to break in all the time. I rent most of them rooms. None a them ever come back down, though. Word is the nasties don't kill them. They keep their prisoners alive so they can interrogate them and feed them to the vamps later."

"That's a relief," Shamus said sarcastically.

"It's all lies! Balderdash!" insisted Hollow Monk. "There are no such things as nasties and vampires."

Goldie shrugged, "O.K. Whatever ya say." She turned to Shamus, "Anyway, this is the Adventure Tours Trail. It leads to what's left of the Heart of the Woods. If we stayed onnit, we'd eventually hook back up with the main road to the sanitarium. So instead, we head north from the Heart to the ridge of the plateau. Once we climb that, we'll be onna property. Then, we overtake the ferryman, cross the moat and we're in."

"Just like that, huh?" asked Lola, her skepticism evident in her crossed arms.

"Yeah, just like that," said Goldie, her confidence evident in her square stance and fists balled on her hips.

A circle of huge stone pillars decorated with crude paintings of animals, spirals, and folk surrounded the Heart of the Woods. Each was easily twice the height of Shamus and, in total, covered an area of about one hundred feet.

"They say these stones tell the story of a Tree Folk's journey into the afterlife. These stones ain't native to the area, neither. In daylight they're stark white. Nobody knows where they came from or how they were erected without modern technology," Goldie said in reverence.

Hollow Monk examined the stones with an expert's care, "They're from Regret. An Outlandish city near the sea that was destroyed when the gods fell. Most likely, the Tree Folk used a crude sled system with ropes, pulling the stones along using teams of men."

"Pulled giant stones from Regret to here with ropes and wooden sleds?" Goldie wasn't buying it, "I ain't buying it. Do ya know how much these things weigh? No wooden sled could carry stones this heavy."

"It's the only rational explanation," huffed the monk and stepped inside the circle of stones.

Within the stone circle, the ground was bare of vegetation except for a single oak tree standing in the exact center. Four different colored lines, one for each cardinal direction, lead to the tree. The line to the North was paved with white pebbles, to the South with yellow, the West was paved with red, and the East with blue."

"How is this so perfectly preserved?" Bewilderment crept into Hollow Monk's normally rational mind frame, "There haven't been Tree Folk here for—"

"Hundreds of years," finished Shamus for him.

"We take care of our history," said Goldie proudly, "This monument is one a the things that gives the town life and purpose. We cherish it as part of our spirit. There is *life* here. There is *magic*. Can ya feel it?"

"Yes," murmured Shamus sadly, for the giant now stood in the remnants of the Heart and he could feel the steady flow of Gaia's lifeforce beneath his feet. He realized it was easier to feel the earth now that he was closer to it.

"No," said Hollow Monk matter-of-factly because he still couldn't feel anything other than the cold harshness of rationality.

"I feel orbs on us while we're standing here wasting time," said Fa Lona pragmatically because she was a Ninja without Harmony and thus couldn't focus on anything for more than a few ticks of the tock.

"Yeah," said Goldie quietly. "Let's be onna way. We ain't got much time." She walked along the white line and into the darkness of the forest.

"We're almost there and haven't even glimpsed anything remotely nasty," snapped Lola. She sounded almost disappointed.

"They're here," Goldie barked in a rough whisper. "They're just waiting."

"For what?"

"Fer us to get too far inta flee to safety," said Goldie. "There's a small clearing just ahead. I used to picnic there with my…" she trailed off briefly and then regained her composure, "We should face them there, inna open."

The moon's voluptuous luminescence illuminated the clearing with silvery rays. The clearing was circular, about twenty feet in diameter, and carpeted in soft grass. A young spring flowed through the clearing's center from east to west adding a pleasant and lively touch while splitting the circular clearing into separate hemispheres. Two werewolves waited across the stream in the clearing's northern hemisphere.

Once the small party of heroes was in sight, the werewolves began to violently pace and snarl. Their bodies, covered in short fur, rippled with muscles, gliding with dexterous ease as they stalked back and forth. Red evil flared in the orbs of the dog-men and rage dripped off their razor sharp fangs in slow rivulets.

"Wwwwooooooohhhooooooeeeeeeeaaaaaaaaaaa!!" Hollow Monk screamed a proclamation of denial. You see, the irrationally rational mind doesn't handle paranormal or supernatural experiences well at all. As a matter of fact, the overly rational mind will reject such occurrences and obstinately refuse to admit or acknowledge them. Thus, when faced with the reality of the unreal, if unable to explain it away, their minds simply break. Shut down. Makes one wonder how rational supposedly rational folk really are. The monk fell immediately to his knees and began chanting repeatedly, "This isn't happening. They aren't real."

Lola Fa Lona scoffed at him, "Don't worry, I'm *sure* they aren't real. Conjured from the simple, superstitious imaginations of country yokels. Why don't you run over there and shoo them away for us? Confront fantasy with reality."

The monk ignored her and continued to pray with hands covering his face and head lowered.

"What are they waiting for?" Lola asked Goldie.

"Fer us to go over there," said Goldie without ever looking away from the bloodthirsty monsters. "Fleabags can't cross water."

"Why not?" asked Fa Lona.

Goldie shrugged, "Dunno. Maybe it keeps them from spreading. Maybe it's cuz they are made of stone during the day and any way ya cut it, stone sinks like…well…a stone. Here," said the warrior. She reached into her pack and pulled out three wooden stakes. "When ya knock one down, be sure to stick this innits foul heart, or cut its head off, else it'll get right back up." She handed a stake to Fa Lona and Shamus.

Lola nodded. "Ensure a finished product."

"Exactly." Goldie smiled as the old feeling of battle anticipation consumed her again. "Keep yer wits about ya. I ain't never seen flea-bags roam in packs smaller than four. Something ain't right here."

Lola Fa Lona drew her blade and licked her lips with unabashed eagerness. If there was one thing the ninja princess *lived* for, it was whooping canine tail.

Shamus unstrapped the axe from his back and hefted it with a whimper. Without his massive size advantage, the former giant doubted his abilities.

Hollow Monk remained prostrate and chanting, "This isn't real. This isn't happening."

"Let's do this." Goldie let loose a glorious battle cry and charged across the creek with Lola and Shamus close on her heels.

No sound. When Hollow Monk looked up, he was alone. The dark gloom of the clearing had been replaced with warm sunlight trickling through the branches. A squirrel bounded across the clearing and leapt fearlessly into a tree at the forest's edge. The sounds of chirping birds caught the monk's ear as did the bubbling laughter of the infant spring that played across the clearing's landscape. The moonlit sky had been traded out for one colored a magnificent blue.

Hollow Monk rose to his feet in utter confusion. Where had everyone gone? He could've sworn that he was traveling through a werewolf infested wood in the middle of the night to rescue a particularly bumbling misfit. But now, there was nothing or no one of the sort. Just an empty clearing on a warm and sunny day.

The preacher smiled to himself. "I *knew* none of it was real. It was all just a crazy dream. I must've fallen asleep while on the road," he said aloud, audibly confirming his thoughts. After all, *if you speak it; you can seek it* is one of the precepts in the Good Paragraphs. Thoroughly convinced, he was ready to return to work. He dusted himself off and set out in search of a road that would lead him to a town full of folk willing to part with their dingle for a morsel of spiritual bread.

Hollow Monk aimlessly wandered uphill enjoying the day and taking in the natural beauty of his surroundings. Soon, the forest gave way to rocky hills overshadowed by a craggy mountain range. At the top of one of these craggy cliffs stood a huge white building that kind of resembled the sanitarium from his dream, with a few noticeable differences. The moat was missing, replaced with a fence constructed of gray, metal webbing. He could see through the fence and into the grounds of the building. Which wasn't a very economical use of fencing in his mind. Off in the distance, Hollow Monk saw lots of white shapes bustling back and forth. The top of the structure was free of stony nightmares and it actually looked to be a somewhat inviting place. When he reached the front gate, Hollow Monk noticed it was manned by a single guard asleep at his post. A sign on the gate read: "Sunny Shire Mental Health Facility."

*That's odd.* Hollow Monk peered at the guard dressed in a very dark blue material and had something resembling one of Goldie's pellet shooters in a holster on his waist. The guard snored softly in his chair; feet propped up on his desk. Hollow Monk decided this meant that admittance was open, so he walked into the facility's yard.

Well-manicured dark green grass covered the grounds. Scattered about, old trees acted as silent sentinels and offered pleasant sanctuary from the sun's heat. Stone walkways crisscrossed the entire property and folk in white coats scurried along them no doubt on some errand or another. Folk in white robes ran and played as happy and content as children. Others sat in wheeled chairs staring blankly into space. These folk were accompanied by one of the white-coated individuals who whispered to them and pushed their chair around the yard.

"Vampires, indeed," laughed Hollow Monk to himself. "If these simple and happy folk are vampires, I'm a giant albino chicken!"

"Father? Excuse me, Father?"

Hollow Monk turned around and a very thin, very handsome older gentleman wearing a white coat smiled at him. His white hair survived in patches, clinging to his scalp with the tenacity of a man who refuses to admit defeat. His piercing blue orbs spoke of a dangerous intelligence lying in wait behind them. His face was slender and angular, all of it apparently organized around the sharp protrusion of his nose. His most prominent feature, however, was his moustache which drooped heavily down his face desperate for attention. "I'm Dr. Eugene Flickett, warden of Sunny Shire. You must be Father Murphy from the, uh, parish," the doctor said with an unusual wink.

"Yes. Yes, that's me," lied Hollow Monk. Living without faith makes it much easier to lie.

"You aren't exactly on time," said Dr. Flickett, glancing at a watch strapped to his wrist instead of on a chain and tucked in a pocket like normal folk. "No bother. Follow me. It's almost time for the ceremony."

"Yes of course. My apologies," said the monk and followed the warden into the hospital.


As the brave warriors crossed the creek, the beasts let out a monstrous howl that summoned four more wolf men to their side! This only halted Goldie and Lola for a fraction of a second, but Shamus was a different story. Upon seeing the numbers shift toward the other team, he stopped dead in his tracks. Frozen in place, his mind flooded with doubt and indecision. It took every ounce of the ex-delivery prole's courage *not* to run screaming into the night like a frightened nancy.[26]

Goldie fired her pellet shooter at the werewolf directly in front of her. The lead ball landed with a satisfying thud between the beast's orbs, and it collapsed like a sack of sugarberries. The enraged woman stooped beside the wounded beast, stabbed it through the heart with her stake, and drew her other pellet shooter in one fluid motion.

Not to be outdone, Lola Fa Lona hurdled the stream (so she wouldn't get her feet wet) and hit the foremost werewolf square in the chest with a flashy jump kick. Despite her tiny size, the momentum from her speed caused the dog-beast to lose its balance and topple backward. The princess followed the beast down, becoming ever more vertical while the werewolf became horizontal. Drawing and slicing in a single action, she neatly separated the creature's head from its body before it hit the ground.

From her crouched position, Goldie fired at the first of the lycanthropes to burst from the forest. The pellet struck the creature in the left shoulder and sent it sprawling. The Fighting Marine cursed and rushed the beast while pulling a jagged knife from her belt.

Lola caught movement in the corner of her vision. She turned and saw a werewolf trying to flank Goldie on her blind side while the innkeeper hacked at its comrade. With an expert toss only a Ninja could accomplish, the princess threw her stake at the shifty canine, piercing the creature's heart.

The beast fell forward and expired with a painful howl.

But she didn't have time to gloat. Lola's sensitive ears alerted her to the approach of something from behind. The Red Dragon Ninja smiled viciously and her orbs flashed with yang. She leapt into the air and back flipped over the sneaking lycanthrope, neatly decapitating it on her descent. She landed and spun around to meet a hairy paw as big as her head sailing toward her with inescapable speed. The stupid mutt had snuck up on her! Disappointed with herself but proud of her fight, Lola closed her orbs and braced herself for death as all good Ninjas should.

Shamus watched the battle in slow motion. He watched Goldie barrel into a wolf-man she had wounded and attack it with nothing more than a dagger. He stared at the innkeeper in a mixture of awe and fear. One-Orb Goldie was no longer a grieving mother and widow. She had morphed into a focused battle machine bent on

---

[26] A "nancy" is what we call weak or cowardly folk in the Realm.

revenge at any cost. McFamus almost felt sorry for the dog-beast suffering the innkeep's wrath. Goldie already claimed the werewolf's life and still she continued to attack it. The warrior woman was in such a fury she didn't pay attention to her blind side and the werewolf's companion was taking advantage of Goldie's moment of weakness.

Before he could utter a cry of warning, Shamus saw the tiny princess toss the stake almost casually in the direction of Goldie's would-be assassin. Amazingly, the stake struck its mark and the beast was no more. But the Red Dragon Ninja wasn't out of danger. Two werewolves remained and they rushed Fa Lona while she had her back turned. Shamus wanted to yell a warning but his mouth was frozen shut with the shameful cold of nanciness. Luckily, the Ninja's keen senses warned her of danger. She leapt gracefully into the air and swiftly decapitated one werewolf when she came out of a back flip. That left one werewolf, and it had the initiative on the princess. Lola spun around as the beast lifted its rippling arm to smack the Ninja into the next world. An odd sense of selfless bravery swelled inside Shamus.

*Fight now!* screamed Commander Gali, his Sacred Fish, and Shamus snapped out of his daze. Sometimes we need the help of our Sacred Fish's still, small voice to goad us into action. Otherwise, we'd just stay rooted in place, frozen and dumb, unable to move. Shamus took one large step toward Lola while raising the axe high above his head. The werewolf swung its clawed hand toward Fa Lona and at the same time Shamus brought his blade down in a wild, but powerful chop. Rock hard muscle met deadly metal and the axe won. The beast's arm severed at the elbow, mere inches from the princess's skull. The arm fell harmlessly to the ground and the werewolf went mad with pain.

"Stab it with the stake!" Goldie screamed.

Shamus rushed the wounded creature and impaled it before it had a chance to recover.

Lola opened her orbs and saw the paw lying at her feet. The rest of the werewolf lay a few paces away with a stake through its heart. Shamus towered over Lola, axe dripping with blood.

"What got into you?" Lola asked Shamus. "Found some machismo all of a sudden?"

Shamus didn't reply he simply stared at the werewolf's corpse with wide, unbelieving orbs.

"Where's the preacher man?" Goldie asked.

"I thought I saw him wander off into the woods while we were fighting," said Shamus.

"I knew it! Filthy nancy!" Lola yelled into the night. "Leaving us here to die! He'll pay. I'll see to it."


Sunny Shire Mental Health Facility was everything Hollow Monk's rational mind expected. The dominating theme was that of stark sterilization from every angle. The place reeked of clean. As a matter of fact, the place was so clean that Hollow Monk actually felt guilty for intruding on its germless perfection.

The main lobby was littered with couches and Chatter Boxes. Patients lounged or dozed on these couches in various stages of drug-induced numbness to reality. These folk were truly a sight to behold. Hollow Monk noted the patients as Dr. Flickett commented on them. Each had a label. A rational explanation for their distorted views of reality. Labels like Paranoid Schizophrenia, Narcissistic Personality Disorder with Histrionic Tendencies and Clinically Depressed fell like a love poem from Dr. Flickett's lips.

"Fascinating," said the monk. He wasn't sure what the labels meant but he appreciated and understood their ordered and complex rationality. "But do they have names?"

"They certainly do," laughed the warden. "The one with Paranoid Schizophrenia is Ben, Randi is the Narcissist, and darling Susan suffers from Clinical Depression," he recited the names as if he was reading from a roll sheet. It was obvious to the monk that the doctor's passions lay with his labels and not with the patients these labels were supposed to correct. "We pride ourselves on the doctor-patient relationship here at Sunny Shire."

"What makes them like this?" asked Hollow Monk.

"Lots of things. But nothing we can't handle with therapy and lots of drugs," said the doctor with a wink. "See, what we do here is help folk to *reconstruct* reality whenever they lose touch with it."

"Based on whose perception?"

"Excuse me?" Dr. Flickett was taken aback.

"Reconstruct reality based on whose perception?" reiterated Hollow Monk.

"Not *whose* perception of reality. *The* perception reality. The consensus reality that comprises human existence. Not the subjective false realities constructed by the patients in their deranged mental states."

"Some would argue individual perception *is* the sole perception of reality," said the cleric scarcely believing that he had uttered such superstitious and irrational nonsense.

Dr. Flickett smiled, "Keep talking like that and we may have to prolong your stay, Father."

"Yes well," Hollow Monk cleared his throat, "About the ceremony."

"Of course! This way." Dr. Flickett disappeared into a short hallway that led to two ornate wooden doors. A sign above the doors read: Ball Room.

"Where are we now?" asked Shamus. They had decided to rest a bit and warm themselves by a small fire before continuing.

Goldie sat on a fallen log near the fire reloading and winding her pellet shooters. "Pretty close. 'That's the ridge right there," Goldie said and pointed at a dark shadow to the north that sliced through the moonlit night like a wicked talon. "We top that, we're at the moat."

"Are you guys positive we want to go in there? I mean, I know I pushed for it and all, but in retrospect..." and just like that doubt wormed its way back into Shamus's heart while his Sacred Fish rested. It really is that easy, dear reader. We awaken for a moment, in a burst of inspiration or energy, and then just as quickly, perhaps more so, we slip right back into sleep.

"Positive," said Fa Lona. "We have to avenge Infinity Jones. Plus, there's vampires in there. I've never seen a vampire, have you?"

"Well, no," admitted the tiny giant sheepishly.

"Don't you wonder what they look like? Smell like? What it's like to take your blade and—"

"No!" interrupted Shamus, "I've never wondered about any of that stuff."

"Why not?"

"Because, that's not things normal folks wonder about."

"Whatever," Lola rolled her orbs, "What makes *you* so normal?"

Shamus's voice secreted false humility, "I have taken a vested interest in promoting the good of the Realm. I have literally scaled up and down the ladder of society. I have been a pauper and I have been a king."

Lola laughed. "You're a freak. Normal folk don't do things. They do not have 'vested interests' unless they are ill conceived. Normal folk don't scale social ladders. They aren't paupers *or* kings. They are just...folk. They're all blah being blah and blah blah blah. Normal folk are blah. Oh, and normal folk certainly *aren't* enormously large giants who sell their greatness to every smooth-talking peddler who comes along."

"Now wait just a minute!" Shamus roared and sprang to his feet. "That's uncalled for!"

"Shhh! Did you hear that?" Lola's ears perked up, "Leaves rustling. Twigs breaking. Someone's coming."

Shamus cocked his right ear skyward, "I don't hear anything. Quit changing the subject," he growled.

As if to prove him wrong, the foliage behind McFamus exploded, covering him in leaves and branches. The giant whirled around to meet the attack, but something large and scaly bowled him over. Lola instinctively jumped to the lowest branch of the tree she was sitting beneath. Goldie rolled off the log and into a crouch her pellet shooter aimed at the threat.

The thing unraveled to an impressive eight feet in height and stood near the fire swaying with a hypnotic rhythm. From the chest up, the creature resembled a scaly human woman with writhing snakes for hair, but the lower torso was that of a serpent. In her hand she held a nasty blade with jagged teeth lining the edge.

"Maiden of Lilith!"[27] exclaimed Lola from her perch. That outburst seemed to break whatever trance the creature was in and she darted for Goldie in a blur. The brave fighter barely had time to fire her pellet shooter before she went rigid and turned to stone. The pellet flew directly into the Maiden's mouth and exploded out the back of her throat. The snake-woman collapsed clutching her neck and gurgling.

"What in Mark's name was that?" shrieked Shamus.

"Maiden of Lilith," Fa Lona said and jumped down. "Used to hunt them as a kit. They'll stone you dead just for looking at them. Odd to find one this far south. Must be an import."

"Is Goldie…" began Shamus but his trembling voice wouldn't allow him to continue.

"Dead?" finished Fa Lona flatly. "Not yet. They don't really *turn* you to stone; they just kinda cover you in it. So, she'll be alive in that stone tomb for a few days until she dies from dehydration or something. S'how my uncle went. We better get going." Lola had only

---

[27] The Maidens of Lilith were once very beautiful women. They made a pact with Lilith, one of He In Grammatical Error's queens. The Maidens were granted 50 years of unsurpassed physical beauty in exchange for 150 years of servitude as a snake-like Maiden. During their 50 years of beauty, the Maidens of Lilith are some of the most sought-after women in the Realm. But during their 150 years in service, they are some of the most wicked and foul beings to crawl the earth. Only 100 Maidens are in existence at one time and as odd as it seems, there is actually a waiting list. Some folk will give anything to be beautiful even for a moment.

taken a few steps when she froze in her tracks. She heard the twang of a bowstring and dove forward. "Duck!" she yelled.

Shamus tried, but even with his reduced giant height of ten feet it was still very difficult for him to "duck" any approaching airborne objects and the arrow lodged in his shoulder. Shamus's orbs rolled up in the back of his head and he landed with a thud.

With a vicious cackle, another maiden emerged from the shadows holding a bow. The cursed beauty slithered over to Shamus and rolled the giant onto his back. He was unconscious but breathing. The evil monster then turned her attention to uncovering the ninja crouched in the bushes. She readied her bow and her snake hair began to thrash about in different directions scanning the underbrush for signs of the Ninja.

Lola knew she didn't have much time before she was discovered and disposed of just like her friends. Thinking quickly, she pulled two small white bags off her belt and threw them in the direction of the Maiden. The bags hit the ground and exploded into a huge cloud of thick smoke. Within seconds, choking white fog covered a thirty-foot area.

The serpent-lady tried to scan the fog, but the smoke confused her senses and blinded the snakes sprouting atop her head. In panic, the monster dropped the bow in favor of her sword. Lilith's slave never knew the tiny death that sought her out in the mist while she wildly swung her blade and spun in circles. A sharp pain in the Maiden's neck was her only sensation before the whiteness was overtaken with eternal black. Her lifeless body slumped to the ground.

The Red Dragon Ninja gouged the creature's orbs out and dropped them into a belt pouch without looking at them. For a Maiden of Lilith's gaze can stone, even in death. After she had finished the beast off, the princess attended to Shamus.

"Hey. Wake up, big man!" Lola yelled and slapped the unconscious giant in the face. "Wake up you stupid fool!"

Shamus opened his orbs with a gasp, "What happened?"

"You got shot by a Maiden's arrow."

"Is it bad?"

"Well, the wound isn't, but the poison will harden you sure as their gaze will."

"Am I going to die?" asked Shamus, his voice quivering from restrained sobs.

"Yeah. But the good news is, you'll die a lot more slowly than One-Orb over there," she jerked a delicate thumb in Goldie's direction. "You get the luxury of slowly turning to stone as the poison works its way over your flesh. It'll take a few hours for you to turn completely."

"And then?" Shamus asked. Tears streamed down his face.

"And then you wait to die of dehydration while trapped inside your stony shell. There's nothing that can be done. Sorry. Don't worry though, I avenged you."

"I don't want vengeance! I want to live!"

"To repay the death of a fallen comrade by slaying his murderer is the greatest honor you can do him; this is the Way of Red Dragon Ninja," recited Fa Lona, her gaze drifting off into other Where's and When's. "Anywho, my saucer is spilling over with vengeance this evening so I must be off." Lola disappeared into the brush and left Shamus propped up against a tree weeping.

"I don't want to die alone," he sobbed into the night.

"You aren't alone," Lola spoke from the darkness, "Goldie is there. She can still hear. And there are always whatever gods you pray to. Try them. Who knows? You may have better luck than the monk at getting them to listen," Lola snickered and then all faded into silence.


The Ninja princess collapsed at the base of the Ridge, her breath coming in hot gasps. She scanned the dark forest with her excellent night sight—there was no pursuit.

Frustration seeped in as she pondered her situation. All of her comrades were as good as dead. Even Jones was a goner, but she'd known that all along. What she really wanted to do was at least see a vampire and maybe start a few fires on her way out. But plans had changed. She was a single Ninja against an unknown number of nasties. There was no way she could storm the front gates alone despite her unsurpassed skill. She would surely be overwhelmed. The little Ninja had almost made up her mind to quit the mission altogether when something like a whisper carried on the wind tickled her ears.

"Infinity Jones is alive. Fleabags can't cross water..."

"Then how did they get across the moat?" Lola asked aloud. Light bulbs exploded in her head. A tunnel! Most likely a tunnel with an outlet that gave easy access to the woods. Lola sprang to her feet. If there were a secret tunnel, then there was absolutely no reason that she shouldn't be able to find it. Filthy canines were stupid. The tunnel couldn't be *that* hard to find or else the wolfmen would forget where it was. With that in mind, the Red Dragon princess began to scour the base of the ridge for an entrance.

The ballroom looked like it had vomited red. Red carpet, red walls, even the tables and chairs were red. Dr. Flickett and Hollow Monk entered the red room to uproarious applause from a mixed crowd of doctors and patients. The doctors wore surgical masks and white gloves and many of the patients were restrained with some sort of knotted coat with buckles that restricted movement of their arms.

At the north end of the Ball Room was a stage. Displayed on the stage was a large stone table with a smaller metal table next to it holding an obsessively placed array of knives and other questionable implements. A huge fireplace spanned the length of the north wall and illuminated the room in an eerie orange glow.

Dr. Flickett led Hollow Monk down the center isle and directly to the stage. He stepped up to a metal pole with a wire protruding from its back. When he spoke, the doctor's voice filled the room with an unsettling vibration. "The priest has arrived!" he proclaimed and the crowd cheered. "Your turn. Say something to them." Dr. Flickett stepped back and nudged Hollow Monk forward.

The preacher cleared his throat and the sound was magnified by the metal pole causing a few doctors in the crowd to chuckle. Hollow Monk stepped away from the device. He didn't require such pathetic aid in order to be heard. He possessed the Voice. "Good folk," he began and his voice crashed against the emotional shorelines of his audience, "We are gathered here today in celebration." The crowd roared in agreement. "And as I look around me the color *red* comes to mind," Hollow Monk paused in anticipation of laughter, but all he got was an uncomfortable cough from Dr. Flickett. The monk continued, "I bring a message to you today. A message of Truth and Peace. I speak to you with HIS authority," Hollow Monk's voice boomed off the walls and vibrated with life in the chests of those present. "The path to enlightenment is a path of sacrifice. The way is one of struggle and torment. For no one ever reached the Divine by staying in comfortable places. No! Advancement means exactly that. Advancing. Moving forward into dark, unexplored frontiers. I am touched by the trailblazing spirits that plunge headlong into the uncharted and chaotic places of your collective mind. Perhaps one day *you* will be seen as the true pioneers who gave of themselves that others may benefit and learn, and leave behind the harmful labels that are used to disqualify you from society."

"Ahem," said Dr. Flickett nervously shuffling his feet, "That's quite enough, father. You test the bounds of common decency." He stepped up to the metal pole, "Let the ceremony begin!"

The ballroom doors opened and two large doctors wearing black hoods began dragging a half-naked brown-haired man toward the stage. The prisoner hung limply between the two doctors. He raised his head and looked at Hollow Monk in pleading desperation.

The priest's heart raced as the severity of his situation slowly sunk in. His vision wavered and he felt a knot in the pit of his stomach. Hollow Monk looked again at the man being dragged to his doom. It was Infinity Jones!

"Monk?" I asked and the universe shifted back.

Hollow Monk shook his head in disbelief.

The hooded doctors carried the man up the stairs and strapped him to the altar with tough leather bands.

"Who is that man?" Hollow Monk asked Dr. Flickett.

"Just some traveling salesman we found loitering around the premises. Nobody that will be missed, I assure you." The doctor winked.

"Is his name Infinity Jones?"

"No. It's Dean Kirkpatrick or something of that nature. Now, we broadcast the ceremony live via closed circuit cameras to televisions in the Patient's Commons. That way everyone gets to participate."

"Yes, of course. Um, what exactly is the premise?"

"The premise is simple," said Dr. Flickett as he scanned the assortment of knives, "It is the belief of this institution that most, if not all, mental disorders result from episodes of uncontrolled rage caused by a repressed primitive attraction to violence. At our core, humans are very violent creatures, father. We revel in slaughter and war; it is part of what makes us human and we aren't meant to repress our humanity. But civilization demands it in order to pretend like society actually functions properly. Sadly, for some folk this repression causes the mind to…fracture…if you will, and the violence seeps through the cracks in the dam. Slowly at first, but soon, the dam bursts. When the unconscious can no longer suppress it, the primitive instinct washes over the mind in a torrential flood. In response, the brain initiates certain defensive mechanisms to keep it from being completely overwhelmed and these mechanisms manifest as disorders. Enter psychosis, nervous breakdowns, etc.

"Through extensive scientific research, we discovered that live displays of violence actually *curb* many of the symptoms found in our patients by acting like a flood wall, if you will, absorbing and deflecting much of the bloodlust. My team and I discovered that once our patients were given certain aggression enhancing drugs and allowed to experience live brutality in a structured setting, they projected themselves, if you will, onto the wicked acts being played out for them. Thus, they get the experience of brutality with none of the responsibility. Afterward, the patients were noted as having a sizeable increase in mental stability, overall cooperation and even a decrease in certain paranoid delusions and hallucinations." The doctor picked up a metal saw and examined it for a moment. He shook his head and returned it to the table.

"We began with animal sacrifice. Chickens, dogs, cats, cattle, creatures of that nature. With each sacrifice we did something more brutal and more violent. Mutilated the beasts in creatively horrendous ways. For awhile this was enough, but you know the human capacity for desensitization. Therefore, we had to up the ante, if you will, to keep the improvements the same." The doctor selected a knife and presented it to the monk. "I'm sorry, but I thought you were briefed by your superior about the nature of our work before he sent you," said Flickett, his orbs narrowing in suspicion.

"Yes, yes," stammered Hollow Monk, "I just wanted to hear it from you." With trembling hands, he took the blade from Dr. Flickett and turned to the terrified young man on the table.

"Unsteady hands for a servant of the Darkness," noted Dr. Flickett

"Where, uh, where do I cut first?"

"I like the eyelids. That way they have to watch the entire time. Are you sure you've done human sacrifice before?"

"I-I-I don't know what's going on," Hollow Monk felt another nauseating jolt and the universe jerked him back into the Realm of Possibility.


The knife fell from his grasp (knives are non-universal) and he saw Infinity Jones strapped to the altar. Hollow Monk looked away and discovered his surroundings had completely changed. He was still in a large room, but it wasn't decorated in red. The walls were made of large stones stained dark with dried blood. Dirt and sawdust covered the floor. This place was *filthy*. The stage was a small replica of a step pyramid, with a stone altar positioned atop it and next to that was a metal table. The confused anti-holy man scanned the crowd. The patients had all been replaced with slavering vampires, muzzled and wearing mittens, but unmistakably vampiric. He turned to Dr. Flickett and found that he had also been replaced. A very round man with rimless glasses and beady orbs stared holes into Hollow Monk.

"Give us blood!" the round man yelled.

"Give us blood!" the crowd chanted in response.

Behind the fathomless shadows masking his face, Hollow Monk squeezed his orbs tightly shut and said a silent prayer for help. Seconds later, an ear-splitting boom heralded the imploding of the chamber's doors followed by smoke rolling over the stones like a stormfront. Lola Fa Lona emerged from the smoke and gracefully bounded over the rubble. She saw the monk and Yang blazed in her gaze.

"You die first monk!" she screamed and began making her way to the stage by skipping lightly across the heads and shoulders of the agitated crowd.

Hollow Monk's vision wavered and reality jolted.

Once more, Hollow Monk found himself in Sunny Shire Mental Health Facility. Dr. Flickett had returned and the warden stared at Hollow Monk, fury and accusation telegraphing from his gaze. "What's going on?"

"*I* am Father Murphy. I'm telling you that man is an imposter," said a voice. Behind Hollow Monk stood a man dressed in a long black robe covered with arcane symbols. The wiry priest had a thin moustache spread across his upper lip that looked like a small, yellow caterpillar.

Hollow Monk actually laughed. It was an eerie sound, half hopeless, half crazed. "What are those silly drawings all over your robe, *father?*"

Father Murphy's thin yellow moustache quivered with anger, "I'll have you know these are symbols of power. I bend unseen forces to my will with these 'silly drawings.'"

"You do no such thing. Whatever paltry ability you possess was gleaned by dealing with entities who took more than they gave. In the end you are doomed," retorted Hollow Monk.

"Who are you to claim such things?"

"Only a simple man who has followed a similar path."

Dr. Flickett placed a firm hand on Hollow Monk's shoulder and spun him around, "If you are not Father Murphy, then whom do you serve?"

"I don't think you really wish to know that," spoke the cursed monk. "I think your demands are the result of pompous self importance. I think the reality of such terrible knowledge would fracture your mind, doctor. Open the floodgates, to borrow from your quaint metaphor. Shall we test my theory?" Hollow Monk lowered his hood.

I don't know what Dr. Flickett saw when he looked Hollow Monk in the face. That particular horror was thankfully masked in the shadows cast by the flickering firelight. But whatever it was turned the warden's white moustache black from the roots down, literally scaring the color *back* into the man's hair. In haunting contrast, his face went instantly white and his orbs froze wide with fear. A low scream began in the diabolical doctor's throat and grew into an expression of sheer and unimaginable terror. The warden fell to his knees gibbering and sobbing, his mind shattered into a million unrecognizable pieces.

Hollow Monk lifted his hood and turned to face Father Murphy who had armed himself with a jagged dagger from the metal tray which he brandished boldly.

"Tuatha Dannan!" he screamed and thrust wildly at Hollow Monk. The blade deflected harmlessly off the monk's oversized symbol of He Who Is Not A Pronoun.

Hollow Monk grabbed the Father's right arm and stepped left. Using Father Murphy's momentum, Hollow Monk slung the hapless priest into the huge fireplace. Father Murphy went up in flames, his arcane powers doing nothing to save his life.

The crowd went wild with cheering and applause.


The monk's vision wavered and he stood atop the step pyramid. He held a bloody dagger and stared down at me. Dr. Wickett lay on the floor nearby in an expanding pool of blood.

The vampires howled with bloodlust and began to resist the efforts of the staff to corral and calm them. Heavily armed and armored sanitarium guards weaved through the crowd, forcing their way to the stage.

Hollow Monk shook his hooded head as if waking from a trance, "What happened?" he asked and quickly cut me free.


I scrambled to the prostrate and sobbing Dr. Wickett and pilfered the Orb from his coat pocket. The man gushed blood out from an unseen wound and the scent of it drove the vampires to insanity.

"I really was trying to help," he kept muttering.

"Trying to help who?" I asked. I stood up, using the altar to steady my wobbly legs. The doctors in the crowd had disappeared, and the vampires slowly pushed their way toward the stage further hindering the progress of the guards.

*Man, that was a funky smelling pocket. Put me on, Jones. There isn't much time.* The Orb glowed blue and pulsed in my hand.

I have to admit, I was torn with indecision. If I put the Orb back around my neck, I would be its thrall and subject to its command once again.

"If you don't; we die!" yelled Hollow Monk sensing my struggle.

The guards hoped to clear a path by physically attacking the crowd to make an opening. This only angered the vampires more and they quickly turned on the guards slaughtering the hapless rent-a-cops with supernatural precision. The guards were soon overwhelmed and many of the survivors slit their own throats to avoid the horrible end of death-by-vampire. Using confiscated weapons, the vampires tore muzzles from their faces and mittens from their hands and rushed the stage howling with hunger. Lola was nearly toppled as she jumped over the last few heads and landed on the miniature pyramid.

"Vengeance for nanciness! This is way of Red Dragon Ninja!" yelled Fa Lona and struck Hollow Monk in the ribs with a forceful roundhouse kick.

Hollow Monk crumpled to the ground, clutching his side.

I sighed and put the accursed Orb around my neck. Instantly, it lit up in a radiant blue glow that enveloped me, the monk, and Lola. In a flash, we were gone.

Momentarily stunned by the bright light, the vampires gazed at one another in confusion. But the scent of fresh blood wafted into their nostrils and their hunger would not be denied. Dr. Wickett could only hope that he bled out before his mutinous charges converged upon him. He didn't. His death screams were drowned out by the howling of blood-thirsty vampires. Ah, karma. Eventually it catches up to you.

## *Bonus Section: The Fate of the Sanitarium*

To make a long story short, the vampires now run the Sanitarium. But their victory would be short lived. Once word spread about the uprising, the government ceased supplying prisoners. And to make matters worse, the vamps couldn't leave the Sanitarium without being invited and no one wanted to invite vampires anywhere. They were trapped. For a while they capitalized on the influx of vampire hunters that appeared after the riot, but even that traffic soon slowed. Eventually, they ran out of live blood *and* the spicy tomato juice substitute. On that dark day, the frustrated blood-suckers turned on one other like *Express Go!*™ junkies fighting over a shot. The townsfolk of Velhampshire trembled for weeks at the terrible screaming and howling from the Sanitarium. Then, suddenly, all was quiet. Only eleven vampires survived the civil war. Those survivors swore a pact of

brotherhood and made a bold decision. They began devoting themselves to a monastic lifestyle founded on experiencing the Divine
through the elimination of desire—and it worked. That's right, they
became monks. Vampire monks. Crazy, but true.

The blue light subsided and we stood around a metal door in the ground.

"What crap," snapped Fa Lona. "Couldn't we be magically whisked back to the inn?"

"In all fairness, there were three of you," the Orb spoke audibly to Lola.

The princess's orbs widened in amazement and then glinted with anger. "That thing had better never speak to me again. Ever. I don't trust talking barbles. And neither should you, Infinity Jones."

"Where's this door lead?" queried Hollow Monk between painful inhalations.

"Out. It's how the fleabags get past the moat. But before we go, we conclude our business, you filthy traitor!" Lola raised her sword.

"I have no fault," said Hollow Monk in defense.

"Lies!" hissed the Red Dragon Ninja. "You fled when the dog boys attacked so you could sacrifice Infinity Jones to your god, Man Man!"

"I beg your pardon!" said Hollow Monk, "I—"

The hungry mob burst from the building, scouring the grounds for any gardeners, night watchmen, or escaped doctors. They inched closer by degrees; no doubt following the scent of live meat.

We fled into the tunnel making sure to secure the metal door behind us.

The tunnel was in ruin. At one time, stones had lined the walls giving them support. Now, roots grew from what remained of the crumbling walls and disintegrating fragments of stone littered the hard dirt floor. Rotted wooden beams supporting the ceiling threatened to collapse under the strain of their unbearable burdens. We walked cautiously, careful not to touch the walls.

As we walked, Hollow Monk related his experience.

"Sounds like spastic shifting. It's what happens when you're stuck between two universes and can't decide which one to stay in," I said.

"So I was in two places at once?"

"Kinda. More like two versions of you were in two places at once. Your Sacred Fish kept shifting between them uncontrollably while your mind tried to grasp what was happening. While you were in one place, the other you was on auto pilot."

"What happened to the other me back at Sunny Shire? Am I still there?"

I shrugged. "Honestly, I'm not sure. Oh, there are theories and speculations as to what happens to alternate selves after spastic shifting. But no one knows for sure."

Lola burst out laughing. "Liar. That's crazy nonsense. Universe hopping like that."

"It is no such thing," huffed the not-so-holy man, "Makes perfect sense to me." Then he changed the subject. "Might I ask where the rest of our companions are, princess? Perhaps calamity befell them at your hands?"

"They are frozen in the woods right now," she said, without a hint of concern, "They got jumped by a Maiden of Lilith. Two actually."

"Aye, and you shall be meeting them soon," added an incorporeal voice. We rounded a small corner and came face to face with the white lady flanked by two gargoyles.

"Jewel, I take it?" I asked, already knowing the answer.[28]

"At your service, Mr. Jones," she said with a mock bow. "I see you have been reunited with your artifact. It seems Dr. Wickett can't be trusted with even the smallest of tasks. No matter. I will just have to remove it myself. We'll do it my way this time, none of that bloody potion."

The apparition floated towards me, and I stood rooted to the ground by her enchanting stare. As she neared me, I could feel the frigid cold of the grave radiating off her. Jewel brushed my cheek with her porcelain hand and excruciating pain snapped me out of the trance. I didn't have a barble, so I blurted the first cantrip that came to mind.

"I swing a bunch but I'll only hit once," I recited and began whirling my left arm in wide circles gathering energy. "You won't see it coming, a nasty gut punch!" I sent a concentrated vibration of energy from my whirling fist into Jewel's stomach.

The demoness doubled over and tumbled back down the tunnel, but regained her composure. Jewel smiled a mirthless and evil smile.

---

[28] I should note that Jewel was a special case from the other stone monstrosities that guarded the asylum. She didn't turn to stone, as such, instead, her ethereal form inhabited the stone statue of her above Velhampshire's gates. How Dr. Wickett managed this remains a mystery.

"You really expect to harm me with Fair Folk's Tricksy? Those parlor tricks are not arcane. *This* is arcane." She stretched out her right arm, curved the first two fingers of her hand and quickly flicked her wrist.

A ghostly hook sailed through the air and imbedded itself in my chest. The hook found my fishome, and Jewel violently jerked the incorporeal fishing pole inside my chest, sending me to the ground in agony.

"Isn't it absolutely delicious?" teased Jewel as my body contorted with painful convulsions. "I call it, the Sacred Fishing Pole. I'll yank your Sacred Fish right out of its fishome and swallow it whole!" She laughed, a hideous sound that conjured images of screaming birds. "Take care of those other fools," she commanded the gargoyles.

The stone monstrosities growled and lunged past, briefly blocking me from Jewel's view.

That was my only chance. "Snip Snip," I wheezed and used the first two fingers of my left hand as scissors. Jewel's thin line of magical energy severed and my pain melted away.

But my liberation was short lived. The succubus's attack had drained me of energy, and as a result I was having difficulty getting on my feet. Jewel hooted victoriously when she realized my plight and redoubled her advancement with outstretched arms. Her fingers sought my tender flesh like razor sharp proclamations of revenge. And I could do nothing but stare dumbly as she determined to carry out her death sentence on my being.

Hollow Monk stepped in front of me and faced Jewel's onslaught. He raised his staff and commanded, "Be gone abhorrent demon! I banish you in the name of the Flawless He! Return to the Nothing that birthed your foul form!"

Jewel didn't slow. She slammed into Hollow Monk and raked at his face, but the instant her hand met those impenetrable shadows, she recoiled in pain. "*You* are Nothing!" she hissed in fearful awe.

"Demon whore!" boomed Hollow Monk. "I am Everything!" The cleric swung his staff in a wide arc splashing the evil succubus with a holy light.

Golden droplets showered Jewel with divine purity. The demoness screeched in pain as her features melted away like ice cream on a hot sidewalk. She dissolved into a puddle of white ectoplasm, never ceasing her furious howling as she died.

"Wow," said Hollow Monk. "I really didn't expect that to work."

"Then why'd you try it?" asked Lola. At her feet laid the bodies of Jewel's gargoyles, each peppered with multiple stab wounds. Lola was a bit scratched up herself, although nothing looked too serious. She stepped over the stone corpses and helped me to my feet.

"I rationalized that if the existence of demonic manifestations was factual, then the Church's methods for combating such creatures must also be truthful. So, I doused my staff in holy water and attempted an exorcism. And here I thought holy water was good for nothing more than trivial blessings."

We exited the tunnel as the sun rose over the trees. Lola led us to the spot where the stone forms of Goldie and Shamus rested. At some point, Shamus had crawled over to Goldie and put his arm around her in apparent consolation.

"Horrible," sputtered Hollow Monk, "utterly horrible. They did not deserve such a fate."

"Yeah," agreed Fa Lona, "S'how my uncle died."

"Can anything help them?" asked the monk, "Healers? Sorcerers? Clergy?"

"Nothing I ever knew about," said Fa Lona. "All our healers forgot the secrets. They just gotta wait to die inside there."

"Nonsense. He Who Is Not A Pronoun will heal them." Clearly, the clergyman was on a religious high after his successful encounter with Jewel. Hollow Monk raised his hands to the air, bling twinkling in the early morning light. "Oh mighty He Who Is Not A Pronoun, hear the supplications of your chosen. Restore these good folk, these devoted servants that they may complete thy works."

A bird chirped happily in the distance.

"I don't think he's listening," Fa Lona snickered.

"Please Lord," continued the monk undaunted, "Hear me. Please send the Excitement! I am your humble slave. Use me!" Still no response. Hollow Monk decided to try a different route. "In your name I rebuke my false life!" he declared and began stripping himself of his bling and tossing them into a growing pile of accessories at his feet. "I am unworthy! I am unholy! I do not come to you in arrogance! I do not appeal to you with pride and self-importance! I only wish to bask in your presence."

As he threw his last ring to the ground the monk went rigid, "This is His will," said a powerful voice that was not Hollow Monk's own. This voice was full of authority and goodness. This was a voice that incited creation. "Let what evil has done, be undone by the purity of good." Hollow Monk stiffly leaned over, picked two golden rings from the pile at his feet and slung one at each statue.

The rings struck true and exploded into a shower of light that became webs crisscrossing the stony forms. Cracks appeared across the rocky tombs of Shamus and Goldie and stone fell in large chunks at their feet revealing the living flesh beneath. Once free of their entrapment, they fell to the ground unconscious and Hollow Monk followed suit.

"Go figure," mused Fa Lona. "Stupid monk's on a roll."


We gazed over the Yawno Plains that abruptly exploded from the forest's tree line, as if fleeing the ancient wood's grasp. Soft, yellow grass blew gently in the breeze beneath a vast sky that mirrored the expansiveness of the plain below it. Herds of antelope grazed peacefully next to large herds of wild bovine, while scores of foozlebunnies scurried about, careful to hide from the deadly hawks circling above in anticipation of a meal.

Hollow Monk kept his distance from us, lost in thought. And if that wasn't blessing enough, he didn't sermonize. He didn't lecture. He didn't produce a single sanctimonious syllable for the better part of a day, which for Hollow Monk was the conversational equivalent of a vow of silence. He simply walked and looked at his hands occasionally as though he expected to find something written there. Whatever he saw, or didn't see, he kept to himself. I could tell he struggled to accept the reality of the unreal and wrestled with the assault against his mental bastion of materialism.

When he did speak it was only to say, "I did no such thing." Like if he spoke the words, they would somehow alter reality, or at the very least, create a comfortable lie for him to exist in.

But Lola wasn't having any of it. She immediately snapped back with, "Yeah, you did. You got all stiff and talking in a boomy voice and you threw your rings right at the giant and the one-orb."

"Impossible! I don't recall any of that. I remember praying unsuccessfully to He and then I must've passed out from exhaustion and been picked clean by your sticky fingers as I slept!"

"I didn't take your mammon-bling," hissed Fa Lona. "They're ugly and smell like Fake. No self-respecting princess would be caught dead in such adornment."

"I'm missing two rings! No doubt pawned in the last village for a few measly dingle before we left town!"

"Even if I did try to sell it, no one would buy that junk. Besides, how do you explain Goldie and Shamus being miraculously unstoned?"

"Enough!" roared Goldie. "Ya jacks cut it out already! Who cares what happened? All that matters is that we're all free and healthy and back onna road." After our encounter in the sanitarium, we explained everything to the innkeep, from escaping Lum Chow's dungeon to disguising ourselves prior to entering Velhampshire. Upon hearing our adventures, Goldie decided to accompany us in case we "ran into any more trouble and needed bailing out."

We shouldered our packs and headed across the great Yawno Plains. The sun was at its pinnacle when we spotted a seemingly infinite field of shapeless black forms in the distance. As we drew closer, we saw they were enormous black mosquitoes with huge suckers plunged deep into Gaia's flesh. Curiously, each mosquito had *Shamuscorp* stenciled across it in huge white letters.

"What's that about?" asked Goldie.

"They're called Big Rigs," said Shamus fondly. "One of Russel Bugtussel's best developments."

"What're they doing?"

"Getting Black Sludge from Gaia."

"What's that?"

"Well, it's what puts the 'Express' in *Express Go!*™. We refine it at the plant in the City of Lost Causes to extract the zing. After a few more scientific processes, you have drinks, brownies, quickfood, chewing gum—shoot, you can put zing in anything," he paused briefly as he gathered the remnants of his pride about him like a tattered cloak, "Did you know that we actually passed a law in the ULS prohibiting edible or inhalant substances from *not* having zing in them?"

"Why would ya do that?" Goldie shook her head, unable to fathom such lunacy.

"At the time, it was all about the dingle. Mark's Lesson Number 117 said it would secure the market."

"Did it?"

"Yeah…but that's Man Man's problem now." Shamus wandered through the rows of black mosquitoes lost in memory.

"I just thought of something," piped up Fa Lona. "If these things are getting the zing sludge or whatever for Man Man then why don't we just…break them?"

Shamus's jaw dropped, stricken with horror, "Are you joking? Do you have any idea how much one of these beauties costs? How many of my folk have given their blood and lives to make sure the Big Rigs are running smoothly and extracting the maximum amount of Sludge? Folk have died, young miss! And now you propose that we eliminate the very reason these brave citizens gave their lives? For what? To put a small thorn in Man Man's side? And a small one indeed! Destroying these technological marvels will do little more than give Man Man one more reason to focus his far-reaching influences in our direction."

The Red Dragon Ninja's orbs burned, "You really are spineless! Worried over breaking some crappy suckers because you don't want Man Man to find you. Well, *I'm* not afraid." The little princess drew her blade and scurried up the leg of the nearest mosquito. She positioned herself just over the creature's head and thrust her blade into its brain. The mosquito shrieked horribly and lashed about. Lola withdrew her blade and leapt to the next Big Rig before the dead one hit the ground. She hopped from creature to creature repeating the process. But before she could kill them all, the insects got wise to her plan and took to the air, flying in the direction of the desert.

"What have you done?" yelled Shamus. "They're going to report, you know! You've doomed us all!" The giant stormed off in a huff.

"What in all the Great It just happened?" swore Goldie. She had an affinity for creative swearing.

"Um, I'm not quite sure," I admitted. "From what I can tell, Shamus had a fit of spontaneous situational morals and Lola took it upon herself to act when Shamus couldn't."

Goldie shook her head in disgust and we took off after the tiny giant.


We made camp at dusk and Lola took first watch. She still seethed from Shamus's outburst and needed some time to bring herself back to the Yin.

"I see fires!" exclaimed Fa Lona as twilight settled into darkness. "Over there! I'm going to investigate."

The princess returned a few hours later. "It's a village full of teeny folk twirling around like half-drunk mountain monkeys and sacrificing piggies. You guys gotta see this!"

"They're called Chopsilians and I would leave them be, if I were you," advised the cleric. "Chopsilians are nasty little curs that will slit your throats with avaricious delight."

"Shut up, monk," spat Fa Lona. "Nothing's going to happen."

"Suit yourselves. I'll stay with the wagon," said Hollow Monk.

Lola led us to a camouflaged village populated with small, hairless folk. Hairless, that is, except for thick tufts of hair that began just below their ears, traveled down their cheeks and stopped about an inch apart on their chins.

In the center of the village a huge bonfire roared encircled by mud huts and animal hide tents. Numerous spits with roasting pigs surrounded the bonfire. At one end, drummers gathered around a bloody altar facing west. In front of the drummers stood two tribesmen dressed in pig skins, making rooting noises and chanting something like: "**Hum** diddy diddy **hum**." I understood them to be the chief and shaman of the tribe. The shaman was wearing a clay amulet fashioned in the semblance of a demonic looking boar with six tusks. The chief wore a headdress crafted from pig tusks and crow's feathers.

We were watching the ritual from our hiding place when two Chopsilians burst into the midst of the ceremony waving their spears and gesticulating. The ritual came to a halt and the chief and shaman conferred with the excited guards. "HOOP!" roared the chief. The grass parted and more Chopsilians appeared with Hollow Monk leading the horses by the reins and they, in turn, pulled the wagon.

"Hootenanny Hoot Hoot!" trilled the chief and motioned for the guards to rifle through the cart.

The guards unbridled the horses and led them to the altar. The priest followed, carrying a club he'd procured from a tribal warrior.

The shaman raised his arms to the sky. "Hoot woot hoot!" he proclaimed to the heavens. With a wild howl the priest swung the club into the first horse's leg.

The poor beast whinnied as the club met its knee with a sickening crunch that sent it to the ground. The shaman quickly drew a dagger and slit the wounded animal's throat. As it bled out, the equine giant gazed at the Chopsilian with fearful orbs. The priest slaughtered the other horse in the same manner and commanded a group of Chopsilian males to skin the bodies and cook the meat along with the sizzling pork.

"Well, there goes our ride," whispered Goldie. "What should we do?"

Thankfully we didn't have to worry about any sort of plan. "Hoop! Hoop," barked voices from behind us. Out of the tall grass emerged a small party of Chopsilians brandishing spears. "Hoop. Hoop. Hoop," they demanded, thrusting their spears at us and corralling our party. We surrendered without resistance.

All glances turned in our direction as we were escorted from our hiding place and into the middle of the plainsmen's feast. We were brought before the chief and made to kneel. The Chopsililan leader orbbed us with a calculating stare. "Hoop! Hoo-Hoo-Hum-Hoop," he chirped and clapped his hands twice.

Our captors bound us with knitted grass ropes and put us next to Hollow Monk, situated near the fire next to the drummers.

I scooted over to sit next to the monk. "Does your pious rationality know anything about these little scamps?" I whispered.

"They are a race of near-hairless Cuddlies. They were forced from their island home to the plains a few centuries ago by the West Feather Trading Company and fell into worshipping the feral pigs that roam here."

"Cuddlies? So, they'll kill us?" I asked.

"Most likely. As soon as the ceremony is over."

*Wonderful,* sneered the Orb, *it appears my fate is once more to be a jewel cast before swine.*

"Hush," I snapped.

"Well, there might be a way…" Hollow Monk spoke up.

"What is it? What's the way?"

"Well, someone challenges the chief and drinks Pig Spit."

"That's it? If I could slurp down Lard Sauce, I can drink Pig Spit," Shamus offered. "Let's challenge."

"Uhh…Hoop…whoop hee…hwoop," called the monk in broken Chopsilian.

The chief rushed over and orbbed the monk. "Hoop whoop hee hwoop?" he asked, then added, "Hoo whoopsie?"

"Hoop diddy," responded Hollow Monk and nodded at Shamus.

"Hoo Whoopsie!" yelled the chief and clapped his hands three times. The Chopsilians cheered and gathered around. The chief served Shamus a foul-smelling brew in a hollow pig tusk that he swallowed in one gulp.

"What is that?" said Lola wrinkling her nose at the smell.

"Pig spit," Hollow Monk said, "it's an alcohol only Chopsilians know how to brew. It's supposed to shrink taller folk down to Chopsilian size in order to even the odds of a challenge. Shamus will shrivel down to about half his height, be given a spear, and made to fight the village champion. If he wins, we live. If not, we join the pigs and horses roasting on the bonfire."

"Hey now," McFamus protested, "You never mentioned shriveling and having to fight champions and whatnot."

"If I had, would you have agreed to challenge," asked the monk.

"Probably not."

"Well, there you go."

When the magic potion kicked in Shamus's reality unraveled. He couldn't see himself getting smaller, only perceive it with some little-used sense of "the way things should be." At the sight of his physical handicapping, the Chopsilians erupted in deafening applause and cheer.

Once the giant was properly shrunk to a dandy five feet tall (still nearly a foot taller than the tallest Chopsilian), he was assigned three guards and led into a tent where they outfitted him in ill-fitting boar's hide armor. Then they gave the teeny giant a spear and shield and escorted him to a large field behind the stables. The field, a circular clearing about twenty-five feet in diameter, had a shallow pond at its center. At the north end of the field sat a raised platform proudly displaying a throne made of tusk. The chief, shaman, and their entourage were already seated, hooting in unmistakable sadistic glee.

The rest of the Chopsilians gathered around the perimeter forming a large, but tight, circle. They herded us to the south side of the field at spear point. Shamus joined us and was instructed to wait through forceful hand gestures.

"I like your armor," sneered Fa Lona. "Makes you reek like pig instead of nanciness." She laughed until an attentive Chopsilian guard nudged her into silence.

The crowd parted and a large boar with a saddle was led over to Shamus.

"Pigs!" exclaimed Goldie. "They use the pigs fer mounts!"

"Duh. Pig is definitely the motif around here," said Lola.

"Why do I need a pig?" Shamus asked the monk who seemed to know much more about the situation than he was letting on.

"Pig jousting. Followed by hand-to-hand combat if you survive. Winner takes first pick of the dead guy's loot and choice of appendages. Can you ride a pig?"

"I'm not sure," he admitted. A stable boy handed him the reins and disappeared into the crowd. The awkward giant's first attempt at mounting the swine was unsuccessful as he immediately slid off the opposite side. This was very amusing for the crowd and they laughed at Shamus's lack of skill for quite a while before he managed to secure himself atop that feral beast. Shamus took the boar for a few practice runs around the field and then returned to "his side of the ring," as it were.

"This should be no problem" he boasted to Goldie. "I've picked it up rather quickly."

The plainsmen erupted into a riotous cheer and a very fat Chopsilian entered the ring, adorned with pig hide armor bearing various trinkets and body parts as decoration. The champion rode a large boar that matched his size and carried his weight effortlessly. He took a few laps around the ring to soak up the admiration of his audience before positioning himself at the end of the field opposite Shamus. The crowd cheered and hooted; and in response, the champion lifted his spear into the air and roared a primal battle cry.

"Are they kidding? I can't tell which is bigger, the rider or the mount. How do they expect to joust?" I was soon answered.

The chief stepped forward and made a hooping speech with a few whoops thrown in and then took his place on the throne of tusks. Two sharp drum beats alerted the audience that the battle had begun.

The champion lowered his spear and spurred his obese mount. The fleshy duo moved much faster than should be possible for beings burdened with so much mass.

Shamus spurred his own mount and it shot forward, carrying the giant into battle heedless of his commands. He bounced in the awkward saddle, fighting to keep his balance the entire time. If the situation weren't so serious I would've laughed. But Lola didn't mind laughing at all. Before he could lower his spear into a secure position, the giant was confronted with the champion's jagged spear tip sailing directly for his left orb. Shamus instinctively ducked and the spear passed overhead. Instinct, it turns out, is considerably more reliable than skill. A fact Shamus would go on to demonstrate repeatedly in this battle. But such is the way a fishome grows.

"Hoo! Hoo!" the crowd yelled angrily.

The champion reached the other end of the field and spun his mount around for another pass. McFamus followed suit, only this time, he was better prepared. The giant lowered his spear and raised his shield as he rushed to meet the Chopsilian. When they clashed, it felt as if Shamus were clashing with a stone wall. Shamus's spear shattered as he was thrown backwards off his mount while it continued forward—without him. Shamus flew a good ten feet before crashing to the ground with a thud. Attentive members of the crowd lifted him to his feet, handed him another spear, and pushed him back into the fray.

The champion dismounted and approached Shamus with a grin of assured victory plastered across his face.

The fat Chopsilian and the quivering giant circled each other, poking and prodding with feints and half-thrusts, studying each other hoping to locate weaknesses, but were unable to find an opening or distraction. Such is the way of things when you're fighting for your life. You tend to pay attention in those situations.

The Chopsilian spectators hooted in frustration at the lull. I was just glad for a moment to catch my breath.

The crowd's reaction prompted the champion to act. In a surprising rush of speed, he lunged toward McFamus with a powerful spear thrust.

The giant used the haft of his own spear to knock the champion's attack aside and responded by stabbing at his fleshy torso.

The Chopsilian parried and attempted another lunge.

Shamus sprang backward and the spear point missed his gut by mere inches.

"Keetch whoop keetch," the champion said to Shamus and smiled, "whoop whip whoop!"

The obese champion and the giant began their dance of circles once more. I could see on the champion's face that he was unsure of Shamus's skill. He had obviously risen to the top of his primitive ranks by throwing around his weight. But the giant offered him a great challenge as they were both about the same size.

The champion's muscles tensed in preparation for another attack and with a wild yell, he rushed the giant with spear out. Shamus skipped a couple of steps to the right and lowered the tip of his spear. The champion's feet became intimate with the giant's spear and decided to stay a while. The fat Chopsilian crashed to the ground landing face first in the shallow puddle.

Shamus yanked the spear from betwixt the champion's feet and grazed the tip against the base of his skull. "Do you yield?" he demanded.

Shamus waited for an answer, standing straight, in command of the situation. I was never prouder of him than I was in that moment. In response, the champion lay motionless.

"I said, DO YOU YIELD?" he yelled, but still got nothing.

A few Chopsilian warriors separated from the crowd and made their way to where the champion lay. They rolled him over and discovered that during his fall, the champion had impaled himself on his own spear.

"Keetch! Whoop Keetch!" one of the warriors yelled to the chief and made a cutting gesture across his throat.

"Hoowoop! Hoowoop," said the chief jovially. He clapped his hands and the rest of us were unbound and led back into the village where we were escorted into the chief's hut.

The hut was almost five feet tall and was easily the tallest building in the small plains village. The main room was furnished with small mud stools around a fire pit. Here, we were served heaping plates of sizzling pig by bare-headed Chopsilian women. As far as swine is concerned, I've never eaten better before or since. It was bitter and smoky but it had been cooked just right and still maintained its juiciness. It was served with a side of plainstaters and riceroot done up in the proper fashion.

The chief popped in to check on us. He spoke through Hollow Monk since only he understood their language.

"He says you are a great warrior," he translated for Shamus and the Chop-in-Charge nodded in stoic agreement. "He says it'll be a great honor to have you as their new champion."

"What!" Shamus exclaimed and jumped to his feet, "I can't be their champion!"

Hollow Monk related this to the Chopsilian and the chief hooped angrily, shooting looks in Shamus's direction. "He asks why not."

"Tell him because I'm not a Chopsilian for one; and for two, I'm Shamus McFamus! I've got places to see and things to do. Not that our visit to this lovely village hasn't been most enjoyable," he added quickly. "But I've gotta move on."

Hollow Monk did the best he could to translate. The chief looked at Shamus and then spoke to Hollow Monk.

"He says he completely understands. A champion is required to go on a quest for the glory of the tribe in order to prove his ultimate worth, anyway. You've be given permission to quest with the understanding that any wealth you acquire must be handed over for the good of the entire tribe." Shamus's face wore skepticism like a well-fitted suit. "Look McFamus, the only thing keeping us alive is the fact that you are the champion. These little buggers mean business. It would behoove you to play along for the sake of your life and ours."

It was obviously impossible to communicate through cultural barriers. He'd have a better chance getting his point across to the pigs these folk adored. "Fine. I agree," he said finally.

Hollow Monk nodded and the chief beamed.

"Hoop!" he squealed and shook each of our hands before returning to the ceremony outside.

"Alright, monk, come clean," said Fa Lona. "How is it you know of these folk so intimately?"

"I don't see any reason in keeping it from you," the cleric said. "I've nothing to hide. During the early years of my service to the Flawless He, I was part of a mission team sent here to convert the Chopsilians. There were six of us handpicked by Pompus I, himself. Father Prudebert, myself, Brothers Playa and Hay Seuss, Sister Florentine and Sister Silence. We studied every aspect of the Chopsilian's recorded culture. We knew they were violent and distrusting scamps all along, but we just didn't understand the reality of it.

"After a year of training, my team and I set out across these very plains in search of the Chopsilians. They found us soon enough and bound and escorted us much as we were tonight. The Chopsilians wasted no time in slaughtering Playa and the gibbering Sister Silence, putting their carcasses on those huge splits around the bonfire. I think it was panic that forced Prudebert to blurt out the challenge like he did. That changed everything.

"Suddenly, the Chopsilians went from glowering to all smiles and kindness. Prudebert was given the Pig Spit and treated like you, Shamus. Everything happened much like it did this evening, only Prudebert was impaled on the first pass. He never even lifted his spear. Knowing certain death hung over our heads those of us who remained seized the opportunity to flee into the plains while the Chopsilians were busy celebrating and congratulating their champion.

"The little beasts mounted pursuit in a flash, hunting down and killing my companions. I alone escaped. I could hear the cries and pleas of my sister and brother as they were murdered by these cannibalistic savages!" Hollow Monk clenched his fist. "We were only trying to awaken their Fish! They needn't kill us!"

"Maybe they're happy how they are," I offered.

"Don't be a fool, Jones. All the Realm's inhabitants are ignorant and blind. They need strict moral guidance if they are to reach the light."

"That may be true. But sleeping folk often get angry when they're woken. They enjoy the peace and contentment of their naps and dreams."

"How long does this stuff take to wear off?" Shamus asked trying to change the subject.

"I'm not sure," admitted Hollow Monk. "Prudebert was dead long before it had a chance to wear off."

"I'll sleep outside, just in case," Shamus grumbled.


The terrified squeals of swine and the hysterical hooping of Chopsilians tore me from my slumber.

The chief burst into our sleeping chamber. "Hoopie Hoop!" he screeched.

"He said something about a fire," translated Hollow Monk, groggy from being jerked out of sleep.

"Mr. Jones!" yelled Shamus from outside. "You better get out here!" I was surprised to discover that sometime during the night, the Pig Spit had worn off and Shamus was back to his regular reduced size of ten feet.

The village was in an uproar. The grass surrounding the small village was aflame, threatening to incinerate the entire community. Chopsilians scrambled to and fro, heaving containers of water on their structures and around the perimeter of the village.

"What are they doing?" I asked. "There's no way they can put out that fire."

"They aren't trying to put out the fire," answered Hollow Monk. "They are wetting the boundaries of the village and their buildings in hopes of keeping the fire out."

"Will that work?"

"It has in the past, so I've read. We should probably assist them lest we barbeque along with these sadistic little monsters."

"Let's go!" yelled Goldie. She rushed over to the well and pulled water twice as fast as the team of Chopsilians assigned to the task.

"She really is strong," Shamus said with an approving stare. "Just the kind of woman a guy needs by his side during a fight…"[29]

Hollow Monk and I joined the effort and Lola sat outside the chief's door sharpening her blade and ninja claws, exuding an air of noble indifference. Suddenly, the Chopsilian's hooping switched from frantic to alarming. Many of them pointed to the sky. We followed their direction and noticed a large winged figure leisurely circling above the flames. The figure periodically swooped down to snatch a prone Chopsilian on the fringes of the village. It soared high into the sky before dropping its prey into the blazing inferno with a horrific laugh.

"Fantastic," said Lola dryly as she rose to her feet, "it's that dragon. This'll get his attention." She pulled three ninja stars from her tunic's sleeve and hurled them at the beast circling above. Two harmlessly deflected off the dragon's thick hide and one sliced through the thin membrane of his wing.

Slither snarled in pain and landed near Shamus with a rough thud. "Imagine meeting you here," the bounty hunter said and drew his wicked blade. "Are you enjoying my midnight blazzze?"

Shamus's orbs flashed with anger, "This is your doing?" The giant's fishome began to boil and something wonderful finally happened. His Sacred Fish, Commander Gali, finally burst the dam of fear that held Shamus at bay for so long and courage flooded the wee

---

[29] One of the first things folk do when their fishome starts to grow is to fall in love with someone who's currently emotionally unavailable. I'm not sure why this is, though I do have my theories. Perhaps, in their excitement for growth and aligning with the spirit of life, they want to share it with others who were hurting as they were. Perhaps their new internal construction project gives them the audacity and courage and just the right amount of foolishness to think that they have it within themselves to change another. Regardless of the reason, it's a fool's errand. I don't recommend it. Of course, I'm speaking from experience, but that is another story…

giant's heart once more. "I'll have your head for this!" Shamus radiated strength and confidence.

"Good. I wasss hoping you'd sssay that." The dragon raised his sword and rushed the giant before he could pull the axe from his back.

"Halt!" Hollow Monk Voiced and stepped into Slither's path. The dragon stumbled back a few steps, but the cleric's abilities certainly didn't have the same effect on the dragon as it did on the Traditionalist Guards. That's because dragons are very magical beings and the more magical a being is, the less susceptible they are to magical energies. "You've upset the rules of honor and fair play," the monk explained weakly.

The bounty hunter laughed robustly, scrutinizing the monk through razor thin orbs. "That'sss Sssome Voiccce you posssss--posssss—have," Faust blurted in frustration. "It mussst have been really powerful…onccce. Perhapsss that isss how you managed to acquire ssso much wonderful bling? Tell me, wasss it a fair trade?"

"No," said Hollow Monk as if in a daze. Slither had turned the tables and enthralled the cleric with his dragon-born talents of charm and hypnotism.

Slither smiled, "I will ssslay you, falssse priessst, and pick bling off your corpssse!" He swung his blade, intending to separate Hollow Monk's melon from his head-pole.

Mother Death's grasp was averted by Shamus's axe blade as the giant's swing met the dragon's sword in a shower of sparks that rained down upon the preacher's hooded head. Hollow Monk passed out cold from fright. Goldie and I pulled him to safety. Shamus and Slither stood face to face.

The bounty hunter laughed and his orbs sparkled with battle-lust. "You cannot defeat me giant. It doesss not matter that you have acquired a new toy or machisssmo. It will not sssave you."

"Then I expect today will be a good day to die," said Shamus in a firm voice that surprised even him.

See, at his core, Shamus was a very courageous and noble being with bravery and a goodness of heart that few could match. The problem was that the further he got from his core, the less noble and good he became. And soon, Shamus's calculating and self-serving mind overrode the noble intentions of his Sacred Fish. When this occurred the giant did unbearably stupid things like hooking entire populations on potions that did them more harm than good just to make a few more dingle.

But Commander Gali was done passively swimming around while Shamus's brain went and ruined everything with its rash and selfish decisions. It was time for action and Commander Gali made a bid for rule of Shamus's senses, which he won after executing a brilliant coup. Once more, bravery and gusto saturated the giant, as if he had gone through a midlife crisis at the green age of 750.

The giant smiled wickedly and swung his right elbow into Slither's left temple.

The bounty hunter stumbled back in dazed confusion. That blow actually *hurt*. Slither had obviously underestimated the strength and skill of his opponent. That was a mistake he could only make once. The combatants withdrew and orbbed each other with calculating stares.

The hunt finally got interesting for the dragon. Too long had he languished in boredom with the ease of capturing his inferior prey. He might as well have been spearing fish as they slept in a barrel. Faust's ego had grown to such proportions that he actually thought himself invincible and without equal. His bounties all lacked the necessary skill to give him a good fight. Even the recent battle with the gypsies disappointed him. He had slain them all save their leader, Fallen Tree. But this giant was an enigma. The nanciness that plagued McFamus had been mysteriously cured and replaced with an unknown zeal.

Slither's forked tongued danced across his lips. He drew his arm across his chest and swung down hoping to cleave the giant's torso in two.

Shamus parried with his axe and Faust responded with a kick to Shamus's gut. McFamus exhaled and stumbled backwards.

Slither immediately sought to skewer Shamus before the giant could recover.

McFamus swung desperately and knocked aside the dragon's blade with the haft of his axe.

The warriors once again retreated and watched each other with predatory intentions.

*You're doing fantastic*, said Commander Gali, *He fears you now.*

*I'm kinda worried*, replied Shamus mentally, *he isn't what I expected from a dragon.*

*Don't heed Fear. Fear and Death are close companions and each supports the other. Fear opens the door of men's hearts to Death, just as Death opens the door of men's hearts to Fear. Now is not your time to lie down. Now you fight!* Shamus leapt at the bounty hunter with an executioner's swing.

Faust barely had time to lift his blade and intercept the deadly blow. He responded by circling his blade and forcing Shamus's axe to the ground then lunged for the giant's chest.

Shamus swung his axe up and knocked the thrust away. Without delay, he swung at Faust's left side and the bounty hunter's deft deflection is all that kept the thirsty axe from biting into his scaly flesh.

But the dragon could not recover fully, and on Shamus's backswing, the giant's axe dug into the dragon's right shoulder, severing Slither's arm.

Slither fell to his knees, clutching his bleeding stump. "Mercccy," he pleaded with his head down, "I am unarmed." The dragon's tongue played across his lips.

"Only those willing to give mercy deserve it themselves." The enraged giant raised his axe and swung with the intention of ending the vile bounty hunter's life.

Faust rolled and drew a blade from his boot. The dragon tossed it underhanded at Shamus, hitting the giant just below the belt.

Shamus exhaled in pain and surprise as his axe fell from his grip. He looked down to find the dagger hilt protruding beneath his navel. "No!" he and his Sacred Fish screamed simultaneously. Pain threatened to overtake the giant and the dark oblivion of unconsciousness crept toward the edges of his vision. "It will not end like this," he said through gritted teeth. His vision burned red and pain was forgotten as he drew upon long forgotten primal rages. The giant withdrew the dagger and plunged it deep into the top of the dragon's skull as Slither tried to stand. Slither collapsed heavily and expelled his final hiss. "Jackass," grumbled the giant and collapsed.

Goldie rushed over to the unconscious hero and tended his wounds with a softness henceforth unseen.

"How is it?" I asked kneeling beside her and checking the giant's wound.

"Bad," she answered. "The dagger had a serrated edge. Tore a hole in his gut. This wound can't be healed with salves and herbs. Needs blessing and healing."

"I can try something," I said. I rubbed my hands together to gather energy like the old gypsy Grammy had taught me. Once my hands were warm and pulsing with active energy I placed them above the wound mere centimeters from actual touch. I closed my orbs and visualized the wound sealing aided by the energy flowing from me. I heard Goldie gasp in wonder. The gash had completely closed and an ugly scar stood in its place. Shamus was still unconscious, his breath shallow but steady. It would take some time for him to recover from the magical healing.

"How'd ya do that?" stammered Goldie.

"Nature magic. I'm not exactly sure how it works," I admitted. "I learned the technique from a gypsy."

"Are ya a wyzyrd?" she asked. The ex-mercenary gently ran her fingers across the scar and the unconscious giant stirred.

"I'm a lot of things," I said. "He needs sleep and we need to see about this fire. He'll be O.K. as long as he stays here near the center of the village."

The fire reached the village limits and popped angrily as it met the wet earth and tried to overtake its natural enemy. The shaman gathered the Chopsilian drummers together and set them to a particular beat that he began dancing and hooping to.

"They are trying to strengthen the boundary by appealing to their protector spirits," explained Hollow Monk after he regained consciousness.

The drumming continued for the remainder of the evening. At one point the smoke grew so thick that it threatened to choke everything in a deadly cloud, but the boundary held.

At dawn, the East Wind carried off the smoke, and we witnessed the damage of the hungry fire. As far as the orb could see, the grassy plains had been reduced to a smoldering wasteland.

Shamus awoke feeling stiff, but otherwise healthy. He gathered the breastplate and sword from Slither's corpse and added them to his possessions. The dragon's corpse was dumped in a shallow grave far outside of the Chopsilian village.

After we helped the tribesmen bury their dead and repaired what we could, the chief led us to the village storage pit. A group of Chopsilian women was loading supplies onto three sleds made from pig hide stretched over large tusks. Each sled was tethered to a team of five feral pigs.

"Whoop Hoopsie Hoop," the chief said as he proudly displayed the sleds.

"He said these are his best pigs and personal sleds," translated Hollow Monk.

"Hoo Whoo Chopsilian Shh! Hoop si Hoop Whoopsie."

"Umm," Hollow Monk took a moment to sort out the much longer phrase, "He said they are made from the Great Mammoth Boars that roam in secret places known only to the Chopsilians."

"Hoopsie ti Hoopsie Keetch Chopsilian. Keetch Hoopsizzle," he said and pointed to Shamus.

"He said he's giving them to you for slaying the evil demon that slew his folk and set the grass ablaze. It's quite an honor, Shamus."

The giant bowed in thanks and the chief continued, "Eee whoop whoop keetch Chop si whoopsie."

"He said that you are also being given the dead champion's pig and your choice of his appendages as trophies."

"The pig is fine, thanks," said Shamus.

The swine was saddled and led over to Shamus. Surprisingly, he fit pretty well in the saddle. The sow's girth was such that it kept his feet from dragging the ground by a few inches. "What's the pig's name?" Shamus asked.

Hollow Monk relayed the question.

"Hoop Lilly," spoke the chief clearly. "Hoop woo hoop woo keetch whoopsie."

"He says that one day she will bear many strong boars with a fierceness for battle. She is literally the village's prized mount. Accept her graciously," the cleric warned.

Shamus bowed in thanks from the saddle. Hollow Monk was given his own mount. A young boar about half the size of Hoop Lilly named Apples. Lola, Goldie and I each mounted a sled and we were on our way once more. I must say, it was quite a sight. Two men riding oversized swine in the company of sleds pulled by feral pigs and manned by a motley crew. The pigs were amazingly sturdy and strong and carried even Shamus's excessive weight with relative ease. We made excellent time over the scorched landscape in our trek westward toward the uncertainty of the Desert of Lost Causes.

We made camp when the scorched plains finally gave up the ghost and admitted they weren't going anywhere interesting before sunrise. The pigs were watered from skins and staked out at a respectable distance from the fire. Feral swine being what they are, a man sleeps better not wondering what's snuffling around his boots in the dark.

It was quiet around the campfire that night. For quite a bit had happened and the shock of everything had frazzled our nerves. We had survived many things that would've killed most folk and still needed time processing the mental paperwork on all of it. Lola drew doodles in the dirt with her dagger. Shamus and Goldie kept looking at one another without trying to let on they were looking at one another. And I sat listening to the Orb relate things that I hadn't been around to witness. Hollow Monk sat apart from us for a while. I noticed him looking at his hands again in that particular way he'd been doing since the sanitarium. It is precisely the way a man looks at something he doesn't recognize but is fairly certain belongs to him. Eventually he settled himself, pulled his hood up against the night air, and cleared his throat with the unmistakable authority of a man who has decided that what this moment requires is a parable.

"We are afraid. Uncertain. Traumatized. This is a hard place to be. But I know something that could help. There is a story," he began, "that the clergy of He Who Is Not A Pronoun tell to young initiates. A story of a pilgrim and his path to the temple on the mountain."

Lola made a sound that was not quite a groan and not quite a sigh but contained elements of both.

"I'll allow it," said Goldie.

I poked the fire and listened. I had heard the story before. At least, the version told to me by other Brothers of He. I was curious on how similar they would be to one another.

Hollow Monk took a deep breath to fill his lungs with the necessary pomposity and then spoke, "What is a pilgrim? What kind of person undertakes a journey that will test the very limits of their being? A pilgrim is a person who has peered through the veil of deception and looked into the heart of the unknown. A pilgrim is an individual who is always seeking to become a better person. A pilgrim is someone who has traded in everything he or she has ever considered real in order to awaken their slumbering Sacred Fish. Most importantly a pilgrim is a person who possesses the courage and the determination to plunge head first into the enigmas of truth even though it may cost him his sanity…or his life. I know a story about such a person.

"He was a disenchanted young lad. A boy who had never fully trusted the world as folk tried to build it for him. He was incessant in his pursuit of knowledge and sought after it to the exclusion of all else. It was late one night that he was awoken from a dead sleep by a faint whispering in his dreams. His orbs popped open and he bolted upright in bed bathed in a cold sweat.

"'Who's there,' he shouted into the night.

"'Just the wind…just the wind…just the wind,' said the wind.

"'What do you want,' said the lad in a quivering voice.

"'A message…I carry a…We carry a message,' whispered the wind.

"'Tell me.'

"'The door is open. Just step outside,' urged the wind gently. The boy got out of bed, walked over to the front door of his spartan quarters, and laid a trembling hand on the knob. He took a deep breath and threw open the door. Amazement spread across his face when he found himself not staring into the hallway, but at a bright sunlight day illuminating a path with green hills rolling into a beautiful valley and then disappearing into a dark and foreboding patch of woods beyond. The trail reappeared on the other side of the woods and climbed up a great and craggy mountain halting at a small gray structure on the mountain's topmost peak.

"'What am I supposed to do,' he asked the wind.

"'Follow it…Follow it,' answered the wind.

"'Why?'

"'Because there are things to see…' laughed the adventurous West wind.

"'Because no one ever got anywhere staying where they were…' howled the impatient East wind.

"'Because all trails deserved to be followed,' whispered the soothing South wind.

"'Because you need to be tested,' grumbled the harsh North Wind and then all was silent.

"The pilgrim gazed at the path in fear of the daunting task before him. He took a deep breath and looked to his feet. Oddly, he found three acorns lying there.

"That's odd, he thought and without really understanding why, he reached down and gathered up the acorns. He returned inside and took only enough time to dress and pack a few important items before he started on his quest.

"His first destination was The Valley, a warm and pleasant place full of golden light and carefree happiness. The wind sang joyfully as it tickled the soft grass with its passing. A pacific pond is situated in the middle of this place of peaceful sanctuary, and legends say that griffons and unicorns sometimes come there to drink.

"This is the place that mankind's most joyful memories are kept. This is where those memories come alive and dance before enraptured gazes like golden fairies skipping across flower petals.

"'This isn't so bad,' he said aloud, 'It's warm and inviting and comfortable. I could learn to like it here.' After he'd lunched, he laid back on the soft grass and dozed off. He dreamt of more innocent times and simpler places when a rustling sound woke him.

A white foozlebunny[30] sniffed at his face showing no signs of the mistrust and fear that usually infects that particular species. The

---

[30] Foozlebunnies are as common in the Realm as pigeons are in yours. In fact, we call them Grass Pigeons here. They're everywhere. And what's worse, they don't shut up. Ever. That's why the one in this parable is so abnormal. It's actually paying attention to the conversation and not filling the space with asinine prattle. And this the real lesson in humility the pilgrim passed. Usually, folk just pelt foozlebunnies with whatever is nearby until they leave. Trust me, they really are that annoying. One of my worst adventures ever involved a family of foozles

pilgrim smiled and selflessly gave the bunny one of the acorns he'd found.

"'Thank you for your generosity,' spoke the rabbit.

"The lad's orbs widened, 'How is it you speak to me?'

"'All of nature speaks to those who want to hear it,' said the rabbit, 'And folk who find themselves in this valley are folk who desire to hear. This is the beginning. This is the sanctuary of those who walk the paths less traveled.'

"'Shouldn't there be more folk here?'

"The rabbit laughed, 'Certainly not! This is merely the beginning! There are many paths yet to travel. Consider this a rest stop on your way to your destination.'

"'But I like it here,' whined the traveler, 'Why can't I just stay here where it is warm and comfortable and pleasant?'

"'Because no one would learn anything if they stayed where they were comfortable,' snapped the foozle, 'Life isn't about being comfortable, it's about finding your Sacred Fish. And that, my friend, is no comfortable task.'

"'Your wisdom is blunt, but you are right,' said the pilgrim, 'I can see that I must move on if I am to complete my journey.'

"The bunny smiled, 'Your first test is passed. That is the test of humility. If you are ready to learn, I will lead you to the next part of your journey.' The foozlebunny hopped to the trail and made its way into the dark forest ahead. The pilgrim shouldered his pack and followed the bunny into the welcoming embrace of Destiny.

"The forest was old and dark. Shadows played tricks on one another until they conjured a terrifying drama of uncertainty before the pilgrim's frightened face. The dense gloom of the forest caused time to stretch out like a piece of taffy only adding to the already uneasy traveler's discomfort. He put his head down and followed the foozle, determined not to stray from the path.

"The foozle turned sharply and scampered off the path into the darker shadows of the forest, leaving the pilgrim with difficult a choice. Does he choose to have faith and follow the foozle off the path into the haunted forest? Or does his resolve crumble and cause him to flee back into the safety of the sunlit valley?"

"Is this a rhetorical or hypothetical question," I ask, while elbowing Shamus awake.

---

who needed to be relocated so a farmer could plow his fields. Some nights the terror of it will still rip me from sleep and live in my head until dawn.

"Both," replied the monk and continued, "The traveler does not succumb to fear. Nay. He keeps his orbs on his guiding blessing and steps off the path. He delves into the depths of the forest until the foozle leads him to the Great and Holy Wise Man. The ancient figure welcomed him with a smile of pure love and joy.

"'What is it I can do for you, child,' asked the Wise Man, and the pilgrim caught the impression of a loving and caring grandfather who bounces children on his knee while he tells them fantastic stories.

"'How do I reach the temple atop the mountain?'

"'You must catch the Excitement. Dig it. Open yourself to it and catch it as it rides the Lost Lyrics of the Silent Song.'[31]

"'Just like that?'

"'Aye, just like that.'

"The pilgrim sat before the Wise Elder and closed his orbs. He took seven relaxing breaths and surrendered himself to the Excitement. It whisked him up and out of the forest. He saw with a griffon's glance the vast green canvas of trees, and he was whisked over it in the wink of an orb. His faith and determination allowed for him to land him at the base of the mountain. His gaze followed the mountain, his head-pole craning as far back as it could before he finally caught a glimpse of the temple on the summit. The pilgrim shouldered his pack and began to climb.

"He climbed for days conquering obstacle after obstacle until he came to an impassible valley packed with boulders. Defeat crept in to the traveler's spirit, when lo and behold, a squirrel materialized and perched itself atop a nearby boulder. He reached into his pack and retrieved yet another acorn and offered it to the squirrel. The grateful critter gleefully chattered and clapped his tiny paws. He snatched the nut from the pilgrim's hand and then bounded away, leaping from boulder to boulder. The pilgrim followed. The squirrel zigged and zagged through the Valley of Unsurpassable Rock, following a path that none but it could navigate. The pilgrim emerged on the other side of the rock valley. From there, it was only a small climb to the summit. Our hero breached the summit to discover a small and simple temple built of stone. Inside was naught but an equally simple stone altar. He knelt before the altar and placed his last remaining acorn on it as he mumbled prayers to He Who Is Not A Pronoun. The Lord smiled upon this and blessed the faithful pilgrim with health and wealth unto

---

[31] The mundanely invisible currents of energy that permeate the Realm and give it life, meaning, and hope. Without them, the Om couldn't vibrate and the Realm wouldn't exist.

the end of his days. The moral being that one's Sacred Fish is met mainly by giving critters acorns and listening to the wind. Thus, be simpleminded not simple," Hollow Monk fell into an expectant silence.

"Huh," grunted Shamus with a yawn, "Sounds a bit like moralistic propaganda."

"Yeah," I concurred, "And I've heard your story before and that's not exactly how it goes. For one, he doesn't meet the Great Wise Man or whatever in the forest, he meets the Great Mother Tree and she tells him to catch the Flow not the Excitement. Oh, and when he places the final acorn on the altar, the Benevolent Chaos as She Who Becomes, blesses him with a kiss and Divine Fruit."

"Paganistic hogwash," sputtered the quasi-holy man, "That is a parable of He Who Is Not A Pronoun! Not some wicked utterance of that unholy wench!"

Now if there is one thing I cannot stand it is intolerance bred from ignorance. Statements like that are a breeding ground for hate and retaliation. This time was no exception. My face flushed red with rage and I rose from my seat. "You will apologize for that, sir," I said reaching for my blade.

"You dare raise steel to one of His disciples?"

"Aye. I won't have you blaspheming She Who Becomes's name in my presence. Your beliefs are yours to own, but you won't be condemning me for owning mine."

Hollow Monk lowered his head, "I shall guard my words more closely from now on." However, he did not retract his statement about the Lady.

The Desert of Lost Causes isn't what you might expect from a vast arid wasteland. For one thing, not all of the desert is a sea of sifting sand dunes. That's only toward the center where the land was particularly barren after the farming colony's depletion. The outskirts are actually a teeming desert biosphere. Brown, prickly cacti fashioned after bucks' racks or thorny paddles thrive in the harsh environment. Groves of mesquite fight for precious water alongside yucca. Small animals and predatory birds ensure the continuation of the circle of life and offer desert dwellers sustenance. Dust devils whirl mischievously across sun-scorched earth, kicking up great funnels of dust as they pass.

It was here, on the edge of the Great Mesa overlooking the desert that our party discovered a black tower that shot far into the air and came to a point at the top in the manner of an obelisk. Sunshine glinted seductively off its perfect obsidian surface. At the base of the tower stood two huge doors and an inscription emblazoned in the brightest white could easily be read from where we stood: "It's not who you are, it's what you know."

"What's that?" asked Fa Lona in wonderment.

"Snoot Tower," I replied dryly.

"What's Snoot Tower?"

"It's where the Snoots live. They moved here centuries ago after," I glanced at Shamus, "the desert was created."

"How was it created?" the inquisitive Ninja asked.

"It was my bad," admitted Shamus. He then explained the rise and fall of his Land of Farmly Paradise.

"Exactly how old are you?" asked Fa Lona.

The small giant blushed, "Well, you see, the taller a giant is, the longer he lives. I was kind of bigger than all the other giants so…"

"So how old?" persisted Fa Lona.

"Seven hundred and fifty years."

"Oh. My. Gawsh! You're, like, older than my gramps."

"It's right for my size," huffed Shamus, "It's only about twenty-five in Ninja years."

"Well, that's still old."

"Please, Infinity, continue your explanation," interrupted Hollow Monk. "I know little of this place. The residents wouldn't grant me entrance."

"Yeah, well Snoots aren't much for piousness or rationality," I said. "They are more scholastically oriented in their pursuit of knowledge."

"We don't sound so different."

"Yes, you are. Different like night and day. You said Pious Rationality's main goal was to understand the Divine by hording material possessions and acquiring knowledge of the mundane."

"Correct."

"Well in general, Snoots don't believe in the Divine. And they horde knowledge to increase their status. They see less intelligent folk as inferior and treat them as such."

"Still doesn't sound too different," Lola threw in. The monk turned his hooded head in her direction, and though his face was obscured, he projected annoyance like Hawking radiation emitting from a black hole. The princess ignored him. "Can they ever horde too much knowledge? Or do their brainpans just explode after a while?"

I couldn't help but smile at that. "Snoot heads don't explode. The more knowledge a Snoot absorbs, the bigger his or her head swells. Eventually, their noggins get too large for their head-poles to support and the heaviness causes them to lean backwards, forcing their orbs and noses up in the air. It's crazy. They literally *have* to look down on folk to see them. That's why they moved out here."

"Why?" inquired Hollow Monk.

"Because it hardly ever rains. Rain is very deadly to Snoots because they walk around with their noses in the air like this," I mimicked walking around with a heavy head and my nose in the air to demonstrate. "It'll drown 'em outright."

"What of the tower itself?" Hollow Monk was very curious about the Snoots, which was very curious in and of itself.

"It's obviously a multi-floored structure. It has twenty-one floors, and each floor houses a specific field of study and each field has its own color.[32] Except for the bottom floor and the very top floor. The

---

[32] The colors are: Maize for the Agriculturalists, White for the Arts and Letters, Drab for Commerce and Accountancy (fitting I always thought) Lilac for Tooth Manipulators, Copper for the Consumptionists, Light Blue for the Educators, Orange for the Engineers, Russet for the Naturalists, Crimson for Humanities, Purple for Solicitors, Lemon for the Bibliophiles, Green for the physicians, Pink for the Musicians. Silver Grey for the Loquacious, Olive Green for druggists

bottom is where the Great Library is and the very top is where the Keeper of Knowledge lives."

"How is it you know so much about all of this?"

"I was a Snoot for a while. Still am, technically. I never got properly banished, just blacklisted by my field."

"For what?"

"I just…kind of…left one day."

"Was it an emotional break down?" asked Hollow Monk in a very head-shrinking tone.

"Of sorts. I couldn't stand acquiring knowledge just so I could brag about how smart I was. Plus, the conventions are real sleepers. Especially after lunch. Nap central. But I mainly left because I needed to empty my brain. Release my knowledge and turn it into wisdom."

"I see," said Hollow Monk. "Couldn't release come from imparting knowledge to others?"

"If only it were so easy. Snoots don't share knowledge with the pure intention of educating others. They use it as a platform to express their intellectual dominance. Not one Snoot has ever written an anonymous paper or given a presentation from behind a scrim. They do it to be noticed and recognized as Supreme Snoots. For then and only then are they conferred the coveted status of Master of Knowledge Piled High and Deep. But that doesn't release any knowledge; it just relieves pressure and makes them feel good for a while."

"Yeah, I think you're lying, Infinity Jones," Lola said, capping off the conversation, "That sounds like a place too boring even for you."[33]

Ignoring her, I gazed on that tower and a wash of unsettling, repressed memories flooded over me. "We should go around. I don't want them to see me."

After a detour around the smooth black monolith of Snoot Tower, we spent a harrowing four days in the desert during which we were brutalized by the arid landscape and violent weather. It was at

---

and the philosophers wore Dark Blue, The Categorizers wore Golden Yellow, the Theologists sported Scarlet robes and the animal docs like Gray.

[33] She was right. I was lying. I was a rather popular fugitive at that point. The Snoots put out a bounty years before Man Man ever did. And for good reason. My mission at their tower was one of espionage. I sought and won their most prized possession—the Orb of Power. But while in that place of dry knowledge and even drier humor, I learned much about who I didn't want to become. And oftentimes that is just as important as learning who you do want to become.

sunset on the fourth day that my tired band came upon the outskirts of a ruined city so old that stone and marble served as walls for the fallen monuments.

An eerie gloom blanketed the city. Nature had crept back in and, despite the arid landscape, a soft grass covered the ground within its borders. Shrubs, weeds, wild flowers, and even domestic flowers gone wild littered the cracks of the perfectly straight stone roads or hid amid the crumbling ruins that served as a reminder of civilization's temporal presence. Huge trees with leafy hands drew a canopy of foliage above that guarded against the angry heat of the sun and provided the city with its eldritch gloom. In certain places sunlight burst through that ominous ceiling of sylvan defiance and peppered the cityscape with soft radiance.

"What place is this?" asked Lola Fa Lona as we wandered the parameters of the city. Inscribed on the archway above a main entrance was the word, "Remembrance."

"An old place. A place that was here long before Shamus ever showed up and scorched everything. The Tree Folk whispered that this was the dwelling place of an ancient power: an oracle that showed you the future if you proved your courage."

"If you believe that sort of nonsense," Shamus snorted.

"You mean you didn't believe them?" asked Lola.

"Are you kidding? They were *Tree Folk*."

"So?"

"So, Tree Folk are superstitious by nature. Believing in spirits and magic and whatnot. But I figured there might be some truth to the legend, so I sent an archeological team in to investigate."

"What'd you find?"

"Nothing. They never returned."

"That doesn't bode well," whispered Hollow Monk.

"You think? I figured some rogue band of Tree Folk clipped them before they got back."

"Did you ever stop to think that maybe something clipped them when they got *here*?" asked Lola.

"Of course not," said Shamus defensively. "That would mean that—"

"Yeah, what?" challenged Fa Lona. "It would mean that the Tree Folk were *right*. And you couldn't have that could you?"

Shamus's complexion swelled into a fantastic shade of red giant (like the star) and he strode away from her in shameful silence.

"Nut-less Nancy!" Lola yelled after him.

"Leave him be," I said to the fuming princess. "At least he's learning."

"Is that what it takes for one selfish giant to learn? To ignore the utter death and destruction of everything around him? Is it really necessary for him to cause suffering just to learn from his own example later?"

"Yup. Unfortunately, that's the only way most folk learn, giant or otherwise. The problem with giants is that they can't help but make such an impact."

"Well, just because the Tree Folk were right, doesn't mean that McFamus was wrong," said Lola. "Those ruins are probably loaded with treasure and that treasure needs guarding. Monsters and traps make the best security for ancient treasures. Which is why the giant's teams never came back. They were probably those nancy rational types off on a quest to put their names on something they dug out of the ground. Like your Snoots. Never even occurred to them that there may be things here that wanted to kill them. Good thing I'm not that stupid. When do we go in?"

"*We* don't," I said. "Shamus does."

"Why does he get to?" complained the Ninja princess. "C'mon Infinity! Be fair!"

"I am being fair. This is something Shamus has to do by himself."

"But why?"

"Don't worry about it," I snapped and walked over to converse with Shamus in private. "It's your destiny to go inside."

"By myself?" worried the giant.

"Yes. This is your test."

"Why do I have to be tested now? And like this? Haven't I already been tested enough? C'mon Mr. Jones! I don't wanna traipse about some ruined city looking for an old dude to tell my fortune. Let's just send the Ninja in to root around for treasure and be on our way."

"I can't believe I'm hearing this! You know what? Forget it. Never mind. Don't even bother! Why don't you just sit here and whine some more? Maybe we *should* send Lola in." I stormed away fuming and unpacked my pigsled.

"I'll show you worthless," Shamus grumbled. "I'm no coward Mr. Jones!" he yelled at me.

"Prove it," I challenged.

"Fine. I will!" Shamus donned the turtle shell breastplate he'd claimed from Slither, grabbed his axe and plunged into the ruined cityscape of Remembrance in stoic silence.

I smiled. That was easy enough.

"So, what're we supposed to do?" asked Fa Lona.

"Wait."

"Well then that gives us time. Which one of you lazy jacks is brushing my hair?" Lola announced and plopped down where she stood.

Most of the buildings were once dwelling places for various deities or spirits. Some ruins were positive and gave off a warm and pleasant vibe. Others secreted negative energy and Shamus hurried past them lest he become consumed with their oppressive evil.

Shamus only traveled a short distance into the city when a creature spun right from the yarns of the darkest nightmares materialized from the shadows. It had the hind quarters of a hippopotamus, the body and front legs of a lion and if that isn't odd enough, it had the head of a crocodile to top it off. The beast halted in front of Shamus and growled.

"Welcome, intruder, to Remembrance," said the abnormality in a voice that sounded like rocks falling from a high cliff. "It has been a while since any have ventured near."

"Who are you?" demanded Shamus.

"Once, I was Ammit, Eater of the Dead. But since my banishment, I am the Fishmonger."[34]

"Well, Mr. Fishmonger, I seek the Oracle," McFamus proclaimed.

"It's *Miss* Fishmonger and if you want to see the Oracle, I must have proof of your worth."

"What kind of proof are you looking for? Like battles and fights and stuff? I just killed a dragon a few days back. This is his armor."

Ammit laughed, a strange choking sound. "Fascinating. I'm sure it was a struggle for survival, but the Oracle demands his own proof. You will be tested, your courage and ability driven to their limits. Do you accept?"

"I suppose," said Shamus.

"So be it. The outcome for this test is simple. If you win you will be granted audience with the oracle…if not, you die. Any queries?"

"No, no. That's pretty straight forward."

---

[34] Ammit's origins are well documented in the sacred texts of several Realms she has been banished from. What is less documented is her disposition since the banishment, which is considerably more pleasant than her reputation suggests. The Eater of the Dead was, in her prime, a genuine terror. The Fishmonger mostly just guards the ruins, argues with Pan about scheduling, and has developed a fondness for riceroot tea. Time changes everyone. Sometimes for the better.

"Good. Then let the test begin."

The universe shifted and Shamus stood in the center of a grassy field. In the near distance, the crumbling remains of many inns and hotels blighted the ancient cityscape. To the south of where he stood, he could make out the ruins of caravansaries huddled near the city's west gate.

"The Grand Marketplace," growled Ammit. The abnormal creature appeared beside Shamus. "Used to be the heart of the city. Folk traveled countless leagues to trade here. But those were the good old days, as they say in other Where's. Now, it serves as a field of battle. The ground where worth is tested."

"Who do I have to battle?"

"You're a hero, Shamus McFamus, and all heroes must defeat fantastic creatures of myth and legend. It's part of coming into your own."

"My own is fine where it is."

"Nonsense. Like most folk, you cannot see yourself as you truly are. Despite your progress, your own is still puny. Has the stench of weakness clinging to it…still reeks of uncertainty and indecision. Those are traits that will get you sent up the River Styx if you aren't wary. A hero cannot fear his Sacred Fish. He cannot hesitate as you are wont to do. A hero must fight! He overcomes adversity because he himself is an adversary of those seeking to impede his path. Best to perfume yourself in the sweet nectar of battle-sweat and wash away the weakness by bathing in the blood of your enemies."

"That's gross," said Shamus.

"That's life," retorted Ammit. "Your Wheel of Fate is spinning. Prepare to become a legend or die." The fishmonger blinked out of existence and Shamus was alone.

The trees above him rustled in a breeze that arose spontaneously into creation.

"Ahem," coughed a sudden voice at the giant's feet.

Shamus glanced down and noticed a small man dressed in a vest made of leaves and pants of brown grass. About his head was a crown of mistletoe resting lightly atop sharply pointed ears.

"Can I help you?"

"Oh you most certainly can," said the being. "You're Shamus, right?"

"Right," admitted the giant, "And you are?"

"Pan. I'm here to test your worth and all."

"You?" Shamus stammered in disbelief.

"I know, I know. It was a surprise to me too. Actually, I'm the substitute assessment advisor. The normal worth checker is actually a gigantic Cyclops covered in red tattoos with a huge horn jutting from his brow. Got these huge muscles, at least twice as big as yours. He carried this monstrous wooden club that must've been the size of an Ironwood Tree. And the club had these awesome metal spikes sticking out of it."

"Wow," said Shamus, "Pretty frightening."

"I know," agreed Pan. "He was quite an imposing figure."

"Apparently. So where is he?"

"Yeah…he couldn't make it on account of his untimely death."

"What happened?"

"Stabbed in the orb with his own horn. Nasty brawl last night during a game of dice at the local inn for guardian spirits and lost gods." Pan danced around making stabbing gestures in the air before him.

"Are you saying that *you* killed the Cyclops?"

"Of course I did," said Pan in a huff. "I don't tolerate cheaters. As a general rule."

Shamus gave the imp a slanted stare.

"What's the matter? Don't I look the part?" Fair's Child raised himself to his full height of three-feet and three-inches and flexed his tiny muscles in a display of machismo.

"No. No, I'm really not seeing it," admitted Shamus.

Pan scowled at Shamus as meanly as possible, "How bout now?"

"Nope. Not now, either. It is awfully cute, though."

Pan visibly deflated. "Cute? I'm not cute! How come everyone says I'm cute?"

Shamus shrugged, "Beats me. Look, I mean no disrespect, but can we move this along? How are you planning on testing my worth?"

"Well, I had this fantabulous battle planned where me and you slugged it out in grand form. I was going to throw magical barbles at you left and right and there were going to be these vines floating down from the sky. And when they touched you, they'd grab you tight like ropes and then sprout thorns that dug into your flesh."

"Sounds uncomfortable."

"Oh, I've been assured that it is. Anyway, then I was going to magic this crazy big plant monster into being that sprung up out of the ground and attacked you. It would've been brilliant I tell you! Brilliant! I was going to kick your teeny giant ass twixt your dopey giant ears."

"So, what happened?"

"I rewrote it."

"Rewrote it?"

"Yes! I can do that, you know. I have *license*…just don't tell Infinity Jones."

"How do you get license?"

"Rigorous training process. Most folk don't make it through alive."

"So, what's the rewrite? Even bigger plant monsters or something?"

"Pish! You wish! No. The plant monster was in no mood to fight seeing as how he hasn't been fed in a while. Instead, I've uncovered a game from other Realms that requires a true test of skill and courage. This game has brought nations to their knees and rerouted the very course of history itself."

"What is it?" asked Shamus.

"It is called Ping Pong to the Death!"

"Ping Pong? That doesn't sound very scary."

"Just you wait," Pan said and drew a barble from his mag. He took a few steps back and rolled the barble between Shamus and himself.

*Sing along, to my battle song,*
*Ping, ping, pong. Ping, ping pong.*
*Oh, it won't be long, it won't be long,*
*Ping, ping, pong. Ping, ping, pong,*
*'Fore you head is gone and I move along,*
*Ping, ping, pong. Ping, ping, pong. "*

Green glitter exploded from the tiny sphere with a brilliant flash of light and when it cleared, a green table appeared between Pan and Shamus. It was rectangular in shape and had white lines painted along the sides and down the middle. A small net was strung across the center of the table. On Pan's side sat a wooden bench that Shamus guessed would help Pan's height handicap.

Shamus noticed a small wooden paddle covered in a strange red material had appeared in his hand. It was almost spongy to the touch. "What is this?" he asked Pan.

"It's your paddle," Pan said as he hopped onto the bench. "See, you hit the ball back and forth with the paddles. The ball has to bounce once on your side before you can hit it back. You score a point if you hit the ball and the other person can't hit it back. We each get five serves. Whoever has the most points at the end, wins."

"What happens to the loser?"

"I'm going to chop off your head and feed it to my plant monster. I did mention he was hungry. Ready?"

"Rea—" Shamus's response was cut short when the ball delivered a powerful blow to his chest that knocked him off his feet. Hairline fractures spread quickly across the surface of his turtle shell breastplate and it fell to pieces around him.

"I call that one 'the zinger.' Can't trust armor too much. Has a tendency to fall to pieces when you're relying on it most. I hope that wasn't expensive," mocked Pan from across the table.

"No, it was only a priceless trophy gleaned from a battle that tested the very limits of my skill," Shamus said as he got to his feet and dusted himself off.

"Must've been a short battle. One point me. Ready?"

Pan immediately sent another ball zipping across the net. It slammed into the center of Shamus's side of the board like a tiny meteor.

Shamus tried to swing, but he was too slow. The barble deflected at a ninety-degree angle and flew off before Shamus had finished his swing.

"Two points me, zero points you," Pan cackled. "You really suck at this game!"

"Well, in my defense, I've never done this before."

"Whatever. That's the oldest excuse in the book. That one's been trashing up the Realm of Possibility since the days of the Chaos Unfolding.[35] You'd think the threat of imminent death would motivate you to play better." Pan shrugged it off, "Whatever, you can just stand there and die like the nancy you are. I'd actually prefer it."

Pan whacked the Ping Pong barble with his paddle and sent the third serve of the epic struggle of life and death over to Shamus.

Shamus hadn't taken Pan's comments well. He thought he *was* growing, that he *was* becoming more courageous. And here this shrimpy little miscreant was accusing him of nanciness because he was two points down at some alien game called Ping Pong.

*Don't take that from him,* huffed Commander Gali, *He's a scrawny Child of Fair! Show him just how giant you really are!*

This time, Shamus was ready. Anger sharpened his focus; and when Pan's barble came zipping toward him, he sent it flying back.

---

[35] The Chaos Unfolding was an early time just after the Great Nothing and Everything spoke the Realm into existence. Many gods and spirits roamed the Realm and the dark recesses outside its borders in those days and these supernatural powerhouses often battled for supremacy over the land and its fledgling folk.

Pan returned the barble and it hit on the very corner of Shamus's side of the table before it flew off into the darkness. "On the line is in," Pan chimed. "Three points me, zero points you! You just wanna give me your head now?"

Shamus glared at Fair's Child and hunkered down. "Serve," he said, a cold determination frosting his voice.

Pan obliged and the Ping Pong barble zipped through the air. Shamus returned the barble and the volley began. Pan zigged and Shamus zagged. Shamus crissed and Pan crossed. Pan went right and Shamus went left.

Paddles were naught but a blur of motion during this exercise in survival. Sweat began to pour from giant and elf alike and one stinging drop of sweat saved Shamus's life.

The mutinous bead of sweat charged from Pan's brow down his crinkled forehead. It was neatly rerouted and flowed down his temple, past his orbrow and into the corner of his ocular cavity. Salt dug into the little man's sensitive orb and he instinctively clenched it shut.

At that instant, Shamus returned the barble. The globe struck Pan's side of the table and flew past his closed orb. The trickster attempted a feeble swing, but missed horribly.

"Ha!" Shamus bellowed. "I got you!"

"You got lucky," pouted Pan, "I had something in my orball."

"Whatever. That's one of the oldest excuses in the book."

"Shut up," Pan snapped and served his last barble.

It bounced lazily on Shamus's side of the table. It was an easy return for Shamus and his overconfidence cost him. The ball bounced gingerly across the table and caught in the net.

"Four points to none," Pan said triumphantly. "Beat that."

"I will. Let me see one of those Ping Pong balls."

"It's a Ping Pong *barble* and it's already in your hand."

Shamus opened his left hand and discovered a bright silver ball resting in his palm. "Oh. Thanks." Shamus smacked the barble with wicked force and the true test began.


We set up camp at the oasis just outside the city walls. It had a fresh water well and we filled our water skins and tended to our swine mounts. As the sun set, we started a fire and prepared to wait for Shamus's return. We dined on a nice assortment of sweet cacti and some wild Desert Doves that Lola had killed with a few deft tosses of her throwing stars.

We were enjoying an after dinner riceroot tea when Lola perked up. "Hsst! Did you guys hear that?"

"Hear what?" whispered Hollow Monk.

"Sounded like something scraping against stone." She bolted erect and drew her blade in one smooth motion, scanning the area with her sharp vision.

"Maybe it was nothing. Maybe your ears were playing Tricksy on you," suggested Hollow Monk.

Lola whirled around to face the anti-holy man. "Listen here, I am a highly trained Ninja warrior! My ears *don't* play Tricksy on me! I *know* I heard something."

As if to prove Lola correct, five monstrous figures emerged from the gloom into the firelight. They were human in form, but not in entirety. From the shoulders down, the men were lean and bronzed like the desert dwellers who have chiseled a life out of the unforgiving landscape. But from the shoulders up, where human heads should be, were instead the heads of ibises!

The bird-headed horrors gripped smooth wooden spears that ended in points of barbed metal. On their belts hung wicked curved blades that were small, but quick and deadly in battle. They wore no clothes to speak of, save a loin cloth and some sandals. Around their head-poles, beautiful ornaments made of gold and other precious metals splayed out in a layered pattern, like scale mail, and fell about the creatures' chests.

"Now there's something you don't see every day!" I exclaimed, "Bird headed aberrations that reek of primitive grace. Fantastic! This'll make for great tale spinning!"

"I don't see what you're so happy about, Jones," said Fa Lona. "They'll probably kill us…well, kill you anyway. I'm sure I'll escape while they're distracted."

The Ibis-men spread out and surrounded us never letting their spear points out of striking range. The bird men made strange cooing noises, but they refused to attack.

"Get our backs to one another and gather round the fire," Goldie ordered.

"What's going on?" growled Lola. "Why don't they do something?"

"Maybe they're waiting for someone," I offered.

"Who?" asked Hollow Monk, "The Ibis Lord himself?"

"Perhaps," I said in all seriousness.

"I don't like the way they're orbing me," said Fa Lona. "They got freaky bug orbs." Her fingers twitched near her sheathed blade.

"Don't ya do it, princess," warned Goldie.

We heard the sound of someone or something approaching and the strange Ibis men grew quiet. Their solid black orbs rolled back and forth as Ammit stepped into the firelight. She was accompanied by a small brown ape holding a handful of rolled parchments.

"Welcome strangers, to Remembrance," growled Ammit in much the same way she growled at Shamus.

"Uh, just a small point of fact," said Hollow Monk. "But we aren't actually *in* Remembrance. We're just waiting for someone."

"I'm aware. The little giant," said the Fishmonger. "Indeed, at this very moment he struggles for his life against a most worthy opponent. Which is why we are here."

"Why's that?" asked Goldie.

"In the event that your boy loses, your lives are forfeit as well."

"What!" exploded Hollow Monk. "That's crazy! We only came here so that our companion may seek the Oracle's advice!"

"Indeed," said Ammit. "And in doing so you've decided to share his fate. We might as well make ourselves comfortable. We're going to be here a while. Got any more of that tea?"

The barble was a comet that left a tiny crater on the table's surface before it hummed neatly past Pan's ear.

"Hey! No fair! I wasn't ready!"

"That's weird," said Shamus, "You looked ready to me. That's one point to four."

Pan's almond-slanted orbs narrowed to dangerous slits. "That's fine," he said a bit too sweetly, "I'll give you that one."

Shamus's next two serves also ended in points. The first occurred after an exciting volley back and forth that ended when Pan drove the ball into the net. The second serve earned Shamus a point when Pan was unable to reach the barble despite an epic lunge on the elf's part that resulted in his tumbling off the bench.

Pan gathered himself up from the grassy ground. "I thought you said you've never played this before," he accused.

"I guess I just got motivated to live. Or maybe I'm just a natural at this Ping Pong game."

Pan snorted derisively. "You're a natural at being a weak-willed pansy. That's what you're a natural at."

Shamus smiled, "That's three points to four."

Shamus served and Pan's return was so quick that Shamus didn't have time to react. The ball bounced off the table and flew past Shamus with a zip.

"That's still three points to four. And this is your last serve. You nervous?"

Shamus didn't reply, he simply served. He struck the ball with all the strength he could muster. The barble landed on Pan's side of the table and deflected toward the wide-orbbed elf's forehead. Pan ducked and swung. The barble didn't even flinch. It flew through Pan's paddle like an asteroid through a dust cloud and left a smoking hole in the center.

"That makes it four points to four points. Looks like we tied."

"We did no such thing!" Pan yelled. "You cheated with your super strength!"

"I don't have super strength! I'm just better than you," retorted Shamus.

"Is that so?"

"That's so."

"We'll see about that. The tiebreaker is one game of hunter-bearninja[36] winner takes all."

Shamus nodded in agreement.

The Ping Pong table disappeared in a puff of silver smoke and light. Shamus and Pan stood back-to-back.

"Before we do this, I think I should tell you that I've never lost a game of hunterbearninja in all my centuries of life," bragged Pan.

"Neither have I," Shamus lied. He was actually awful at hunter-bearninja and hated the game entirely. But the Wheels of Fate spin equally making princes into paupers and vice versa. Much of life is hinged on how the Wheels turn and Shamus's Wheel was overdue for a fortunate spin.

"Ready?" Pan asked.

"Ready," Shamus said.

"One, two, three! Hunterbearninja!" both combatants shouted and whirled around to face each other.

Pan posed as the bear and Shamus as the hunter.

"Hunter kills bear!" Shamus yelled triumphantly. "I win! I win-nnnn!"

"By all the Incarnations of Princess Plum!" swore Pan. The little man waved his hand and a miniature guillotine appeared before him.

---

[36] This game is played much the same way that parchmentdaggerstone is played except it requires more physical action on the participants' parts. The participants stand back-to-back and yell "hunter, bear, ninja," simultaneously and then do a 180 degree jump in which they face their opponent and make their pose. Hunter holds the crossbow and kills bear. Bear raises claws into the air and growls and kills Ninja. Ninja adopts a fighting stance and slays hunter.

He pathetically flopped to his knees and laid his head in the crook. "Just pull the rope and get it done with," he instructed Shamus.

"I really don't feel like I should kill you after that game. There was no real combat involved. It doesn't seem…honorable."

Pan twisted his neck like a corkscrew so he could see Shamus. "You won and those were the rules."

"Can't we change the rules?"

Pan sighed in disgust. "Change the—? No. Forget it, I'll do it myself!" The elfin miscreant unwound his head and reached for the release rope that dangled just out of reach "Will you hand that to me please?"

The giant reluctantly obliged and Pan jerked the rope. The blade fell swiftly and Pan's head dropped into a nicely woven wicker basket on the opposite side of the guillotine made especially for catching severed heads.

"Now why did he have to go and do that?" Shamus wondered aloud.

"Cuz I *had* to," chirped the severed head from the basket. "Contractually bound to follow my own rules. The Oracle is a real jackass about those sorts of things." While he talked, the trickster's headless body rose and walked around the guillotine. It retrieved Pan's head from the basket and placed it in the crook of his arm. "Shamus McFamus, you've proven your worth and may advance to the Oracle," the fairy's head said sulkily. Without another word, Pan's body spun around and marched into the shadow shrouded city of Remembrance.


"It is done," said the ape abruptly. He strode forward and laid the scrolls at my feet. "These are for each of you. The Oracle speaks through these written words." That being said, he turned his back on us and melted into the shadows with the Ibis men and Ammit following on his heels.

"Who was the monkey?" asked Lola.

"Not sure," I admitted. "My best guess is that he was an incarnation of the Oracle. He appears in different forms," I said as collected the parchments at my feet.

The scrolls were addressed to us individually and I handed everyone their own.

"What do ya think they say?" asked Goldie.

"Probably just some stupid crap like a fortune cookie," said Fa Lona. "That's all this seeing into the future stuff is. Crap." She unrolled her scroll. "Hey!" she squealed, "The paper is blank! What a jip!" As soon as she finished that statement, her orbs glazed over and the Red Dragon Ninja actually grew quiet for a while. Pictures sprang up in her mind's gaze and flashed across her imagination while an ancient voice echoed inside her head.

"You are a true Ninja with skill possessed by few."

"Tell me something I don't know," said Fa Lona.

"As you wish. You mourn the loss of your Harmony in vain. The power to reclaim it has always been within your grasp. Disharmony reigns in ancestral lands. Your clans of old are no more. The ravages of Man Man have seen to that. Even as I speak, two new clans have risen from the chaos. Yin and Yang. They battle each other with bloodlust in their hearts. Each trying to win dominance over the other. Balance must be restored. Heed this: To correct disharmony you must forge a bond with ancient foes. The Oracle's voice faded away and the Ninja princess snapped out of her daze.

"Whoa," she sighed, "You guys gotta try that!"

Hollow Monk looked at his scroll, then to Fa Lona, then back at his scroll. If he had a face, we would've seen him swallow a lump in his throat and then break the parchment's seal.

"The Void inside you is a gaping maw, faithless one," said the Oracle. "You've paid dearly for your lessons."

"I have," agreed the cleric.

"And yet your debt is yet to be completed. You seek the return of your faith, of your true faith?"

"I do."

"Then you must pass through many Trials of Fire to prove your worth."

"Haven't I been through enough? I've learned. I've changed. I've tested the very edge of reality and then fell over."

"You have done these things. However, your trials are not over as long as you remain a slave to cold logic. Understand that the Realms don't run according to logic and reason alone. Within the countless Realms, many things exist outside the scope of rationality. The rational brain accepts this. The rational brain understands its own limitations and welcomes the chance to expand said boundaries. Heed this: Ignoring the unexplained doesn't mean that it doesn't exist, it just strengthens ignorance."

"Well?" Fa Lona snatched the scroll from Hollow Monk's hands, "Yours is blank too! Did you see it? Did it talk to you?"

"It did," admitted the monk.

"And? What did it say?"

"Sentimental hogwash."

"That doesn't sound like the Oracle," said the Orb, "As a matter of fact, that's offensive to Oracle-kind. Open yours next, Jones."

So I did. And a thick darkness fell upon my vision. Out of that darkness spoke the Oracle's voice.

"Black is the color of oblivion, of forgetting, of things uncreated. It is the color of disgrace, defeat and shame. This is what we must endure. We who were once a proud race of beings generous and terrible each in our own right. Then slowly came the shadow, whispering deceits among us. One by one we became angered and bitter toward our own. Weakened by this, the Usurper was able to sweep over us like a purifying plague. White is his colour. The square his shape. He seeks to structure and contain. He has no use for compromise, so unnervingly proud is His ego. The Usurper he calls himself because that is what he desires to be. But he forgets that immortality cannot be unmade. So he banishes us instead. He emptied Hades so we could have a prison to occupy. All of us. Many of my Brothers and Sisters and I now find ourselves bound to this land of perpetual shadow. Cloaked in black to announce our disgrace, our fall, we wander this bleak landscape relentlessly mourning the loss of our children."

"That's terrible," I said aloud, and my words fell like stones in that blackness.

"So it is. The Usurper still battles, although the number of his enemies quickly dwindles. He is powerful and cunning after all these aeons. But his watchfulness over his prison grows lax from arrogance. Thus, my Ilk and I are sometimes able to escape."

"So there are others like you."

"Indeed. Those of us who escaped fled into the many realms of legend and imagination to wait, to sleep, to recover ourselves. Ammit and I chose to guard this resting place and wait."

"Wait for what," I asked.

"Those secrets aren't for the ears of men,"

"Fine. Keep your secrets. The only secret I wanted an answer for was about the Orb, the millstone around my neck."

"That's not very nice," said the Orb.

"You seek answers to the Orb of Power, Infinity Jones. Answers I cannot give."

"What is this crap? That's no answer!"

"Do not profane holy ground. You asked for wisdom and I gave you a truth: all lives are a story, Young Infinity."

"So then my life has become part of this story?"

"Yes, and many others besides. You've yet to see that and understand your part as a man chosen to remember the stories we write."

"I hope it went better for you than it did for me," said Hollow Monk as I returned to the waking world.

"It probably told him what an insufferable jerk he was," said Lola, "That's why his face looks like he just ate a raw lemon."

Goldie looked at us and her face set in determination. "Whatever it is, I need to see it." And she unrolled her scroll.

"You've lived a warrior's life. Ferocity. Determination. Loyalty. These are your defining traits, Goldie Lox. You cling to them at night when sadness and loss threaten you with tears. You call upon these strengths to raise the warrior within. You use them in order to survive. Yours is a paradoxical existence. Your pain is monumental and only matched by your will to live. You bear the loss of your loved ones as chains around your heart."

The hardened warrior's tough countenance cracked and tears began to fill the fissures of her pain with soothing waters.

"Don't worry. Your pain will soon be relieved. Heed this: Emotions are cruel overlords. You must rule them lest they rule you."

I never expected to see Goldie cry, she didn't have that constitution. But cry she did. Tears flowed unbidden down her cheeks as she stared off into the middle distance while the Oracle delivered its message. When she looked at us, I saw behind her mask to the real woman who she tried to keep hidden. And let me tell you, that woman had a beauty that couldn't be rivaled.

We didn't say anything after the scrolls. We simply sat around the fire, lost in our own thoughts, awaiting Shamus.


Shamus entered the Temple of the Oracle. Out of all the buildings in the city, this temple remained the most intact and continually glowed with a soft, unreamly light. Walking through the doorway caused tiny pinpricks of energy to race up and down Shamus's spine.

"Hello?" he called into the still air.

"Greetings and congratulations, brave Shamus," spoke a voice from everywhere and nowhere at once. The fabric of reality in front of Shamus ripped and a majestic figure stepped out of the Nothingness. The Oracle was dressed in flowing white robes and also bore the head of an ibis. However, sprouting from atop the Oracle's head were two curved horns that magically suspended a crescent moon between them. In his left hand he held a scepter and, in his right, he grasped an ankh.

Shamus's knees gave out from fright and he fell to the ground. "Who—who are you?" he stammered without looking up.

"In other Realms and earlier times, I was Tehuti. I was representative of the Divine Intelligence, master of art and science. It was I who uttered the words of creation.

"But those times are no more and I have been forced to find sanctuary in other places. Thus, I came to be here. Now, I am the Oracle and it is my duty to test the mettle of Realmly folk and bestow the worthy with the gift of foreknowledge. History cannot be made without my guidance. I am an inevitable destination on the paths of all true heroes and adventurers."

"I'm not trying to make history," said Shamus.

"But history is trying to make *you*, young giant. Now rise and receive your gift."

Shamus rose to his feet, but kept his head bowed.

"Your mind seeks to end the tyranny you have allowed to grow, but your heart seeks other answers. It wishes to know if you will ever regain your former stature, does it not?"

"Yeah. How'd you know?" asked Shamus.

"There is little that escapes my sight. But be warned. Stature is not measured by physical size alone. It is greatly measured by one's willingness to accept his destiny with a steady heart. Do you understand?"

"Yes," mumbled Shamus.

"Good. Now in order to regain your stature, you must undo Man Man's evil."

"How?" challenged Shamus.

"Start by destroying the *Express Go!*™ refinery to staunch the flow. Without *Express Go!*™ saturating the land, Man Man's control and size won't be so total. He will become vulnerable."

"But if I destroy the refinery, that's going to destroy the hard work and lives of my folk," countered Shamus.

"They aren't your folk anymore," the Oracle pointed out. "Man Man is controlling the Shamusans with his devious potions and they no longer have the capacity for long term memory. They only remember you in vague legends distorted by Man Man in an attempt to demonize you."

"But even if the land isn't mine anymore it still bears *my* name. It was my dream that drew the Shamusans to the ULS and my prodding that led them to their descent into addiction. I am still responsible for them. What's going to happen to the populace when their reality disintegrates before their very orbs?"

"The society's bottom will fall out and the folk will come crashing down with it. The whole place will turn into forced a rehab center.

The entire country will come to a screeching halt. Chaos. Anarchy. Revolution. But you have seen worse. What Man Man has done to the Shamusans is a fate much worse than any fate to arise from the ashes of Chaos. Indeed, there is sacrifice, but at least their lives and their Sacred Fish would be theirs once more."

"Shouldn't they have that choice?" asked Shamus.

"They have no choice now, so you must choose for them. Would you rather they spend the rest of their existence trapped in a lifeless daze or would you rather liberate them, though the cost is great, that they may regain their Sacred Fish?"

Shamus underwent a visible internal struggle and finally broke down. "Alright. You're right. They are my folk and I set out to undo Man Man's evil. That's what must be done…at any cost."

"There is greatness for you yet, giant. And love too… you are on the path returning to your past. This path leads to sorrow but ends in peace. Your Sacred Fish is your true self. He will guide you to destiny. Heed this: The means to end the scourge can be found with Skittle-shanks the Gnome." That said, the Oracle dissipated and everything went white.

We awoke, though we didn't remember going to sleep, and found we were camped at a small oasis some leagues from the City of Lost Causes. The oasis was strangely devoid of any travelers or nomads, save us. We took this as a reward from the Oracle and spent a languid morning packing camp and tending to our teams of pigs. Off in the distance, the outline of the City of Lost Causes shimmered in the heat—a touching monument to forlorn hopes.

The city was nestled in the grip of the barren Muerto Mountains that loomed precariously above it like skeletal claws threatening to close at a moment's notice.

"The City of Lost Causes!" exclaimed Lola, "I don't believe it!"

"Neither do I," muttered Hollow Monk, "Perhaps a wormhole…" He wandered over and absently took down his tent, mumbling to himself.

"All this stuff is going to drive him crazy," said Shamus sympathetically.

"He was already crazy," I said. "He's just trying to stay that way."

"So did you get to see the Oracle?" Lola asked Shamus.

"Yes."

"What'd he say?"

"He said that we had to destroy the *Express Go!*™ refinery and stop Man Man's totality of control."

"What!" exclaimed Hollow Monk from across camp. He stalked over to where the rest of us were standing. "That's insanity! That's crazy talk! Just think of the consequences!"

"I have," said Shamus somberly. "And it *has* to be done. It's the only chance we have."

"You'll kill us all! And for what? The mutterings of some pagan degenerate?" He turned his shadowed face toward the heavens. "Oh mighty He, why have you cast my lot with these insane miscreants?"

"I can't believe you. Where I'm from, monks like you are killed for public sport." Lola turned to me. "So what are we going to do now?"

"Well, if we really have to shut down the refinery, we need inside the city. We gotta get to the road and get in line," I said and pointed off in the distance where a great mass of color stretched from the city's gate into the desert.

"What's that?"

"The Trans-Aridia Trade Route. The only road into the city and through the desert. Not surprisingly, the route is preyed upon by bands of vicious bandits who are in turn preyed upon by clans of merciless desert nomads. They appear in great clouds of dust and disappear before it settles. This makes the road dangerous and the few oases that dot the desert landscape are downright deadly. The trade caravans that slowly lug goods or slaves across miles of open desert are easy targets for the swift horses and sharp blades of the bandits. For this reason, caravans arm themselves heavily and travel with as many folk as possible in order to better defend against attack. As you can see, they tend to arrive at once and congest the city."

"Well, we can't just run up there and get in line. Think about it: ya guys are wanted criminals heading into a hive of mercenaries and bounty hunters who'd love to collect," Goldie reminded us.

"No worries," I said and dug my stage makeup out of my sack, "We'll just get dressed up. That should serve us until we can get to an inn."

Shamus was disguised as a dragon bounty hunter. Goldie was an island-dwelling strong woman, and I was magicked into a young nobleman styled after the fashion of the City of Allure. Lola was a gypsy acrobat, and Hollow Monk once again refused the makeup, citing reasons relating to the safety and security of my Sacred Fish or some such gnomesense.


Our tiny band merged with the great river of beings inching along at a disgustingly slow pace. Instantly our senses were assaulted with the multicultural soup before us. The crowd was a perfect menagerie of the Realm's inhabitants. Sun-hardened nomads dressed in loose garments and turbans stood alongside pale nobles in velvet jackets and frilly shirts. Ninja clans rubbed shoulders with Outlanders. Here and there, dragons towered above the crowd, and a few Cuddlies darted amongst the forest of legs grown by the throng of pilgrims.

The Chattering Winds couldn't compete with the cacophony of languages assaulting the air like an apostolic miracle. The gruff barbaric dialect of the Frozen Folk danced with the lilting language of the Winged Folk from the Place Where Angels Die. The lazy Outlandish dialect clashed with the sharp and angry sounding language of the High Azens. Cuddlies sang, dragons roared, horses whinnied and camels spit.

Riding on either side of the road, to keep order and defend against any brazen bandits, were some of the Queen's guardsmen mounted atop Armored Toads.[37] The guards were tanned dark from a lifetime in the desert, with crops of dusty brown hair and faces devoid of sympathy or mercy. All that remained in their orbs was the evil glow of smoldering hate. The guardsmen wore chain shirts emblazoned with a bright green sword piercing a golden sun (the Queen of Swords's coat of arms) and carried nasty looking spears. On their hips they boasted wicked rapiers rightly dubbed, "Scorpion's Tails," for their points were coated with a deadly poison.

The Armored Toads were squat creatures with spikes of varying browns covering their bodies from head to tail. Despite their apparent encumbrance and squat statures, Armored Toads were quick and could use their tongues like deadly whips. These filthy monstrosities ruled over the desert's Shimmering Dunes and were known for slaughtering any parties unfortunate enough to cross their path.[38]

"There's all sorts of folk trying to get in here," said Shamus from his vantage point above most of the crowd.

"Well," began Hollow Monk. His voice took on a magniloquent tone as he geared up for another one of his sermon/lectures, "bastions of Sin and Debauchery such as this have a tendency to attract a particular type of element. As a result, racial and cultural barriers are often overlooked. Don't get me wrong though, I'm sure the city's populace is divided into cultural sub-groups and some of those most likely interact exclusively with their own ilk. This tendency stems from the necessity of survival. In a place such as this, weaker folk wouldn't last long on their own. They would naturally seek out others like them or attempt to find a group to accept them. They develop trust for

---

[37] Armored Toads are native to the Shimmering Dunes and are among the more peculiar creatures the Realm has produced. They grow naturally occurring plates of calcified hide that cover their backs and shoulders like a saddle built by someone who has never sat a horse. The Queen of Swords's cavalry discovered early on that Armored Toads could not be domesticated, reasoned with, bribed, or frightened. They could, however, be given something to chase. The cavalry still considers this a victory. The Toads are indifferent to the arrangement.

[38] The Shimmering Dunes are located in the middle of the Desert of Lost Causes. There the sands are pure white and shimmer in the sunlight like dazzling jewels. And indeed there are jewels there. Very rare Star Jewels that are craved by many for their aesthetic, healing, and magical properties. Armored Toads roam here and attack any who try to explore the Shimmering Dunes.

their new clique and that trust in turn mutates into distrust for any outside the group."

"Holy Hooded Honchos! Will ya shut up? Frigging walking encyclopedia," growled Goldie. "That nonsense don't do us no good!"

"The ignorant scorn the opportunity for knowledge," retorted the monk. "And there is no need for blasphemy."

"Hey!" exclaimed Fa Lona. Her ears perked up. "I hear Azen! Can you guys see where they are?"

"Up ahead a ways," said Shamus, "I can see three of them."

"I need to talk to them. Be right back."

I stopped Fa Lona. "That's not a good idea."

"And why not?" she snapped.

"Cuz. The guards won't let you out of line and those ahead of us would just as soon gut you as let you go before them. Best wait till we get inside."

"Gah! That's stupid! I'm not trying to cut in line. I'd come right back," she whined.

"Just chill out ya little brat," Goldie chastised.

Lola glared at Goldie and spun around to ignore us.

After countless hours in line, we finally passed through the gates of the fabled metropolis. Folk stuffed the narrow cobblestone streets and it took me a bit to reacclimatize myself with their unsettling civil planning. The maze-like city streets were ideal for trapping unsuspecting outsiders and travelers, making visitors easy prey for the local denizens. Some say the Queen had designed it that way. Remember the motto inscribe above the city's gates? "Survival first, Civility later." Now you know why I don't trust talking alleys.

The City of Lost Causes was a massive cluster of tightly packed buildings. Most of the buildings were single-story adobe structures with flat roofs. However, merchant houses and some of the more reputable inns rose three stories high and were constructed of imported stone and wood. Above them, noble houses erected with expensive marble and even rarer woods spread across the barren foothills that skirted the palace.

The Palace of Swords was fashioned entirely of polished crystal that intensely reflected the sunlight. Looking directly at it was nigh impossible during most of the daylight hours. At night, the palace emitted a cold gray light from within. Here, the Queen of Swords plotted wicked fates for her subjects, and her only daughter sighed at the moon, longing for naught but uncomplicated happiness.

The refinery rested on the banks of the River of Destiny and the waters around it had taken on an odd iridescent property, much like dragon's hair. Trees clustered abundant near the riverbank and offered some cover from prying orbs. The refinery itself was a square metal structure with gigantic cylinders stretching high into the air constantly puking black smoke. Wafting on the dry desert breeze, this smoke birthed the foulest stench to ever rage against one's nostrils, causing an instant gag reflex.

The side facing the city was lined with huge bay doors from which streamed scores of wagons constantly being loaded with crates marked *Express Go!*™. Workers entered through huge double doors from the south as drones would enter a hive. To the north spanned a stone lot littered with all kinds of fancy carriages. The entire structure was surrounded by a five-foot wall.

"Ack!" spat Goldie, "That smell is awful."

"It is," agreed Lola.

Shamus inhaled deeply. "That's the smell of incomprehensible amounts of dingle."

"How do folk stand it?"

"The workers all wear masks to cover their noses and mouths. So do the guards. The cityfolk become nose blind after a while."

"How many guards?" Goldie asked.

"I'm guessing at least thirty after that stunt with the Big Rigs."

Lola consciously ignored the comment.

"And some of those are undoubtedly patrolling with dogs. Beyond that, I can't tell you," Shamus finished.

"This ain't gonna be easy," Goldie said.


High above our heroes, the Queen of Swords stood at the windows of her chambers overlooking the city from her palace of crystal. Trembling viziers loitered in corners and shadows, avoiding direct orb contact with the Queen as best they could. At her feet, the headless corpse of a messenger slowly spread a pool of blood. The Queen hadn't taken the news of the Big Rigs well.

"I'm telling you! I don't trust that weasel, Man Man!" The Queen of Swords paced her throne room in vexation. Servants scurried in to remove the corpse and mop up the blood. "He's building an army of mindless drones and spreading his material influence Realm-wide. He's got plans!"

"My queen, might I suggest something?" asked a trembling vizier. Much like messengers with bad news, many a vizier had fallen under the queen's blade when delivering unpleasant tidings or making bold suggestions. They had to choose their utterances carefully and even then, their safety was never guaranteed. They lived under constant threat of spontaneous decapitation. This is why they trembled incessantly.

"As you please," the Queen of Swords waved a nonchalant hand and gazed out a large window overlooking her city.

"Man Man is our ally. His refinery offers jobs and stimulates our economy, not to mention it supplies him with *Express Go!*™ and a nice dingle profit. Surely, he wouldn't risk such an important asset."

"You speak foolishly," retorted the queen and the vizier flinched. "*Shamus McFamus* was my ally and he was usurped by Man Man. I know enough never to trust a usurper. They are vipers lying in wait to strike. The destruction of the Big Rigs has set back production at the refinery, and I fear Man Man will use this as an excuse to plot some retaliatory action. Then where will we be? I sense the Wheels of Fate have spun in another direction. We must prepare."


"I'm gonna find my kinsmen and maybe pick up some dingle lying around," Lola said and melted into the crowd before I could protest.

"We need to find a place to stay!" roared Goldie above the din.

"I know of a place. Follow me!" I yelled back and began to fight my way through the crowd.

"The Forked Tongue" was located near the city's south wall.[39] An old structure, it stood a mighty three stories tall and boasted some of the best desert ale in the entire Realm. The inn was constructed purely from polished birch wood and had a two-tone paint job, red and black. The proprietress was a female dragon hailing from the Outlands named Sibilance.

As far as dragons go, she was high class and beautiful. She was a Draco (the tailless dragons) covered in smooth emerald green scales that sparkled seductively in the dim light. Deep green orbs accentuated hair that fell in iridescent waves down her back. She stood a curvaceous seven and a half feet tall, her lithe form swaying under a satin slip-dress.

The Forked Tongue's large common room housed many wooden tables and benches that had seen a barroom brawl or two. Huge

---

[39] The Forked Tongue is the finest establishment in the City of Lost Causes that one can enter without being recognized as a wanted person. This is not because it is particularly reputable. It is because Sibilance, its keeper, has a long-standing policy of aggressive non-observation regarding the identities of her guests. This policy has served both parties well for a number of solar spins. It would continue to do so right up until the day it didn't. That day would come soon.

lanterns suspended from the rafters offered little light but plenty of smoke.

"Last time I was here, the west steps took you down to the gambling room and the north steps took you up to the...*private* rooms. The doors by the bar lead to the boarding rooms," I explained as we made our way to the bar tended by Sibilance.

"Well what have we here?" hummed Sibilance as my troupe approached the front desk.

"Evening madam," I said in a fake accent, "My company and I require lodging. What have you to offer?"

Sibilance orbbed me closely and sniffed the air. "Infinity Jonez," she said, "You can hide your appearanze, but not your szent. I'm hurt you would fool me..." Her natural speech impediment had been corrected when she was a child—a sure sign of a well-to-do dragon.

"Now lady, take no offence," I dropped my accent, "but the disguise is necessary."

"Of courze," she purred, "I have offerz for your capture hanging on my wall." She pointed to the wanted posters casually. Our bounty increased to fifteen thousand dingle a piece and we were now wanted in connection with the destruction of the Big Rigs.

"Well, well. Getting more popular by the day it seems," I said. "That being the case, we need discreet lodging and stabling for our pigs while we take care of some things."

"Pigz?" queried Sibilance. "How iz it you ride zwine?"

"This one here did us the favor of becoming the champion of a certain plains-dwelling tribe," I said and motioned toward Shamus. "And they outfitted our party so their champion wouldn't be wanting."

"Shampion eh?" Sibilance's tongue flickered lustily across her lips. "Of courze I can howze you dizcreetly. How can I expect your payment? In dingle? Or..." she sized up Shamus with the avaricious hunger of a cannibal orbbing a missionary. "You know, that one makez a good dragon."

It was then I realized we didn't have any dingle. "I, well, let's see what we have," I stammered and dug through my pack looking for items to barter.

Sibilance was orbin' Shamus the entire time.

"Look," I pulled the giant aside and whispered, "we don't have any dingle. You may have to take one for the team."

Shamus gulped. "Umm...please no. She looks like she could hurt me."

"Oh, she can and probably will," I admitted. "But once you get through the pain, the pleasure is pretty intense."

A wild uncertainty sprang up in Shamus's orbs. Fear lined with morbid curiosity. "I don't know…"

"Dammit man! We need a place to stay and this is it! We don't have any dingle and no one else will house us without turning us in."

"But, but, but—"

"Is this enough?" Lola appeared beside me as if by magic and hefted a large sack of dingle on the counter.

Shamus's sigh of relief was none too tactful.

Sibilance picked up the dangle and tested its weight. "Yez, thiz'll do," she said with the faintest tone of disappointment in her refined voice. She laid keys on the bar and motioned towards the doors on the left. "Back there," she said and returned to tending her bar.

After we had a moment to settle in, we met in the common room to discuss our next plan of action over a bit of dinner and some ale.

"So how we gonna do this?" asked Goldie. "Sounds like way too many folk and weaponry for a smash-em-up job."

"Yeah, that's where I come in," said Shamus. "The Oracle told me that a Gnome named Skittleshanks could help."

"You've got to be kidding! That makes absolutely no sense!" I exclaimed in exasperation. "You mean to say that the only being in the entire Realm of Possibility capable of helping us is a Gnome? And Skittleshanks the Gnome at that!"

"What's wrong with him?" asked Shamus.

"'Gnomes are Gnomes are nasty little jackals,' my grandmammy used to say. They're obsessive collectors and ruthless businessmen who would cut off their beards before they cut you a deal. Fair's Folk may be guilty of harboring vexing tendencies and using Tricksy, but Gnomes…There's a reason they were banished, you know?"

"So you fault them for being wily businessmen?" asked Hollow Monk.

"No. I don't fault them for being wily businessmen," I sneered, "I fault them because centuries ago Gnomes managed to hoard nearly all of the Realm's Enchanted Whatnots and Secret Potion Recipes. Their obsessive and possessive natures dominated the market and gave them an unfair advantage over their natural enemies, the Elves, not to mention everyone else. When greed and power-lust consumed them, the nasty little buggers attempted to conquer the Realm. Did no one listen in ancient history class or what?"

"That's not history, Jones, that's a creative legend," informed Hollow Monk.

"Legends are history. They're just a more interesting version of it," I corrected. "Now as I was saying, the Gnomes declared war on the Realm and would've certainly been victorious if the Pantheons hadn't intervened. In order to even things out, the gods shifted the Elves and Gnomes to Over There. It was the only thing they could do. You see, Magical Whatnots and Potions are non-universal and by shifting the Gnomes to another universe, the gods effectively stripped them of their unfair advantage."

"But why the Elves too? I mean, it was the Gnomes who cheated, right?" asked Shamus.

"Yeah, but then the whole Realm of Possibility would be overrun with Elves. There'd be nothing to keep them in check. Trust me, nobody wants that. So, the Pantheon of Chaos willingly banished the Gnomes and in return, the Pantheon of Order willingly banished the Elves. There you have it."

"So what's that have to do with Skittleshanks?" asked Shamus.

"Everything! Skittleshanks is a Gnome who escaped Over There and returned to Here. Not only that, the wind whispers that Skittleshanks traded his Sacred Fish to the evil He That Is In Grammatical Error in exchange for his escape. That means he's a devious and dangerous Fishless fugitive living in a city full of desperate folk and thieves."

"Do you know him?" asked Shamus.

"Yeah, I know him," I admitted. "I've run into him a few times during my travels. He's not easy to find. I'll take you tomorrow. We'll use the makeup to get around." However, I wasn't pleased about it. I absolutely hate dealing with Gnomes. "Stupid Oracle sending us after stupid Gnomes," I mumbled into my clay mug of desert-ale.

Skittleshanks's shop was truly a place of artificial wonder. Shelves covered every available inch of the small building and floor space, naught but a skinny walkway, was arranged around large gizmos of wild imagination.

"I wonder what this is?" Shamus examined a miniature carving of a horse-drawn covered wagon.

"That, sir, is an interesting item, indeed. It happens to be an *Instant Wagon*," said a very small man with an extremely long white beard. He wore a sharp blue suit and a matching brimless hat. "You say the words and the statue instantly comes alive! Great for nifty escapes from unpleasant scenarios, if you get my drift." The Gnome playfully nudged Shamus's knee. "That's odd. Your scales don't feel like scales! They feel like skin!" Once Skittleshanks realized the stage makeup's Tricksy, it was no longer effective on him. "Enchanted stage makeup? Honestly! Does anyone still expect that to work?"

"It has up till now," said Shamus defensively.

"Why, you *do* look familiar," he studied Shamus, "Give me a moment and I'll place you." He turned to me and recognition lit his face. "Infinity Jones! I thought I smelled the stench of Fair's Tricksy! Worse than the smoke the refinery burps. No matter. Now, what did I do to deserve such a fortuitous visit?"

"Are you Skittleshanks?" asked Shamus.

"Why yes I am," said the Gnome with a dramatic bow. "And you must be Infinity's traveling companion in crime, the wee-giant Shamus McFamus. There! I told you I'd get it!"

"So, you know of our bounty?" I asked.

"Who in the city doesn't? Your mugs are posted in every public building and on every street corner from here to the riverbank. *Someone* wants you very badly." He looked us with calculating scrutiny and his gaze fell to the Orb around my neck. "Why, is it true? Can it be the Orb of Power? Here? In my humble shop? And in your bumbling possession?"

I grasped the Orb defensively. "Aye. Tis. And you'll have none of it, you rancid scoundrel!"

"Tell that creature to keep it's orbs off me," snapped the Orb, "Or else I'll turn it inside out and leave it for the crows."

"Testy artifact you have there, Jones."

"Tell me about it."

"Don't worry. I'm not asking for it. I know its history and its curse. You are welcome to both. I have no desire to bear it." However, that reassurance didn't keep him from gazing lustily at the artifact.

*That's it! I've had it! I will not be treated like a common bauble!*

"I'm sure you'd sell it before you bore it," I said and tucked the Orb into my tunic before it could sling any hurtful insults. Gnomes are notoriously sensitive.

"You know me well, Mr. Jones. So, what brings you into my domain today, gentlemen?" the Gnome asked, turning the conversation on a dime that seemed a bit more cheerful than his orbs admitted.

"I was told you could help us," said Shamus.

"Oh? Were you now? And what were you told I could help you with?"

"We need to fix a problem."

"So mysterious," said the Gnome. "Need to fix a problem, do you? Now I wonder what problem that could be? What problem could the wanted *former*-CEO of Shamuscorp and a wandering rogue scholar possibly have in the City of Lost Causes? Unless…of course! Your usurper holds quite an important asset here, doesn't he, Mr. McFamus? And with the 'mysterious' destruction of the Big Rigs a week ago, tis that much more important now, isn't it?" Skittleshanks cackled. "I'm afraid your informant was correct. I have just what you need."

"I'm afraid of that too," I said.

"Tut, tut, Mr. Jones. Follow me." We followed him to the counter. "Wait here," he said and disappeared into the back room. The Gnome returned moments later holding an obsidian box about the size of Shamus's palm. He sat the box on the counter and carefully undid the clasps. Inside was a statue of an ivory elephant painted pink.

"What is it?" Shamus asked.

"What does it look like?" snapped the Gnome. "It's a Pink Elephant."

"What does it do?"

"It gets ignored."

"That's stupid. What's so bad about this elephant that everyone wants to ignore it so much?" Shamus asked skeptically.

"No one wants to be connected to it for fear of humiliation and utter ruination of their reputation. Let's ask our somewhat noble friend, Infinity Jones, to enlighten us. What is worse: An acne bubble on the night of Winter's Ball or a Big Fat Pink Elephant in the middle of the room?"

"The Pink Elephant," I admitted begrudgingly.

"See? I told you," Skittleshanks said to Shamus. "You ever tried getting things done with a Pink Elephant in the room? Doesn't happen. Folk put all their energy and effort into ignoring that embarrassing Pink Elephant in the middle of the room. And does it go away? No! It literally feeds off the lack of attention. It grows and grows until it completely fills up the place. And here's the juicy part: once the elephant gets so big, it's impossible to ignore. When that happens there're two options. The first involves finding scapegoats to pin the whole thing on. Sacrifices, if you will. The whole blame is cast upon them and they are tossed at the feet of the Pink Elephant. They die in shame so that more important folk can continue to live in hypocrisy."

"And the second?" asked Shamus.

"The second option is more fun in my opinion. It involves no sacrifice at all. The Pink Elephant just explodes in everyone's face…figuratively speaking of course. No outright violence to speak of. Though violence does usually follow on its heels. Humiliation and public ruination do tend to infuriate the pompous and popular. And such things can only be quelled through gratuitous violence."

"Fascinating. I'll take it," Shamus said.

"Great! That'll be fifteen thousand dingle," said Skittleshanks. "Shall I wrap it up for you?"

"Fifteen…Um, Skittleshanks, sir, I don't have fifteen thousand dingle."

"Is that so?" asked Skittleshanks with a wicked gleam in his orbs. "Why, surely you have true blue friends who would happily loan you such an amount. I mean this is an important purchase. Saving the Realm from evil despots and all…"

I shook my head, "I'm broke."

"What a surprise," said the Gnome with undisguised contempt. "But it just so happens that I *could* use a hand picking up a few items I'm seeking…nothing hard really. Just make a few stops to pick them up from their previous owners. In return, I'll *give* you the elephant. How's that sound?"

"Sounds like a trap," said Shamus. He'd certainly learned from his dealings with Man Man.

Skittleshanks raised his hands, palms out, in a pathetic attempt at innocence, "I protest, sir! Here I am trying to help out disadvantaged amigos by getting nothing more for this rare artifact than having a few minor errands run and you accuse me of treachery!"

"Right. I'm not so foolish."

"Why then, allow me to prove my good intentions. I need three items picked up. In return I'll give you three items from my store. The Pink Elephant, of course, plus the *Instant Wagon* and this nifty box of snake pellets." The Gnome placed a wooden box decorated with a black cobra on the counter. "Simply put fire to a pellet and a deadly Black Desert Cobra rises from the flames to attack your enemies."

"I'm still not sure about this. What do you think, Jones?"

"I think we'd be foolish to think we have any other choice. That's the way these things are constructed, you know."

"What you lack in wealth of dingle you make up for in abundance of wisdom," Skittleshanks told me with a bow. I was almost certain he mocked me, but you can never be sure with Gnomes. By the gods, I do hate them so.

"Fine. I accept your offer," Shamus informed Skittleshanks and gathered his new possessions off the counter.

"Good. First things first." The Gnome produced a stack of papers and handed them to Shamus.

"What's this?"

"Purchase order for *Express Go!*™. Need you to pick up a shipment from the plant. Routine stuff really. I have an account, so there's no need for payment right away. Plus, it'll get you inside."

"Why do you need a shipment?"

"Are you kidding? 'Inside sources' tell me *Express Go!*™ is about to become a very rare commodity. And I want to be on the receiving end of the dingle flow. Is there anything else?"

"Yeah," I said. "Got any barbles to trade?"

Skittleshank's face lit up. "Why, I most certainly do!" He produced a fancy mag from beneath his front counter which he rummaged around in until he retrieved a sparkling marble with a deep green spiral in its center. "Bet you never seen this before."

"What is it?"

"It's called 'Nature's Avatar.' Got it off of Pan a while back in exchange for reconnecting his head to his body."

"What's it do?"

"Summons a rain cloud that makes a wrathful plant monster grow and slay your enemies, or some such stuff. The monster withers after the rain stops. Bout ten ticks of the tock. One caveat, it is hungry and as such, in a very foul mood."

"Interesting. I'll trade you a Dream Weaver for it."

The Gnome thought for a while. "Deal," he said finally.

We exchanged barbles and Skittleshanks disappeared into his back room.

"He wasn't *so* bad," Shamus said as we left the shop.

"Yeah, well, we haven't had to 'run his errands' yet," I retorted.


"What are we going to do with a stupid statue of a Pink Elephant?" yelled Fa Lona. She had been irate ever since Shamus and I returned from Skittleshanks's with our meager loot.

"It's the only way it can work," explained Shamus.

"Whatever. He could've given you a big fat bomb!"

"How many times do I have to say it? I'll not be responsible for killing the innocent and oblivious! I'm done with it!" roared Shamus.

"Screw them! It's what they get for being involved. No one forced them to work there!" The Ninja's orbs flashed with Yang.

"Let's all calm down," I interrupted. "The Pink Elephant is a good option. Stories say that it was created by an evil vizier sorcerer in order to overthrow his Outlandish sultan. He was going to place it beneath the sultan's throne and discreetly leave before it blew up. Then he'd return to pick up the pieces and claim the throne. But on the night before he was to hide the elephant, the vizier was murdered by the sultan himself."

"Why?" asked Fa Lona. Shamus was forgotten as her natural curiosity led her elsewhere.

"Because the sultan desired the vizier's only daughter. She was a beauty above beauties. A rare treasure. The sultan sought to include her in his harem. A desire her father was not keen on filling for his master."

"So, in an ironic twist of fate, the sultan's greed saved him from the greed of others," Hollow Monk said.

"Basically," I concurred.

"Not a good lesson for the young ones."

"Yeah. But that's how it went and that's how it goes. Anyway, the Pink Elephant has seen much political and social intrigue in its illustrious history. The mere mention of its name can make an emperor's brow bead with sweat."

"Will it work," asked the monk, "Or is it just a legend?"

"Only one way to find out now," I said.

The plan was simple. We'd use Shamus's *Instant Wagon* and Skittleshanks's purchase order to gain entry to the plant via the loading docks. Goldie would drive the cart, Hollow Monk would ride crossbow, and Shamus would ride in the back. Lola and I would position ourselves in trees just outside the gate and serve as a distraction if things blew up. Shamus would plant the elephant while he loaded the wagon and leave as if nothing had happened. We'd deliver Skittleshanks's order and head for the Forked Tongue, holing up there while we waited for history to be made. Simple right?

The morning of the caper, Shamus summoned his *Instant Wagon* into being. Two beautifully white Clydesdales lumbered into existence tethered to a large ironwood wagon with huge wheels. The whitewashed wagon was a good fifteen feet long and seven feet wide and covered with a huge tarp after the fashion of settlers' wagons.

I only had a single application of stage makeup left and we decided it'd best be used on Shamus to disguise him as an Ergo slave. "You're Ergo name is Groll. Don't forget it." I handed Shamus the bearskin loincloth and iron shackles he was to don for his role.

"What're these for?" he asked.

"They're your Ergo costume."

"A loincloth and some manacles? Surely you jest."

"If only, dear giant. If only. Authenticity is the key. As you may or may not know, Ergo hail from the Barbarian Tundra. Thus, a dense coat of hair carpets their bodies for warmth and protection. The loincloth is more for decency's sake. However, they have been known to kill Frost Bears for the sheer joy of it, hence the manacles."

"Where did you get them?"

"Sibilance."

Shamus opened his mouth for an undoubtedly tactless question, but I stopped him short. "Don't ask."

"Well, where am I supposed to hide the elephant?"

I shrugged. "I'll leave that for you to decide. Be creative."

The giant took his costume with a grumble and went to change.

The wagon rolled up to the loading gate and stopped at the command of two guards. One bearing the markings of a sergeant approached Hollow Monk.

"Purchase order?"

Hollow Monk handed the sergeant the purchase order and the officer scanned it over. "Twenty-five barrels to Gnomesense Distribution? That's quite an increase from your last order."

"The boss's been doing well fer himself," growled Goldie. "Is there a problem with that?" Her good orb dug into the guard's comfort level like a burrowing mite.

"No. No problem at all," said the sergeant, clearing his throat. He returned the purchase order to Hollow Monk and quickly motioned the wagon through.

"That was close," Hollow Monk whispered as they pulled up to the docks.

"Shhh! Holy Screaming Loins! Are ya trying to get us popped?" Goldie snapped.

Goldie let the wagon's tailgate down and Shamus bumbled out in his loincloth and chains. Meanwhile, Hollow Monk handed the purchase order to the dock manager for review.

The manager glanced over the documents and motioned Shamus and Goldie to follow him inside the plant. The floor manager directed the pair to a stack of *Express Go!*™ barrels and returned to his business, leaving Shamus and Goldie unattended.

The inside of the foundry was a technical marvel henceforth unseen in the Realm. Big Rigs dumped Black Sludge into a large main tank. From there, it was distributed through a convoluted series of pipes to various hydrotreaters and vacuum tanks where the Sludge was refined with chemicals and complicated processes. From those smaller tanks, the refined Sludge was pumped into numerous types of holding containers. Some tanks held *Express Go!*™ while other's held lamp oils, supercharged hay juice, and zing that had been chemically solidified or compressed into a gas.

The refinery bustled with activity. Workers rushed around in a frenzy checking meters, product quality and equipment operation. No one seemed to notice Goldie and Shamus standing around like slack-jawed yokels.

"What now?" asked Shamus before he loaded the last barrel onto the wagon. "Where do we hide it?"

"In plain sight. Put it right there next to that big tank," Goldie whispered back.

Shamus knelt down near the main tank and deftly set the elephant on the floor. Instantly, folks' gazes shifted to avoid the sight of the

Pink Elephant. They absolutely refused to look upon or acknowledge the enchanted pachyderm that had appeared in their midst. The area around the Pink Elephant became a magical ground zero and easily tripled in size as workers went out of their way to skirt the wretched artifact.

The job done, Shamus and Goldie climbed onto the wagon and made for the gate only to be held up by a small regiment of angry guards that spread out and surrounded the conspirators. Three guardsmen bearing crossbows aimed at Goldie and Hollow Monk stood on the loading docks. In the distance the excited baying of large dogs pierced the air and grew incrementally closer.

"Where do you think you're going?" growled the sergeant.

"Um, we're leaving," said Goldie. "We got our product. Now we deliver it. Do ya'll mind?" She tried to urge the horses on, but the sergeant grabbed the bridle.

"Actually, we do mind. Just a quick question. What were you doing on the work floor inside?"

"Just checking things out," Goldie explained nonchalantly. "Never really seen the inside of the place. Heard it was some kind of marvel. Just wanted to get a peep at it, ya know?"

"That's odd. Because shortly after you 'just checked things out' the workers became very tense and distracted. Any guesses as to why?"

During the interrogation, guardsmen herded a constant stream of other wagons inside the yard and out the gates in a calm and timely manner.

Goldie looked at Hollow Monk and the cleric shrugged. "Maybe they need a long weekend?"

"Or maybe you left something. Turn around and come with us. We'll get this figured out once we get the dogs here. Close the gates and pull them off that wagon!" yelled the sergeant.


Lola and I saw a guard run out of the plant and whisper something to the sergeant. The sergeant reacted by gathering his men and surrounding the wagon as Goldie tried to leave. All the other wagons were escorted out the gates. We couldn't hear the conversation, but what we saw told us plenty. After a brief exchange, the guards swarmed the wagon. Goldie drew her pellet shooter and fired at the first guard that tried to pull her from her seat. The sentry fell backward with a smoking hole twixt his orbs. The rest of the guards redoubled their efforts and Goldie and Hollow Monk soon fought to keep from getting pulled to the ground. In a few short ticks, our companions would be captive and our simple plan ruined.

"We've got to get them out of there. They'll be offered up as scapegoats for sure," I said.

"Here," said Lola and handed me a squishy barble from her belt pouch. "Don't look at it, just throw it."

"What is it?"

"Maiden's orb. Throw them at the gates!"

We tossed the Maiden's orbs at the closing gate. They splattered against the gate immediately transforming it into slabs of stone that ground to a halt. The egress had closed about half way, which was just enough space to fit the lumbering wagon through.

"Well, that was my idea," said Lola. "What you got?"

I quickly drew my newly acquired barble and spoke the words that would release the magic as I threw it inside the refinery's fence.

> *"Green is Gold*
> *Fire is wet*
> *Future's told*
> *Avatar's met!"*

Within moments, a miniature cumulus cloud gathered directly overhead and rain began to fall. A humanoid shape sculpted from convoluted foliage grew from the ground in thick serpentine strands. Arms and legs became distinct, a large round head lifted slowly, and two glowing orbs alight with the fury of Mother Earth opened with singular purpose. Once the plant monster had grown to fifteen feet, it ripped its rooted legs out of the ground with a howl and attacked.

"Sound the alarm!" screamed the sergeant. Three strikes of a gong signaled the highest level of urgency among the refinery's regiment—full-scale assault.

Every last man in the *Express Go!*™ plant's garrison converged on the loading docks to battle with the unnatural threat. It was an ugly fray. Weapons were nigh useless against the monster's pliant flesh and the frantic attacks of the guards only served to infuriate the horrible abnormality further. It attacked savagely, knocking guards hither and thither or gathering them up and ripping off their heads with all the ease of uncorking a bottle. Blood mingled with magical rain and the ground was soon awash with muddy crimson brooks.

Goldie exploited the commotion and charged recklessly through the gates deflecting the desperate blows of guards trying to halt the wagon. A flurry of bolts ripped the tarp to shreds, but the wagon and its passengers remained intact. The sergeant gave hasty orders to mount pursuit before he was scooped up and dismembered by Gaia's angry son.

"C'mon!" I shouted to Lola. "The plant monster will wither once the rain stops. Follow the wagon!"


"Chariots!" Shamus roared soon after they'd broken free of the gates and began their hectic flight to safety.

Two bronze chariots manned by a pilot and a crossbowman and pulled by a pair of Armored Toads quickly closed the gap with the wagon. The mobile platforms had blades extending from their axels that added a high-pitched whirring sound to the low rumbling of the wheels.

Thinking quickly, Shamus heaved a barrel of *Express Go!*™ into the path of their pursers. The chariot drivers dodged the splintered debris with expert precision and spurred their mounts on with a wicked smile. Shamus tried again with two consecutive barrels. Again, the charioteers deftly maneuvered away from his attack and drove the scuttling toads parallel with the wagon.

"Monk! Behind you!" Shamus warned.

Hollow Monk looked back and discovered a chariot bearing down on him. The cleric swung out with his oak staff and caught the pilot under the chin. The man went sprawling to the ground and his chariot crashed into a nearby merchant's stall.

The remaining chariot pulled up beside Goldie. The crossbowman fired while the pilot tried to direct the blades into the nearest horse's prone legs. Goldie veered the steed away, but not before taking a crossbow bolt in her side. The gruff innkeeper slumped over and would have lost the reins if not for an impressive grab by Hollow Monk.

Shamus saw Goldie's injury and his vision turned red. With a powerful roar, he leapt from the back of the wagon and onto the chariot, knocking the passenger under the horses' pounding hooves. The ironwood wagon passed over the guard with little more than a rough jolt, but his mangled mass became tangled in the chariot's light weight wheels. The moving platform toppled over, spilling the pilot and Shamus to the ground in a cloud of dust. The frantic Armored Toads righted themselves and sprinted off dragging the broken chariot behind them.

The chariot crashed near the Bazaar and the commotion gathered a curious crowd which hemmed in Shamus and the pilot, hoping to force a bit of action. Some of the more civic minded spectators called for guards, but the din of the Bazaar muffled their shouts.

Shamus and the remaining charioteer faced each other—two vaqueros in a standoff. The smothering presence of battle tension filled the air, and the crowd urged the combatants into a fray. The driver drew his Scorpion's Tail and lunged at Shamus with brash assurance.

Shamus flung his hands up and blind luck caused the point of the Scorpion's Tail to deflect off the iron manacles on his wrists. Before the guard could attack again, Shamus introduced the bit of chain between his manacles to the guard's head. Steel links caved in the soldier's temple with a crunching sound and the guard collapsed in a heap.

*You're getting better*, said Commander Gali. *We'll make a warrior out of you yet, Shamus.*

The crowd gasped and muttered, for they saw an Ergo slave attack one of the Queen's guardsmen, the penalty for which was death. A few of the grizzlier looking men growled and threatened to overtake Shamus. Blades were drawn and Shamus found his circle getting smaller by the moment.

Lola and I came upon the scene in the nick of time. We shoved our way through the throng of bystanders (hoping no one would recognize us) and found Shamus standing over the dead guar frantically searching for a way past the vigilante mob.

"Groll!" I shouted at Shamus and marched over to where he stood. "Bad Ergo! You know it is forbidden to slay within the city! Do you know who this man is?" I pointed to the dead guard.

Shamus played along and shook his head stupidly.

"He was one of the Queen of Swords's guardsmen! They will want your head for this! Come. We best get you to the guard station and turn you in before I lose my head as well." I motioned for Lola to grab Shamus's chains and she complied, but not without shooting me a dirty look for bossing her around.

The crowd reluctantly dispersed and we walked calmly toward the Bazaar until the sound of barking dogs reached our ears. At which point calm walking was replaced with frantic sprinting into the first alley we saw. We hid in tense silence, waiting for pursuit.

If anything, the Queen's goons were persistent. I suspect they feared death at her hands more than death at the hands of others. I barely had time to unlock Shamus's manacles and hand him his axe (I had strapped it to my own back, just in case. I like to plan ahead) before Lola sensed danger.

"Hsst," warned Fa Lona and raised a closed fist, "Guards coming! They have mutts with their noses to the ground!"

"They're coming from this way too," Shamus informed us as he peered around the other end of the alley.

The dogs barked and pulled at their chains as the guards neared our hiding place. We'd soon be boxed in.

"Up!" Lola snapped and used her ninja claws to scale the side of the nearest building. Shamus boosted me, but before he had a chance to climb, the guards and their dogs flooded the narrow space from each outlet.

"Go!" he roared at us. He drew his axe in a flash, the runes crackling and sizzling with anticipation. An unnatural battle lust entered the giant and Shamus's Sacred Fish seized the moment to act accordingly and further sharpen Shamus's dulled battle-sense.

The double-bladed war axe became a blur of blue-gold metal. The giant quickly decapitated the first dog to lunge at him and took its master's left leg with the deadly backswing of that magical axe.

"We better make sure the giant doesn't get himself sent to the coffin farm," said Lola. Her orbs flashed with Yang and she drew her throwing stars.

The Red Dragon Ninja laughed while she rained deadly steel on the foes behind Shamus. The guards tried to retaliate, but their crossbow bolts clattered harmlessly against the side of the two-story building that served as mine and Lola's perch. When the hapless guards and their dogs had fallen prey to Lola's disharmony, she jumped nimbly to the ground and retrieved her weapons (and any valuables) from the corpses.

Shamus deflected the attack of the remaining dog with the flat of his axe blade and buffeted the guard upside the head with a meaty left fist.

Lola jumped in and finished off the stunned dog with a cackle of Yang-ish glee.

The dazed guard turned tail and fled into the Bazaar, but a quick toss of Lola's shuriken ended his life.

"Let's go," said Fa Lona, "I've already cleaned the dead of dingle and valuables."


We navigated our way through the Bazaar's expansive ocean of folk to Skittleshanks's shop and were immediately set upon by the infuriated Gnome.

"Are you jacks crazy?" he screeched. "I asked you to pick up an order, not instigate a skirmish! Dead guards? Plant monsters (he shot me a deadly glare)? An investigation will surely follow. And if that isn't bad enough, I'm three barrels short! Who's going to explain that?"

"Well, you see," started Shamus, "When the chariots attacked, I had to distract them."

"And you 'distracted' them by tossing *my Express Go!*™ out the back of the wagon?"

"Well…yeah," the giant admitted. "It was all I had on hand."

Skittleshanks screeched again. The sound was the culmination of all the anger and frustration simmering just beneath his salesman's veneer. All it really takes to push someone over the edge is a gentle shove in the right direction. Fate and momentum take care of the rest.

"I suppose you have the city patrol hot on your tails?"

"Not so much," said Shamus. "I mean, we did, but we kinda threw them off."

"How?" asked the Gnome.

"We killed them in a dark alley."

"No survivors? No way my description could get out?"

"No," stated Fa Lona. "Ensure a finished product; this is the way of the Red Dragon Ninja."

Skittleshanks nodded in approval. "Alright, follow me. Your companions await you in the store room."

The back room of Skittleshanks's commercial super-store was a huge warehouse filled from ceiling to floor with aisles upon aisles of shelves loaded down with an eclectic menagerie of trinkets. The whole place had an air of vast cluttering and could potentially arouse sensations of claustrophobia if one were to wander for too long.

The *Express Go!*™ kegs were neatly stacked near the large bay doors that served as the back entrance and the wagon was conspicuously absent. Goldie lay on the floor doing her best to staunch the flow of blood from her torso and Hollow Monk paced about nervously muttering to himself.

"I can't heal it," he kept repeating.

"Let me take a look," I offered and leaned down to examine our wounded friend.

The bolt had pierced Goldie between her ribs. It missed her lung, but that was little consolation. Every slight movement caused the battle-hardened widow to wince in pain and the pool of blood around her grew a bit larger. "I can't pull it. Went too deep," she inspected the wound with the expert gaze of a battlefield veteran, "I'll bleed out like stuck swine. Can ya fix me, Infinity Jones? Like I saw ya fix Shamus?"

"I can. But it'll be painful. The body isn't meant to be mended magically. It's unnatural."

"I don't care. Do it," she said through gritted teeth.

I took a moment to gather the Energy into my hands before I grasped the bolt and yanked it from between her ribs. Instantly, blood began spurting from the wound like a fountain. I quickly pressed down on the puncture with my right hand and visualized the wound closing like the old gypsy had taught me.

Goldie cried out in agony as the magic seized the wound. Tiny threads of golden energy acted as stitches and began to repair and pull the flesh back together. The puncture sealed within a minute and the mercenary collapsed into a deep sleep brought on as a result of the magical healing.

"Now what, Mr. Jones?" worried Shamus.

"Now, we need to get back to the Forked Tongue with an unconscious woman."

Slither's drakehood (that's childhood for dragons) was tumultuous at best. As I mentioned before, he was low class. That much was obvious from his sibilant speech and chosen profession. I'm not trying to water down facts with circular pussyfooting here, that's just how it was. Class distinctions are an inevitability of life in my Realm and, I dare say, in your Realm too. Once social structure is established, it has to be maintained at all costs. Folk who step outside the conventional boundaries of society are ostracized from the rest of the herd. That's the way it goes. Conform or die!

As a result, folk subvert their individuality and place others above themselves in order to have a place in the hierarchal bubble of society. Sadly, the very nature of such bubbles doesn't promote equality. The strong are leaders and lawmakers while the weak are followers and subject to the laws of their leaders. The powerful gain prestige and are recorded in legends; the weak fade into oblivion without so much as a nod given in memory of their service.

Slither had a chip on his shoulder for this very reason. His father was a humble potter with extraordinary talent. In fact, Faust's father had quiet desires to revolutionize the potting industry with the invention of an "unbreakable pot." You'd think this'd be a good invention—a useful one that saved precious resources. But Those in Charge saw it differently. You see, when folk have dingle on the brain that's all they can think about. Dingle this, dingle that, dingle, dingle, dingle! There's a saying that goes, "Not even the sun would rise if he weren't making dingle for it."[40]

Those in Charge didn't care about the usefulness of the unbreakable pot. They reasoned that if everyone had unbreakable pots the potter's industry would be put in dire straits.

"Broken pots keep potters in business," Those in Charge mumbled amongst themselves while smoking fine cigars and drinking cognac in their private clubs.

---

[40] Incidentally, I once asked the sun about the remark and he told me: "I work for purpose, not dingle. And if dingle is your purpose, well, that is vapid purpose indeed." Then he burned me for asking such a foolish question. I maintain it was worth it. The sun, whatever else one might say, does not mince words. But I digress.

That statement is an outright lie. Broken pots kept potters busy with menial work and never gave them the chance to improve themselves or their craft. They could've made all sorts of other things: unbreakable plates, mugs, aqueducts, and etc. and actually improved Realmers' quality of life. But it's not about improving the quality of life; it's about improving the size of dingle hordes.

All of this became apparent to Potter Faust as he tried to sell his unbreakable pot. The frustrated potter voiced his discontent, quietly at first, and when no one listened he grew louder and louder until his ranting threatened to pop the social bubble and he gained the attention of Those in Charge. When a bounty was issued for the capture of Potter Faust, the fugitive gathered his wife and son and fled to the City of Lost Causes to hide and start anew.

Initially, the sight of his father's wanted posters put a heavy lump of fear in the bottom of Slither's stomach. But before long, cogs began to turn in his reptilian think-sponge. He rationalized that Those in Charge were very powerful and influential and lesser folk would believe and follow their dictates out of ignorance and fear. This didn't bode well for revolutionary potters or their families. Slither concluded that if you can't beat them, you best join them in hopes of getting close enough to knife them as they slept.

Understanding this, the Drake Slither turned his own father over to the authorities and even attended the public execution with his mother. With the small bounty he received for his fratricide, Slither bought a sword and began his infamous career as a bounty hunter. As Slither grew so did his skill and reputation. By the time he was a youngly adult dragon, he had secured a position as the most ruthless and feared bounty hunter in the Realm. Of course, this reputation did absolutely nothing to aid him in scaling social ladders.

Slither realized too late that Those in Charge thoroughly enjoyed being as such and wouldn't readily step aside to share their position with a dragon potter's son turned bounty hunter. Slither was merely another pawn to be manipulated by the Powers that Be. At best, the bounty hunter was placated and tolerated because of his usefulness, much like a ferocious guard dog. But as soon as he was no longer useful, Slither knew Those in Charge wouldn't think twice about disposing of him. The effects of this epiphany were twofold. It enlightened Slither and infuriated him. Those in Charge *had* to pay. Slither *must* have his vengeance!

Cold and evil orbs opened to absolute darkness. Slither almost panicked—almost. He'd been buried alive, that much was obvious. And without a coffin to speak of. What an insult! Folk would pay for that disgrace. Slowly, with claws fueled by revenge, Faust dug himself out of his premature grave and burst into the cool night air with a mighty roar.

The Chopsilians had dumped Slither's body in a shallow grave far outside of their village. The tiny tribesmen didn't roast the dragon's carcass because they were fearful that ingesting the flesh would infect them with his evil. Their superstitious fear ended up being the death of them. Anyone who is three plus one knows that dragons regenerate unless you burn them or hack their bodies into small pieces.

The Chopsilian sentries heard Faust's bellow and scurried to the chief's hut to relay their discovery with fear-soaked words. The chief immediately ordered a running team to find and inform Shamus. The rest of the small tribe was broken into two groups. The women, children and elderly were led by the shaman and some braves to the Hidden Places to seek the protection of the Great Boar. Any male Chopsilians of fighting age were armed and awaited their deaths with a primitive acceptance.

It certainly didn't take long for the Pink Elephant in the room to do its job exactly as Skittleshanks said it would.

All the guards involved in the fiasco had been killed during the battle, leaving no witnesses to accuse my troupe of involvement. After things settled down, Those in Charge of the refinery gave everyone an extended weekend. Upon returning to work, whisperings of the Pink Elephant's origins began to circulate. At first the workers believed the plant monster *was* the Pink Elephant, but when the elephant didn't leave the building after the Avatar dissipated, that idea was quickly discarded. Before long, wild theories and conspiracies cropped up and the Pink Elephant's appearance was blamed on everyone from Man Man to the Snoots, but no concrete evidence was ever uncovered. The refinery workers eventually buckled down and returned to work, wary but determined to move on. They managed to ignore the elephant for a while, but the more the proles ignored the elephant the bigger it grew, until the "you-know-what" was constantly in their faces despite attempts to overlook it. Fearing they would be blamed for the elephant's continued growth and presence and thus sacrificed to it, the workers quit in droves.

…And the Pink Elephant continued to grow…

Eventually, the rumors of the "you-know-what" found their way into the haunts and alehouses of the refinery's proles.

Here's a conversation I overheard:

"Did you hear about the refinery?" a drunken worker asked a silk merchant over ales at the pub.

"No. I've only arrived in town. What of it?"

"A scandal has broken out."

"Verily? Do tell."

The prole leaned in very close and whispered into the merchant's ear, "A 'you-know-what' has shown up."

"From where?"

"No one knows, though many have ventured to say. It all started with an attack by some kind of plant monster. After that, things got so bad that us workers had to leave our jobs. But you mustn't breathe a word of this to another Sacred Fish."

"My lips are sealed," said the merchant somberly and finished his ale.

The silk merchant rushed right home and told his wife who told her friend, the Queen of Swords's personal cook. The cook told the queen's dress maker who told the queen's lady in waiting who told the viziers who finally whispered it into the ears of the Queen of Swords, Matriarch of the City of Lost Causes.

"What?" the Queen bellowed and sprung from her throne. "First the assault on the refinery and now this?"

The viziers cowered before her, "We are sorry, oh mighty queen. We know not how it came to be. But the 'you-know-what' is growing at a mighty rate. Something must be done. We must find some escaped goats to throw at its feet before all is lost."

"I'll do no such thing! I told you fools! I told you and you refused to hear me! As I said before, Man Man cannot be trusted. This is his fault and his doing! It's his plant, let him fix it. Send him word demanding a sacrifice before this thing blows up in everyone's face!"

...And the Pink Elephant continued to grow...


When the workers fled, the floor masters and managers quickly followed suit. No working-class proles wanted a job at the refinery for fear of the Pink Elephant and the consequences that being too close to it could bring. Having no proles to work for them, management had the daunting task of running the refinery themselves. They quickly became overwhelmed with the daily operations of the plant and lack of proper manpower. Not to mention the looming and imposing presence of the Pink Elephant constantly at the fringes of their awareness. Management quit out of exasperation and sheer exhaustion.

Those in Charge could do naught but sweat nervously, watching as the "you-know-what" sought to overtake their lofty offices of plush luxury. When the floormasters fled, Those in Charge blamed one another. Not surprisingly, none were willing to go down with the ship. Having no lesser goats to scape, they liquidated their assets and left the city.

The Pink Elephant completely swallowed the *Express Go!*™ refinery a few days after Those in Charge fled. The small, pink statue had grown into a veritable behemoth perpetually on the edges of the citizens' vision and a tense desperation gripped the City of Lost Causes. Sacrifices had to be made lest the Pink Elephant explode over the entire city.


"Um sire," Media Tron said into Man Man's ear. She was a plain looking woman, not unattractive, but not stunning. Pale brown hair cropped off at her slender shoulders and she wore a well-tailored suit much as a man would. Her job was to be the voice of Man Man since he'd grown too big to speak directly to his subjects without bursting their ears. Folk literally ran in terror at the sound of his mighty intonations.

The evil peddler's orbs slid open, "What is it?"

"It appears there is a…problem with the refinery."

"Problem? What problem?"

"Whispers of a…'you-know-what'…"

"No!" Man Man gasped. "From where?"

"Not sure. It appeared unexpectedly a few days ago. It happened shortly after a skirmish with a magical foliage monster that led to the death of the refinery's entire garrison."

"Foliage monster? Strange…Those words don't fit well together. Something else must be going on. Send a team of Peanuts out to investigate and retrieve whatever *Express Go!*™ remains. We'll need to stockpile lest I lose influence. What of the Queen?"

"Well, she's furious. The refinery vice presidents have all fled the city and the 'you-know-what' has grown exponentially over the past few days. It's starting to affect other areas of the city. The time is drawing near that it will demand sacrifice. She fears ruin and demands you supply an escaped goat to throw at its feet."

"Hmmm…No, that won't do. We're taking an official stance of noninvolvement. We'll send her some dingle to aid her in her time of need. Beyond that I have no part in this. Nor do I have any knowledge of whatever it is. Just in case, amass a small regiment of Gaunties on the border of the Desert. They'll act as a warning buffer if Pandora comes to play."

"Most Omnipotent Master, perhaps that isn't such a wise idea. The Queen is threatening—"

"That is all, Tron." Man Man's orbs slid shut.

"Yes milord." Media Tron bowed and left.

...And the Pink Elephant continued to grow...


We barricaded ourselves in our rooms while waiting for things to cool down. I called a meeting in Goldie's room to check on her progress and discuss our next plan of action. Goldie had recovered nicely. She was still tender and moved with a bit of stiffness, but all in all, One-Orb Goldie was back in full form with an impressive scar to add to her collection. During her recovery, Shamus had rarely left her side. He repaid her earlier gentleness with some of his own. Once Goldie regained consciousness, she and Shamus could be heard talking and giggling like love sick schoolmates. The low rumble of Shamus's voice would permeate through the walls and then be shattered by Goldie's robust laughter. The rest of us suspected something was brewing betwixt the unlikely pair. Needless to say, I was astounded, Lola was dumbfounded, and Hollow Monk was confounded. We thought it best to leave it be.

"When are we leaving the city?" asked Fa Lona.

"I've still got to get a couple of things for Skittleshanks for letting us have the elephant," said Shamus.

"I didn't make that deal," retorted Lola matter-of-factly. "That's on you. I've got to get my Harmony back. The Oracle told me it was in High Azen, so that's where I'm going."

"Just like that? You'd abandon us?" asked Shamus a bit heartbroken.

"I'm not abandoning anyone. You are all welcome to come along...even the monk," she conceded, though she did so through clenched teeth.

"I've got to see this through. Can't you wait for just a bit longer?"

"No," said the princess.

We all looked expectantly at Shamus.

The giant shuffled his feet and stammered for a bit before he made a decision. "I guess we could leave and hit up Skittleshanks on the way back through."

Hollow Monk guffawed. "On the way back through! Good one. Like we'll be coming back through!"

A soft rapping on the door brought us to attention. "Infinity Jonez," whispered Sibilance. "I would zpeak with you." The dragoness had done an expert job at rerouting any inquisitive guardsmen and even a few of Man Man's Peanuts. As grateful as I was, I knew we'd only owe her more for her loyalty in the end.

I opened the door a crack and Skittleshanks shoved through before I could close it again. I shot Sibilance a reproachful look. "And here I thought only a feline would sneak a Gnome in through the back gate."

She shrugged, "I'm zorry. He juzt kind of…appeared out of a mizt.

"A Gnomish mist. I can appear anytime, anywhere and don't you forget it." Skittleshanks slammed the door and glared at us menacingly. "Word on the street is you plan to leave town before fulfilling your contract with ol' Skittleshanks," he accused, "Good thing I stopped by to hand deliver your next assignments and wish you well in person." The Gnome handed a parchment to Shamus.

Shamus scanned it over and his face turned pale. "You're kidding! We can't go to the Shimmering Dunes!"

"Of course you can! Getting in isn't hard, it's getting out that's the problem. But I have all the faith and confidence that your intrepid group will pull through with flying colors. Now, might I suggest you and yours leave at an accelerated pace? Perhaps get a jump on the job and all?"

"You could. But why would we?"

"Word on the street is someone gave an anonymous tip to the city guard as to the location of a certain shrunken giant and his friends. That should put some fire in your pantaloons!" The despicable little gnome laughed and dissipated into his gnomish mist.

"He's not kidding," said Lola from the window. "I see guards all over the place. And they're headed this way. We better leave soon."


"He sent what?" bellowed the Queen.

Her viziers cowered in fear before her throne. "Dingle, my Queen," mumbled a prostrate vizier.

"What am I supposed to do with that? I need a sacrifice not more dingle!"

"Man Man has denied knowledge or involvement, milady."

The Queen shrieked in unadulterated fury. "Denied? He dares deny *me*?" Grabbing her sword from its sheath by her throne, she thrust it into the back of the prostrate vizier who'd been unfortunate enough to deliver the news.

The man expired with a groan.

"Call the generals and amass the army. We go to war with Man Man," ordered the Queen. "His denial will cost him dearly."

…And the Pink Elephant continued to grow…


"No, *you* listen," I snapped at Sibilance. "You led that disgusting little jack right to us and now he's directed the guard here. If we're caught, we're all as good as dead, including you, because I guarantee your name was mentioned in his anonymous tip off."

"What of your shampion? Can he not zecure our freedom?" Sibilance smirked with a playful glint in her reptilian orbs.

"Stop acting like an insipid shrew! This is serious!"

A rap, rap rapping at the inn's door interrupted the conversation. "Open up by order of her majesty, the Queen of Swords! We have warrants! Keeper Sibilance! Do you hear me?"

"Maybe you're right Infinity," she purred. "Perhapz I zhall lead you to zafety. Gather your cohortz and meet me down ztairz. The gaming hall iz clozed during the day. I will deal with the guardz and collect your zwine."

Moments later we were in the inn's gaming room awaiting Sibilance and our pigsleds. Above, we heard the trampling of armored feet on the wooden floors and the harsh yells of guardsmen. All was quiet for a moment and then furniture crashed and wood splintered. Sibilance yelled something incoherent that was cut short by a heavy thud. Shortly after that, the door leading to the gaming room was assaulted.

"Oh my," said Hollow Monk, "We're done for, aren't we?"

"No. We aren't." said Shamus. "Mr. Jones, I need a bit of flame."

I handed him a book of matches I snagged off a gaming table. The Forked Tongue's insignia was printed on the outside cover. Shamus rushed up the stairs, matches in hand.

He stopped at the door and pulled out his box of snake pellets. He lit two and quickly pushed them under the door. Frenzied screaming erupted on the other side of the door quickly followed by heavy stomping.

"Stupid dragons and their snake pits!" a muffled voice yelled. "Those're Desert Cobras! Leave it be! Let's torch the place and go!"

A mass exodus of booted feet moved across the floor above and all was quiet.

"I smell smoke," Lola said almost immediately.

The door upstairs opened and thick clouds of smoke rolled in. The inn was aflame. Fire's shadow danced voraciously across the inn devouring the dry wood like a quickfood addict at an all you can eat zing buffet.

Sibilance stumbled out of the smoke and into Shamus's arms, bleeding from a wound on her head. "Againzt the back wall," she mumbled dazedly, "Juzt walk through. Zecret pazzage." She collapsed into unconsciousness.

"Let's go!" ordered Shamus as he heaved Sibilance over his shoulder. "The place is burning down!"

"I smell bacon," said Fa Lona as she sniffed the air. "Does anyone else smell bacon?"

…And the Pink Elephant continued to grow…

The secret passage behind the gaming room wall was exactly the sort of passage secret passages aspire to be: cramped, smelling of mildew and bad decisions, and lit by exactly zero torches. Walking through a secret passage is much like you'd expect. A whole bunch of fear and uncertainty bookended with the feeling that someone is following you. That is to say, it's not a leisurely stroll. Especially with a giant, even a small one, who had to nearly double over to keep his head from hitting the top. He did this a dozen times. And each time, his painful outbursts increased in sincerity and profanity.

The passage deposited us into a narrow alley between a fishmonger's stall and what appeared to be a very reputable hat shop.[41] The smoke from the Forked Tongue had turned the sky the color of a bad omen and the distant sounds of the city guard were still very much audible.

Shamus set Sibilance down against the alley wall with a gentleness that was frankly out of character for a man who had spent the last ten minutes hitting his head on the ceiling of a jagged stone tunnel and

---

[41] Appearances can be deceiving. This particular shopkeeper fled the City of Allure after his hat bands developed the annoying tendency to turn wearers' foreheads green and make them break out in hives. It even happened to yours truly. And I do love a good hat. Trust me. Nothing but nothing makes a statement like a good hat. Bold, adventurous, and irresistibly alluring, are just a few compliments I've received because of my hat. So, if you don't have a hat, by all means get one as soon as you're able. Just make sure you're getting it from someone who knows what they're doing and doesn't follow Gnomish recipes for hatbands.

cursing about it the entire way. "Those jacks really did a number on her. She needs a physician," he said.

"She needs to learn when to keep her mouth shut," said Lola, who was nevertheless crouching down to inspect the wound on the dragoness's head with sharp and practiced orbs. "It's not deep. She'll live to make poor decisions again."

"This'll help." I produced a small vial of Wakey-Wakey Juice from my pouch and handed it to Lola, who uncorked it with her teeth, sniffed it with all the enthusiasm of someone smelling a boot, and administered it to Sibilance, wafting it under her nose with a sadistic glee. Within moments the dragoness's orbs fluttered open.

She took in our collective faces hovering above her, then the smoke darkening the sky, then Shamus's expression of intense relief.

"My inn," she said.

"Gone," I confirmed.

"My gaming tablez?"

"Were they inside your inn?"

"You know they were, Infinity Jonez."

"Yeah. Then also gone."

"And you didn't leave me to die? After what I did?"

"Well, Shamus had a lot to do with that. Mostly due to the fact that he was the only one strong enough to carry you through that tunnel."

Sibilance looked at Shamus for a long moment. Shamus looked back at her. Neither of them said anything. It was the loudest silence I had ever heard, and I once attended a philosophy lecture.

"We have a pig," said Fa Lona helpfully, having retrieved a lone pigsled from somewhere behind the hat shop. She did not explain how. The pigsled was in good condition, though down a few boars to pull it. No doubt the "bacon" Lola had smelled before our journey through the secret passage. But any win is a big win when you've been knocked down.

"Just the one," Shamus asked, "What about the other sleds? Hoop Lilly? Apples?"

"What you see is what you get," snapped Lola, "I'm a Ninja, not a wyzyrd."

Hollow Monk cleared his throat in the manner of a man who is about to say something sanctimonious and knows it. "Perhaps we might use the remaining moments before the guard regroups to make our exit from this wretched city. Just a thought."

"For once, the monk is right," I said. Hollow Monk beamed. "Don't let it go to your head," I added.

Shamus helped Sibilance to her feet. She was unsteady for a moment and then steadied herself against the alley wall with a dignity that suggested she had never been unsteady at all. "I zuppoze I am without a purpoze now," she said, "And a fugitive to boot." She managed to make this observation sound almost unbothered, which is a considerable feat when one has just watched one's livelihood turn to cinders.

Shamus opened his mouth, closed it, opened it again, and then said something that surprised us all, including himself. "Come with us."

Sibilance looked at him with large, golden orbs. "You are going to the Zhimmering Dunez."

"Yes, among other places."

"You know why that dizguzting Gnome zent you on that errand, correct? Becuz nobody who'z gone in to the Zhimmering Dunez haz come out. Ztar Jewelz are rare for a reason. The last person Zkittlezhankz zent in ztill hazn't returned."

"Well," said Shamus, and he squared his small shoulders in a way that would have been imperious if he had been his original size, and was instead simply determined, which is a considerably more useful quality anyway, "we're not the last person. We're this person. And this person has a pigsled, a Red Dragon Ninja, a bard who knows his Tricksy, and a monk who the Lord occasionally speaks through, and I'm told that counts for something."

Fa Lona made a noise that in a less composed person would have been described as a snort. "It's not the way I'd stack a deck, but beggars can't be choosers. The Dunes are on the way to High Azen. What say you help me and I help you?"

I had been leaning against the alley wall with my arms folded, watching this small drama unfold with what I considered to be admirable restraint. The Orb had been equally restrained, which meant it was saving something truly cutting for later.

"I'm coming," decided Sibilance quietly. She straightened her spine with the particular composure of someone who has decided that burning inns are merely a setback. "I have a gift for zertain thingz the Dunes will require. And Zkittlezhankz'z betrayal can't be overlooked."

I pushed off from the wall. Above us the smoke was thickening and somewhere in the direction of the main gate the guard had apparently found their organizational footing. It was, by any reasonable measure, an excellent time to stop having feelings in alleys and start moving.

"Right then," I said. "Desert of Lost Causes. Shimmering Dunes. Armored Toads. Afterward, we'll pass through High Azen to collect whatever the Oracle has left for our princess, settle accounts with a Gnome who deserves considerably more than settling, and avoid starting a war with the Queen of Swords, who has already started one without us."

"What could possibly go wrong," said Fa Lona. It was not a question.

"The Orb interjected, "Better to wonder what could possibly go right? The answer to which is not much. If I end up buried in some sand dune because you got eaten or die of thirst, Infinity Jones, I will not be a happy camper."

"So, no change from the usual," I said. Then to the group, "Shall we? The road isn't going to travel itself."

And so we went. Out of the alley, past the fishmonger who pretended not to notice us, through the fine merchant district, and eventually through a gap in the city's eastern wall that Sibilance knew about because dragons always know the secret ways out of places. Historically, they have been on the receiving end of angry mob brutality with staggering consistency. Not without reason, genetic memories die hard, dear reader, and dragons don't have many good memories among Realmers, genetic or otherwise.

The pigsled carried Sibilance and Fa Lona. Hollow Monk walked because he had taken a vow of self-imposed hardship, hoping to realign him with the Holy He that was slipping ever so further from his grasp. Shamus and Goldie walked beside the pigsled and I walked beside Shamus, and for a while none of us said anything because sometimes the only adequate response to escaping a burning building, outrunning a city guard, surviving a Gnome, and deciding to march into a desert full of armored amphibians is a companionable silence.

"Mr. Jones," said Shamus, after we had put a comfortable distance between ourselves and the city walls.

"McFamus," I replied.

"Back there. In the gaming room. That thing I did with the snake pellets."

"A solid bit of thinking under considerable pressure. Not everyone manages that. I daresay you saved our hides with that stunt. You've grown and that's impressive."

The former giant was quiet for a moment. Somewhere behind us, a plume of smoke rose over the City of Lost Causes against a purple dusk. Ahead, the road stretched east toward possibilities that were, in all likelihood, going to be spectacularly inconvenient.

"Have I really grown, though? I used to be big, the biggest thing in all the Realm…and I was a coward the whole time."

I considered this. It was, as observations go, accurate and therefore worth something. "Size," I told him, "Is the most overrated measurement in the known Realms. What matters is the dimension of the Sacred Fish, and yours, Shamus McFamus, appears to be growing. I'd keep watch on that fishome of yours. It's going to need more room before this is over."

Shamus nodded slowly. He seemed to be trying the idea on to see if it fit. From the look of it, it did.

…And the Pink Elephant continued to grow…

The End

"So?" I asked the young man as I leaned back and sipped my coffee. "What do you think so far?"

"Pretty cool story."

"It's not a story," I corrected. "I told you; it's a *retelling*. The difference being, this actually happened. If anything, it's at the very least a tale. And not even a very tall one at that…unless you count the giant before he shrunk."

"My bad."

"Yes, well you are a bit green around the aura. I'm allowing certain concessions for ignorance and whatnot…for the moment. But let's be sure to learn and grow from our mistakes, eh? I've lost all patience for folk who insist on perpetuating the harmful life cycles they put themselves in. Like a ravenous of foozlebunnies. You aren't a foozle are you?"

"I don't even know what a ravenous of foozlebunnies is," the lad replied.

I sighed, because sometimes that's the only way to release frustration. Then I answered, "You see, when foozlebunnies become too large, or family groups clash, their constant chatter drives even them mad. With no other recourse, they turn on themselves, devouring each other until their numbers dwindle back to tolerable levels. Then they start the whole process over again. Hence, a ravenous."

"That's dark as hell."

"Yes, well, foozlebunnies are only cute when they're seen and not heard. As a matter of fact, that's probably a general rule of thumb you need to check while in the Realm. The cuter something is, the more deadly. But you've not answered my question. Are you in a ravenous? Are you a foozle?"

"Not the last time I checked."

"Good. Keep checking. And at the first sign of foozleness remind yourself that all your foozle pals are heading toward the same repetitive self destruction. And when they get there, one after the other they'll devour one another just like the other suicidal foozles before them. That's what they get for following the crowd. Sometimes, being an outsider isn't such a bad thing."

Jay-zun was quiet for a moment. He turned the coffee mug in his hands as though it were a barble he was trying to read. "Can I ask you something?"

"By all means. However, I make no guarantees regarding the answer."

"Shamus," he said. "He used to be this enormous, terrifying giant. And now he's just…small. And all these terrible things happened to him. Seems like every time he gets ahead, something knocks him down. But he's still going. Into the desert. Toward the toads. Why?"

I set down my mug and regarded him with an attention I do not give freely. "Because the road is still there. Heroes know this and keep walking," I said. "And because when you have spent a long time being enormous on the outside and hollow on the inside, the moment you begin to fill up, you find that a hollow thing and a full thing weigh very differently. The full thing moves. It cannot help but move. The weight of a growing Sacred Fish is a remarkable motivator."

Jay-zun looked out at the street where the horseless carriages continued their senseless zooming and the busy folk continued their senseless scuttling. "I think maybe my Sacred Fish has been asleep for a while," he said. He seemed surprised to hear himself say it.

"Most folk's have," I told him. "The trick is not to panic about the time it was sleeping. The trick is to start filling your thirsty fishome. Right now. Today. With whatever water you can find. Even a mud puddle will do. Ask Shamus. He'll tell you."

"But I can't ask Shamus. He's not real."

I gave Jay-zun the look I reserve for folk who say things that are both incorrect and a waste of a perfectly good breath. "You wrote him down. That means he's as real as anything on this table. Realer, possibly, than that extraordinarily mediocre muffin you've been ignoring since I arrived." I leaned forward. "Stories are more than just fanciful tales. They give us a picture of what we will face in the world and instructions on how to handle it when we get there. Now. Why don't you fetch me some more of your coffee and I'll tell you what happened after—" I didn't finish that statement.

The universe jolted and I was again sitting on the Countess De'Lis's balcony overlooking the Sea of Confusion. The shift left me disgustingly nauseous. I rushed over to the balcony's edge and retched into the crashing waves far below. Not a flattering behavior for a gentleman entertaining a crowd.

"Infinity Jones? Infinity Jones, are you alright?" asked a musical voice. I felt a delicate hand on my back and turned to see the Countess De'Lis staring at me with worry in her big emerald orballs.

"I'm fine…I'm fine…I just…What happened?"

"You were right in the middle of one of your fantabulous retellings when you suddenly went off in a daze. You stared out at the sea for a few tocks before you ran over and garped off the balcony."

"Where's Jay-zun?"

"Who?" asked the Countess.

"Jay-zun. The author. I was giving him a retelling of Shamus."

"There's no one by that name here, Infinity," the Countess said apprehensively. "Are you sure you're alright?"

"I'm fine…It must be exhaustion. I've only recently returned from an adventure, you know."

"Yes, I know. Here let's get you comfortable." The Countess led me back over to my chair and sent for another glass of vino. "Now who is this 'Jay-zun' you are speaking of?"

"A skald from another Realm. Would you like to hear about him?"

"Oh yes!" exclaimed the Countess and clapped her hands. "Pray tell we could meet this character?"

"Perhaps, perhaps. Who knows when or where the universe will shift?"

A servant handed me a glass of aged sugarberry vino from the Barony of Sometimes and I sipped it in exquisite delight. "Baron von Sometimes makes a fine vino, does he not?"

The crowd agreed and each ordered their own glass of the delicious nectar. What foozles. I'd have to be on guard for a ravenous in this crowd. Nobles are often the most ravenous foozles of all. Some might say they are prone to it.

"Now," I said, "Where was I?"

"Jay-zun?" offered the Countess.

"Ah yes. It begins here, ladies and gentlemen. This tale of other Realms has roots here in the Realm of Possibility in the great City of Allure. Amidst the emerald green hills that roll like rocks into the sea, with picturesque cottages and colorful colloquialisms I found myself sitting on the balcony of the beachside estate of our generous hostess, Countess De'Lis. As I sipped vino and entertained this modest crowd, I was interrupted by the nauseating jolt that accompanies the more severe universal shifts…"

But, this tale will have to be saved for other times and different places. My lantern is burning dim and the imps of exhaustion plague my sight. The time draws near for me to explore those ever-fantastic realms of Nod and Dreamyland.

Remember, dear reader, the experience of life is one riotous adventure after another. Live them all until you die.

Until our next encounter,

*Infinity Jones*

Acknowledgements

The amount of help and support I received from friends, family and various professionals along the way has been tremendous. I daresay that without them, this book could never have happened.

I'd first like to thank God for giving me the drive and passion for writing. Even if it is to the exclusion of all else.

I'd like to thank my parents. My father for initially seeding this whole story and my mother for her unwavering support (and finding an artist).

I don't have enough words to express my gratitude to Marilyn Lyons for bringing my imagination to life through her artwork.

Thank you to Chris Deichman for the cover design and to Rob Ewing for the cover image.

Thank you to my son Aidan, who was named into the Realm before he was born and who read sixty pages of the proof copy in one sitting and came home with questions. That's all an author needs to know. May you never grow too old for fairy tales. Welcome to the Realm of Possibility!

And thank you, dear reader, for not only reading the book, but this acknowledgement page as well. You just never can tell when you might miss something important. May you find a new home in the Realm.

Finally, thank you Infinity Jones for setting me straight on a few things.

If I've forgotten to mention you and I should have, I apologize. Don't hate me because I'm forgetful. Love me because I'm eclectic.

About the Author

Jason DeGray has been writing from the Realm of Possibility since a universal shift deposited Infinity Jones at his table at Sugar Browns in Lubbock, Texas sometime in the early 2000s. He has never fully returned. He publishes through Outlaw Star Press in Albuquerque, New Mexico where he diligently works at keeping the reality of mythology alive and well.